CW00862543

Also by Alex wolf

Lut-Par Saga

Vatican

Under the name Lucie Parfitt

Jilted - Recovery in 2020

SON OF SONG

Lut-Par Saga

Alex Wolf

Élan © 2021 Alex Wolf. All rights reserved.

Cover art by Gabrielle Ragusi

The right of ALEX WOLF to be identified as the author of this work has been asserted by her in accordance with the Copyright, Designs and Patents Act 1988.

All rights reserved. No part of this publication may be reproduced, transmitted, or stored in a retrieval system, in any form or by any means, without permission in writing from the publisher, nor be otherwise circulated in any form of binding or cover other than that in which it is published and without a similar condition being imposed on the subsequent purchaser.

All characters in this publication are fictitious and any resemblance to real people, alive or dead, is purely coincidental.

ISBN: 9798527782288

For Nightwish, the band who gave the Son of Song his voice.
For Anne Rice, who gave vampires their bite.

CONTENTS

GLOSSARY

Fae	A species that mainly lives in the Faelands in Lut-Par (normal-sized). They are known for their vast history of tales and mischief. In Élan's generation, magick was less common due to the problems it had caused in history, such as mistrust from other species.
Faeling	Young fae are considered a faeling until the age of 16 years.
Pixie	Similar to vampires, a creature that prefers to live during the night. Unlike vampires though, they prefer to eat meat as well as drink blood, making them less vulnerable to daylight. A highly intelligent species that is ambitious and rather industrial compared to the other species in Lut-Par. They mainly live in the Pixie Province.
Subsidium	A title for fae that are considered to be in a transactional contract with a vampire - giving blood in return for an agreed payment.
Taikatalvi	This translates to magick winter - a story about a faerie that faced the gods in a storm and used their magick to prove their honour. It became famous as the origin story of winter.
Vampire	A species that mainly lives in the Vampire Nation. Weakened by daylight and prefer to live during the night. Drinks the blood of humans and fae.
Yule	A seasonal festival celebrated during the winter.

NAME PRONOUNCEMENTS

Alain	*[ae - l - ain]*
Diafol	*[dee - ya - fol]*
Élan	*[ee - lan]*
Merlough	*[muh - low]*
Subsidium	*[sub - sid - eye - um]*
Taikatalvi	*[tie - ka - ta - vee]*

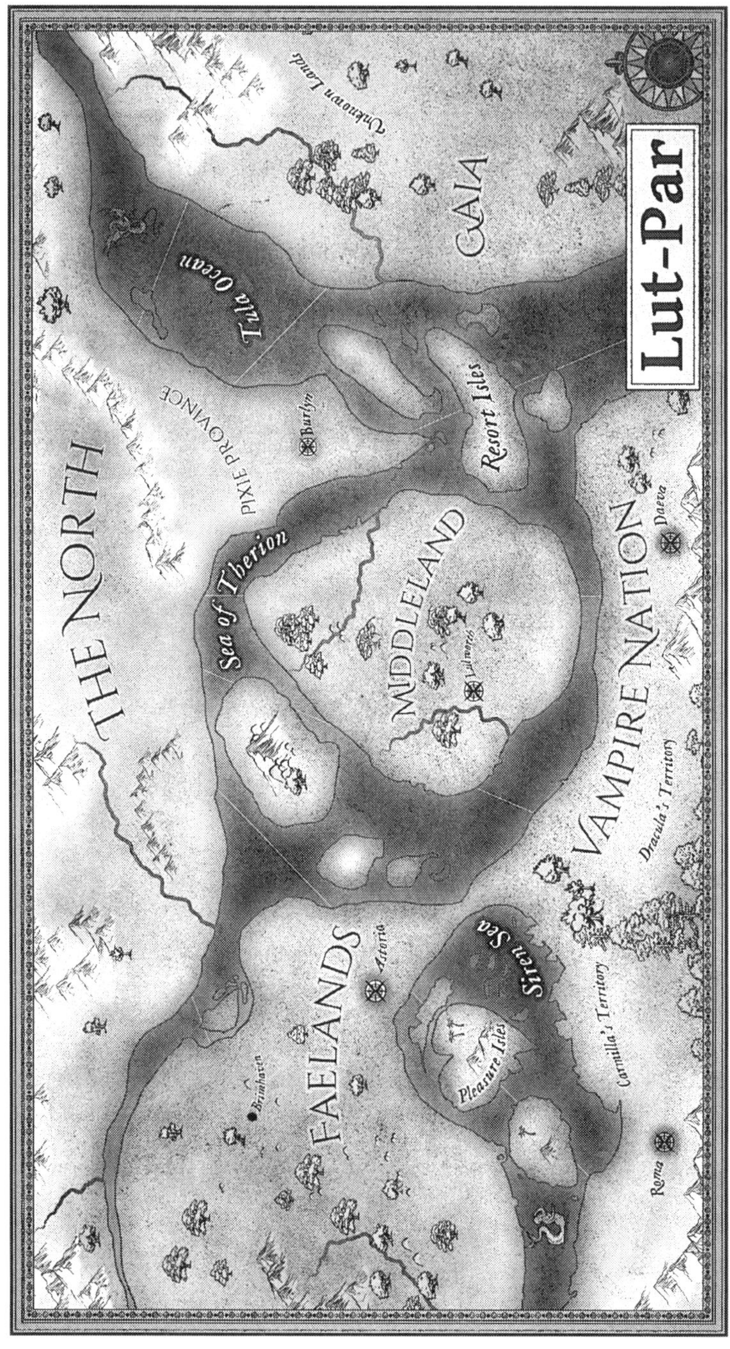
Lut-Par
THE NORTH
GAIA
Unknown Lands
Tula Ocean
PIXIE PROVINCE
Burlyn
Resort Isles
Sea of Therion
MIDDLELAND
VAMPIRE NATION
Daeva
Dracula's Territory
FAELANDS
Astoria
Siren Sea
Pleasure Isles
Camilla's Territory
Brimhaven
Roma

Content Warning

Please be aware that the following fiction contains; Physical abuse and slavery.

Prologue

A crash of thunder startled the young faeling awake. Confused and disorientated, he cried softly. Wrapped warm in the thick winter covers, embraced by the walls of a strong cottage home, he remained frozen in the large hand-carved bed. He trembled as the thunder faded to a grumble. His small body was swallowed by the deep darkness of the night. Even before he could utter the weak words for his faerie mother, the very being was by his side in an instant. A candle lit up her face with her warm eyes and pale complexion. She was smiling softly, reaching for him. A flash of lightning ripped a scream from him, and tears fell.

"Hush, my faeling," she whispered, her warmth soothing the small shuddering body. Slowly, she pulled him to her, transferring the small body from the hand-woven covers to her warm body. Her soft nightgown held a familiar scent that soothed the faeling. Thunder soon followed the lightning and the mother held her son strongly to her, constricting his trembling. They sat there in tense silence, waiting for the storm to erupt again. The faeling felt his mother sigh as another roar of thunder drew a shudder from him.

"You must not cry, my youngest," she said softly.

"I'm scared, mother," he cried, unable to move from his mother's chest, even though it was almost suffocating him in the tight embrace.

"It is natural to fear the gods," she whispered softly against his small, pointed ear. "But you must not be afraid, dear one, for they are here with us and they will protect us," she continued. This caused the faeling to stir and he drew back from his mother to meet her warm brown eyes.

"Why would they do that?" he asked, confused. The gods, he knew, were selfish, dark beings who only knew how to manipulate and conquer souls. His mother smiled secretly as if she knew something he didn't, drawing him out further from her hold.

"Because, dear one, you are blessed. Blessed by the gods themselves. The gods of rain, wind, and thunder," she said in a secretive voice. The faeling frowned. His mother seemed to catch herself and held back on the rest of her words.

"Come, let us sit by the fire and warm ourselves," she said, standing, already facing the fireplace that held a small fire on the opposite side of his room. After a slight hesitation, the faeling followed her.

A flash of lightning quickened his pulse and he leapt to sit next to his mother on the long cushion near the fireplace. She wrapped a woollen blanket around them and pulled him to her so he was almost in her lap. She felt a little sadness knowing he was already getting too big for it. They sat in silence, watching the flames dance and flicker softly. His mother held him firmer as more rumbles of thunder arrived.

"Have I ever told you of the story of the Taikatalvi?" she asked as the growls of the thunder died down. He looked up at his mother with wonder, excitement not far from his mind at the idea of a story when it was long past his bedtime. "Then I must continue for it seems the gods wish it be so on this night," she said, pulling him closer. He wasn't completely comfortable with the angle at which his mother held him, but he refused to prolong the story any longer. His mother sat, watching the fire, gathering her thoughts. The faeling's excitement grew as he felt a single drop of magick curl around them. The thunder seemed to subside, and the lightning softened. His mother sighed deeply, staring into the flames. The faeling too, focused on the flames. It was there that the story began…

The thunder was replaced by drums, the rain by piano keys, trickling around him. The fire danced in front of him, to his mother's words, with a music only he could hear. A tune only he knew. It was there he learned of what she meant by the gods blessing. The magick surrounded them as the story was told.

Before the faeling knew it, he was no longer a young faerie, but an observer on a mighty quest. He watched as a hero faced danger and saved the innocent. His heart thudded in his chest as the drums rumbled around him, the piano showering him in melodies. The faeling would recall little of this night, but it was enough to soothe his fears and banish the impact of the thunder. He laughed in wonder and stared in awe at the flames performing for him and his mother. Her hold was no longer physical; only by her voice did he know she was there with him.

"Fear not mighty hero, for you are blessed by us and all that be," his mother's voice rang. The faeling, mouth agape, continued to watch the dancing flames, entranced. Soon the fire faded, as if tiring from the show.

"And so, the hero faced his greatest challenge yet. A creature of darkness and old. A beast that ruled the night and stole all things that we hold dear," his mother's voice hardened and he shivered.

"Vampire," he whispered. His mother paused and looked at him, the dying flames reflected in her gaze.

"Yes, little one. A vampire," she said, her voice deep with sadness. She stared at him until he fidgeted from the silence, the flames low to the coals.

She continued the story, her voice sounding hollower than before, until the flames eventually died and they were small buds of light against the black coals. Her son's soft, dark head lay against her, the spell having lulled him into a soft sleep once more. She sat there until her aching bones could no longer hold them both.

Gently, she lifted him into his bed once more, aghast at how big he had grown. A hidden, dark thought thudded in her breast.

A creak at the door made her gasp and cower against her sleeping child. Moments passed and she laughed at her own foolishness. She kissed his soft head, enjoying the fresh scent of the forest on him.

"*Mine*," she thought in her motherly pride as she left the room, letting the soft glow hold the spell a little longer than needed. The thunder was now a distant grumble like a beast above them. The lightning had moved on.

Carefully, she closed the hand-carved door and turned to walk the dark hallway. Goosebumps rose on her skin, missing the fire's warmth. The candle she had used had gone out and was not necessary as she could see in the dark. Yet, her senses told her she was not alone in her dark, quiet hallway.

As she moved from the door, her nerves tingled and sensed a presence, which was not a pleasant one. A creak to her left started her heart and she grit her teeth in fear. She moved slowly, knowing not to give in to the darkness that mocked her. As soon as she moved again, a nasty snigger caused her to freeze. Sickening recognition sank her heart.

"Stop tormenting me. I know you are here," she said, fighting her chattering teeth. A louder chortle followed, causing her to tremble with despair.

"Ah, such dramatic accusation from a child. Ah, yes, but clever though! One of my cleverest…" came the voice, crawling up her spine. She forced herself to move slowly into what she thought would be a more normal stance, less frightened.

"Why are you here?" she asked, unable to ease the tremble in her voice. Another snigger came.

"Well, for the story, of course, you know I can't resist them. And that fire trick! My my, yes! You are my cleverest," came the arrogant voice. The mother faerie held her tongue, knowing better than to give in to his bait.

"And the faeling…" he drawled. She shivered more, unable to pinpoint his location.

"Leave him be; he isn't yours yet," she bit out, unable to resist the bait he threw at her. A bark of laughter shook her. It was never good when he laughed.

"That may be, but the boy must know soon. He is almost of age," he hissed, making a lump swell in the mother's throat.

"I need more time," she said softly, clutching her elbows. Sorrow swirling around her.

"A deal is a deal. You knew this time would come, I have been patient. Nurture him, train him, tell him stories. I do not care! Never forget what you promised me," the voice turned into a growl.

"Yes father," she replied as silent tears fell.

By the time she had returned to her bed, the sky was brightening with the promise of a clear morning. The air was already ripe from the retreat of the storm. As she lay down, she struggled to get comfortable, the bed too soft, the covers too thick and constricting. Her husband sighed in sleep and replaced his arm around her, his scent soothing her. As her being stilled into comfort, a small itch remained in her mind. A darkness forming.

"*Mine…*" Said a voice that was not heard, but came from her mind. The voice wasn't her own.

PART 1

Music

Present Day - 10 years later

Darkness surrounds me. I am alone yet comforted with myself. This is what I want; this is what I am meant to be. My heart pounds to the promise of music.

Once, this darkness scared me. I felt tormented with its blinding potential. My young mind used to recreate the creatures from stories and frighten me with them. I found out how real they were.

Yet here I stand, in quiet anticipation, my confidence and self-assurance anew. I was ready for this. My body aches with the thought of what was to come. I catch the distant noise of a crowd and the excited yelps. I smile to myself as the drums start their warm up. Almost time.

My fingers begin to twitch as the piano joins the drums, swallowing the noise of the crowd. Soon I am to be there. To be

where I belong, where I was born to be. My legs, taller now, judder in anticipation. It takes all my will not to move too soon.
I open my eyes and register the darkness around me. My heart pounds harder, not with fear but from excitement, a contrast to my past. The electric twang of the guitar tears through the current melody, escalating to a new level. My breathing comes harder as the music rides through the pleasant wave of song. Almost there.

I take a deep breath, my voice ready and eager after my warm up. My magick swells within me, threatening to burst through my chest. My hands fist as I feel the upcoming moment. It is here!

The music stops, swamping the stadium into silence; this is my cue. I jolt and run onto the stage, elated it has finally come. Screams in the crowd pick up as the first few see me emerge. The lights blind me as the roar of the crowd shatters the silence. As the initial excitement dies down, the instruments begin. I hear the climbing melody luring my voice free. Ignoring the will to unleash my voice all at once, I let the music draw it out teasingly, my magick a soothing caress of assurance.
Soon, the crowd is overtaken by the music and surrounds the stadium. The song kicks into full power and I unleash my spirit, my will, and everything I am. Like a siren, my voice pulls others into the music. Together, our energy dances and the magick is unleashed.

The audience is dark, but I see them well, enough to acknowledge the mix of species. My heart swells with appreciation at the size. Never before have fae and dark creatures alike joined together to listen and celebrate music. *My* music. The music I was born to create.

Together, my band of vampires and I, a faerie, have created a symbiosis of music genres. With instruments, chords, and beats classically of vampiric style, combined with my voice of the fae, these powers create an energy, a magick that has never been seen. Everyone present witnesses it. A power, a connection that resonates in every being.

My microphone is the sceptre and I rule their hearts. I sing my words in perfect melody, spinning tales with the frequencies. Everyone is singing, dancing, or joining in, in their own way. I look around and my musicians are enjoying it as much as I am. Like me, they are in awe of this power, this connection, and together we take them on a journey.

A world between the fantasy of faerie-tales and the passionate romance of vampirism.

Reluctantly, I return to my reality by the end of the concert. This is never smooth or subtle. I walk back off stage, buzzing and oozing with magick and energy. We all smile at each other and congratulate ourselves on another success.

As I embrace them, I see their fangs in their smiles. Smaller than I thought as a faeling and much less intimidating in person. The vampires in the old tales were terrifying monsters and I swoon at the idea that I am close friends with these creatures now. How distant they seemed to me as a young faerie, a creature lurking in the shadows on the other side of my nightmares. I am happy to find that they are actually quite pleasant to be around now.

But not all vampires are the same. This was my painful lesson. I walk past the studio rooms, and I catch a couple feeding off each other, an intimate act that I feel guilty to have witnessed in the moment. As I walk on, feeling the blood rush to my face, my hand carefully goes to my own neck as I remember my dark past.

Seeing this act a year ago would have undone me. Such foul memories lie beneath the surface of this part of my life, which I must squash down. It is over now; I am not the innocent faeling anymore. A flash of red from their eyes remind me of my own personal villain, a deathly snap of his sharp fangs. I withhold a shudder, keeping my memories from overwhelming me.

I yelp as I hit a hard chest. The family scent envelopes me suddenly and I calm in relief.

"Gods! Sorry brother! I guess I was—"

"Daydreaming again? Yes, you have always done that. Particularly after singing. In fact, many struggle to bring you back to the ground." He chuckles lightheartedly, his voice pleasantly warm. Oh how much like my father he is! His presence is so comforting, though we are both faerie males, borne in the same lands, we differ in looks completely.

Where I am shorter and light in stature with dark hair, he is strongly built, tall and fair in complexion. His eyes, a warm brown contrast my own pale green. Rolo is my elder brother and only sibling. A practical and down to earth male, with unrelenting loyalty to anything he cares about.

Though we look different, we share the same love for music. His own reflects a more organic, folk-faerie-style that is hard not to love. He gives me the sense of homely warmth and familiarity that I strive to express in my own music. Unlike mine, his music is not tainted by the darkness. The darkness is powerless against his light and it is something I know I will never achieve myself. I am too immersed, too far into its grips, made anew from my past. And I am okay with that.

"Élan, are you sure you're okay? You haven't been listenin' to a word I've said, have you?" he asks incredulously, his faerie district twang coming through. I love it and it reminds me of home.

"Sorry, I'm fine. What did you say?" I ask, my voice not showing any sign of waning from the giant performance I've just done.

"I said I came back here because I was worried. There is word that *he* is here. He is either here or nearby. I don't like it. He shouldn't be coming and botherin' you straight after a performance," Rolo grumbles, his handsome face crumpled in irritation.

I smile sadly at his concern. Appreciating his frustration, it was impossible to stop *him* coming if he wanted to be here.

"He is nearby; I can feel him. Worry not, dear brother, for when you are me, he is always nearby," I replied, patting him in thanks. He sighs sadly.

"It's not right, you know. You need to be your own self You're old enough now, brother, to be without his darned presence," he grumbles, standing aside to let me walk ahead. I snicker at his words. I admire his boldness, and wish I had the same growing up, perhaps then things would not have happened as they did…

"Dear brother, offending him will only force his grip on me to tighten. I endure him because I am his; I am his at least until this spring," I replied casually. His protectiveness towards me is a comfort, I am lucky to have a brother like him.

Growing up, we were close up until my eighth year. For reasons you will soon learn, I moved away and no longer saw him as often. I missed him greatly and always wondered, if I grew up with more of his influence, how would I differ now?

But there is no use pondering these meaningless thoughts. What happened, happened. And as my eighteenth birthday arrives, I intend to see him as much as I did as a faeling.

I assure my brother that I am fine, and we eventually separate. I arrive to my studio room, the scent of lavender hits and relaxes me. The flower of my homeland. I smile knowing my mother left them for me. I admire their presence on my table and feel the buzz in me begin to fade.

A shadow catches my eye, but I don't react, not anymore. I feel the presence, but say nothing, knowing it is no use. I pick up a different energetic buzz and tilt my head slightly. A flicker draws my eye and I look before I can stop myself.

Next to the pot of lavender sits a gold coin. *The* gold coin, his mark. Now that my eyes have caught it, I struggle to draw my gaze away from it, staring at it forebodingly. It is at this same moment that I realise how quiet it is. I can't pick anything up from outside my room, which is strange. I feel no magick, yet I am not as naïve anymore to his tricks.

I turn quickly and take my clothes to the joined bathroom and change out of my costume.

I dress hastily, feeling as though I am being watched, and walk to leave the studio without looking back. I grab the doorknob and freeze when a voice stops me.

"Are you not going to take my gift?" the voice gloats with dark humour. Slowly, I released the door handle and turn. I fix my gaze on the floor in front of me.

"I am sorry, but I cannot accept it," I reply tonelessly. He clicks his tongue.

"Such a way to address your grandfather? Where's the warmth that was on that stage? Not good. No, this won't do! I have missed you, dear one. Come forward." I let the magick pull me to the mirror above the table. Invisible strings tugging me closer, putting me in place. The magick leaves a sharp taste on my tongue, like having just bitten a raspberry.

I reluctantly meet the gaze of the figure now behind me in the mirror, knowing who stares back. My grandfather, Diafol.

Don't be fooled by the title. He defies the meaning of the kind, elderly figure who nurtures and treats you. This faerie, or *being* I should say, is all tricks. All magick and cleverness. Many of the fae look up to him, a creature of power that is one of few that remain as the last of the old and magickal. No one really knows his age, but he is known throughout the lands. His power and ability to manipulate the most innocent of reason. He is also what you could call a villain.

A creature that survives on his own needs and pleasure. He enjoys using others like a grand puppet-master of the fae realm and watches their lives play out like the director of a film. This we all know and hear, yet I cannot hate him. Oh, how I would love to. He who has done so much to me and my family, his own flesh and blood. He who has let danger and despair befall us, without using his own power to help.

Yes, there are things I disagree with. I cannot condone many of his actions, if any. But, he is part of me. Whether it is biological or goes further, I dare not find out. All I know is that I simply cannot hate him or wish him ill. The curious faeling within me is still in darkness and watches him in fascination. Watches for his next move and what he will do.

I see him now before me, in his mystical glory. Not many have seen him and believe that if his looks reflected his terrible personality, then he would be the worst kind of demon.

But he is simply mystifying. His hair, a dirty mop of once brown but now grey with dust. His skin I find most fascinating, with a greenish tinge freckled with a glitter-like substance that sparkles like scales. People whisper of this being, of his close lineage to the Mer in the sea, a rumour he likes to redirect back to me for talent in my voice. A siren's voice.

Although my brother sneers and says he just doesn't wash properly. My eyes meet his and I feel the hold that I always do in his gaze, his eyes a glowing yellow that would remind you of the blazing sun as it descends beyond the horizon. Death's eyes.

In the light of the room, his pupils are small pinpoints that hold me in place. I look nothing like him, which makes me wonder where my looks come from. He insists I resemble my grandmother, a young male version of her. She passed long before I was born, but without seeing images of her likeness, I struggle to believe him.

He is dressed in his normal attire. A neutral shade of brown on his shirt with a vest of dull scales that he said is from a dragon he had slain in his youth. Dragons have been long extinct, so either his age is beyond what anyone can know, or he is lying. The latter is most believable. Even for someone who cares for him like I do, I know that I would be a fool to believe his words. I trusted him once; I have come to regret that. He taps his long dirty nails impatiently.

"I'm sorry. I didn't mean to be rude. You startled me and I do not want to take your gold," I reply, sounding younger than I am. He grins, showing his sharp, pointed yellow teeth—a grin I like to think is of endearment, but then I have seen him pull the same face when looking at a corpse.

"Yes, yes, good boy. Always my good boy. Clever! Oh, so clever like me. You know better than to take my gold. For having my gold comes at a price, doesn't it dear one?" he replies, his voice gravelly and in his singsong way. His accent is also unlike ours, more articulate and harder to place.

"What do you need of me?" I ask innocently as I take note of his good mood. Something that could be good or equally as bad for me.

"Ah but I am only here to congratulate you, my boy! On another wonderful performance. Bewitching creatures alike. It was particularly enjoyable watching those stupid vampires slobber over such talented magick," he giggles, something he does more than he talks. I smile, genuinely happy he liked it. The part of me that is still faeling is relieved to hear this.

"I'm glad you are pleased, Grandfather. I owe it to you for this inspiration," I reply. I am getting better at lying to him and it scares me. It scares me as it feels that in doing so, I am becoming like him. I am honest in almost everything, but lying to him seems to make it easier. He giggles again, which has a self-gratifying ring to it. He looks at me knowingly.

"You know it boy! Together we will unleash our magick upon the world. Those creatures adore you and soon, everyone will. You are my star!" He sighs happily. I smile and swallow down how much my heart rises to his praise. I remind myself it is all lies.

A knock at the door startles me.

"Urgh, it is that blasted, oaf brother of yours," Diafol growls.

"One minute! I'm nearly ready, Rolo," I call.

I turn back to find his face hard in thought. I remain silent, knowing better than to disrupt his thinking. As the silence draws out, I resist turning away even though his expression makes my skin crawl. If I pull my attention away, he will surely punish me.

"What will you do after spring?" he asks softly, sounding almost sad. His question catches me off guard. For a moment, I try to pull together an answer.

"What will I do? Continue my music, of course! Why would that change?" I ask, surprised and not knowing where he is going with this. Yes, spring marked my eighteenth year and freedom from him, but that didn't stop my love for music or my band.

For whatever reason, I don't like where this is going. I know him well enough to know this is a touchy subject. He nods slowly, taking in my answer, his gaze frozen in thought.

"Let's hope so. Gods' know you don't owe me anything. Not anymore…" he says, again his voice soft. It puts me on edge as I realise it's regret that he feels. Regret for what happened to me. I am amazed knowing very few, if anyone, has seen this side to him. A side that teased me into believing that he had a heart, a soul. Something that connects us to our family more than he's let on.

Suddenly, I remember Rolo is still waiting for me and my heart races. The worse thing now would be for Rolo to barge in. Diafol would inflict his rage for disturbing our tender moment. As if reading my thoughts, Diafol narrows his gaze at the door.

"At least that oaf is still of use to us. To you. He will protect you while I am unable to," he growls as if that fact disgusts him.
"He will, but I do miss you, Grandfather," I reply, half meaning it. In reality, I have enjoyed the new freedoms that led to my independence.

"Not to worry, dear one. I will certainly be with you again before the time is out!" he answers, returning to his devilish self. I nod, smiling in my most charming way as if I were on stage once more.

"Then I will see you soon?" I ask, relieved that he is showing more of himself.

"Sooner than you think, little devil, for I know you look forward to your freedom. Don't even try to deny it! Who wouldn't, for I am not some stupid creature, no sir! Do you think I hold all this responsibility, this amount of soul and respect, from being a dumb creature? No! I am the great Diafol and even when your life is yours again, I will still remain in your shadow. Do you understand, boy?" he asks in his ranting way, his voice raised. I swallow heavily, worried over his words, his sudden ill mood, and the fact that my brother may have heard him and come in at any moment.

"Yes, Grandfather. I know, worry not, I will never forget who I am. Why I am here or what I am," I reply, my mind pulling the words from what I know would please him. It has its effect and I panic, wondering if I am spinning a spell of my own.

"Oh, dear one, you have no idea what you are capable of. You are my greatest. This, I know. Just like your mother, you have outdone yourself and strive to be the best, and like her, you will remain with me even after our time is up. Mark my words," he says, his voice fading, his image losing its opacity. I am haunted by his words and I nod, too scared to say the wrong thing.

As he fades, the last piece remaining is his glowing eyes and grinning shark smile. I pull away when it completely goes, knowing if I did it too soon, I would regret it when we next meet. I feel his magick tugging at me, pulling my soul as if it wants to take me with him through the mirror. It is not painful, but rather uncomfortable, and leaves a bad taste in my mouth.

I run and open the door to Rolo with his arms crossed.

"Sorry I—" I begin.

"No need. I know better than to disturb your precious reunion. We need to go," he says shortly, already turning to leave. My heart sinks at his disappointment in me.

As I follow him, I shiver at the memory of my grandfather's words. The hidden truths in them, the mystery yet to be known. Family issues is an understatement.

Home

Growing up, I was blissfully unaware of the impending storm around me. The secrets of my birth were unknown to me. I was a faeling in the country, the region where the forests ruled the skies and the land was plentiful in its greenery. Houses were few and far between, everyone knew everyone, and spending the day without getting grass stains or mud on you was impossible. It was wonderfully fresh and like all young faeries, I took it for granted. It wasn't until the spring, around my eighth birthday that cracks in our strong foundation started to show.

Spring was slowly transforming the Faelands and increasing sunlight was warming the land. I was helping my brother with his field, despite my mother's protests. It annoyed me that she seemed more protective of me than my brother. I thought it was from being her youngest, not knowing the dark, hidden fears that she secretly guarded. My brother, older by six years, knew what she feared too. Yet, despite this, he avoided treating me any differently, always involving me in his games and work.

I was his little shadow, his friends used to say, always wanting to join in, and my brother encouraged it. This brewed tension between my mother and brother, but I did not notice this until much later. Otherwise my mother seemed carefree, an avid gardener who controlled the attention of plants everywhere as if they were waiting for her approval, bowing to her every whim. With this talent, she created wonderful remedies and grew flowers that seemed entirely unique. The neighbours gave up competing with her garden long before I was born.

My mother was in the garden, her face serene in the presence of her loving subjects. She glowed with something more physical than pride and bloomed like the sunflowers. She wore her hair long in fine strands of light green that shimmered in the sun. Her eyes, a warm brown that my brother inherited. Her frame, long and thin but strong like a mighty stalk. The embodiment of a flower and her namesake, Azalea. She wore thin, flowy clothing, as did many wives of the fae village. Nothing of fashion reached the borders of our secret little haven and we liked it that way.

I can recall, on a specific day, running up to her amidst her flowers.

"Hush! He is coming," she whispered in a conspiratorial tone. The flowers seem to nod and turn to me as I arrived.

"Mother, Rolo caught a rabbit!" I gasped, my young face flushed, having ran as fast as I could to report to her with pride. She smiled and patted the soft grass next to her.

"It was so cool! He is the best hunter I ever saw!" I gasped excitedly. I loved my brother immensely. Naïvely, I strived to become like him one day, strong and brave.
My mother laughed. "His has your father's wits. Rolo has always been good at helping your father," she says casually, inspecting a flower. I deflate a little, disappointed by her casual response.

"I hope to be as good as him one day," I said, pouting at her. She laughed again and turned to me. Something clicked in her mind and she caught herself.
"My dear, we cannot all be hunters of the world. Some of us are born with other talents for greater things," she said, sobering. I frowned at her words, not understanding what she was saying. She confused me sometimes. I always seemed to be on another level. Not knowing what she knew, it created a small wall between us, something she only let down when she chose.
"But mother, he was so good. Even father didn't help him this time. It was just me and him and we got it! We—"
"You were alone with your brother? Where was your father?" she cut in, turning to me suddenly. I frowned at her concern.
"He's gone fishing like he always does when the water is quiet. No bad omens today. Why? What's wrong, mother?" I asked, seeing the fear in her eyes. She sighed heavily, sounding exhausted.
"You are too young to be on your own, even with your brother. Your father was wrong to leave you both," she growled, annoyed. This upset my little heart. I felt she didn't think I was able to look after myself, me the mature seven-year-old faeling.

"But mother, other young fae can do this. Why can't I be with my brother alone?" I asked, confused. She sighed and looked at me in thought.

"Because your brother doesn't watch you properly. You need someone there in case…you get hurt," she said. I frowned, fully confused.

"But Rolo can protect me. He stopped that Davy Woodthorpe throwing mud at me before," I said pridefully, convinced my mother had the completely wrong idea about Rolo. It upset me that she didn't think Rolo could look after me, let alone I could look after myself. The protectiveness was too much for me to comprehend. Little to no danger was around us, yet she feared for me as if she believed in the beasts she told me stories about.

"Yes, well, worse things can happen." She grimaced. I sighed feeling defeated and deflated. After minutes of thoughtful silence between us, she turned to me, shaking off her dark mood.

"Enough of this talk. Take these inside for me. I will join you soon and we can start making dinner together," she said, smiling at me encouragingly. As a child, I easily fell for her distractions, making dinner with her was a favourite pastime of mine. Many afternoons and evenings were shared creating meals together. The young male faelings of the village used to laugh at me and say I was doing 'female faeries' work. I used to reply that they never had a mother like mine to enjoy the time with. And it was true.

Despite all her faults, she was still a wonder to me. A beauty and delight to those she met, and as much as I aspired to be like Rolo, I also wanted to cook like my mother.

My father was always outside, working on something and getting resources on the outskirts of our little village. He was well-known by the fae and respected for his hard work and good soul. When my brother began schooling in his eighth year, I proudly took his place on my father's boat and helped him fish. It was his favourite activity and to no surprise, he had amazing talent. Very rarely did he struggle to catch fish on the still waters of the lake near our house. I helped him with pride, knowing it used to be my brother's job.

Ah, I remember those days well. Especially in the bright summers, the waters were almost smooth like stone and my father relaxed and was happiest on his little boat. I enjoyed his company and we talked about many things. He has lots of stories about his days before settling with my mother. Stories of sailors and tavern fights. A mermaid or too was thrown into the stories to make me giggle with faeling delight. Like dragons, they had not been seen for years so everyone assumed they were gone.

"Father, tell me how you met my mother," I asked excitedly; it was my favourite story. He turned to me dramatically and sat opposite, making the boat rock a little. He took my hands in his, big and tanned from many long days on his boat. His nails were bitten short as it was easier to handle squirming fish and calm chickens in storms. I looked at him, his eyes as blue as the water. My father, being a sailor, had ancestry that the fae believed was from the mer creatures in his stories. Watching him handle fish made me believe this. His hair white with age, my father met my mother later in life, which is why he had so many stories to tell me, his face lined with time and his smile warm and comforting.

In the boat, he held my hands in his and began his tale about meeting my mother—his rose among the thorns, he called her. It made me laugh, knowing her name is Azalea, a flower that was nowhere like a rose, showing his lack of knowledge with plants.

My parents met when my father fell ill on a particular voyage. They stopped at a dock where she and my grandfather lived. She was famous for her healing abilities and healed him in the days he stayed there. She made a lasting impression on him and he vowed that after his business was complete, he would return to her. They eventually did see each other again and were in love. My brother, Rolo, was born a few years after.

"But we were not complete," he sighed, making me fidget in childish excitement. "For you see, we were missing something, something that we could not figure out until…" He paused for dramatic effect. I was grinning stupidly, knowing where this would lead to.

"Until one day, your mother heard something. Do you know what she heard?" he asked me.

"A song!" I burst and hushed myself, forgetting that we were waiting for the fish. He chuckled under his breath at my excitement.

"Indeed little one. But not just any song. A song of the heart, of family. A soft yet hopeful tune, as if coming from a flute of the soul," he said. He looked at my hands and turned them as if admiring them.

"But I did not believe it. I did not hear it. I thought your mother mad, having spent too long in the sun. Until days later, on a day like this, guess what?" he asked, looking back at me expectantly.

"You heard it too," I whispered in wonder. He grinned at me through his beard.

"Yes! And on that day, I discarded the fish, ran back to your mother, and told her that she was not mad for I heard the song too," he said happily, making me giggle. The next part was the best part.

"And she told you she was pregnant," I said excitedly. He laughed happily, not caring about the fish for the moment.

"Yes, she told me of the promise of what you would come to be my dearest Élan. My beloved second," he said, sighing happily. Never afraid to show his feelings, his eyes watered slightly as he admired me.

"Oh, we were so happy…" he sighed, stroking my dark hair softly.

"Were? Father we are still happy." I giggled, enjoying my hair being ruffled. His eyes glazed over for a second, too quick for my young mind to pick up.

Looking back, it was more prominent to me now, that fleeting look bright in my memory. He soon regained himself and smiled.

"Of course we are. And soon it is to be your birthday. The mighty age of eight, the age for faelings to be schooled and—"

"Father! We got a fish!" I gasped, pointing at the rod distractedly. We turned and tended to the catch. I laughed excitedly as I thought of showing Rolo my latest catch, my innocent, young self missing the sadness in my father's smile as we reeled in the fish.

"But Rolo, mother said I am not meant to go alone with you," I whined, fearing my mother's wrath. Not for myself but for my brother. Leading up to my birthday, my mother seemed more tense than usual. In the blissful land of ours, this seemed most peculiar, and it worried my little mind.

"Nonsense! We are only going to get another rabbit like last time," my brother chided me as we walked. I grasped his arm tightly as we walked.

"But Rolo—"

"Élan." He leaned to level his eyes to mine. He was always taller than me, which frustrated me, but also why I was more prone to trust him.

"Do you want to prove to mother that we can do this together, just you and me?" he asked, his face serious. I nodded firmly.
"Then worry not. She fears for no reason and we can prove this," he said, almost to himself as we entered the forest behind our house.

Hours later…

The sun burned the sky red with its descent. Rolo ran to the cottage alone.
"Father! Mother! Élan's gone," he shouted, angry tears threatened his eyes. He proceeded to tell them what happened; Azalea broke down crying, while Maurice was deathly quiet.
"You lost him," Maurice finally spoke.
"He disappeared! He was right next to me and then he was gone," Rolo cried.
"Gone?! How could you be so stupid!" Azalea shrieked, her face wet with tears.
"Stupid? How am I supposed to stop that? He disappeared, I say! No doubt from your damned magick," Rolo yelled, his face red.
"How dare you!" Azalea hissed, breaking the remaining peace between them.

Faerie's magick varied from one to the other. For example, Maurice had little if any, which he used for his activities in the field and waters. Whereas Azalea had the highest amount a faerie can hold, no doubt from being directly related to Diafol himself. Rolo seemed to be the same as Maurice in most ways, and especially when it came to magick, and he was glad for that. He had never seen the use for it beyond the necessary uses upon the land and waters, and never understood why his mother loved it so much.

So far, in regards to Élan, little had been discussed or revealed as of yet, but there were whispers that he was to be as powerful as his mother.

"Enough," Maurice said firmly, the calmest out of all of them.

"It is almost dark. Rolo, stay here in case he comes home. Your mother and I must seek him out." He gathered his coat and fishing blade.

"Yes, let's go," she responded in a trembling voice, ignoring Rolo's presence.

"Luck to you," he called, pacing, not knowing what to do with himself, restless yet exhausted. Azalea had left as if the wind pulled her away. Maurice turned to his eldest.

"We will find him, worry not," he whispered and embraced Rolo, something they rarely did.

"I'm sorry father," he mumbled, sounding younger than he was.

"Hush. We will find him. Stay here and stay safe," his father consoled, his voice soft and nurturing. Maurice left, holding a torch, his wife already out of sight. He knew better than to hold her back from looking for Élan, her magick crackling in the air around the cottage.

"Gods, Élan, be safe," he muttered to himself as he struggled to catch up to her, following the small sparks of magick that lay a path to her location.

They found Élan around midnight. He was deep in the forest and they were both exhausted.

"Maurice, I see him!" Azalea called, already running to her youngest faeling. They had heard him before they saw him; he had been laughing.

"Mother! What are you doing here?" Élan asked, confused. She grabbed him by the shoulders and pulled him into a tight hug.

"Gods, Élan! Where have you been?" she asked, her heart beating against his cheek.

"I heard a song mother, like the one in father's story," Élan replied innocently. His mother pulled back to meet his face.

"A song?" she asked, her eyes wild. Maurice had just caught up with them.

"It is good to see you are safe, son," he said, breathing hard.

"Yes, a song, a great song that I followed here and—" a snigger broke Élan off. Azalea froze, clutching him so tightly it hurt.

"I am so happy you liked the song, dear one. It was awfully fun to play!" Diafol cackled, walking into view.

"Get away from him," Azalea growled.

"But Mother, Grandfather found me! I followed the song and got lost. I was s-scared and he found me," Élan explained, upset with his shameful admission.

"You see, dear one? I found our poor, lost faeling. Do I deserve your anger? No, I do not! So spare me those beastly looks of a mother bear and greet your father with the respect I deserve," her father said, his voice louder as he walked towards them, into the firelight of Maurice's torch.

"Father, I-I thank you for helping us in finding Élan," she said, though she didn't sound convincing, not even to Élan.

"I am sorry I scared you, Mother, truly," Élan said, looking up at her.

"Ah, there. Now you see! Such a good boy. A good faeling to admit he has done wrong. Not many faeries can do that, no! But this boy—this boy is good and has such a good ear for music," Diafol said, his last words sounding more like a sneer. Azalea looked back up to him. She read the meaning in his words.

Gently, she held Élan close and whispered words into his ear. Slowly, Élan fell asleep and Maurice took him into his arms, the torch now floating from the magick in the air.

"You led him here. Why?" Azalea asked, knowing her faeling to now be asleep.

"As I said, dear one, I wanted to see if his ear for music really was that good, and oh yes, it was! Such great magick in such a small body. Just echoes of what is to come. What wonders he will do." He grinned at the sleeping faeling.

"Now, sir, you need to leave. It isn't time yet," Maurice said bravely. Azalea gripped his arm in warning. Her father turned his deathly gaze on him lazily.

"Maurice, oh, is that you? You are looking so old now. I am surprised you can make it out here with all our magick mingling. Must be making those old, tired knees buckle." Diafol grinned.

"Please," Maurice begged softly as he clutched his sleeping faeling closer to him.

"Look here, you useless fish-man, if you weren't holding the boy I hold most dear, you would be gone in a flash! I will go, yes, I will go for now. But remember! On his birthday, I will be back. And I will be leaving *with* him." He patted Élan's sleeping head, making his parents jolt.

"Mine," he said, menacingly. Azalea whimpered.

"Father please—" She was cut off as Diafol's hand gripped her throat, stopping her coming any closer to her son's sleeping form.

"Azalea!" Maurice shouted, frozen as he held his son, the spell keeping Élan asleep.

"Stay right where you are fish-man," Diafol growled and grinned back at Azalea.

"Listen to me, child, and listen well, for I will not say it again. You made your choice, your very selfish choice all those years ago. Yes, yes, you did. And I was kind in my agreement, yes, so kind. For you see, I could have had that oaf of a first son you have but no, I asked for your second. And your second, your most beloved second with all his little magick, will be mine. Why? Because you asked of me and I gave you what you needed. And what did I say?" he asked, grasping her up still.

"Y-you said—" Azalea rasped. Diafol dropped her so she could speak. He held out his palms encouragingly.

"Yes, dear one?" He grinned nastily.

"That magick always comes with a price," she cried, a tear falling. Diafol chortled.

"Yes, oh yes, dearest daughter. Indeed it does. And neither you nor your silly husband can stop that! Now go! I doubt there is

anything worse in this damned forest than me but I am bored and cold and will take my leave!" He started to walk backward, out of the light.
"Yes, father."

Quietly, Élan's parents walked back to the cottage, Azalea's tears dried from her face.
"Come now, beloved. He is safe; he is ours," Maurice spoke softly, a desperate attempt to lighten the mood.
"For how long, Mauri? How long before he is taken from us? My faeling," she touched the sleeping form on her husband's chest, her voice broken.
"Let us not dwell on that then dearest, and focus on him. He will need us, our strength. Teach him magick that he can use for himself," he said softly as he walked through the dark. Azalea went quiet in thought.
"What if I go with him?" she asked. Maurice stopped and turned to his wife. "Listen, I know it's not the best, but there isn't time now to teach him. Let me ask my father to go with them and watch over him. Therefore, he will not be alone and I can care for him," Azalea explained quickly.
"Mauri?" Azalea asked after he doesn't respond. Maurice laughed bitterly.
"So, I am to be without a wife and a son? And what of Rolo?" he asked. Azalea huffed, defeated.
"As I said, it's not the best, but what choice do we have?" Élan shifted in his sleep, distracting them both.

"Let me think on this. For now, let us return home," Maurice murmured, the cottage coming into view. Together they walked back solemnly in silence, holding hands.

The creak of the front door startled Rolo awake. He gasped as his parents lumbered into the house, Maurice groaning wearily from carrying his son a great distance.

"Gods, I feared you would never return," Rolo gasped, staring at his brother's sleeping form. His father continued to carry Élan to his room silently, as Azalea warmed her hands by the fire. No word was spoken as Élan was tucked into bed.

"May the gods watch over your resting soul, my son," Maurice whispered to his faeling as he tucked in the covers. Softly, he kissed his head and left, bones weary.

"Rolo, go rest son." His father sighed as he returned to the fire at the entrance room, a space where Azalea kept her books and few small chairs. The fire comforted the forms that stood in its light. Rolo stood and looked at Azalea and took in the grim mood.

"What happened?" he almost growled.

"Leave it, son. It is too late to discuss," Maurice whispered, his voice croaking with tiredness.

"It was him, wasn't it? That toad of a man," Rolo spat, his angry gaze not leaving his mother. Slowly, she looked up at him, the fire's blaze reflected in her gaze.

"Watch your tongue, boy. You know nothing of what you speak," she hissed.

"Tell me then!" her son barked back, which caused Maurice to raise his hands.
"Calm, Rolo. He is safe and let it be done," his father cautioned. Rolo fisted his hands, pain crumbled his face.

"For how long, Father? I know what is to come on his birthday. You both talk when the moon is high as if your faelings fall deaf. I know what will happen. That creature, that despicable thing whom we are to call 'Grandfather' is to take him! And what are we to do? Stand by and let it happen?" he asked, disgusted. Azalea laughed darkly.

"Ah yes, Rolo, I see. What are we do? Oh I know, why not let the brave first son take his place, is that it?" she let the question hang in the air, stale with sarcasm.
"We know this. We cannot do anything, even if we wanted to, son. We have made our choice. Now we must abide by it," his father added calmly, anger stirred from the others.
"We? *We* made our choice? No, Father. No, do not take me for a fool for I know it was not me and certainly not you who made this choice. So who could do this? Who would cause this heartache?" Rolo narrowed his gaze to his mother. Azalea stared back just as deathly, threatening whatever potential peace to return in their tense relationship.
"Enough, Rolo. Leave us," his father growled, sounding angry for once, sparking surprise from Rolo. Out of respect, Rolo smartly bit his tongue and stomped back to his room.

Hours passed, it seemed, while the couple sat solemnly by the fading fire, Maurice's head bowed in thought, Azalea's face grim and weary, the promise of more tears to return.

"Alright. Leave with him. I cannot bear it. The thought of him being alone with...with him. It must be done," Maurice croaked looking at his wife, holding her gaze. Grateful, Azalea's tears fell, a small smile broke through her face.

"But you must promise me one thing. Promise me that under your guidance, under your tender care, he will *not* become a creature like him. Make it impossible for the very semblance to be made between. If this happens, my wife, I fear we will lose him forever. Our son may as well be dead to us," Maurice said darkly, holding his wife's hands tenderly in his.

Quietly, Azalea cried, knowing the truth he spoke. She took his hands and placed them on the sides of her face.

"I promise, my love, I will do everything in my power to make this not so," she said, firmly kissing his palms afterwards.

Maurice stood suddenly and turned to face the fire, its once bright flames now faded as the sky lightened outside.

"Then it is done," he said bitterly as if cursing the flames.

Celebration

Oblivious to the events that led to the day, I grew more and more excited for my birthday. As every faeling did, I felt more mature, more aware of what lay ahead for me (or what I thought). A party was to be held in my honour, any excuse for the neighbours and villagers to gather and eat sweetmeats. This year though, things would be different.

My mother seemed shaken, but less worried for me now. I barely remembered that night in the forest and in a childish, illogical sense, I thought I had proven that I was capable of being alone and more independent.

For the few weeks leading up to the event, I was allowed everywhere and to do anything I wanted. I went on big hunting trips with my brother and father. I spent long afternoons baking with my mother and even coming to market with her to pick fresh ingredients. I was overcome with the sense of it all, the thought of ageing more and feeling closer to the elders in my life that I cherished.

I didn't hear anymore songs, but rather, sang my own. My father insisted I learned from him the old folk tales, sailors chants and shanties that he swore had protected him against evil spirits on the water. I learned tunes that my mother sang to the flowers and impressed everyone with my talent. I even made joke songs with my brother, spinning silly tales that would leave us both rolling in the grass, tears of laughter streaming from our eyes. Even my mother and brother seemed at ease, both making an effort not to fight around me, my brother taking an interest in baking (although I suspected it was for Mary over in the next field, a fae girl the same age as him).

Soon, the day finally arrived that I officially turned eight. I felt it took an eternity yet also no time at all. The birds' song greeted me on my birthday day.

"Awake, my youngest, for it is your special day," my mother whispered, kissing my head. I gasped and wrapped my arms around her neck, embracing her gleefully. She laughed happily, hugging me firmly to her. I noticed she had already dressed in a shimmery gown of gold, a gown of celebration.

"Happy birthday lil' sprite!" Rolo called from my door, making me laugh.

"Hey! I am no longer little!" I shout back, laughing. My mother looked at me lovingly, a lazy smile on her face.

“Where is father?” I asked excitedly. She smiled, stroking my face affectionately.

“Why, gone to get your breakfast of course! We cannot have a growing faeling eat boring oats on his birthday.” She chuckled, standing, the morning rays making her dress sparkle. I stared in awe at her suddenly realising I had nothing special to wear. Seeing my gaze on her dress, she laughed, almost embarrassed. Taking my hand, she led me into her small closet and showed me a suit of green velvet.

“I cannot have a son of eight years wear rags, can I?” She chuckled as I gasped and hugged the hand-tailored cloth. Being my mother, she knew my sizes by heart and was an excellent seamstress.

“Mother you are a wonder!” I gasped, enjoying the softness on my skin. It fit perfectly, the green cloth bringing out my eyes. I admired my reflection, feeling like the prince of the forest.

“I believe my son has bewitched himself, shame I will have to devour his breakfast myself!” My father laughed at my door. I ran to the main room to join my family.

The neighbours and villagers nearby all gathered and decorated the land for my birthday. With flags and pretty bunting that fluttered in the wind with excitement. The tables held special recipes of sweetbreads and sugary treats as a fayre took place for celebration. As noon came and went, musicians took up their small modest instruments and played a tune, encouraging all ages to dance and jig. I laughed and danced, having the most fun, everyone making an effort to talk to me, even the ones who usually shied away from me.

Even as a faeling, I knew some avoided me, at first I did not understand why. It had made me feel wrong in some way. My mother just shrugged when I told her this, and said that some fear the powerful, as she casually ripped weeds from soil.

The faelings all came to admire my suit of green and begged their parents to have one for their day of birth too. I felt pride as I shared my mother's talent and was gawped at by the younger faelings. Our small, grubby hands filled with cakes and treats, we gathered around my father, who sat on a chair he had carved himself as he prepared for a story. He waited for all the faelings to hush and began in a quiet voice, making me shudder in anticipation, excited to have my father share his talent with the other faelings on my special day.
At some point, I noticed my brother was missing and looked around. I spied him near my mother's garden. A girl stood next to him in a pink party dress, her red hair tied in ribbons to match, their backs to us as they admired the towering sunflowers. I was going to call for him when he turned to speak to her and I saw his face, red and blushing. It stopped my voice as I remembered he found it harder to speak to girl faelings than I did. Especially Mary, whom I now noticed was the girl who stood with him. I left him be, feeling good things were taking place.

Everything was perfect, the air and energy combined. By late afternoon, faeries from further away had joined us, making a larger crowd that covered the land two-fold. I felt so honoured to have everyone be there on my special day. Soon it seemed

they were waiting for something, waiting to see someone that wasn't me. I noticed this as an elderly faerie man approached me.
"Happy birthday, dear Élan. Many good wishes to you," he said, smiling at me.
"Thank you, sir. Please, enjoy yourself," I responded for the hundredth time. He nodded, grateful. Then he hesitated and turned to me again.
"Do you know when *he* will be coming?" he asked me excitedly. I frowned, unsure of who he meant.
"Who, sir?" I asked innocently. The faerie laughed gruffly.
"Your grandfather, of course! Everyone is here to see him. Why it has been…what? It must be eight years since he last came!" he answered. My heart sank for a reason my young mind could not understand.

"Oh, I do not know, sir. Soon, I hope," I answered honestly, deflated. The faerie sniffed and wandered off in disinterest. I walked through the crowd, the conversation having tainted my celebratory mood. A hand on my shoulder stopped me.
"Hey, why the sad face?" my brother asked, looking at me, concerned. Small lights switched on around us with magick, in preparation for the fading light. I looked around sadly, sobered as I saw the merriment around me.

"They are here for him, aren't they? For Grandfather," I stated sadly, pouting in disappointment. My brother huffed, crossing his arms.
"Well some old fools may be, but I sure as heck am not. I am here for you and you alone," he said, patting me in comfort.

"You are certain it is not Mary you are here for?" I bit back in jealousy. My brother's face blushed red in shock.

"W-who?" he asked, looking around as the energy had picked up, voices raising around us. Annoyed and upset, I walked away, feeling it was a better option than to shout at him on my birthday. I pushed past others, feeling my frustration build. I felt foolish in my green suit, my pride ruined. I collided into my mother.

"Gods, Élan. What's the matter?" she asked, taking my shoulders. My face was red with frustration and I turned away from her embarrassed.

Before she is able to confront my behaviour, an unnatural scream ripped through the air, a shooting light soared across the evening sky. It exploded above us and captured everyone's attention, including my own. I took my mother's arm, not sure how to take the sight before me. I heard others gasp in surprise, some in awe.

The lights, as they fell, were multi-coloured and beautiful. I felt my mother tense next to me. Before I could question her, a shout distracted me.

"Greetings, fellow faeries, it is I, the devilish Diafol! How are we this evening?" I followed his voice and saw him standing on a small dais next to where a tent had been erected. Faeries gathered immediately, pushing past us, answering him with greetings and welcomes, cheers on his return. I pouted, annoyed at the shameless attention they gave him and how well he received it. A few times, I had encountered my grandfather

(though more than I remember it seemed) and each time he had left me feeling confused, mystified, or forgotten.
Despite this, I still liked him and felt proud to have such an important being related to me. Suddenly, I realised my mother had not moved since the appearance of her father.
"Mother?" I asked, though I was drowned out by the crowds' cheers. He was telling some story about his journey here, causing laughter and more questions from the onlookers. I sensed my mother's distress and although I could not place it, I gently tried to tug her away from the crowd.

Before I could get her to move, a sound stopped me. A gentle song pulled me from my current focus and I looked around curiously, feeling strange from its lure. It sounded like a gentle flute; the melody calmed me and stirred my faeling curiosity. I walked out of the crowd, forgetting my mother and her worries, the song giving off a welcoming pull.

"Ah, there he is! The faeling of the hour! My dearest and youngest! Come here, dear one," my grandfather called. The music stopped. I shook my head, frowning.

Faeries made space as I made my way to him. I looked up at him in awe as I ascended the stairs. He was dressed for the occasion in a dark blue velvet suit, studded with what looked like small stars that glistened against the torch lights. His hair looked slightly less knotted as if he had run his fingers through it. His greenish skin looked almost orange against the lights, his eyes glowing yellow-gold. He put out his hand to me as I approached and shook it quickly, almost so strongly that shook my small body.

"My, my. What a fantastic skin of velvet you wear, dear one! Must be of your mother's design?" He grinned, his sharp yellow teeth scaring me a little in the evening light. I turned then to look at the crowd, over two hundred faeries now gathered, watching us converse. I nodded, answering his question. My voice wavered as my heart thudded.

As if to comfort myself, I spied my mother, my father joining her. But their tense expressions uneased me. What was wrong? Why weren't they happy? My grandfather's snort drew me from my thoughts.
"Ah, indeed. What a talent she has! I always said she should make more of it than she has. But enough of her. Yes, enough. It is your birthday, dear one, and what gift would you ask of me?" he asked, leaning down to my level. His question caught me off guard and I stuttered an answer, not knowing.

Again, I looked to my parents and found no support on their faces. Were they afraid? Perhaps the light was tricking my eyes.

"Ah I see, a lucky faeling such as yourself would have most things he needs. Yes, a very modest life you live, dear one. But perhaps I can give you something you don't have, yes? Say perhaps some gold?" he asked, giving me another toothy grin. The crowd had grown quiet as if anticipating my choice. I heard my mother cough as if distressed. I frowned at Diafol. Something in me thudded wrongly at his offer.

"Gold? Why give me gold? Gold is rare and eight-year-olds don't know what to do with gold," I said curiously. Before me, he flipped a gold coin and caught it at my eye level. It glistened in the firelight, reminding me of his eyes. I stared at it, feeling a tug on my soul. Its lure suddenly clear to me, yet a part of me felt offbeat with what was going on.

"Why, what boy does not want gold? And this is not just any gold, dear one, but magick—filled with my protection! Yes, a very good gift. The best, yes?" he asked with excitement in his voice. I stared at it some more, feeling hundreds of silent gazes on me. Anyone knew better than to turn down a gift from the great Diafol, yet the tugging in my soul was uncomfortable and felt wrong. There was no music; I felt nothing looking at the cold metal.

"I'm sorry, Grandfather, but I have no need for it. I know it is special like everything you have and give. But I cannot take this from you," I replied, blushing as gasps broke out through the crowd. I bowed my head, ashamed. Diafol remained quiet and stood to his normal height. A giggle drew my gaze back to him. He smiled down at me, humour lit in his eyes.

"Yes, I see, I see! Such cleverness, yes, cleverness, dear one. Very good, very good, my boy. For you see, gold is powerful and pretty, oh so very pretty, but take it when it is not needed. No. This is greed, dear boy. Greed! And we would not want Élan to be a greedy faerie, would we?" he asked and I sighed in relief. A test! A tricky test, gosh he is the damnedest creature as I recall these memories of my youth.

"No, you see, we have a much better gift for you, yes much, much better! But that is for a later time." The crowd, who were stood in confusion, booed quietly for missing out on my actual gift. Playfully, he wagged his finger at the crowd.

"For now, let us continue the celebration into the night! The day may be to rest, but the night is greeting my grandson on his eighth year! Let our spirits take to the skies!" he called, another screaming line of light shooting into the sky before it exploded, causing the crowd to scream in joy and cheer loudly.

As they stared at the lights in the sky, and danced to some unheard song, my grandfather knelt down to me on the dais.

"Tomorrow we shall talk more of this; tonight, enjoy yourself," he said rather sombrely. I nodded and left the dais, noticing my mother and father were now smiling sadly at me.

Azalea sat watching her youngest stuff his mouth full of cake, Rolo laughing at him. Both were overtired as it was late into the night, but she dare not ruin their fun.

A small breeze raised goosebumps on her bare arms, as a presence drew near. Knowing who it was, she remained uncaring, watching her children.

"Aren't you going to thank me, dear one?" Diafol sneered, his arms crossed.

"Why did you do it? Why give us this night?" she asked, unable to tear her gaze away from her children.

"He is a clever one, that faeling. I am proud, daughter. He passed a difficult challenge. He can last one more night without my instruction." He sighed, the breeze lifting his dusty mop of hair.

"What will you say tomorrow?" she asked, shivering slightly.

"That is between me and him. You will catch on I am sure of it. For now, leave it. Enjoy these hours with your son," he said and turned to leave. Azalea began to walk away.

"And daughter? Whatever I use him for in the future, remember this night, this solace I gave to you, and think me not a complete monster," he said, all humour and games gone from his features. He left his daughter standing there in shock, mouth agape, speechless.

Purpose

My birthday seemed to have no end. I stayed up the latest I ever had. My gift from my grandfather was forgotten until midday the next day. I recall my mother holding me for an extra long time that night and I enjoyed the love that flowed from her. She seemed almost free of fear and stroked my head as I spoke, jabbering excitedly about my day. In my childish heart, I enjoyed the attention and loved the day thoroughly. The day that followed would change my life forever.

I had passed out early the morning after my birthday and was left to sleep until noon. The sun was high in the sky when I woke, eyes aching from the long day. I felt tired but excited when I remembered it was not completely over yet. I ran down into the main room to find the place empty. The smell of the morning breakfast already fading.

"Mother?" I called, confused, fear already building in me. Was this a dream? Never before had the cottage been empty upon my waking.

Softly, music began to play. It was the same song as the night before. I followed it, not knowing what else to do. It led me onto the top of a large hill that overlooked our cottage and neighbours. It was quiet, with soft birdsong and insects already fully into their day. The music suddenly stopped as I felt a tap on my left shoulder. I quickly turned, scared. A giggle to my right turned me back to face the hill; Diafol stood at the top. He waved me over and I ran to him, my heart pounding.

He sat down, cross legged on the grass, staring out into the lands below us, a lazy smile on his face. The wind fluffed our hair and freshened our faces. We sat there, quietly admiring our view, neither of us in a hurry with what was to come.

"You enjoyed your birthday?" he asked, surprising me.

"Most certainly, Grandfather. It was most memorable!" I answered happily, my mind alight with thoughts of it all.

"Wonderful, but the best is yet to come, dear one. I want the best, the very best, for you!" he said gesturing to the land ahead of us.

"Thank you, Grandfather. I am honoured to be so beloved by you," I answered, blushing. I truly was grateful. Not many can say that a being so powerful as Diafol is beloved by them. He laughed loudly as if finding my admission hilarious.

"Sweet. Such sweetness. Oh, you will do well, yes, very well. I have such plans for you—big plans!" he said gleefully. I looked to him eagerly.

"Élan, dear boy, do you know what makes you different from every other faerie down there?" he asked, gesturing to the land below. I frowned, thinking hard. As if to help me, the song quietly picks up in the wind. I gasp and turn back to him.

"The music! I can hear the music, Grandfather!" I said excitedly. He laughed, clapping his hands.

"Yes, dear one, yes! You hear it, you hear the music of the gods. No one else, no one here but you and I can hear it. Even when your mother held you in her belly, it was you listening through your parents," he said, putting his arm on my small shoulders proudly. I feel the weight of his arm at the same time as his words.

"But what does that mean, Grandfather? Why can I hear the music?" I asked innocently, for this had plagued my mind on many occasions.

"Because, dear one, you are my blood, my most powerful faeling and you are blessed, oh so blessed, and destined for great things. Such great things!" he said excitedly.

"Like what, Grandfather?" I asked, frustration hardening my voice.

"You have the power, yes, such great power and magick within you. With this power, we can travel the world, you and I. We will travel and spread this great music far and wide. For that is what you were born for, my faeling," he explained, gesturing widely. I am unable to hide my surprise.

Suddenly, I see a vision of me singing and making music around a world outside of Brimhaven. The image bright and bursting within me. Like a vibrant dream, I see myself spreading the talent far and wide beyond my imagination. I feel the first simmer of my magick in response, making my arms goose pimple.

"To travel? Me? Into the other lands?" I asked, unsure. I never even considered leaving here before this moment, let alone venturing into other lands, especially ones not in the Faelands.
"Indeed, this is truth, such a great truth. And my gift, the gift I want for you on your eighth year, is important, oh so important, Élan! The gift of knowledge," he said, facing me fully now, his eyes pinning me into place. I frowned, unsure of what he meant.
"Knowledge?" I asked, confused. I watched as his pupils dilated and his mouth hardened.
"Yes, dear boy. With power, such power and magick that you have, there must be knowledge. Knowledge of other lands and creatures. What is power without knowledge? A waste, I say! Such a waste." He spat. I stared at him, completely captured by his words, for this was the most he had said to me and I hung on his every word. His voice became the only sound to reach me, my body feeling like a wall from me to him.

"Will I be great? Great like you and mother?" I asked, breathless, completely charmed by him. He grinned at me.
"Why yes, most definitely greater than your mother," he snorted and laughed loudly at his own words.

"And this is what my family wants? What mother and father want for me?" I gasped, amazed, the vision of me, clearer before me than the village below us. Diafol nodded and grinned widely.
"And who knows? Maybe you will even be greater than me! Oh yes, such promise. But this is important, and yes difficult, difficult like that test you had last night, yes. For you see, you cannot stay here," he said quickly. I was be-spelled with all this promise and wonder, I missed the meaning in the last words. Slowly, the words sank in and my brow furrowed slightly.
"Leave…here?" I asked hesitantly, looking out at the village before me. It was coming into to focus in front of me once again.
Leave home? Leave Brimhaven?
I was hesitant. I knew this was unusual for a faeling so young. Though if not me, then who? Was I not the grandson of Diafol?

After all, my mother did not grow up here. Perhaps I was also meant for other adventures outside this land. It seemed beings with greater magick came from outside this land of simplicity. Even those very thoughts had my heart pounding with excitement.

"Yes, ah yes, see? This is tricky, so tricky, but you see, knowledge cannot be found here, knowledge must be learnt with me, away from here," he explained. I remained quiet in thought, not knowing how to take this news. Did mother know this? Did my mother want this? For she has never mentioned such a thing before…

"Ah ha! But you see, your mother can come with us, yes, she is to come and help you with her knowledge and together, we will teach you," he said.
"But what about Rolo? And Father?" I asked sadly, my thoughts torn as I realised this meant being without them slowly sank painfully into my gut.

Yet the vision of my music, being spread through the world beyond what my faeling mind understood, made my heart soar and my first sense of simmering magick tingled my very bones.

"Knowledge is not needed for them no, not them. But you see, they need to stay here and look after the land, for I know they are good at this. Just like you will be good at your power and music, they will be good at this. Everyone has their purpose, little one," he said, gesturing boldly to the land before us in the bright daylight.

I bravely swallowed down the sadness that overcame me. I will miss Rolo and father dearly, this I knew. Am I really meant to leave here? I looked out on the thriving fields and flowers.

He proceeded to tell me of his plans and the tutors he had sought out to teach me knowledge and worldly things. That this would mean I would be staying in the Capital of the Faelands, Astoria. When I began to hesitate, my thoughts still on my brother and father, Diafol assured me.
"Worry not, dear one. Worry not one bit! You will miss them but it will be good, oh so good for you. And we can still see them, yes, let us see them on special days, any days that you wish," he

said, holding my shoulder, looking at me fully. I pondered his words and smiled, assuring myself that this was what growing up was about. I was to follow my destiny, be brave, and help my family by doing my best. They wanted this for me.

We continued to speak on this for the rest of the day. I was bursting with questions about the Capital and what I was to do there. The more I heard, the more I began imagining myself there. Whenever my thoughts returned to my brother and father, my heart would drop and I began assuring myself that it was for the best; after all, my mother would be with me.

"When do we leave? I need to ready myself," I asked, noticing the afternoon transitioning into the evening.

"We leave at sunrise tomorrow," he answered, the news dropping like a stone in my belly. So soon? I wanted to ask, the shock freezing my voice in my throat.

"You mother approaches," Diafol said, pointing below us. We stood and joined her. I hugged her tightly, my head only reaching just above her navel.

"Say your farewells and I will collect you both at dawn," he said as I clutched to my mother. I heard him walk away and wondered where he rested when he was visiting, for I have never seen him stay at our cottage, even though there is space for him.

My mother held me to her for the longest time. I stood, content to take in her scent, letting my grandfather's words run through my mind.

We quietly walked back to our cottage, hand in hand. I took in my surroundings as if it was my first sight on the land. The scent of the grass, the fresh wild flowers. The sound of the bees and distant sounds of sheep grazing on the hills around us. The sky faded to a pleasant orange and the air was colder now.

"Mother, I am happy you are coming with us, for I will surely miss you all too much if I were to be with Grandfather on my own," I said cheerfully in my young optimism. My mother stopped and crouched down in front of me.

"And I am so glad to be with you, my dearest. My brave boy, I am so proud of you," she said, a sad smile on her lips.

I hugged her hard, overcome.

"But won't you miss Father? And Rolo?" I asked, pulling back.

Surely, this meant it was important for me to leave, if my mother insisted on coming with me, leaving father and Rolo behind? I watched curiously as small tears fell on her pale face.

"Why yes, dear one, I shall. But helping you will be a great honour. Your father and brother know this," she assured me, holding my blushed face in the wind.

"Because everyone has their purpose?" I asked, quoting my grandfather. My mother hesitated.

"I suppose so," she muttered. We walked quicker back to the cottage; no other words were shared.

That evening, I felt weary, the days catching up, my energy drained. My thoughts of leaving the next day were fogged with drowsiness, making me unaware of the tension around me. My father sang a song accompanied by his lute as my mother cooked quietly. His voice slow and sadder than normal, it eased me into my tiredness. Rolo returned with arms full of firewood, face flushed from the cold wind. He joined me by the fire.

Sleepily, I asked Rolo about his day. He answered with little interest, distant in his demeanour, eyes staring into the fire. I would have noticed his off-tone if not for my drooping eyes. Plates and bowls clattered on the small table, calling us to supper, a warm soup waking my heavy body.

"Sorry it's not much. I had little time," my mother muttered breaking bread for us. I smiled lazily at her, happy to have something light and warm to eat.

"It's fine, dearest. We appreciate the comfort." My father smiled softly, placing his hand over hers. She smiled sadly at him and squeezed his hand in response. I hummed happy at the warm earthy taste.

"Is this really to be our last night together? A rushed meal and sleepy brother?" Rolo growled into his bowl.

"It is what is, son. Be at peace with it," my father warned.

"Oh, is it? Truly? And how am I to be at peace with it, Father? That monster taking away my brother was no choice of mine," my brother said, emboldened with anger.

Suddenly my mother burst into tears. Something I'd hardly seen and now I was fully awake. In a childish response, I felt my own eyes watering, my brother's tone tightening the air around us. Looking back, I wonder if it was guilt that my mother now cried for...

"I'm sorry, Rolo. The choice was mine. It was selfish. Maybe I should not go," I said quietly, feeling my throat tighten, the realisation that I had caused this.

"No, son. You must go," my father said softly.

"Yes, you must," my mother said brokenly. My brother thudded the wooden table with his fist, making me yelp as he rarely did such a thing.

"As if he has a choice! You are wrong, brother," he growled, looking at me. I frowned, making my lip tremble. The firelight behind him lit him up like some demon, and I considered him being possessed as he did not make sense to me.

"What do you mean?" I pouted, voice shaken.

"What he means is—" my mother started.

"What he means is that we want you to go, son. There is nothing for you here, not in a way that will be of use to your potential. You need to go, go and live your life that you were meant for, one full of adventure and magick," my father said, kissing my mother's palm. This got a snort from my brother but he said no more about it.

"Yes, Father. If you feel I should, then I will. I want to make you proud. All of you," I turned to my, brother who had discarded his soup.

"Brother please don't be upset with me. I mean well; I will come visit you I promise," I said softly.

He sighed heavily, sounding as tired as I feel. Quickly he stood, roughly putting his bowl in the sink. He strode next to me, the room is small, so it seemed in a flash, he was there. He took my shoulder roughly.

"You know nothing," he hissed at me and left the room.

"Leave him," my father spoke, although none of us made a move. My mother sighed, her tears silent. I remained sitting, frowning at his words. Why was everyone acting so weirdly?

"Is he jealous?" I asked after moments in deep thought.

"Perhaps," my mother said, having resumed eating her soup.

"Worry not, little one, he does not know what he speaks. Now finish your soup and to bed, you have an early start tomorrow," said my father, finishing his own bowl. I obeyed silently.

My brother's words stayed with me days after, the bite in them clanging loudly at something I did not understand. But they rang some unknown bell of warning within me that felt important.

The Capital

By the time I had realised that I had left my childhood home, I was already halfway to Astoria.

I had been bundled into a small, wooden horse-drawn cart, my mother holding me close to her, wrapped in blankets against the morning dew. I briefly heard my grandfather speak and he was gone. I was in and out of sleep as we journeyed past the hills and trees.

Occasionally, my mother would sing softly, stroking my hair. The wind carried her voice so it danced around me in my sleep. Like a babe, I was soothed into a peaceful lull as we travelled away from the only place I had ever known.

Many days passed before I was awoken by loud hooves on the pavement. The hustle and bustle of a marketplace with a symphony of different voices. I peaked out from my blankets, the daylight blurring my vision. More voices joined an assortment of busy faeries moving around us. I noticed they were dressed brighter than the earthy colours of my village, with large hats with feathers. My curious eyes soaked in the vibrant sights around me. Hundreds of hard shoes and hooves struck a beat around me, my head fully out of the blanket now. This place was a busy wonder!

I stared in amazement at the buildings that stood tall as trees and closely arranged mighty houses that dwarfed the humble cottages of Brimhaven. Fine, intricate patterns lined the walls, some carved and some painted. Gold shone through the designs, enticing me to enter. I was most impressed by what I saw, feeling assured about my bold choice to leave the comforts of the Faefields.

My magick tingled as I took in others around me, using more magick that I had seen in Brimhaven. They used it for simple tasks, to enhance their busy lifestyle. I could not wait to find out how to use it more myself! My mother chuckled as she acknowledge my wide-eyed fascination.

The smells were musky and unfamiliar to me, laced with perfumes and powders. My stomach rumbled as I caught the scent of fresh bread.

"A good welcome to you grandson of the great Diafol. Please take this," a faerie male in an apron made an offer to me as the cart halted. I looked to my mother and she nodded, smiling gently. I took it from him with thanks, letting it warm my hands, the pleasant steam coming off it in the morning cold. It would seem my grandfather was popular here too.

We reached a large house, separate from the others in the busy town. Behind it loomed a large forest that had me standing, eager to explore its expanse. My legs trembled in weakness and my mother helped me out of the cart. We drew nearer and the intricacy in the details against the house had me gasping in amazement. Who lived here?

The house commanded the attention of any passerby. In a shimmer of magick, Diafol appeared in the doorway of the house. Gods! This was his house? I clutched my mother in excitement as we walked down the path.

"Is this truly where you grew up Mother?" I looked at her in surprise. Our house seemed so small and humble as I took in her grand childhood home. She smiled down at me, her face drawn from the journey.

"Indeed. It is rather large, isn't it?" She chuckled dryly. Soon I dived into thoughts of my mother growing up here, alone with Diafol. I remembered my grandmother had died when she was very young.

"It must have been lonely," I muttered, feeling a lurch of homesickness. What were Rolo and father doing right now? Instead of replying, my mother led me inside.

Colours and patterns opened up to me as I stepped inside, the hard floor echoing my steps. I couldn't even withhold my gasp of amazement as I took in my surroundings.

The ceiling reached the sky itself! Where the patterns ended, the walls were lined with books held together on shelves that stretched far and wide, all in a variety of shapes and sizes. My heart raced at the idea of reading them all - I loved books! We had so few at home and most were for practicalities such as cooking and gardening rather than entertainment.

It also seemed that while the cottages were made for purpose in Brimhaven, this house was made to stir wonder and inspire leisure. Instruments stood where my father's tools would have been, fine vases and statues of fabled faeries posed where my mother's pots would sit. Even the air seemed spiced with magick, tingling my nerves and drawing a song from my soul. Gods, there was so much to explore!

My mother watched me, a small smile playing on her lips. "It is overwhelming, but you will get used to it, my sweet. There is a lot you can learn here and I am sure you will enjoy all that Diafol has to teach you." Her smile wavered as she drew the blanket around my shoulders.

"The gift of knowledge," I whispered to myself as I toured my mother's childhood home.

To my disappointment, I was allowed little time with Diafol himself. He had constructed a busy schedule with a variety of tutors, as he insisted that I had a lot to catch up on with regards to faelings my own age.

In Brimhaven, there were small classes held where you learned to read and write. These were purely by choice and many faeries were too busy running their pieces of land to attend. My parents had encouraged us to go when we could but these were nothing compared to the extensive sessions my grandfather had arranged for me. Giant books were dropped before me to pore over and read at a pace that reminded me of a Jackrabbits' run. These books contained stories and legends I have never heard of before. Fables that stretched far beyond the Faelands, reaching far to the North.

I attended classes that were held in the town, with other faelings slightly younger than myself. Everyone seemed to know who I was and regarded me as such, a distant respect for one with a powerful and much discussed grandfather. Even the tutors themselves spared me extra patience. When told to read out texts, I heard snickers from the others; apparently my accent was obvious and charming to them.

Being from the forest region of the Faelands, I spoke the same common language—Karing—as all day creatures did, but I had a twang that made me self conscious and shy. Although, anyone who laughed at my expense, was soon severely punished by the tutors. This made me even more uncomfortable and made it hard to make any friends.

I was eager to learn more about my magick but was quickly disappointed when no classes were held on the subject. Apart from what I had already seen of it being used, I was given a book on the War, and was informed that since then, barely any magick was taught. I put away the information, knowing for this to be not entirely true, as my mother was taught by Diafol more than what I had seen.

I was pleasantly surprised to learn that the food here had more variety and flavours to pick from. Being a merchant's town and the capital centre of trade in the Faelands, there were many new fruits and vegetables as well as meats from beasts I had never heard of, available right to our door step.

My mother humbly obliged in cooking me a variety of broths and stews that were tangy and spicier than the simple flavours I was used to in Brimhaven. As I revelled in the new tastes, she smiled softly, her delicate features flushed, pleased with my enthusiasm.

Needless to say, I flourished in Astoria with all it had to offer me. I adored the gift of knowledge my grandfather had bestowed upon me. I could not imagine myself the same, if I had stayed in Brimhaven. My classes soon grew longer, and eventually, I was relocated to my grandfather's house as I surpassed and advanced in my classes, taking everything in that they threw at me, my specialisms needing more attention.

Though my magick was still a mystery, with my mother strangely avoiding the subject, I soon found my new passion—music.

Just a few weeks after I had arrived, different tutors started to visit my grandfather's home. They boasted to be specialists in their field.

I remembered standing there for hours in the large house, repeating words constantly, accentuating and defining my words. They said to come across as more 'worldly,' I had to lose my farm-fae twang. Wanting nothing more than to become 'worldly' enough to travel with my music, I did as they instructed with fierce determination.

When that began to become less of an effort, I had a tutor to teach me how to use my voice, with and without music, for talking and with small, magickal enhancements that helped project it.

With delight, I felt my voice become more tuned and refined. I began to pick up words that the other faelings used and practised them at the house, in the privacy of my room.

Sometimes, when I felt proud of a particular song or passage, I would run to my mother excitedly, who spent her days in a large glass house behind the house full of plants and shared it with her. She would be proud and admire my willingness to learn. She seemed brighter now that she was among her plants, her hands patched with soil, her eyes bright with interest.

Typically, I only saw her at mealtimes and she seemed happier and was getting used to her new life. Occasionally, a small shred of doubt would make my heart ache as I remembered that I took her away from my brother and father, cursing myself for my selfishness.

But seeing her anew with her plants gave me hope and allowed me to ignore the guilt.

The one thing I never got used to, was the damned clothing as well as the regular bathing. Wearing shirts of silk and suits of refined cotton, as was the fashion there—a different colour or style per day! It was so constricting and stuffy. They simply did not bend or fold with my body like the clothing of Brimhaven.

My scrubbed skin felt itchy and tight. The shoes were hard on my feet and made me ache within a day of wearing them. Tutors pushed for a better body stance and position, prompting me when I forgot. "You are a grandchild of the Diafol," they would say.

Sometimes, as if in self-comfort, my mind would wander to my brother and father, wondering what they might be doing. I could not wait to show them what I had learned and grimaced at what my brother would think of my clothing.

My enthusiasm grew when my tutors started to teach me more about music and we began to tour the instruments in Diafol's house together. I was shown each one in detail and taught to study it thoroughly. I was educated on the varieties of music in the world, exploring outside my knowledge of the fae, adding depth to my understanding. It fascinated me and I read books on these topics for long hours, lecturing my mother in turn on what I had learned. She listened patiently, saying little and busying herself.

I began using my voice and playing with control and technicality that I had learnt, impressing my tutors.

Beltane, the time of spring evolving into summer, came and it marked a month of me being in Astoria. Word reached my grandfather in his mystery and business on my progress, and he attended my next classes in music, causing the tutors to be flustered. He stood, emotionless, as I sang and played the lute. I stumbled over the strings while my voice rang true as if to cover up the mistakes, and this drew a pleased grin from him.

When I was finished, he remained quiet, as if waiting for more. Nervously, the tutor asked for his response.

"Well of course, he is perfection! My faeling of song," he boasted, making me blush with pride. He eyed me for a few quiet moments after the tutor was dismissed.

"Perhaps this calls for a celebration! A reward for your impressive enthusiasm. Let us journey to that small pile of mud you call home to show your brother and father what you have learnt," he said in a sing-song way.

"Gods! Truly, Grandfather? I would love to. Please, can we?" I begged, my face hot with excitement. It has been so long since I'd seen them and my heart lurched thinking that I might get to soon. He confirmed as such and I ran to tell my mother. She hugged me tightly, crying happy tears.

As we journeyed back to Brimhaven days later in a carriage that matched the intricate house, my heart soared at the thought as seeing my family again so soon. What had they been up to? Had much happened since I had left? Would they like the new songs I had written?

My mind was flurrying with eagerness and excitement. As I watched the land flow by, I saw myself performing music all around the new lands I had learned of.

I wore my old Brimhaven clothing in anticipation (and comfort) of arriving at my old home. I was weary from staying awake the whole journey with little sleep, but as soon as I saw the hill that introduced Brimhaven, I leapt out of the carriage, causing my mother to yelp at me. She soon laughed as she watched me run, almost taking flight back to our old cottage.

I knocked over my father as I embraced him with the might of how much I missed him. I heard the emotion rumble in his chest as I held him, refusing to forget the feel of his warmth against me. He was almost speechless as I held him like I never had before.

"Dear boy, you have grown!" he gasped when I helped him up again. I smiled at him and told him excitedly of my time in the capital. Listening intently, he led me into the cottage, which now felt smaller than before.

The familiar smells and sights soothed me. I refused to let go of my father's hand, despite my age. He held my hands in his as he sat us down. A small proud smile began to emerge as I told him of what I had learnt and my experience with the classes.

"You have thrived, my boy, truly. A father could not be more proud," he gushed, ruffling my hair like he did when I was younger. I grinned at the praise and began to look around.

"Where is Rolo?" I asked, eager to see him again. The sadness of our last evening had been weighing on me. My father pointed to the fields behind our house.

I slowed my steps as he came into view. His back was to me, busy with his work in the field. I hesitated as I stood there, watching him, the old feelings of pride and sadness returning. How I missed him!

I realised then that in the crowded classes of other faelings and in the big town house of Diafol, I had not met any other faeling like him. That I had really missed the fun we had here, just the two of us. I'd spent most of my days with him, learning all I could, his encouragement something I had not realised I had relied on until it was gone.

Lost in my thoughts, I jumped when he embraced me hard. The bitter feelings of sadness bubbled up into tears. I hugged him back, embarrassed.

"I'm sorry for how I left things. I was haunted by it for days. It was stupid of me," he said, his voice raw. I had forgotten how much taller he was, his body wider and stronger than I

remembered. He took my silence as if I was still upset with him. He drew back, concerned.
"Forgive me?" he asked quietly, his arms still loosely around me. I hugged him again, annoyed he had broken it for foolish words.

"Of course," I muttered into his chest.
"You smell cleaner," he grumbled, making me snort.
"You don't!" I laughed, pulling back. He looked at me pointedly.
"You are good though? Well?" he asked, concerned. I frowned.
"Of course I am! Why wouldn't I be?" I said, finding his concern amusing. He didn't reply and his last words to me flashed in my mind, a question forming on my tongue. A snigger from behind us stopped me.

"Ah! how fitting to find Rolo among the sheep and mud. Miss me, grandson?" Diafol grinned nastily. My brother narrowed his eyes at him.
"I'm surprised you could bear returning here again so soon. Where are your beloved worshippers?" he replied dryly, his arm around my shoulder protectively. Diafol laughed at him.
"Such malice from a boy! Better watch that temper; the sheep may not recognise you soon enough." He shook his finger, clicking his tongue.
"I suppose we better go see mother," my brother said to me, turning his back on him. I looked back at Diafol and worried he was offended, but he was gone.

Beltane celebrations were held over the next few days with music, dancing, freshly cooked meats, and blooming flowers. It felt that all was how it once was, my self and soul remembering how it was here. I saw other faelings and I boasted of my adventures to them by the firelight, my face flushed with pride and the attention I was getting.

My family seemed to have returned to their old ways as if my absence was forgotten. Diafol remained scarce, heightening the illusion that everything had returned to normal and created a sense of peace among us. When he did make an appearance, it tightened the tension around us like a storm brewing, my brother and father particularly on edge. He created a looming presence, reminding everyone that this was a temporary state and I would soon leave again with my mother.

The days flashed by and soon, I was to return to Astoria. Despite my great adventures and my dream of being a worldly musician, I was reluctant to leave the warmth and stability of my family cottage. I pouted childishly as my father held me.

"Be safe, my songbird," he whispered into my fluffy, dark hair. I swallowed the lump forming in my throat and focused on when I next wanted to return. My brother seemed more cheerful, and was there to say goodbye to me this time. I held him the longest, determined to make up for the missed days we would have.

"Make sure that head doesn't grow too big with knowledge, sprite." He ruffled my hair playfully, making me giggle. I left feeling lighter, a spring in my step and hope alight in my heart, determined not to go too long before I saw them again.

I had made such an impression that the younger faelings were up and waiting for me at the end of the path leading to the hill, which marked the end of Brimhaven. They all waved goodbye and begged me to come back soon. I laughed, waving at them, madly answering with promises. I sat back in the carriage, a silly grin on my face, my mother soberly quiet and Diafol absent once more.

Summer came and went with no sign of me returning home. I soon forgot trying to focus on going back home, heart weary from the strain. I decided that using the same focus on my studies to further impress my grandfather would help.

Diafol himself seemed extra preoccupied, only seeing me once within days at a time. This made it extra hard to discuss my next visit to Brimhaven and it felt as though he was avoiding me. My mother was little help as she too, was at a loss. Our last visit seemed to have drained her of her spirit and hope, almost as if she had left part of herself there.

I could relate to this, my thoughts more often on my homeland now. I used this to fuel my voice in song, and I wrote songs on my memories of home, capturing my audiences. Some were happy and some had a sad tone to them.

At my tutors' request, I was given a solo role in a town choir. I excelled and felt excited to tell Diafol. My mother seemed to awaken when she saw my progress, proposing that perhaps I should invite my brother and father here so that they could see and would not have to wait for my grandfather's decision. I happily agreed and together, we excitedly wrote a letter to them, gushing our love in the pages, pleading for them to come as we missed them so. My mother seemed better, hope lifting her spirit once more.

The choir would perform for Yule, the winter festival in the town. This also marked half a year since my last visit home. Awaiting my family's response, I focused on perfecting my part, convinced they would come. My mother met me in the study room where I practised, a letter in her hand.

"I'm sorry, love. They cannot come," she said sadly, tears already dried on her face. I remember being so shocked that I missed what else she told me. She repeated it after I recovered, bewildered as to why they couldn't come.

"You father is ill, taken to his bed, leaving Rolo to look after the land on his own," she explained, my heart pounded with the misfortune. Father was never ill…

"This must be hard for them; they may be struggling Mother," I said sadly. She could say little to comfort me. I stood, determined to find Diafol and demand to see my father. My mother gasped and stopped me.

"Take care, dear. You must not approach him with such firmness. Take it from me—he will not receive it well," she warned me. It deflated me a little, though I understood. I had little time to think on my words as he was there in the next moment, standing in front of us. He leaned casually against the wall, looking at us, interested.

"Grandfather, may I go see my father? He has taken ill and I want to care for him," I asked, approaching him. He remained quiet, thinking, and I resisted the urge to sigh with frustration. Surely, this was not a tough decision to make!

"What of your choir? The tutors tell me you are vital to the success of the performance," he said carefully. I frowned at him; I was losing my patience.

"That matters not, Grandfather. My father is ill! I must be with him," I said firmly, desperation in my voice. My mother hovered behind me. Diafol's emotionless face turned into a sneer.

He rushed forward and grabbed me by the throat, lifting me. My mother yelped.

"Matters not, eh? Well, how about I wretch the very air from your lungs! While you simper over a broken old man, all knowledge is wasted. No, you cannot go, you silly faeling," he growled at me, making me blush as I struggled to breathe.

My mother pleaded with him desperately until he released me. I crumpled to the floor, coughing. Diafol stood his full height, his body rigid now, his anger simmering off him.

"What a disappointment. Such talent is wasted on you, you little cretin. WASTED. No! If you are not careful, you will not return there again. Now calm yourself before you make a big mistake," he growled at me. The look in his eyes seemed to set something within me. I felt my mother's magick cool my anger, leaving me sad and tearful.

"Father, he is young. He will learn. Please, if not him, let me go. Let me go and heal my husband and Élan can stay to make up for his careless words," my mother said carefully behind me. I wiped my tears silently, feeling bitter, unable to look at either of them. Why did it have to be this way? Hadn't I worked hard enough?

"Indeed he will learn. Bah! Fine. Go to your stupid husband. The faeling must remain here until I am happy with his progress." He gestured airily. I bit my tongue on the angry words that tried to spill out. How I hated him at that moment! Him standing there, talking of my family as if they were his to command. Commanding me to remain here as my father lies sick in bed miles away from us. My mother took me to my room quietly and tried to comfort me.

"Forgive me. It was the best I could do." She hugged me hard as we reached my room.
"You will make him well again? Tell him I love him," I said brokenly, unable to look at her face.
"Of course I will. He will know it is not your doing for not seeing him. I am just so sorry I cannot bring you with me love,"

she said sadly, wiping my tears gently. She hugged me again and I quieted, deep in thought.

"You will miss my show," I muttered sadly into her neck. She hugged me tighter then.

"I know, love, but I have seen your performance. I know that you will do well, my youngest. If only I could bring it with me to show your father." She softly stroked my cheek.

I jolted at an idea and ran to my desk. I pulled out the parchment there and handed it to her.

"It's the music and words I will sing. Take it with you, show him this, and tell him to heal well so he can see my next performance," I said firmly, determination in my young face. My mother smiled at me.

"I will, my son. I am sure your father will love this gift." She kissed me happily, pride shining in her warm, brown eyes.

My mother left days later with a swift farewell. I ignored the jealousy burning within me at the thought of her returning home without me. Diafol was nowhere to be seen, which angered me more, his carelessness wounding me.

Using recipes my mother had taught me, I fed myself and practised my music further, to distract my worried heart. At night I tucked myself in, imaging I was back at home with the handwoven covers and the close wooden walls. I fell asleep to soft music I heard in the distance and dreamed of home.

Yule arrived and I felt sluggish and more alone than ever. I rarely saw Diafol, and when I did, it was in the presence of my tutors. He regarded me as my tutors continued to gush over my progress but I no longer felt proud. I remained reserved, wiser to my emotions around him.

With my mother gone, unable to protect and warn me of the unpredictable creature, I avoided him when I could. I felt myself press harder in effort of my songs, the happy ones harder to find in my mind, the emotion feeling forced.

When I had my Yule performance, the initial excitement was gone. I acknowledged Diafol's attendance, but no other seemed of significance to me.

Yet, during the second half, a particular being caught my eye. As I sang the words, rejoicing the winter gods of old, a tall figure emerged at the back. The lights of the stage blinded me, but for some unknown reason, they caught my eye. I continued without showing my interest, but kept my peripheral attention on them. From what I could see, it was a tall male that wore a large winter coat that emphasised his stature. He stood at the back as if the chairs were too small for him. I felt his eyes on me as I sang. They were red.

The applause ended and the lights went up, signalling the end of the show. Despite missing my family, the crowd's appreciation for me left me feeling relieved and elated. Diafol joined me behind the stage as I was readying to leave.

"Sensational! What great wonders we will be!" He giggled behind me. I smiled to myself, despite the initial anger I felt, now it had faded into weariness.

"I'm glad you enjoyed it," I said simply.

"Ah but not just me, no! Many did, many loved you. And that is what we need, yes! He was pleased," he said, almost muttering to himself. I had missed his last words, my family preoccupying my thoughts.

"Have you heard from mother? How are they?" I asked, deciding I could not wait any longer. My mother had been gone for over a month.

"Ah, yes, all is well. She is soon to return, I hear. Very good, yes, for I need to speak to her, yes," he said, giggling at me. Again, I missed the meaning in his words, as I was already thinking about my mother's return.

She arrived soon after and assured me that my father was well. She gave me a letter that my father had written to me. Hugging her tight, I kissed her glowing face and ran to my room to read its contents.

Dearest Élan,

My heart lurched at his writing, hearing his voice in my head.

I must deeply apologise for not being able to come to your show. I know how hard you must have worked for it. Your brother and I were so looking forward to seeing you, damned this illness! It hurt me so to miss such a wonderful event, my dearest. I hope you can forgive me? I have learned I am not in the same young body I once was, and I catch things much easier nowadays. I was lucky to have your mother with me to heal this old soul.

I sniffed, saddened by his shaky writing. It felt as though he'd aged in years since I last saw him.

My son, I am so very proud of you. I know it must be hard being away from us. We think of you everyday. But this will be worth it when you are older and have the world at your feet.

For some reason I thought of Diafol at this. Am I to be like him? Suddenly I doubted my choices and wished nothing more than to return to Brimhaven, to be with them. Missing them didn't seem worth it, not so far.

Thank you so much for the music you sent me! I was so excited to see what you have been learning. To see it written did not hold the same charm as your talent but I must say, it willed my health back, my son, if not only to see you perform soon.

I smiled at this, excited that he will see me perform soon.

Your mother tells me that you are well. I am pleased to hear that you are doing very well in your studies and learning hard for your family. A father could not be more proud. Worry not for I am well again and I am eager for your mother to return soon, for I know how lonely you must feel. It saddens me that you were absent of both parents during this Yule.

I notice at this point he makes no mention of Diafol.

Your brother misses you terribly. He works hard though and I feel guilty for leaving him to work on his own during these difficult months. Worry not though, my little faeling. It will never be easy without you, but we are living on. We miss you, but are not struggling from your absence. I must note there has been change in your brother that I wonder if you will notice. He has grown older, becoming more a male fae than a boy now.

I had noticed this on my last visit, his height surpassing mine further now.

Furthermore, he has grown quite close to that Mary girl. Do you remember her? He talks of you to her a lot and she visits often to help your mother during her stay. She is quite pleasant and makes your brother happy.

I remember Mary from my birthday party. She was the red-haired faerie my brother tried to talk to. It made me happy that she had taken a liking to him. Usually, the faelings stayed around me more as I was easier to talk to, happy to listen, and told stories. My brother was either busy or too quiet for such things. I was eager to ask my brother about her.

Finally, my youngest, look after your mother. Together, you will both pass the time a lot easier if you support each other. Oh, I know you will, but please remember she is there for you. She loves you more than you will ever know. Never forget it. I will see you soon. Until then, stay strong, brave, and bright like you always are.

All my love, your Father.

I read his letter a few more times, enjoying his voice in my head, the comfort it brought me. What little magick my father possessed, I felt it flow into this letter to me, bringing me to tears. I felt it embrace me and then my mother was there with me. She sat with me and together, we read through the letter once more, my mother elaborating on parts.

Long into the night, we talked of Brimhaven and what was to come. My mother shared stories of her youth in the house we were now in and now admittedly, Brimhaven was more her home than here. When she bid me good night, I felt a small sample of the comfort I felt at home, my hope returned to me from my mother's presence, her glow and spirit revived.

Months later, shortly after my ninth birthday, my mother stormed into the study where I was reading a new romance book quietly.

"Élan, we are leaving!" she declared angrily.

"Hold it right there, dear one!" my grandfather shouted, stalking in after her, his face slightly humoured. She turned to him, her arms beseeched.

"Please, you can't do this!" she cried, distressed. Her words made me stand, watching them in surprise.
"Oh, yes I can, dear one! I can do what I damnedest well want! He is *mine*!" Diafol replied, crossing his arms indignantly.
"B-but he is just a faeling!" my mother cried, making Diafol sneer.

"A clever, obedient faeling," he remarked. My mother just stared at him, defeated. Diafol eventually sighed.
"Dear one, this is for us! For our family… yes? Élan said he was willing to help us, is that not so?" he asked, they both turned to me. I saw the fear in my mother's eyes, freezing my tongue.
"You monster!" she roared. In an instant faster than before, Diafol grabs her and pushes her against the wall making me cry out.
"Now, now daughter. Let us not fight in front of the little one," he growled in her face.
"Please don't hurt her," I cried, frozen in place, afraid for my mother. A tense moment passed before he released her and turned towards me.

"Please, I beg you," she cried, clutching her throat.
"You shamed yourself, Azalea! Look what you have become. Weak! Weak, I say! And was it worth it? Is this what you wanted?!" he barked, gesturing around us. He looked at her, fury boiling from him. My heart pounded as I took in his anger. I determined that if he moved for her again, I would do what I could to stop him. As he stared at her, her last resolve broke down.

"I'll do anything!" she cried out, crumpling on her knees. I was dying to know what this was all about. What was so awful that my mother would be so distressed? But my senses knew how close my grandfather was to wiping us both out.

"You should have thought of that before!" he growled at her. He watched her cry for moments before turning to me, a scary, toothy grin playing on his lips, his glowing eyes staring into my soul.

"Élan…Do you want to help your mother?" he asked over her cries. I looked to my mother and swallowed audibly.

"Yes," I bit, making my mother groan into the floor. My heart pounded with worry for her. What was happening?

"And to help your dearest grandfather?" he sneered at me, moving closer. I hesitated but agreed.

"Don't, Élan!" she cried and looked at me desperately.

"Shut up!" Diafol roared back at her, his face crumpled in fury.

"Well?" he asked, his smile returning as fast as his anger had. I stared for long moments at my mother's crying face. She shook her head at me. I feared for her life, her safety, so I agreed.

"I will do what I can to help you, to help our family," I said solemnly, ignoring my mothers defeated moan.

"You see? At least the boy has some sense!" he giggled, satisfied. He turned to leave.

"Wait! You must promise my mother won't be harmed," I said firmly. He smiled and nodded, mocking a bow.

"Good! Very good. It is done," he replied and left without another word.

As soon as he was out of sight, I ran to my mother, still on the floor.

"Mother?" I asked tensely, touching her back gently. My touch breaks whatever resolve she had, and she's shaking violently.

"I have failed. Oh gods, what have I done? He is mad, damn him," my mother muttered into the floor.

I knelt and pulled my mother up, holding her as she ranted. I was determined to calm her, the mystery of it all swirling around me like crows on a battlefield.

"Mother, what's wrong? What happened?" I asked quietly when her cries died down.

"Oh Élan, my dear son. I am so sorry," she moaned, clutching me.

"For what, Mother?" I ask innocently.

"He is going to take you from me—for real this time. That demon who always keeps his bargains," she muttered into my shoulder. I felt alarmed by her words.

"Who, Mother?" I truly felt she had gone mad. At my question, she broke down once more, unable to tell me. Her distress scared me, her words striking my heart with contagious fear.

"Mother I don't understand," I cried, tears falling on my cheeks. She clutched me tighter.

"I know, love. I know," she whispered

"I am to be a what?" I gasped.

"A subsidium," Diafol replied shortly, his arms crossed. We were sat in the study in which I resided most days for my education.

The tutors had increased their times, new ones coming to teach of other worlds, other creatures. I became curious and insisted I be told of the fate that my mother hated so much.

"Which is?" I asked, confused. I had never heard such a word. My guess lay with dark creatures outside of the Faelands.

"It matters not what 'it' is, but what *you* are. You will serve in a very important household, yes! To entertain and…sing," he drawls, grinning at me, his eyes looking at me but not seeing me.

"I don't understand," I say simply, shock already registering. I was to move away. Again. And this time my mother would not be there.

"Oh you will soon, not to worry, not to worry! Oh it's very exciting having our own Élan enter the big, wide world! You will be good, yes, you will sing and bring light to those miserable creatures, make them squirm." He giggled to himself, trapped in his vision.

"What creatures?" I asked, alarmed. Diafol clicked his tongue.

"Why, vampires, of course! No this is not good. A tutor will have to come and teach you of what is to come," he muttered to himself, oblivious to how his words hit me.

Vampires? They were *real*? Dark creatures that stalked and devoured faelings were real?! What in the gods was happening?

"Grandfather, why? Why *me*?" I gasped, suddenly panicking, shadows growing around me making me shudder. In a flash, Diafol held my face to his.

"It must be you! It must! You are strong—a good, brave faeling. You want to help us, yes? You want to sing out into the world, yes? This will be the start of your dream! This will get us better…acquainted with those dark creatures. Oh, worry not; they are not what you have been told," he hushed me, his words threaded with magick. I felt a blanket of calm wash over my panicked being. Visions of me singing in front of the world, bright and glorious.

"Élan, my faeling of song. You have the sirens' gift; this is your fate, why I brought you here, why I gave you knowledge. It is time, time to go into the world and make your mark," he said, his voice sounding so strong and sure, his eyes were the only thing I could see.

"When am I to go?" I asked, swallowing the horror that would erupt from me later, when I was on my own.

"In your fourteenth year, that is when you will be ready," he assures me, his palms feeling clammy on my hot face.

"B-but, for how long?!" I asked, a wave of panic bursting through his magick. He tuts and I feel a strong leash tighten, calming me with an artificial sense. Diafol snickered.

"Worry not about that. You will soon be singing in front of the masses, mark my words."

From then on, my education changed. From music to history and politics. Specifically, I learned of the ways these vampires lived, how they ran as a society. I was taught that within the Vampire Nation, which lay far south of the Faelands, there resided two main territories. One of Dracula and one of Carmilla. Both fierce beings that ruled over the nation where a vampire descended from either bloodline.

It was fascinating to learn of them, brought to reality by these creatures that I believed stalked the night and were beast-like in their ways.

A full cohesive map of the world was laid out before me as the tutors tumbled through years worth of history and facts, honing in on the Vampire Nation. My heart lurched as I absently pinpointed Brimhaven as a tiny dot in the Faelands, far north-west of Astoria. The Vampire Nation a large, looming country that lay to the South, far from home.

"A subsidium? Why would you ask of this?" my tutor asked hesitantly at my question that had cut him off.

"I am to be one."

"Ah, I see…" The tutor frowned, fidgeting with his collar.

He proceeded to explain to me that this was usually a role upheld by a faerie, something a family would offer for return of protection or money from the distinguished family in the courts. I recalled Diafol claiming that mine were closely linked with Carmilla herself.

"But what do they actually *do*?" I asked, regretting the question immediately. The tutor sighed sadly.
"They offer blood. Blood is the pact that seals the connection. Blood in exchange for financial stability, most of the time. That is the way," he said simply, his emotion drawn from him. My hand absently goes to my throat, my heart pounding at the horrid revelation.

This was his big plan? This is what my grandfather would have me do? Tears went to my eyes.
"It is not so bad, child. They only drink so often. It is known not to be a completely terrible thing," he tried to assure me, looking at me with pity.

I am silent as he speaks the rest to me and leaves quietly, my tears and grief descending, my sadness echoing in the empty house.

As another year passed, my education continued. My mother became more withdrawn and looked more like a ghost everyday.

Despite my horrible truth on what we all now know, I thrived in my classes, eager to find something, anything that would help get me through it. I excelled so well my grandfather gifted me another trip home, a place I felt was more unreal than the creatures I would soon cohabitate with.

My father and brother remained blissfully unaware, excited as I told them of my accomplishments in knowledge. Their surprised laughter held my heart with pride. My mother remained quiet, which concerned my father. She insisted there was nothing and refused to share the burden with him, even in the middle of the night, when the candles softened their faces, their hands holding each other in desperation, threatening tears to be spilled.

When we left at dawn, a part of my light remained with them, leaving my future darker than before. My mother held me, though she had no warmth or light left to give either.

Like broken dolls we lay against each other as we returned to the large intricate house, Diafol's giggles sounding like a tune of doom.

Merlough

"It is too soon," my mother growled, fixing my collar.

"I think not, dear one! No, it is perfect timing!" Diafol grinned from across the room, admiring his own reflection in the mirror.

"It's okay, Mother. I am ready," I assured her quietly. She scowled at me as she finished off the suit.

"You are too young; you do not understand." Pain reflected in her eyes. I gripped her elbows, pulling her gaze to mine.

"I am trying, Mother. It will be okay. It is only for this evening, yes?" I asked her, a snort coming from Diafol.

"For now, yes. Can't have the little mouse frightened, now can we?" he teased, pointing at me through the mirror. The light was already fading from the sky, creating an orange glow in the room around us.

"This isn't right. Why tempt the beast if it is not sealed yet?" my mother said, moving towards Diafol. Her words made me shudder.

"Have you met a vampire, daughter? You are clearly misinformed. Now stop frightening our faeling and make yourself useful. Wear this," he held up a green dress filled with ruffles, a style I recognised as more of a vampiric fashion. My mother sneered but said nothing as she snatched the dress from him. Since her revelation on my becoming a subsidium, my grandfather seemed more patient with her emotions.

"Now, do not worry on what she says. Your mother knows nothing. Merlough is very nice. You shall see." He walked to me, his yellow eyes bright in the evening glow.

"I know, Grandfather. I will try my best to make you proud… I-it's just…"

He stopped behind me in the mirror and leaned down, aligning his eyes with mine.

"Yessss?" He grinned, his sinister stare making my heart pound.

"Why do you need me to be a subsidium? F-for the family?"

"Ahhh, the curiosity of young faelings…" he mused, making me blush. His grin did not assure me that I had not angered him.

"To be a subsidium gets you into the deepest depths of the vampire courts. You will be rubbing shoulders with the most full-bodied of vampires. Therefore, you will learn more knowledge of their kind, first-hand! And with you, you shall bring your music. Wonderful, powerful music that will show them the true magick of the fae," he explained, moving his hands expectantly.

At my lack of response, his golden gaze stared at me in the mirror, his hands gripping my shoulders hard.

"You know why it must be *you,* my little songbird? Why else have you been learning the gift of knowledge for?" he asked, his voice softer, yet no less threatening.

I wasn't certain on his words but at his golden stare, his firm hands holding me in place, I relented. He seemed to sense this in me and smiled softer now, tilting his head.

"How about some gold to give you strength? This may help for tonight," he said carefully. My mother appeared in the doorway behind me.

A tense silence passed as he held up the gold coin he had presented to me before. It shone like the setting sun, beckoning me. The magick pulsed from it like a heart, hidden promises whispered around me on how I would benefit from this.

Carefully, I moved sideways and dropped the hand I was unaware I had raised.

"Sorry, Grandfather, I will use my own strength for this. No gold can stop what is about to happen," I replied sullenly, seeing relief flood to my mother. Diafol tilted his head, his smile also looking somewhat relieved.

"Very good, yes, you are ready. He is almost here," he muttered and moved on. I straighten and regained what little composure I had.

Suddenly, warm arms grabbed me from behind, making me yelp.
"Hush, my love, I am so proud," my mother muttered softly into my black, combed hair.
"For what, Mother?" I asked, knowing I had done nothing yet. She turned me and pulled me to her, her dress causing a wedge between us.
"Mother, that dress is huge!" I giggled noticing the ruffles adding weight to her lithe form. Her long hair sat on the top of her head in a style I had seen in portraits of Queen Carmilla herself.
"And you look well, my son. We will get through this together," she uttered in a serious tone. I nodded and took her hand as we faced the door.
"Merlough is also the name of a type of wine, right? Surely that can't be a bad thing," I say, nervously fighting the urge to play with my sleeves. I wore a tailored suit of green with small gems, flashier than the one I wore for my eighth birthday, the material a finer cut.
"Perhaps," was all my mother said. I ignored the tremble in our joined hands.

I stared in fascination as he kissed my mother's gloved hand.

"A pleasure," his voice rumbled as he smiled. His fangs, which were smaller than I had imagined, peeked at me through his thin lips.

Apart from the fangs, he didn't look much different than us. His build was larger and wider, a head taller than my grandfather. I watched as she smiled pleasantly at him, masking her disgust.

"Welcome, my lord, what an honour," she said, any mockery in her voice missed by him. She curtsied at him, her smile frozen in place.

"I have heard many things about your talents, dear one. My family are honoured for this union," he replied, his accent sounding high class, his voice accentuated, not like the beastly growls I had imagined. He spoke common Karing too, which I was told was normal among dark creatures also. Different languages were only used in private company.

I felt myself become more at ease as the stereotypes of my childish nightmares fell from reality. I saw my mother's smile slip at his words, yet he didn't notice as he turned to me. I felt myself blush at the attention, willing myself to look at him, as was polite.

"Lord Merlough Marquis, a delight to finally meet you," he rumbled, leaning down closer to my height. At ten, I barely reached his chest in height. I felt my mother's tension next to me. The floor creaked and I felt Diafol's eyes bore into me, willing to act.

"É-Élan, my lord," I croaked, my throat dry, my eyes unable to move from his hand, which was held out to me. His nails were long and sharp, which reflected like polished glass. I carefully placed my hand into his. My mother clicked her tongue as I realised I had used the wrong hand, making it awkwardly impossible to handshake. A rumble of laughter came from Merlough.

"Pardon, sir, it is his first time," my mother muttered, embarrassed. Diafol just giggled at me. My face fully hot as all eyes were on me, tears threatening. Slowly, as if I were a mouse, he closed both of his large hands onto mine. I tried not to shiver at the coldness of them.

"Worry not, little one, many your age would flee. You prove far braver amongst us elders," he said, his voice, I believed, had meant to be soft, but just continued to rumble.

Slowly, my eyes rose to his, realising I had not angered him. He smiled as I took him in, his large pale face, and long dark hair bound behind his head; it looked almost too shiny to be clean. His eyes, as I'd feared, were dark red. This confirmed his direct lineage to Carmilla herself, the blood disease strong in his veins. A full blooded vampire.

"He will become more familiar in time, I assure you, my lord," Diafol sang in his mocking voice.

"Indeed," Merlough grinned, his smile much like Diafol's, impossible to look friendly with sharp teeth glistening at you.

"Perhaps a tour of the study may lighten the air, my lord?" My mother suggested tensely. I could feel her need to pull me away from him, her magick embracing me in her stead. I felt my heart slow to a normal pace, my tension ease as I became familiar with the sight in front of me, the reality of everything settling in.

"Yes, let's," Merlough agreed, standing swiftly, a musky scent brushing me as my mother took his cloak. He wore formal clothes, a white shirt covered in a vest of red, lined with gold. Black tailored trousers accentuated his long legs. No wings or horns were revealed, to my relief.

We walked around as my mother detailed the depth of my studies, showing examples of my progress, Diafol occasionally adding to give context to previous conversations they had shared. Merlough seemed impressed and praised me, making me smile despite my hidden reserve.

"What a delight you are, boy. Truly a gift to behold at the court of Carmilla," he said, inspecting my small script on the papers my mother gave to him.

"Yes, well, he still has a few years to go," my mother said, almost too shortly, causing Diafol to raise a brow.

"Of course, dear faerie-mother. No need to rush things." Merlough chuckled, breaking the tension sparking around him.

"You cannot deny the boy has talent." Merlough looked down at me, making me catch myself in my staring.

"Speaking of talent! He has prepared a song for you, lord," my grandfather declared, gesturing to the piano and chairs laid out, ready.

"Ah, what a delight! I had secretly hoped to hear his voice again so soon," he answered, mocking a whisper, making Diafol giggle. My mother froze and eyed them both. *Again*, he had said…

I moved to my planned spot in the middle of the room, my thoughts clouded with mystery. The dark figure from my Yule performance two years ago flashed in my mind. The question hung on my tongue as my mother took her place at the piano. The music kicked me out of my thoughts and brought me back to the hours of practise we had done.

With the tune so familiar, I found myself slipping back into the music, my voice drawn from me.

Wishes to dreams, in the dark of the night
When the world is calm, I can still make it bright
I can see, so far in my dreams
I will follow my hopes to wish
Until they come true.

There's a world out there,
No one has time to see
I will go so far to my hopes
Somewhere in my dreams
Until they come true.

"Gods, he's a gift of the faeries," Merlough gasped to my grandfather, making him chortle loudly. Luckily, I was used to his noises and ignored them.

"A gift that I give to you for a price much owed to me in return," he grinned back evilly.

The song finished in what seemed like a flash. As they applauded, I looked to my mother. Her face was withdrawn, emotionless, contrasting my elation.

"Marvellous, dear one! Such promise in my blood," Diafol cheered, elbowing Merlough playfully, making him chuckle. Diafol's cold eyes shifted to my mother.
"Perhaps our lord requires some time alone with the faeling, to get to know him better?" he jeered, humour sparking within him. My mother stiffened, standing a little too quickly.
"Certainly, there is no need for such formalities at this stage. He is barely accustomed to his…presence," my mother said, coming up quickly behind me. I felt her strain not to hold me as she normally would when feeling threatened.

"Calm yourself, dearest Azalea. I see you have great love for your faeling." Merlough smirked, as Diafol straightened, fury threatening to surface. Sensing the danger building, Merlough turned to my grandfather, hand raised peacefully.
"I agree with his mother. Let us not push the boy too soon. I am much pleased so far. Worry not, dear friend," he said patting my grandfather's shoulder. This seemed to ease him, his face slipping back into another sneaky smile.

"Sure, what is one night when you will have many?" he replied nastily, eyeing my mother. I felt her tremble behind me. My thoughts rushed to change the air between us.

"Is it true you live close to the court of Carmilla itself in Roma?" I blurt out, making everyone turn to me. Diafol raised his eyebrow at me while Merlough smiled, delighted.

"Why yes, not as close as some, but close enough to visit regularly. After all, it is to be expected of a descendant such as myself," he explained, moving to sit on a nearby couch.

"And what is it like at court? I have never been to one, you see," I explained, blushing as I moved to sit near him. I am too cautious to sit too close just yet. Diafol moved to sit next to Merlough, my mother replaced herself behind me.

"Ah yes, well, it is hard for one to describe one's home when it is all one knows. It is very large to accommodate all the vampires that roam or visit there. Many know of who I am. Music plays in the dance halls all night, Queen Carmilla herself sings when the mood takes her, otherwise she resides in the main hall, completely in red." He gestured around him as he explained. My mind stretched at the idea of it all. I felt my mother's hand come to my shoulders.

"Azalea, perhaps you should tend to getting our esteemed guest a drink," Diafol cut in. My mother miserably obliged, sobering the mood around us as she breezed out of the room.

"Worry not, great Diafol. It is a mother's nature to fear for her faeling," Merlough muttered quietly when she was out of the room, looking almost embarrassed. My grandfather snorted.

"Then she will do well to remember it is also natural for the young to flee the nest. I am ashamed by her behaviour. Fear not, this boy has much more wits about him," Diafol growled, gesturing to me. I swallow the retort that jumps on my tongue regarding my mother. Merlough raises his eyebrow to me.

"You wish to leave your mother? You want to help your grandfather by suiting the terms we agreed?" My magick crackled around me, threatening to answer in Diafol's favour. The gold coin flashed in my mind. I shake off his energy, determined to answer on my own.

"I do not wish to leave my mother, but as fate would have it, I am so that I can help my family. It is an honour to represent them at the fine courts of Carmilla," I answered firmly, as though it were rehearsed. They both tensed at my words and relaxed as they sunk in. I believed it was too honest for my grandfather's liking but Merlough seemed charmed.

"Truly brave like you said Diafol. Worry not, faeling, for I feel we will be just fine," Merlough assured me, as my mother walked in, quickly handing him a drink.

I decide to ignore what it might be in the glass, averting my gaze from her freshly bound wrist.

Merlough's visit left my grandfather in high spirits. So much so that I got my reward, I could see my brother and father again. I saw my mother smile for the first time in a while that day. She held me close to her, a small promise of her spark returning to me. It spiked tears in my eyes.

"What will you do when I am gone, Mother?" I asked quietly into her chest. I felt her heart pound at my question, reality too real for the moment.
"I dare not think it, my sweet. To be without you is a fate I cannot yet face," she whispered, taking in my scent, her arms shaking as if her body already felt my absence. She held me for a long time and I let her. I wanted to imprint it into my memory.

"You could go back to father and Rolo? I am sure the flowers miss you," I answered trying to encourage her.

Suddenly I had to know what she would do, for I was worried that she would not move once I left and might wither away like a dying flower.

"Perhaps," she said hesitantly, which made me look up at her pleadingly. She sighed sadly, looking at me fully, her eyes wet with tears.
"Brimhaven won't be the same without you, my love," she said softly, tears rolling down her cheeks. I realised then that she felt the same distance with father and Rolo that I had felt. The dark bridge creating a gap where their love reached but with a delay that left it less warm than before. It overwhelmed me with

sadness. Things will not be the same now for any of us. Part of me refused to understand that this was my doing.

It was decided that my father and brother would visit us though I do not know why I couldn't go home. I felt saddened as I wanted to return to the warmth and open spaces of Brimhaven. The small, cozy cottages and friendly faces.

I waited anxiously when I knew they were travelling to us, pacing the study. This was partly due to the fact that they now knew what I was to be—my future as a subsidium—and I had no idea how they would react. My mother had heard nothing from them, but for them to come must be a good sign, right?

My mother joined me on the morning they were due to arrive. I noticed she looked more herself, wearing a woollen neutral dress of Brimhaven, a simple cut, fresh flowers in her hair, which was in a long plait down her back. It calmed my nerves and I hugged her, overcome with gratitude for her presence.

For myself, I wore a baggy neutral top with matching shorts, the only clothing I had from home and growing a little too small for me now. I kept my feet bare, feeling comforted by the soft carpet beneath. Diafol was nowhere to be seen and I was glad. The last thing we needed were his sly words, twisting our reunion.

When they arrived, I greeted my father the same way I always did. I leapt at him, hugging him as we almost fell over. My brother, taller than my father now, moved in beside us.

Excitedly, I showed them around, assuming their quietness was due to nervousness in the large house. My brother snorted at the size.

"More like a damned cave than a house," my brother muttered, looking around with narrowed eyes. I noticed his height again, gawking up at him. His skin tanner than before, his shoulders wider, chest broad. My father chuckled dryly at his comment. I continued to show them around when we finally reached the study.

"And this is where I spend most of my days, where the gift of knowledge is taught to me," I explained, gesturing widely. Again my brother snorted, my mother clicking her tongue at him.

"Do that anymore, Rolo, and you will make us believe you to be a pig," my mother hissed, crossing her arms. He stuck his tongue out at her, making me giggle. I was too happy to see them. My father admired my written texts I had laid out.

"Gods, son! This is remarkable! Such intricacies in the music and words," my father praised me, making me blush.

"Thanks, Father. I had hoped you would like them," I said happily, fidgeting from the buzz.

"Your voice sounds funny," my brother grumbled, crossing his arms, neglecting the paper my father held.

"It does?" I asked, confused. My mother scoffed at him.

"Rolo, we talked about this," my father muttered, his smile dropping. My brother chuckled darkly.

"Ah yes, we did, didn't we? What was it? Talkin' lessons to get rid of his faerie accent or some shit?" My brother sneered. My face started getting hot again. Did I really sound that different?

"Enough, Rolo," my father warned, putting down the papers, my heart sinking at the impending storm.

"Do I really sound that different?" I asked quietly, unable to look at him, feeling ashamed, the distance between us feeling worlds apart. My brother scoffed, making me flinch.

"You sound like a bloody vamp tramp," he bit, making my mother gasp, horrified. I look at him, shocked.

"Hey!" my father barked, moving next to him. Suddenly my anger and hurt hurled up in me like a wave of pain.

"How dare you!" I growled, shaking with rage, hating that I had to look up so far at him. Why was I so short?!

My father moved in front of Rolo, my mother behind me in her protective stance. Such a bitter memory of mine.

My brother laughed darkly, trying to move around my father.

"How dare I? Ah, yes. How dare I? Apologies, my little lord. I forgot myself and that I was in the company of a blood whore," he sneered, his words shooting me like an arrow.

All the denial I held about that fact shattered my mental protection. A dark part of me felt the truth of his words.

I remembered little afterwards, only that I ran. I ran, numb with feeling one moment, then feeling everything at once, it crashing and shocking my system. I heard my mother and father shout after me, but they remained frozen in their own fear. I practically flew to my room, determined to be alone. Collapsed in fear and horror, my brother's words stabbing me all over, I crawled into bed to nurse my wounds.

"How *dare* you ruin this for him. You know it is not his fault!" Azalea cried as Élan ran out.

"No, it's not his fault, is it. Mother?" her eldest sneered, empowered by his rage.

"*Enough*," Maurice muttered from where he was seated in a nearby chair, holding his head in his hands, brokenly looking so tired and old.

"I asked you to come here for him, not to pick a fight," Azalea spat, disgusted. Rolo just snorted in response.

"Azalea is right. We should be thinking of him now," Maurice said wearily. His words stung my mother, the use of her name proved that he was just as upset with her.

"There must be a way to stop it, Father," Rolo implored, standing in front of him.

"You know there isn't, son."

"He's not invincible," Rolo growled.

"No, he is not, but believe me, I have tried," Azalea cut in, making Rolo whip around to face her, his face red with anger.

"Clearly not enough!"

"Listen. The more you try him, the greater risk that he will find out. And when he finds out, he takes it out on your brother. I just can't do it anymore," Azalea explained desperately.

"You are done are you? Given up?" Rolo challenged.

"Rolo, enough." Maurice stood, putting a strong hand on his shoulder.

"But come on, Father! There must be a way to just kill—" his voice cut off, his throat closing.

"Azalea! Stop this!" Maurice cried watching his son's face turn blue, magick freezing the air in his lungs.

"He *brought* me to this, Maurice. You stupid boy. Don't you EVER threaten his life," she hissed, her eyes clouded with magick, her hand gripping the force that held the air.

"Azalea, please!" her husband begged desperately, seeing the light fade from his eldest.

"He won't say it again. Please, for the gods, don't do this." He took her hand, breaking the link. Rolo gasped, choking at the air flooding him.

"You crazy bitch," he said.

Azalea laughed at him darkly. "Oh, Rolo, I don't know why I bother with you. Such a foolish son you are," she said bitterly tearing that last link they had together. Rolo looked at her, sadness and hurt reflected in the brown eyes he shared with her in likeness. She stopped laughing as Maurice went to Rolo and helped him up.

"You know, the last creature to threaten Diafol's life didn't just simply die," she said quietly, her eyes now lost in memory. She turned to them both, her face hardened.
"He was a faerie like us. This fool cursed my father and hoped to be rid of him. Next thing he knew, he was force-fed the remains of his children while his wife watched. Then, as if that wasn't enough, he removed his wife's skin as the faerie choked on his children's bones," she explained simply. Neither replied to her; they stared in sickened silence.

"You think this is bad? He could do a lot worse. I have seen it," she hugged herself, chilled by her own words.
"Now believe her, son. She has tried everything," Maurice said, calmly squeezing his son's shoulder. Rolo huffed in defeat.

"Then there is no hope. He is to be a blood tramp forever." Rolo's shoulders slumped under the weight of his bitterness. Azalea finally broke down and cried, her hands to her face as if she was trying to shut out the nightmare.

"What have we done…" Maurice sighed heavily, long years echoing in his breath.

I felt a heavy hand on my head. My father's woodsy scent enveloped my senses as I returned to this world.
"Forgive our selfishness," he whispered.

I woke fully, startled to find that he really was there. So many times, I had dreamed of him by my side. I stared at him, dazed, taking in his aged self, his smile tired. Carefully, he stroked my bed-mussed hair. The memories of my brother's cruel words returned.

"You both hate me now," I stated solemnly. My father grimaced at my words and hugged me tight to him.

"Gods! For you to think of such a thing!" he gasped sadly. I sniffed, my tears promising to return as my father held me.

After a moment that felt too short, he leaned back, cupping my face with his hands.

"We would never hate you," he said, his own eyes watery.

"But Rolo…"

"Is an angry fool who is wounded by your absence," my father hushed gently.

"He may look like a full-grown faerie, my son, but he still has the heart of a child. We all do until that becomes a child of our own," my father explained softly. Everything he said always sounded right to me; he sounded so sure of himself. It was comforting in my young, unknown world. I had missed it greatly.

"I am told that you are much wiser with your feelings than he is. You must have your mother's strength and spirit," he smirked, kissing my head, making me frown.

"But mother says I have yours," I replied, my voice still dry from sleep. My father laughed, lighting up his face.

"She is also humble with her talents like you. You are both beloved by most you meet. Therefore I have every faith in you, my little one," my father said, cupping my chin, his nose touching mine.

"But I am doing the right thing, aren't I father?" I asked quietly. He went quiet in thought and sighed, his eyes distant. I waited patiently, my heart pounding for his answer.

"You know, my son, we always knew you were destined for great things. Where Rolo was like me in the ways of the land, you were…like your mother, always meant for something…more," he began.

"You mean because of my magick…and music?" I asked carefully. He seemed to hesitate then nodded.

"Yes indeed, your music was certainly the first sign. A sign of being touched with magick. A sign that you were of Diafol's blood more than your brother." Slowly, he took my hands into his.

"Despite this, your mother had great sadness. A sadness that she feared for you, knowing that you were meant for more. Even as she held you in her belly, she felt this fear." He stopped and swallowed.

"She knew you were meant to leave us. You are to go and spread this gift to the world as the gods intended," he said, looking at me with his eyes full of emotion.

"It was the hardest thing, *the* hardest thing we could imagine, knowing this. But we knew and we have waited. It is your time, my son," he said, then put my hands together in between his, spreading his warmth through them.

"Your birth wasn't easy, you know, not like your brother's. I believed your mother's fear spread to you, making you reluctant to leave her. You were late and the healers feared the worst. They thought you dead; even as you arrived, no sound came from you." My father's voice sounded strained, staring at our hands as he re-lived his memory.

"Your mother begged. She and I both begged the gods' for you to live. You who were beautiful and everything your brother was not. The silence sickened me, I felt myself falter, my soul shaken at the thought of your loss."

"Then, as we were to give up on you, you cried." He looked at me then, tears falling.

"You cried and we all did. We cried with such joy. For that was your first song in this world, my faeling, and the gods knew it would be heard far and wide."

I was in awe at his words, my eyes wide with wonder. I had never heard this story before.

"Your mother was tired of course, exhausted even. She used every last bit of energy to hold you for the longest time, to shower you with our love. Gods, Élan, it was a wonderful thing. Since that day, you have never failed us, continuing to amaze and please the gods with your spirit." He stopped and I itched to encourage more words from him. He brought my hands to his lips and kissed them softly. He sniffed and seemed to remember where he was.

"So to answer whether you are doing the right thing, I cannot say for certain. But what I can say is that never before have I seen a child blessed by the gods as you have been. With the wind carrying your song, I believe you can take the fresh spring wherever you tread, whether it be here, or in some dark country across the sea."

My own tears drip onto my arm, making me flinch in surprise. My father smiled and kissed my head softly.

"I am so proud of you. Never be ashamed of who you are. Where you go, you carry us and the gods with you. That way, you are never truly alone, my little one," he whispered, his nose pressed to mine and I was lost in the blue of his eyes.

Once again, I felt the little magick he had in him connect us, repairing the small gap I had felt for months now. The flood of love and warmth made me cry fully in his arms. He held me until the sky faded to darkness, sharing all the stories of my youth, proving to me that Brimhaven was no longer just a place, but a feeling.

The next morning, my brother approached me in the study, his large hulk bunched with shame, my father's smirk lightening the mood.

"I'm sorry for what I said." It was all it took for me to forgive him. I was so desperate to hug him, something I had not done since his arrival. I rushed at him and hugged him tightly.

"Gods, you're like a rock!" I pouted, playfully punching his chest. He laughed at me, tension seeping out of him.

"Yeah, while you grow soft with pretty papers and knowledge, I grow with the strength of the trees and hills." He poked me playfully.

I truly marvelled at our differences then, knowing that I would never be like him, not how I had wanted to be as a smaller faeling. I was coming to terms with the paths we had chosen.

They stayed for a few more days, undisturbed by the tricksy Diafol. I took them to the town and showed them the large shops and market, my brother marvelling at the food available for purchase. My father admired the equipment available at the blacksmith, sophisticated tools for farming and fishing. Rolo grunted and pouted, saying he needed no tools for such work.

My mother spent hours in her glasshouse, showing my father her small plants she kept there. The days passed happier than the first and I soon felt soothed again, comforted by my choices. I felt myself find ground on the path I had taken, my family's love and faith adding a spring to my step. They wanted this for me.

"So, how's Mary?" I asked, smirking one day when I decided to teach my brother the lute alone in the study. My father told me he knew how to play, but Rolo seemed to feign ignorance in order to spend time with me.

"Huh? Oh her? She is okay, I guess…" Rolo said, his eyes avoiding me. I laughed as he started blushing.

"You like her! Does she know?" I giggled. My brother scoffed, plucking the strings in annoyance.

"Shut up, sprite," he warned, focusing hard on the lute.

"Aw come on. It's not like I can tell her...Oh maybe you should ask mother! She can give you some flowers to give to her," I suggested excitedly.

"Enough! I do not need her help," he gritted. I sat down, deflated by his tone. It was too close to anger and we spoke no more of Mary.

Before I knew it, they were gone again. The house was once again large and empty. My mother locked herself away in her glasshouse for days, as if my very presence reminded her of them. I began reading tales of vampires, interested to see what I could learn in time for Merlough's next visit, my future seeming closer to me than my past, my dreams of singing for the world alight in my heart.

Diafol returned to us and took to spending time with me for a few days, taking an interest in my vampire studies, hinting on what he knew and expanding on what I read from books.

Despite the tension I held for him, I felt closer to him during this time. I actually felt care coming from him as he told me stories of the courts and explained what he knew of the feud between Carmilla and Dracula. I was pleased when I recounted the knowledge to him and discussed my own theories from what I had read.

Before I knew it, the leaves crisped and changed to orange, falling in the autumn wind, their fall dance had begun. And with the fading light, another visit from Merlough approached.

It was between Samhain and Yule when he arrived. My mother was more distant, not caring to dress in vampire fashion this time.

When he arrived, she smiled with more bitterness than before, but Merlough seemed to ignore it. I was once again shy in my greeting, getting it correctly this time and finding myself staring at him again. Diafol chattered with us of my education, talking in detail of our conversations together, sharing my theories on the courts and vampire history. Merlough said little in response, his face humoured but he remained silent on the views shared.

"You can smell him, can't you?" Diafol sneered, changing the subject abruptly. Merlough's eyes darted to him, surprised at his perceptiveness. My mother masked her disgust with a polite cough. Before he could answer, Diafol spoke again.

"Perhaps it is time for you to be alone, now that the boy is comfortable?" He tilted his head playfully.

My mother coughed louder and spoke for the first time since the greetings.

"If I may, perhaps I should be with him for his first time?" she said carefully, her first sign of emotion beginning to show. Merlough looked at me then back to my mother.
"Perhaps it would be best if he were alone; he needs to get used to it after all," he replied calmly, straightening in his mighty height.

"But—" my mother started and a look from Diafol silenced her, or perhaps it was magick. Merlough growled, getting my attention, his eyes on my mother.
"I have been patient, have I not? Now let me have what is due," his voice sliced with warning.
It suddenly dawned on me what was to happen and what they were talking about, my eyes going to his sharp fangs.

"Will it hurt?" I blurted out, looking to my mother.
She remained silent, her eyes pleadingly on Merlough. He chuckled darkly.

"Of course not, little one. No, it is only a taste."
"We are leaving then," Diafol declared, his hand pulling my mother with him. She moved stiffly as if her body weren't her own. I looked away, unable to read the pain in her eyes as she looked at me.

My heart was beating fast and I tried to slow it, knowing it may only worsen things. I struggled to do so as I felt Merlough's gaze on me.
"Gods, your heart is like a fluttering bird. Am I really that terrifying?" he asked, frowning. I blushed, feeling self-conscious,

knowing I was only making things worse for myself. I felt panic slither through me.

"S-sorry my lord, its just-"

"Hush now. I promise it will not hurt like you think. A small pin-prick is all." He gestured peacefully. I looked at him but felt it best to avoid his fangs. Nervously, I tugged at my collar, which made him laugh.

"Gods, no wonder you are a mess! No, no, dear boy! Not there, not so soon. For now, it is only on the wrist. As I said, a taste," his last words hissed. He moved closer as I moved my sleeve to reveal my small, pale wrist, which looked fragile to me now. Slowly, I held it out to him, unable to conceal the shudders.

"Ah, such innocence...the sweetness that radiates off you. Close your eyes if you feel it will help?" His eyes were already locked onto my vein. I did as he said, hoping my shaking would slow as I closed my eyes.

After moments of him holding my wrist, he took so long that I opened my eyes again slowly. Just as I did, I saw a flash of teeth and then he was attached to my wrist, his fangs feeling like pins in my skin. I yelped and bit into my other hand, muffling my cry.

I began to feel faint as my pulse quickened further, feeling it in my own mouth as well as his. Just as I began to sway, he laughed silently, licking his lips, having pulled away from me.

"Gods, it sings! The blood sings to me," he swooned, his head tilted to the ceiling.

Carefully, I pulled my arm back, cradling it. I felt it pulsing still, his venom burning me. He swayed like he was drunk, laughing to himself, oblivious to my silent tears. I stared in horrified fascination as my blood lightened his dark soul. His very flesh taking a more pinkish glow.

"Yes, that's it. What delights I see…" He sighed, wiping his mouth, no blood to be seen. I sniffed, unable to hold my breath any longer, which made his eyes snap to me. I saw no recognition and I forgot my knowledge and all that I was taught. I was trapped in his gaze.

Suddenly, he was before me even though I had moved away quietly from him. His arm around me, pulling me so I was closer against him as his deep red eyes levelled with my own.

"See? That wasn't so bad, was it? A shame to have so little now, isn't it?" He hissed, his eyes largely dilated, looking almost black. He smiled as my heart began to pound harder.

"Come now, you offered that pretty neck so nicely to me earlier. Where has that bravery gone?" cooed the beast before me, his arms tightening around me like a snake.

"Please, it was just a taste," I cried softly. He began to speak when a snicker stopped him, his smile gone.

"A taste indeed… I believe we have an accord?" Diafol was suddenly in the room, standing behind me, his scale-like hand stroking my neck, his nail tracing a vein. A growl rumbled from Merlough, his eyes moving with my grandfather's hand.

"You have the taste. Now, how long does he need?" my grandfather asked, his words firmer and louder, his hand stopped on my neck.

Merlough swallowed and slowly regained his senses. He stood quickly, putting distance between us. He thought for a few moments, while Diafol hugged me from behind, an arm snaking over my shoulder, reaching around my throat as if to guard it, while the other wrapped around my waist. He rested his head on my shoulder, grinning at Merlough. His magick ebbed into me everywhere, lulling me into my own swoon. I felt it gather and wrap around my wrist.

"Two years," Merlough said, eyeing us both, his eyes normal once more.

"Two years to mature? It is done. On his fourteenth year, he will be yours."

Unexpectedly, my mother fell into the room as if she had been banging on the door for a long time. She was gasping and looked around, shocked that she was in the room.

Merlough left swiftly without another word, his cloak swooping around him like wings. Diafol giggled, turning so his lips were on my neck.

"Well done," he breathed, his magick overpowering me, making me sway.

In the next moment, I was on the floor, my mother crying over me. She carefully lifted me and took me to my room.

In my dazed sleep, I relived the moments with Merlough, his form taking on a more beastly figure, merging my childish nightmares to my reality. I fidgeted uncomfortably as a cloth was pressed to my forehead. The vampire venom raged in me like a hungry beast and explored its new home within my veins.

My grandfather's magick seeped away, leaving me burning and turning in distress. I heard my mother hushing me softly, other times snapping angrily at who I could only assume was my grandfather. I felt the coldness of a circular object pressing against my wrist, its power throbbing to my pulse. It stung briefly and my mother quieted as did the venom within me.

"He was too young." I felt my mother shudder in my hazy darkness.

"He won't be in two years. It was better that we were here for his first time. It will be easier as he matures; his body now knows his fate," Diafol muttered, sounding more sober than normal.

"I hate you," my mother hissed.

"I know," he replied simply. I faded back into the veil of darkness, the heat gone from my body, leaving me cool and limp.

I recovered quickly soon after, determined to put the experience behind me. As the initial horror faded, I reasoned that perhaps it was a misunderstanding between cultures.

My small scare was simply from not knowing and inexperience, and I felt ready for my next encounter. Diafol assured me that would be the last until I took my leave, my body now knowing the taste of his venom; it would anticipate its presence. It sounded grim and far less elegant than the writing I had read on the act.

Disappointment thudded at the back of my mind, warning me that this was unknown territory, my small faeling form to be cast into the darkness of the world.

Distance

By the spring of my fourteenth year, I had fallen into a routine of reading and music. My mother had once again withdrawn from me, her mind distracted and her heart absent. Diafol seemed in good spirits, his attention on my education. We spoke nothing of Merlough and his 'taste' of me. If I was honest, I avoided the subject at all costs.

I was reading in the study when my mother strode in, looking more animated than usual.

"Your brother is married," was all she said. I laughed.

"What? No! You jest! He can't be—"

"He is, dearest. Married this spring," she cut me off, her long figure stood before me like a tree.

"I-I don't understand."

"No," she said, affirming that she felt the same disbelief.
"To whom?"
"Mary," she sneered. I frowned, the red-haired faeling returning to my memory once more. The image of my brother talking to her, bright and highly saturated with importance.

"Mary?" I asked and she nodded, her mouth grim. "But why? Why not tell us? I asked him-"

Her dark chuckle cut me off.
"Your father believed it was in his right not to tell us if he wished," her voice scoffed in disbelief, the letter she held out to show me.
"Why would he do that?" I asked, confused by my brother's secrecy on such a thing. We shared everything; what had changed?

"Who knows what that fool thinks," she growled, crossing her arms angrily, making her look younger than she was. I swallowed my anger from her bitterness. I wanted to blame her then, for her distance with her son was the cause of this. The deep truth that it was my own doing, weighed like a heavy stone in my belly.

"So it is done. Done without us," I said, defeated, making my mother sigh sadly, her anger evaporated.
"Yes, dearest." She moved to sit next to me.
"I am so confused, Mother. What has changed so?"
She laughed at me then, making me flinch.

"Why, everything has changed," she drawled, her smile bitter as I pouted at her words.
"So am I no longer his brother? And you, not his mother?" I was upset by her coldness.
"So it would seem."
"But he can't just do that! It's crazy! How can Father let this happen?" She looked at me, unaffected by my outburst.
"I believe that distance we felt, my love, has finally reared its ugly head," she said simply as if it explained everything. I remained silent in protest. Had I truly created this? Was this because I had chosen to be a subsidium?

Slowly, she slid her arm around my shoulders.
"We are lost to them, sweetness," she said softly.
"Why?" I whispered, her arm feeling heavy on me.
"You know why," she quipped.
"But—"
"It is done. It seems to be easier for them to continue without us than to mourn our absence. Your father says it was affecting Rolo badly and he is not strong enough anymore," she explained, cutting me off again. My heart pounded in denial.
"But Father said—"
"Listen, Élan! I told you, we are dead to them!" she gritted out, taking my hands suddenly, her eyes wild. I did not recognise my mother at that moment. The disbelief thudding through me.
"No! I do not believe you!" I shouted, moving away from her, my father's words echoing in my head.

"We could never hate you."

"Then you are a *fool*," my mother seethed.

"Better a fool than a coward!" I screeched, anger boiling within me. My mother remained seated and watched me as I stormed away in disgust.

Days later, I apologised, unable to leave things sour between us. I was hurt and she knew me. I began to worry endlessly for her, what would she do when I left? My father's love for her seemed to fade further, a summer breeze pushed out by the winter. I sat writing, deep in thought, when she approached me.

"You must focus on yourself now, love. Worry not for me," she said softly, her hands on my shoulders with the lightest touch. I sighed heavily.

"But I do, Mother! I cannot leave you alone." I turned to her, my voice broken with emotion.

"Oh, my boy, my precious heart," she sighed, crouching down as she cupped my face.

Slowly, she pressed her face to mine, our noses touching gently. We breathed together in sync; I could feel her magick curling around us like motherly branches swirling green.

"You feel that?" she whispered, smiling secretly, for she knew I did. My heart began to beat in time with hers, forming an undeniable connection from her soul to mine. I remained frozen in amazement.

"I do," I replied, my voice reflecting her softness.

"No matter how far you are, this is what we have right here. It will always remain, my love. When you are alone and fear for me in your selfless being, remember this and know that I am well," she chimed, the magick dancing to her voice, echoing with sweet sound. It stirred my own magick into a gentle breeze to follow hers. She smiled with pride as she felt my magick respond.

"This connection can never falter and it is for you and you alone, my faeling," she said softly, her cool breath caressing my face.
"Thank you, Mother." I sighed, lost in the magick, a soft tune already playing to my soul. She kissed my face as I closed my eyes, her old self returned to me.

In the magick, I heard her soothing songs on those long stormy nights back home, her gentle breeze through the wild gardens, the sun's rays drawing the world from its slumber. The Brimhaven feeling returned to me once more.

I woke with a start, finding myself in bed. The darkness surrounded me. The air chilled from the sun's absence. I hugged myself, heart pounding from the sudden return past the veil of sleep. I looked around me, feeling something was off, something not quite right.

No noises or scent helped me find my comfort with my setting. I trembled as I hesitated, considering leaving my bed.

In the end, the curiosity pulled me from the warmth of my heated bed, my legs weak. My bedclothes did little to shield me from the cold. I slowly stumbled to the door, my eyes adjusting to the darkness, my hand reaching for the door.

A shadow from the window blinded my view of the door and I yelped, turning to the window. It was blocked by a body, revealing nothing to me but red eyes, glaring at me.

Before I had time to react, I was grabbed in a vice grip, and then darkness…

I came-to amid the sounds of the forest at night. The large forest behind my grandfather's house, I presumed. My heart leaped, threatening to leave my body as the memories rushed back to me. I pulled myself up and struggled with the cold biting my bare legs, making me shiver violently. The moon looked down at me, the large face bright and haunting. I heard movement and my instincts propelled me forward. I scrambled to my feet and I ran as fast as I could, my bed clothes whipping about me. My chest burned as I struggled to provide the air I needed, the air itself sharp in my lungs. I ran in no specific direction, away from the sounds behind me.

Yes, there is definitely something pursuing me now.

It's menacing presence was taunting me. Footsteps ran in step with mine almost mockingly, making my beating heart pound in my ears. My mind was blank as I denied the reality of this. I tumbled and tripped a few times, my feet unable to move fast enough.

Gods, please help me!

I knew not what pursued me, not allowing myself time to look. I knew that it was after me and it was dangerous and fast. It seemed to lose its playfulness and the footsteps came closer to me and I began to hear growls of excitement. I was being pursued. This monster, this creature of nightmares had me in its sight.

Gods, they were true!

Those tales of shadow monsters stealing young faelings from their beds were true! I felt a tug at my collar and yelped, horrified. They were so close now. The forest seemed never-ending, the moon watching our pursuit with silent interest.

I was pushed to the ground, halting the chase. The growls rumbled loudly against my ear, hungry.
"*Mine*," it hissed, its nails digging into the back of my neck. I could not scream, I could not shout as the air was knocked out of me. I barely remained awake, the darkness dancing around me.

Violently, I was pulled up again and pushed back against a nearby tree, my head pounding with the rest of my aching body. My eyes were open, but I saw nothing. The hand gripping my throat squeezed the remaining air from me.

A rumble of laughter breathed hotly over my face. I felt its face press against my throat, inhaling deeply. It groans in obscene pleasure, making me fidget in panic. Its knee crashes down over my legs, pinning me to the ground against the tree.

"*Surrender now*," it purred and licked my neck slowly. I struggled, more making it chuckle.

"*Yes, struggle. Get it pumping around, make it flood to me*," it hissed. I begged it silently, tears falling down my face, slicing my cheeks in the cold air.

I felt the promise of sharp fangs on my neck and pushed hard, managing to shove half my body away from it. It growled and slammed me back against the tree.

"*Enough games, little mouse*," it growled and it bit into me, my scream carried away by the wind.

I was jolted awake once again in my bed. My hand immediately went to my neck, which was wet with sweat. I yelped at the shadow from the window only to discover it was a tree. The nightmare swirled around my mind, my nerves on full alert, unable to confirm it was a fantasy. I lay back down, hugging myself with the covers. I shivered despite being in the warmth of my blankets, my sweat dripping.

"*Mine*," the voice echoed in my head as I succumbed to my exhaustion.

PART 2

Into the South

I have no memory of the journey to the south. I was under a spell, which was standard when transporting faeries from the land for the first time. It helped them adjust to the different air pressures and sharper weather - or so I was told.

When I awoke, I was in a strange, tall house which was so dark that it took awhile for my eyes to adjust to my surroundings. It smelled musty and the furniture around me seemed a ghost of its original prime and polished version. Shock and anxiety began to replace the magick that was wearing off.

I had left home. Left my mother. This was to be my new life. I tried to swallow down my shock at how dull it seemed compared to Diafol's house. Creaks and groans echoed around me as if the house itself was vocalising dread.

I was greeted by a male servant of the household, a vampire with a willowy stature and plain features. His voice held no emotion as he explained his role and that he was to watch over me during the Master's absence. I remained silent as he approached me carefully.

"Do you know why you are here?" he asked, accentuating his words. I realised then that they spoke common Karing too—which was some small consolation. I nodded, my mind still not quite believing I was here.

"Good, it is easier that way. I must check you now, so hold still," he said, his tone warning. Again I remained quiet as he inspected me carefully, looking into my mouth, then through my curled hair and cold hands.

"Good, you seem to be ready." He moved away as others walked in silently. All of them wore some type of plain uniform that matched their position. I couldn't help but feel intimidated as they lined up near the wall, their eyes moving as I moved. It was unnerving. Merlough entered last, an air of authority floating around him.

"Master, he is well and arrived in fair condition," the male said as he stood with the others. "Good," Merlough seemed to glide in, not giving them a second look. He stood before me and I felt my heart pound with uncertainty.

Was I to stand? Why did this feel threatening when I had experienced his presence before? Slowly, he took my jaw, my eyes meeting those red eyes that read more menacing than before.

"Leave us," he hissed. His staff flowed out swiftly, leaving us in a tense silence. I stiffened as he leaned in and inhaled deeply near my head.

"Ah… like fresh pine on a crisp day. Finally, you are here." He sighed, his fingers stroking my jaw. His voice sounded more familiar and I felt myself ease more into acceptance. He chuckled.

"Ah that beating heart, like a bird in a cage of ivory. Such a delight you are! So far from home…" I remained quiet, hesitant on if I was to respond. My silence hardened his expression.

"Give yourself to me," he hissed, making me swallow audibly. He took a seat beside me and watched me as I angled my throat to him, my body trembling. A sly smile sloped onto his face as he took in my frightened form.

"This may hurt…" He purred as he leaned in. I remained still in my submission, knowing that this was my fate. My mind reeled with reasons as to why I was there. I felt his teeth bite into my throat, slower than he had with my wrist, as if he was savouring my flesh surrendering. I tensed as a reflex, unable to school my reaction. The pulling sensation soon followed, making me sway. His hands gripped my shoulders as he drank, the pulling tugged harder at my heart with each second. I felt my heart strain like an animal on a leash as panic set in. Even as I felt these sensations, I was paralysed with his venom and forced to sit in horror as my body surrendered to his feeding.

Darkness began to swirl in my sight, teasing at my helpless self and sad tears fell. As unpleasant as it was, I felt my heart ease as I felt his tongue seal the wound. He slumped next to me, his arm reaching round to pull me close. My body felt heavy as he clutched me.

"Ah, such sweet songs your blood sings, little birdie." He sighed, his eyes drooping closed.

Moments later, as I recovered myself in the grips of the sleeping beast, a vampire servant boy returned and gently pulled me from him.

"Follow me," he said softly as he steadied me on my feet.

He led me through the house and all that it contained. From the wall structure, the house felt tall but narrow compared to my grandfather's. The darkness seeming to gather and sit in the corners of the rooms.

As we walked the long corridors, I felt the absence of magick that usually lightened the air and freshened my step. Here, the stillness added to the dull and purposeful atmosphere, weighing on me as did my worry. This was my new life? This was were I was meant to be?

Little personality shone through the walls and rooms. The furniture seemed mismatched and aged with neglect. I particularly noticed the lack of plant life or any life for that matter, apart from the sparse house helpers that seemed to have little presence in the house. The windows suggested we were on a street where a flurry of vampires were going about their evenings, the lampposts casting a ghoulish glow on them.

Inside, there were electric lights and small candles dotted around the rooms, which I assumed were lit for my sake as there was only the right amount for necessity rather than the pleasure of light. Faeries were pretty good at seeing in the dark, but not as good as vampires.

As day dwellers, there was simply no need to acquire the skill. I believe now, years later, that my days in that house, and country, encouraged me to train my sight to be more adapted to darkness than the average faerie.

I was shown to a small box room containing a writing desk and a bed, with a window that seemed to have been newly added and larger than others in the house. Metal grates were added just beyond the glass so there was enough for me to open the window four inches or so but no more.

In the evening light, the shadows of the bars loomed on the walls of the room, casting a prison look. I thanked the boy servant and found my small bundle of clothing and items on my bed. Slowly, I open them, a waft of home wrapping around me. The bed groaned as I sank down, hugging the items to me. I cried quietly as my heart wrenched from the loss, my reality a hard crash of bitterness.

My days changed to suit my setting. I was encouraged to get up and wash around midday, then I was left to entertain myself with dusty books until my master rose. He would sit and wait on the couch that I would soon come to hate, the same place he fed on me on my first day.

He would wait, tapping impatiently as a servant would collect me from my room and bring me to him. As I would enter, the servant would stand along the side of the room a good distance from him, their eyes respectfully diverted from us. I could feel their distaste like a subtle scent in the air as he drank from me in front of them. Sometimes he would taunt them, whereas other times he would ignore them completely as he took from me.

At first I had felt self-conscious of their presence until I eventually learned that it made little difference to the experience. Whether they were there or not, the pain was present. The sickening pulling and the powerless surrender, which seemed so far from what my grandfather had intended. Were his words lies? Had he truly wanted this for me? What of the songs and music? I hated to believe that I had been tricked, that I was foolishly cast out for some unknown gain. I knew my grandfather and above all else he was a hard negotiator. What I had been traded for must have been incredibly important, I believed, as I sat like a stringless puppet, being drained almost to sickness.

When my master went about his business, I was made to sit quietly, to be present and available for his needs. Usually he took from the wrist once or twice a night, and by the throat at three day intervals. Whether it was from the wrist or the throat, the servants seemed to show a distaste, knowing the master himself was too distracted. But I saw them, I saw their faces, their eyes narrowed as if threatened, my blood scent making their nostrils flare. What must it be like to have me walking around, living amongst them as a constant reminder of what they could not have. I had learned in my education that only highborns were legally allowed to have subsidiums. Instead they had rats or small birds to feed on, otherwise cold, congealed blood, which explained their greyer complexion.

On some nights, my master made me sing, mainly when he was feeling angry, having visited court and come home frustrated or worse—when he could hear voices that weren't there. I reminded myself this was my real reason for coming here. To sing and hopefully make it to court.

My voice would soothe and calm him, making him more approachable and like the Merlough that I had met in the Faelands. It was a service that I enjoyed the most and came to appreciate as I felt it held its own magick and gave the place some life. It could never match the shine and shimmer of faerie-land life, but the small glow that was left after my songs was enough to make my own hope awaken.

Even the servants seemed to linger in the room when I began my soft songs, their movements becoming more smooth and fluid. I sang small songs of the forest and the sky, fresh of hope. It lightened my new dull world.

On a particularly bad evening, when I was in my room waiting to be escorted, the master was ranting and raving at a voice no one else heard. As his shrieks and growls grew louder, I became more and more anxious, feeling the servants silent flurry of distress and hesitation to come to me. All too soon, a quick and desperate knock banged on my door.

"The master is in need of you. Come quickly."

"*Where is my birdie?"* The words drifted to me then, his voice seeming to come from the walls themselves. We ran to him quickly and I found him pacing in his study.

"It's not fair, no! I can't be treated like this," he growled as we arrived. The servant coughed politely.

"The boy, Master," he said almost solemnly.

In an instant, I felt his fangs in me, somehow harder and deeper than before. His drinking was in strong messy pulls, making my heart beat erratically out of sync. I yelped and whined at the pain, feeling the difference in his feeding. I saw the servant's concerned look, which caused me to panic further. I hated them as they watched. We were all powerless to him as he drained me.

For the first time, I felt my body fight him and in turn, he gripped me harder, his nails having their own taste of my flesh. I begged him silently, feeling my sight wane and fade. My legs began to falter and I felt someone take hold of me. I felt Merlough growl at the hands that held me but continued to drink. It felt endless, yet at the same time, impossibly fast as my body strained to survive under his demand.

"Master you will kill another!" a voice warned. Merlough growled again but stopped. His withdrawal created my blackness.

"Gods, Merlough! Are you a baby bat?" the unknown voice said, using a term for a young vampire.

"Try him yourself and see if you can resist," came a growling reply. The voice clicked his tongue. I felt a warm cloth on my face, drawing me further into the waking world. The man shushed me as I struggled, my nerves waking to an ache that I couldn't place.

"He is just a boy," he grit, removing the cloth and reapplying it with more heat. The comfort it gave to my shuddering bones made me sigh. Merlough chuckled.

"I did everything that was in my right; it was the family's will," he replied, sounding further away.

"That may be so, but you have not used him the proper way. Fancy taking him by the throat when it has been a mere few days, curse you," the voice growled, taking extra care to apply the heat to my throat.

"Again Doric, you are not here to lecture me or give me advice. I am well aware on how to use MY subsidium. Now, is he well?" Merlough hissed, moving closer. I felt this Doric lean over me, carefully looking at my face.

"He will be well, in due time," he muttered, his cool breath ghosting over me.

"You must not use him until then, do you hear? Otherwise, there will be further complications," he ground out, turning to where I assume Merlough stood.

I woke slowly, the room brighter than normal, the bedroom alight fully with candles and hastily plugged in lamps. The vampire sitting on the bed next to me was pale with long warm blonde hair tied at the nape of his neck. He wore a white coat that resembled a doctor, and was turned to the end of the bed where Merlough stood. Merlough met my eyes and pointed at me.

"See? He seems well enough." He motioned casually. Doric tsked again and turned to me.

"Here. Drink," he said softly, handing me some water. His warm brown eyes reminded me of my mother and I felt calm in his presence. His eyes indicated that he was not a full blooded vampire like Merlough, but a lesser species. One that is bred on the outskirts of the courts, their bloodline a far cry from the source of vampire royalty.

He watched me silently as I drank thirstily, then took the cup off me afterwards. Carefully, as if not to frighten me, Doric placed fingers at my throat and lowered his head as if he was listening.

"Good, you are stabilising nicely," he muttered as he raised his head.

"I told you he was stronger than the others," Merlough grinned and Doric grimaced and looked at him sharply.

"And I have told you that I am not a *faerie* doctor. You cannot keep doing this. Learn some self-control," he hissed, a sign of genuine anger for the first time. Merlough seemed unaffected by his words, and shrugged.

"Just taste him and see what I have to offer for your wonderful services," he sneered, stalking closer to us.

Doric looked back at me, eyes alight for a moment. I must have looked frightened for he turned away ashamed.

"The boy needs rest. Another time," he said quietly standing from the bed. Merlough laughed, patting him on the shoulder, both looking like tall, pale giants in the small lit room.

"Once you have a taste, you will regret missing this opportunity, my friend. He is a delight. Can you not smell him?" Merlough grinned, leading Doric out of the room.

"Truly, it is almost maddening. I do my best not to involve feeding when working; it is in poor taste," I heard him reply as they left. My heart softened at his words, suddenly sad that he was leaving. I thought then that I admired him for his restraint.

Soon after, a servant returned and cautiously handed me more water. I fell asleep again and did not rise until the next evening. Merlough seemed to keep to the orders and resisted feeding from me until I was fully regained a few days later. I took that day as a lesson and was more cautious around him, aware now of my affect on the creatures. Merlough himself also seemed a bit remorseful, taking extra care to drink from my wrist with small, slow pulls. It seems I forgave him soon after that.

Carmilla's Court

Months passed and soon Merlough was again summoned to court. This time he wished to take me along, determined to prove my existence and how 'delectable' I was. Doric's wincing reaction confused me.

Would they not like to hear my voice? To see a faeling from the Faelands attend their court? From what I had read, the courts were welcoming and built for hosting parties. I was nervous yet excited to see the wonders I had read about. Even a chance to meet Queen Carmilla in all her glory was enough reason to get to excited.

I tingled with anticipation as a seamstress came to measure me, making a new outfit in the court colour—crimson. I felt it washed me out terribly, my skin pathetically pale against the bold colour, but Merlough seemed impressed with the contrast.

"Perfect. She is going to be so pleased." He grinned at me. I was unsure of how to react so I remained quiet, aware of how quick his temper could be.

We took a long, shiny black car, something I had not been in before. Such machines were sparse in the Faelands. Here, cars were the main mode of transport for they were built with sun protectors in order to not weaken the dark creatures. From what I knew, they could go at a speed that excelled any horse. I took in everything around me in quiet awe. I could smell the leather from the seats. What would Rolo think of me being in one of these?!

Merlough petted my head on the way, as I tried to ignore the coiling in my gut. Having only seen drawings and faded images of the court in the fae archives, the building itself impressed me the most on my dark journey. Like an imposing palace, it stood as far as the clouds swam. Long, tall, black castle-like turrets and glowing windows looked menacing against the red evening sky. I fidgeted as my clothes felt tight, the fortress making me feel more worried.

"Be still," Merlough growled, pulling me to his side. I noticed then how fresh he smelled, having washed before we left, his clothes the same silk shirt and red vest he had worn when we first met. His long hair freshly combed and tied at his nape as was the fashion. I calmed myself in my thoughts, thinking of how much this night meant to me, to my family, and my dreams.

I was so close now! Merlough continued to pet me, murmuring to himself.

The car lurched to a stop and startled me out of my reverie. We had arrived at the steps and I came out unsteady on my legs for having sat for so long. I felt Merlough's hands come to my shoulders, his lips to my ear.

"Be a good little birdie for me now. This is the pinnacle of your family's efforts, so behave," he hissed warningly. My eyes were upwards towards the peaks, which disappeared through the clouds. I felt his nail tease my throat warningly as he sniffed me. My heart fluttering in my chest at the scale and size of the sight before me, Merlough's words pressuring me. The place was as tall as a mountain!

Merlough broke away as another greeted him and we were led into the mighty Court of Queen Carmilla herself.

I was too much in awe to react frightened or scared for that is surely what I felt inside. I distracted myself with the fine intricate works that lined the huge walls of patterns. The hard floor sparkled with hidden gems of rubies and garnet in a sea of what looked like marble. Long, thin candles lined the walls, making shadows around us dance and gave the rooms a pleasant glow. Merlough moved through the rooms at a familiar pace, causing me to almost run behind him as he spoke avidly to the other vampire.

This was amazing! Gods, I could almost feel a song ready to burst from me with inspiration from my majestic surroundings.

We came to elegant double doors that were pulled open upon our arrival. A warm gust of air and music hit me. It was the largest room I had ever seen, alight with gold and red. The music throbbed with detailed string instruments. The room was full of highborn vampires, from the gleam in their red eyes to the soft shine of the silk they wore, all competing in some silent fashion on their elegance and flamboyant style.

On a dais at the far end of the room, I saw a large red throne that shimmered with the same gems as the floor. It looked more intimidating than comfortable. My eyes dancing around the room, fascinated by the spectacles before me. This was a vampire court. This was the heart of vampire society.

Before the dais, couples of all backgrounds danced to the elegant music, their bodies swerving with grace, their bright silken clothing floating around them. It was truly beautiful. I was so entranced I lost Merlough's trail a number of times, not that he noticed. I stumbled to keep up with him, unable to tear my gaze away from the creatures before me. He was deep in conversation with the vampire, his small faeling forgotten in the sea of predators.

When was I to sing? Had Merlough arranged something?

As I looked closely, I noticed very few other faelings and wondered if it was normal. Where were they kept? How many lived at court?

The thought of me being the only faerie in sight made me blush and feel self-aware as I caught hungry glances aimed my way, the red gazes varying in shade.

Suddenly I felt lost, so lost that I did not know myself or why I was here.

What is this place?

I continued to look around, dazed, searching for some unknown answer.
"*Élan*?" I heard a voice and frowned as the name struck a chord in me. I looked around but could not find its source.
"Élan? Élan, look at me." A hand held my face and my vision blurred. I gasped, my memory snapping back into place. Doric crouched before me, his brown eyes crinkled with concern.
"Gods, what happened?" I asked, feeling ashamed, shocked as I was in a completely different part to the room than earlier.
"Vampire lures differ to faerie magick, little one. Gods, where is Merlough?" he growled, checking my throat and wrists.
"I'm not sure," I muttered sadly, scared for he would surely be angry when he discovered my wanderings. I didn't recall any mention of vampire lures in the fae archives…

"Worry not, I can hear his stupid cackle nearby. Hold my hand," he said softly, standing swiftly, leading me through a crowded section. I swallowed as I felt a blush bloom on my face as he led me through the crowd.

I had been naïve to come here…

"Ah, there is my little birdie. Tried to fly off did you?" Merlough sneered as he drank from a glass of red liquid.

"Merlough, it was foolish to bring him here. It isn't safe," Doric berated, gently nudging me to him. I couldn't help but feel useless and unwanted. I looked up at them, my face regretful.

"I'm sorry, Master, I got—" I was smacked across the face before I could finish. Gasps echoed around us.

"Speak when spoken to, you little whelp," Merlough growled, making the small group he was standing with snicker under their breaths. I held my face, shocked, my cheek burning.

"Merlough, that is—" Doric began.

"Hey! The Queen has arrived," hissed a nearby vampire. It seemed, all at once, the creatures shuffled in the same direction, anticipation fizzling around them. Merlough grabbed me and held me close. The crowd pushed us tighter together as they strained to follow the Queen as she entered. A blanket of silence and awe fell over us.

Merlough was as distracted as the others, trying to get a glimpse of her. I felt too ashamed to look, willing my tears not to fall. I needed to be brave now, for my family.

"This is it; this is my time," Merlough muttered to himself as he pulled us to the front of the crowd, trying to get within view of the Queen. A vampire male near him seemed to look up and down at him in disapproval as we reached the front. The vampire that had led us into the room snorted and elbowed Merlough.

"Isn't she your aunt? Why are you down here with us, while the rest of your family stands up there?" he chided, making Merlough growl.

"Aunty? Aunty!" he called, his ugly voice slicing the respectful silence. I saw a number of pale faces turn to us and realised with dread that we had caught unwanted attention, that he had caused some faux pas. I fought the urge to run.

Slowly, the few vampires that had restricted my view parted, revealing a goddess in red. Everything from her hair, her eyes, her lips, to her dress was a bright red. A scarlet red that put all other shades to shame. Her eyes were the brightest I had ever seen. Slowly, as she drew nearer, I realised that the silence was necessary, for the power she had, burned off her like a flame.

"Merlough, I told you not to address me as such," came her voice, sharp as glass. I felt Merlough tremble and I withheld my own shudder.

"But Alain—" he began, referring to his cousin.

"Alain is blood of my beloved sister and the Blood Prince. You are the blood of my half-mad brother, a brute who continues to haunt me and be bothersome. I would avoid making the same mistake he did," she warned and gasps whispered around us. I felt Merlough's shame like a bitter taste on my tongue.

Gods, she was beautiful. Dangerous, but beautiful. Slowly she began to turn away.

"But my Queen! This is the faerie I told you about," he blubbered, pushing me before her. I almost fell from the force, fearing that if I touched her, I would turn to ash. My heart pounded and I gasped as I felt her eyes hone in on me.

"Ah yes, what a pretty thing," she muttered, her voice cold. My stomach dropped like a stone in my gut.

"Beloved Carmilla, he is the blood of Diafol! A great specimen for us. Please have a taste," he explained, nudging me impossibly closer. I almost yelped in panic. She towered over me like the building did, impossibly captivating and foreboding at the same time.

"Of that old fool? Why would I want that thief's blood?" She hissed, her eyes narrowed dangerously. To her, I looked like a bug, a dangerous bug that needed to be squished immediately. My lip trembled, feeling the shame of her disapproval. This was all wrong! This was not meant to be! Why did she dislike me already? What had I done to her?

"But Carmilla, he is a prize, truly. Wait, just hear him sing! He could duet with you!" Merlough pleaded desperately.

"I have not got time for this," she said dismissively, freeing me from her gaze. For once, I was relieved that I was not to sing.

"Please, I beg you! It will be worth it, I promise!" He grinned slyly, leaning over me. A tense silence crawled between them, no one in the hundreds that were present moved a muscle.

Finally, she rolled her eyes and huffed.

"Fine. He can sing, I will listen just so you will shut up," she growled and headed toward the dais. Merlough laughed, delighted, pushing me after her.

Slowly, she descended the dais and sat on the throne, a miracle, with the size of her dress fitting in such a small space.

She sat straight, her eyes looking forward blankly, making me hesitate in my song.

Merlough pushed me to face her, my back to the entire room. The *snap* of her opening fan jolted me. I swallowed heavily, letting the silence settle around me.

Miraculously, I begin to sing, a soft tune of the forest, one I knew to be Merlough's favourite.

Mother Earth and Father pine,
Are in an eternal entwine,
As the sun graces the light
And all is bright…

Within minutes, she interrupted me.
"All right, I have had enough," she said dismissively, already looking away. I stopped immediately, staring in shock.

"W-what but why? It was sensational, was it not? What's wrong with him?" Merlough whined, fighting to keep the growl from his voice as he stood to the right of the dais. Carmilla sighed impatiently, looking me up and down with venom.

"There is nothing *wrong* with him. His voice is divine. I am sure he tastes wonder—"
"Then why—" Merlough cut in, causing her to turn to him in fury. Her face seemed to flash red and then return almost immediately.

"*Because*," she hissed dangerously, her eyes flaring at his interruption. Her voice seemed a normal volume yet everyone in the room heard her. I felt the promise of tremors again.
"He is a *faeling*, Merlough. Look at him! Merely a faeling far from home. Why in the gods names take him from such a place of sunshine and stars?" she ground out, glaring at him.

The room's air was stiff with tension. Merlough seemed frozen at her words, unable to respond. She sighed heavily, seeming to regain her composure.

"Forgive me for I do not have a taste for stolen faelings from the Faelands. You play a dangerous, foolish game with them, Merlough. Owning a child, one that his mother is now without for the pleasure of your own greed. No! I will not enjoy this boy, for he does not belong here." And with a wave of her hand, she dismissed me. I swallowed down my own retort, my head low in shame. Merlough's rage reared like a cobra as I reached him below.

"It is legal and it is within my right!" he growled. Slowly she turns her gaze back to us, a dangerous smile on her lips.
"Yes, you are correct; it is legal. *For now.* Movement suggests that it is becoming distasteful. Watch carefully for I will only say this once. I have never liked the damned subsidium system and have taken a particular dislike to this practice. Do you see me with a faeling? No. Oh, but practice your rights and do what you must! But tread carefully in this court for I do not condone such acts or take them lightly. Take the boy home. He is cold, hungry, and too damn frightened to be here any longer. I am disappointed

and ashamed that this is what he sees when coming to this great country." She turned away, fanning herself. Merlough growled low but obeyed, grabbing me by the shoulder and pulling me away.

"Oh and Merlough?" she called suddenly, making us freeze in our departure. "Offend me again and you will regret it. Do you understand? Being the blood of my brother will only save you so many times," she said firmly, her voice carrying through the court. Merlough sighed heavily, his head also bowed.

"Yes, my Queen."

"Alain, my heart," Carmilla gasped as he bowed before her, kissing her gloved hand.

"Beloved Aunt in red, how are you?" he asked in his warm voice. Carmilla sighed wearily.

"Much better now that you are here, dearest," she answered, rubbing her temples. He laughed his light chuckle.

"Indeed that was a spectacle. What is he thinking?" he said incredulously, getting a groan from his aunt.

"I do not know, nor do I want to. Just do me a favour, beloved?" she asked, lowering her voice, others distracted in their dances and music.

"How can I help?" he asked with genuine concern, leaning closer to her.

"Keep an eye on that little sprite, I do not trust his grandfather or that buffoon of a nephew," she whispered, her voice masked, reaching only Alain's ears.

"Wait, Merlough, surely you would not go so soon? There are drinks to be had!" called a vampire as we made our way to the giant double doors. He ignored them and pushed me past them. I shuddered at his fury, worrying about the implications this would lead to.

Surely he will want a drink before the night is out…

"I am sorry—" I began, unable to hold my regret any longer.
"Shut up," he spat, tugging me past a laughing group.
"Cousin! Will you not stay for a moment?" a voice called. It drew Merlough from his thoughts and he stood by the doorway.
"Come to gloat, have you? Beloved Blood Prince," he snarled pulling me to him protectively.

"Come now, I have only just arrived. You do not have to leave so soon," he replied calmly. It was at this moment I gazed at him, as I found my balance after Merlough's rough handling. It is a sight I would never forget.

Before me, as tall and great as Queen Carmilla, stood her blonde equal. A man with fine features, long and straight icy blonde hair that fell past his shoulders, his eyes a bright red to match Carmilla's.

He wore a long coat of red velvet and long leather boots. He leaned casually against the door, his arms crossed. A lazy smile played on his delectable lips and for the first time in my life, I felt it. That throb in the heart that feels like no other. I noticed I was breathing hard and tried to calm myself.

Merlough's growl made me shudder again. The blonde laid his eyes on me and his smile disappeared. At once, he was before me, leaning to my height, his dark cloak laid out behind him like wings.

"And what is your name?" he asked, his voice sounding like a purr to me. My tongue failed me as Merlough growled again and tugged me away from him.

"He is none of your concern, Alain. He is *mine*," he hissed, already trying to turn from him.

"Merlough, really, must you be such a brute? The poor bird is frightened of you." Alain pouted, taking my hand, which trembled for more reasons than fright.

"Your voice was beautiful, truly a gift to behold," he said softly, his lips touching my hand. I blushed brightly and felt my body react to him. As if sensing my reaction, he smiled to me, his fangs enticing me.

"Enough! We are leaving," Merlough cut in, snatching my other hand and pulling me away, tearing apart our moment together. My heart still pounded as he pulled me through the long halls leading back to the entrance.

"Curse your damn pounding," he roared, prodding me hard in the chest. I was helpless as he grabbed me and slammed me against the nearby wall. The candles shuddered with the impact and my head bloomed with pain. The pain rerouted as he bit me hard, uncaring of vampires nearby. His gulps sounded obscene to my ears as he drinks from me. My small moment with Alain ruined as I hung helpless bleeding with the reality of my fate.

A part of me felt betrayed Alain did not stop him. But then why should he? I was Merlough's…

The red and gold intensified and sharpened as I focused on the wall opposite, trying to calm myself as he drained me.

"Stop!" a voice yelled as I faded once again behind the veil of darkness…

Beautiful music awoke me, music I hadn't heard since my life in the Faelands. I opened my eyes to be surrounded by blue, submerged in water it seemed. Yet, I did not need to breath and floated weightless in the water. The music was all around me and embraced me, calming me.

In the distance I saw a tail, shadowed by the dancing light. I turned as another tail caught my eye to the left but it was gone before I could fully focus. The music grew louder, buzzing me pleasantly. The voices were a rainbow of tones, harmony

embodied. A hand stroked my cheek from behind, startling me but then soothing me with its softness.
"*Dear child*," the voice sighed, sounding neither male nor female. Arms hugged me around my middle, a head against my own.
"*Ours, always ours.*" It sighed again and I felt a tail beat ripples behind my legs.

Mermaids. Sirens of the deep.

This is what I thought lazily, spelled by the music, the water holding me in place.
"*You voice is wasted to those above.*" It sighed sadly, sounding upset, its arms tightening around me. A shadow went over us and the soothing hands stopped their caresses and gripped me.
"*No*," it whined and I felt a tug upwards, away from the being. A firmer tug made me gasp and the being cried as if wounded. The music continues around us, weaving its magick.

"*Be brave, my spirit*," it cried brokenly and released. The moment it did, I was pulled up, the break of the water an assault to my senses. I was lying on a beach, the sand feeling hard compared to the water's embrace. I was gasping, the air feeling alien to me, my lungs denying their effect. A shadow blocked the sun and long blonde hair fell around me like a curtain. His scent enveloped me again and I struggled to enjoy it in my rasping breath. I focused on his red eyes, confirming the Blood Prince's face.

A vampire in daylight?

I was confused as his hand covered my mouth. His face looked emotionless as he watched me struggle, my body failing.
The absence of music threaded me with panic. I tried to speak through his hands, my body straining to survive. Slowly he lowered his lips to my ear.
"*Breatheeeee,*" he said softly, his voice never failing to stir me within. I took a long gasp in, trying to slow my panic and I was pulled into darkness once more.

I woke on the other side of the veil, a blurred vision that was once the Blood Prince's face became the defined version of Doric. I tried to sit up stiffly, my court clothes constricting my movement. My breath came in short gasps, my mind jumbled and confused from its journey from behind the veil of consciousness. Doric's pale face above me was pinched with concern.

"Be still; you are very weak," he said, his voice croaked and weary. His hand tenderly held me down, though it felt like a heavy weight on my panicked chest. His words drew me further into reality as I returned to my body, but the numbness concerned me. I felt the familiar lump of my bed beneath me and realised we were back at Merlough's quarters.

"Pfft, seems the great court of Carmilla was too much for the little birdie. Had too much excitement," mumbled a beast which my mind registered as Merlough. He sounded a safe distance from me, avoiding distressing me further. Doric clicked his tongue.

"You should not have fed from him as you did. That was the cause. Fancy feeding from him in the halls of the court? Where are your manners?! Your patience, Merlough?" Doric gritted out, sounding furious. I heard a shy scuff of a shoe on the floor.

"Come now, Doric, the evening was tough on us both. You know full well how much the pressures of court have been getting to me," he muttered ,pouting, sounding further away than previously, as if he were retreating from the room.

"Well, it was certainly enough to concern the Blood Prince. You both caught his attention tonight and you know how dangerous that can be." My heart could not help but do a little leap at his words.

Alain was concerned for me?

Doric frowned as if he heard my heart leap—and he probably could due to his close proximity. I calmed my nerves, conscious of my own responses now. Merlough continued as if he hadn't noticed.

"Pfft, he is always stirring trouble. Sticking his nose where it doesn't belong. The boy is fine as you can see," he grumbled, his court clothes swishing as he indicated to me. Despite his behaviour and my weariness now towards him, I realised how we all still adorned our court clothes and began to wonder how long

I had been unconscious. I watched closely as Doric turned sharply to where Merlough lingered by the doorway of the room.

"It would be best not to get the Blood Prince's attention regarding the subsidium. He doesn't take kindly to the tradition, as you know," Doric warned. I lay still, listening intently, realising I may have caused more of a stir than I knew.

Did that mean Alain did not like fae? He seemed to like me though…

"Bah! What is this family coming to? Soon we will be like the miserable whelps at Dracula's Court. All too scared to step on each other's toes, sipping blood in the dark in shame," Merlough growled. Doric chuckled.

"I doubt it will go that far. Regardless, Merlough, all I am saying is take caution, my friend," Doric's voice was calmer then. I heard more than saw Merlough's wolfish grin, waving his hand with a swish of his silk garments before leaving us alone.

I noticed that once his menacing presence was gone, Doric seemed to sober as he took in my weak state. He began to inspect me once more, taking my pulse and reading my vitals with his supernatural senses.

"Forgive him, little one. He has not had the best of life. Although that is no excuse, I know," Doric murmured as our gazes meet.

"H-how long have you known him?" I asked curiously, my voice raw. Doric sighed.

"A while, more than most, lets say. I met him in college, which he dropped out of straight away, of course. But he seemed to take a liking to me and we made friends during my studies," he explained.
"College? You went to the one here? In the city?" I asked, my curiosity piqued, trying to imagine life growing up here compared to Brimhaven's simple comforts.

"Indeed, it is the place to get the accreditation to be recognised even in the districts further east of here," he explained patiently. He was referring to Dracula's side of the Vampire Nation. It interested me as this was rare for ones that were not closely linked by bloodlines (indicated by their red eyes from the blood disease).

From my education, I knew that both vampire territories were closely guarded and for one to cross into the other, they must be highly educated and recommended. Trusted to a level beyond the average creature.
I quietly pondered the very idea of such restrictions in life. How strange that such a distinct connection made such a difference in your life and how similar it was to my own.

Would I be here now if I weren't related to Diafol?

I shoved away the thought before it pulled me down a dark spiral. Instead, I considered Merlough's clear connection to the higher ranks in vampire society and sighed. Even that didn't seem enough to him.

"Your parents must be proud. I heard it's hard to get into college unless you are a descendant from the Red Queen herself," I commented, bringing myself back to the conversation once more. Doric gave an impressed chuckle.

"Indeed, though luckily I was well educated and with competitive parents like mine, achieving the best seems adequate. Being a doctor amongst the relatives of Queen Carmilla certainly makes it…interesting," he clarified. I nodded weakly, understanding the underlying context. Doric seemed to release the tenuous ground this was leading to and mentally shook himself.

"Well, I must confess, I am impressed that you know so much about us. Coming from outside of our land, I know we aren't the most open with our lore compared to others," he laughed suddenly at his own thoughts.

"But then, saying this, I am forgetting you are a relative of Diafol himself. You have seen firsthand the suspicion other creatures hold towards him. He always seems to know things outside his remit. He can stir even the most secure of creatures such as the queen herself," he seemed to stop himself before he said any more. I nodded again, a question having formed and now burned like a brand in my mind.

"Do you know why I was given to Merlough? What are the specifics that my grandfather agreed that seemed above the average family?" I asked carefully, my breath simmering, knowing it was a brave question. Doric went quiet and thought carefully, looking to the window behind me that was blackened from the night.

"To be honest…Merlough is protective of that information. I have seen the contract, though parts only appear for eyes intended to see it. Powerful magick and damned frustrating," he explained, making my heart thud unevenly. More secrets and hidden information? Something I felt as a bad omen within me.

Why had I not thought to ask Diafol himself when I had seen him last? Doric took my silence as resignation.

"I'm sorry. Maybe you can ask Merlough yourself?" he suggested, though he winced at his own words and rubbed his temples suddenly, looking more tired.

"Actually, best not to. Not yet anyway. He barely shares anything with me at the moment. From experience, it is best not to push him too much too soon." Doric leaned over and pressed a hand to my head.

"How are you feeling? I have to admit, your strength has impressed me. Not many others are like you…" he trailed off as if he had more to say but thought it best not to. I shrug, his hand feeling cold on my forehead.

"I am okay. I had a strange dream…does being a subsidium mean you have dreams? I never used to have dreams before," I said, the faded vision swirling in my mind, the underwater sensation still fresh to recall.

Despite my experience at court, the siren dream refreshed my soul and seemed to empower me. My dream was almost there! I had to keep going.

Doric frowned at my words and tapped his chin in thought. "Interesting. I have to admit, I don't have much experience with the fae. As I said before, I am not a faerie doctor. It is possible that our venom may heighten the subconscious on some level… It is difficult without doing tests. Plus, you have more magick than the average faerie so that may have something to do with it…" he pondered out loud. It surprised me that he knew this, and made me wonder how he could tell.

Now he had mentioned it, it made sense why it seemed that unusual things were happening to me. Clearly faeries in this country weren't as magickal as I was.

Was it my magick that attracted the dangerous and the dark?
Like a magnet, did it pull the polar opposite to me?

"How did you find the court? You seemed pretty entranced by it," Doric noted, looking slightly hopeful. It took a moment to ground my thoughts and focus on his question.

Once my mind caught up, my memories flooded back on the night's events. Hazy and reserved before now, they returned with a red and gold vengeance. I repressed a shudder, conscious not to offend Doric.

"It was…like nothing I had ever seen before. Truly a sight I will never forget," I replied carefully. It was a strange sensation to look back on something that I both feared and admired. It seemed to embody the vampire aura itself. Something that seemed so mysterious and desirable, though it triggered a very base sense of fear at the same time.

Alain suddenly came into my mind, the only vampire I remember vividly from the vampire court. A being who seemed just as mysterious as my grandfather. I decided that despite my interest and curiosity with the Blood Prince, I would not mention him to Doric.

"Well, I am sure you will get used to it. I felt the same when I first went to the court. The sheer size alone is impressive, even to taller creatures like us. Also, the number of those attending can be enough to give anyone a headache!" Doric chuckled, making me smile weakly at him. I appreciated his presence, grateful for the comfort he offered though he did not have to.

It made me reconsider my thoughts on vampires. It was easy learning about vampire society and growing up with the dark stories of my youth, to think of them as dark, sinister beings with only an ambition for their personal gain.

Yet here I was, in my fourteenth year, sitting in the Vampire Nation, being assured by a vampire doctor. It certainly made me wonder where my life would lead. And when had my grandfather first drawn his plans for me in this? Was it earlier than I thought?

As Doric made movement to leave, I decided to call him back, eager to learn more while we had this private moment.

"Have you ever been to Dracula's court? How is it different from Carmilla's?" I asked, making him stop and sit back next to me. Worried that I had pushed too far, I stumbled over the explanation for my question.

"You see, I have read a bit on how they differ but it mainly outlined the political stance rather than an aesthetic one," I said, which encouraged a quirked eyebrow from the vampire doctor. He laughed softly, impressed once more.

"No, I'm afraid not. You certainly are a curious one, aren't you? It is very endearing. No, I believe if I ever set foot on Dracula's territory, my parents would disown me. The idea of crossing over is a very dark and controversial topic, even to the most outspoken of us," he explained. I frowned in confusion.

"But why? You are qualified to treat others outside Carmilla's territory right? Is Dracula really that bad?" I asked, getting a surprised scoff from Doric.

"Bad? Oh no, not bad. Just…different, I guess. To be in his territory is a different lifestyle and approach to vampirism. Something we have built our very foundations on. For example, have you heard of pixies before?" he asked and I shook my head. Vaguely, I remembered reference to them but my studies had focused more on vampires.

"Ah! well you see they are another species all together. But a millennia ago, they were our blood cousins and in some respects, they still are to this day. They look the same as us and shy away from the daylight too. Imagine before the definition of vampires or pixies there was a creature, say a predator, that favoured the night and craved the life force of a day creature," he said and as he did, a hungry look overcame him as if from a primal memory —something that caused my being to retreat carefully as he spoke.

"Now it is said that one day, the horde of creatures split in two, as two leaders began to differ on beliefs. One believed that the life force was best served consistently and through drinking, the other was more ambitious and wanted to thrive in the daylight and believed in order to achieve this, the intake was to be through flesh as well as blood," I swallowed down bile with the explanation, feeling queasy. Doric continued as if not noticing my discomfort.

"And so here we are: Vampires who continue to live as we believe were originally intended to. Guarding our history and knowledge fiercely. Pixies seemed to have evolved and emerged as their own. Lead by another belief system entirely." I remained silent, finding this information fascinatingly horrific.

"A-and that's what Dracula and Carmilla are now? Two opposing sides that split the species further?" I asked, trying to calm my own distaste.

"Indeed. It must be interesting from another species' perspective. For me, it just means more tendons in the family's pressure from all angles. More restriction than liberation," he said, his voice lowering.

"You think it's bad then?" I clarified, fascinated. My education deemed so, but this was much to the caution of a faerie's perspective, where restriction and limitations were dangerous and frightening to us. Doric sighed and shrugged, leaving me to wonder further.

"Like my thoughts on Dracula, it is neither bad nor good. Merely an annoyance that we now must follow. As a species, I personally find it detrimental to what we are trying to achieve, yet it is what we have always done to survive. To follow those in power despite our reservations." He smirked at me as I raised my eyebrow in interest.

"I can see the cogs turning in that head of yours. We are too far now to hold back; what do you want to know?" he asked prodding my creased frown playfully.

"Would Dracula and Carmilla join forces if they had to?" I asked, making Doric pleased.

"Attempts at such have been made but with no success. If there ever was, it was before anyone's lifetime that I know of. They are both too distrustful of the other. Too much history to muddy the water. It is a miracle we don't have a war on the horizon," he muttered dangerously.

By this point, I was fully sitting up in fascination at his words. His depth going beyond anything I knew of in my education or any faerie's for that matter.

It was then that Doric yawned and turned to the lightening sky.

"Well, I best be on my way. It was good to talk to you. You seem well recovered, which is a relief." He stood and stretches.

"Thank you for your help. I feel better with you around," I replied shyly. He huffed with a sad light in his eyes as he shrugged on his coat.

"Be that as it may, I hope not to see you again so soon under the same circumstance. I plan to have another talk with him about his control," he assured. All I can do is nod to him, careful not to say how I actually feel about Merlough, in case the devil himself hears me. Doric gives me one final comforting pat.

"Until then, take care, songbird," he called and left the room. I fell back against the bed, feeling exhausted and drained from the night's events, my mind wondering of vampire lore and how different they were to the fae.

While they ruled the night, we thrived by daylight, the sun praising us with light and embedding magick into us indiscriminately. My memory returned to the moment at Carmilla's court when it felt as though some magick had bewitched me. I had known nothing of vampire magick or that it had existed. It was telling how little we truly did not know about these creatures or how they lived. It made me wonder, with a sinking feeling, did my grandfather know of this magick? If not, what else did he not know?

A Mother's Plea

Yule soon arrived with a bite to compete with Merlough himself. It seemed even the mythical Jack the Frost visited here, glazing the world in bitter white. Although we had longer nights in Brimhaven during this time of year, here it seemed to stretch on further as if to assist the dark creatures in their busy schedules.

Outside the house, there was a flurry of activity, as the festivities and markets were set up to celebrate the extended night. Wrapped in furs, we headed out a few times and I marvelled at the elaborate stalls selling fine silks and intricate carvings. Handmade and traditional seemed to be common here and I was immersed in vampiric culture.

It was my highlight of the dark season, having a small freedom to venture outside the house for other reasons than to

attend court. It was a small distraction from my dim reality that I was away from home and not seeing my family.
What were they doing now? Was Rolo even taller now? What was Yule like without me there?

I wrote to my mother often, but despite my ask of my family, in her replies, there was little mention of anyone else. My loneliness seeped into my songs to Master Merlough, which he enjoyed in a sombre reverie. I noticed that the servants made more of an effort to make the house warm for me, for vampires did not feel the cold like I did. Warm pelts and woollen boots were left for me. Fires were lit in every room and I felt grateful for their consideration.

Even Merlough himself took care of me, only touching me when necessary to avoid my shivers from his cold skin; his feeding felt more gentle but was still often. His care with me made me ease more into feeling comfortable around him.

Sitting by the large fire, his nails stroked my head, lulling me into a sense of sombre silence. I had not taken ill again since the visit to Carmilla's court and despite the lonely well of my homesickness, I had fallen into a quiet habit with him.

As my comfort with him grew, I decided to ask the bold question that burned in my heart. I asked to see my family for Yule. His long, sad sigh made my insides grow cold and extinguished any warmth left in me.

"Sweet birdie, you cannot leave here. You are too important to me and my happiness," he almost purred, eyes on the fire. My back was to him and I remained so, avoiding showing my disappointment. I was weary of his temper and knew better than to question this. Still I felt the need to push further.

"Could they not come here, Master?" I asked softly. His nails paused on my head, making me tense. He remained still and an icy feeling dripped down my back in worry.

Had I pushed too far? My throat tightened at the punishment on my throat this may now threaten.

"Would that please you?" he purred, his nails moving slowly once more.

"Yes, Master, very much," I answered carefully. The silence stretched out before us so I decided to talk further.

"I have been here most of the year now, and I have learned so much from you, Master. I know my mother would like to see me," I said, deciding to appeal to him, using only my mother. Even just to see my mother, made my heart soar with hope. The words sat around us for a long time, the crackling fire being our music.

"What would you do for me in return?" he asked, his voice hard to distinguish in tone.

I turned slowly to meet his red eyes. Despite seeing them everyday, they still gave me chills as I looked at him, my mind blank with what he wanted. We stared at each other as the tension grew. His mind and thoughts were a mystery to me at that moment. What more could he want? What could I give him?

Suddenly the gold coin flashed in my mind but I dismissed it quickly. With no other ideas surfacing, I felt at a loss over how to respond. With mild interest, he watched me struggle, a small smile forming.

"Fine, you may see your mother, but not here.There is an Inn where she can meet you and you can see her for one day. But that is all—not your grandfather and no one else. Do you understand?" he said mildly, his nails coming down to my throat.

"Yes, Master, thank you," I said, swallowing the bitter disappointment, the small hope of seeing my mother being the light in my dark tunnel. I had to sing again at court soon, otherwise what was this all for?

"Come," he said firmly, gesturing to his lap. I trembled as I came out of the warm blankets, the air biting with cold as the fire's heat barely reached us. I awkwardly sat on his lap, having grown taller since I had arrived, with my back to him.

Rarely this was the way he fed and I dreaded it the most. There was little connection and I was more tense with my back to him, this dark looming presence. My heart beat faster and he revelled in its growing rhythm. He slid an arm around my chest, only a little lighter than a squeeze. I took a deep breath as his lips pressed to my throat.

"If you betray me, you will never see your mother again," he whispered, his grip feeling possessive. I felt him smile against my neck as my heart sped up to a heavy thudding in my chest.

Before I could reply, his fangs sank into me, and the vile tugging on my heart began. As my sight blurred with my body's struggle, the thought of seeing my mother pulled me from my dismal situation.

Afterwards, he held me as if I were a child, stroking my hair, my head resting on his shoulder. His other arm on my waist to hold me there. It is quiet as we sit through his blood stupor, my taste making him sigh peacefully.

"You have been a good birdie; you deserve the gift to see your mother," he rumbled, eyes on the fire. Feeling unfamiliar and distant from the moment, I remained quiet. He turned and inhaled into my hair, the scent still holding the forest freshness.

"You can't leave me. You won't," he said softly into my hair, barely audible. I was too tired to react.

"My birdie. Mine."

I saw my mother a few days after, as if just the hint of beckoning from my Master made her fly in to see me. We met at the inn where I was escorted in the early dawn by a silent servant. Being lesser vampires, I had observed they could cautiously go out into the grey daylight of winter with little risk of being weakened, though heavily cloaked to do so.

As soon as I entered, I was almost knocked down by my mother's embrace. The noises and smells of the inn swirled around us as I took her in. Happy tears sparkled her face which she consciously wiped away and led me to the stairs. Her presence soothed me immediately, as if part of me had returned with her, gods, I had missed her!

We had a private room to ourselves which allowed us to talk intimately, the sounds of the staff rumbling below us, dulled by the walls in between. Closed off in the room, my mother embraced me once more, the servant had left to give us this time, as approved by Merlough. I was relieved to see that see resembled more of herself once more, her colour more vibrant, her eyes alight and warm.

"Gods, boy you are frozen! Do they not keep you warm?" she gasped, only half joking. She held my face in her hands, and inspected me worriedly. I giggled at her critical eye.
"Darling, you are thinner. Are you eating enough? What do they feed you there?" she asked, looking concerned. It warmed me and I answered her honestly, saying that it was nothing like her cooking but it got me by.

In fact, they were particular in what I ate. I had to eat enough to ensure that it kept me healthy and my blood in check. It was mainly soups and boiled vegetables that had barely any taste, but I avoided sharing that information, as I knew she wouldn't approve.

"But Mother, you look well," I said after reassuring her of my diet. She smiled sadly, her loose light green hair framing her face. She glowed in this dark place.
"Indeed I am, I have kept myself busy. Here," she said, giving me a wrapped parcel quickly. I gasped and unwrapped it to reveal a special mixture of herbs and berries. The fresh waft of the forest came over me, making me nearly tearful of the absence in my lungs.

Was this really worth me being away from home?

Doubts started to worm their way into my heart, my homesickness overwhelming me.

"Its a special broth I made, one that will aid you during the winter. It helps keep the light within you and also thickens the blood…" she trailed off as I look at it. She sighed and I looked at her.

"It will help," she said softly, her grip tight on my shoulder. I hugged her tightly in return, feeling the deeper meaning in her words. The fact she was supporting me and helping me meant so much to me; surely this meant I had done the right thing in coming here?

"How are father and Rolo? Oh! and Mary?" I asked as we sit on the couch provided.

"They are well, dearest. Pushing through as the cold reaches them even in the north. Rolo does well to help your father and I see them as often as I can," she replied, playing with my hair which had blown array from the winter winds.

"And Grandfather?" I asked carefully, interested as I mildly missed his strange behaviour too. Was he pleased with my progress? Was I doing enough? My mother paused and considered her words as if she had not thought of him recently.

"Ah yes well you know him, only around when he wants something of you. I am pleased to say that is very little with me nowadays. He spends most of his time in the forest behind his

house, no idea why," she said airily. With my thoughts on Diafol, I hugged myself, feeling a cold draft.
"What would you like to do here, Mother? It's a cold day." She hugged me and rubbed my back to warm me.
"I would very much like to stay in here and be with you. That is enough," she said softly, and I felt the familiar tingle of her magic touch me tentatively.

"Are you sure?" I asked, looking up at her, her frame still taller than mine, though just a head taller now. She smiled proudly as if she too took in my growth.
"Yes, now come by the fire." And once again, as if I were her little faeling, we sat in front of the fire, the heat a welcome presence. She hugged me to her, and we sat together, a fur blanket connecting us and sharing the heat between us. We sat quietly, letting the flames dance and crackle for us.
"I'm sorry I did not bring a gift for you mother," I sighed sadly, feeling ashamed. I had looked in the markets but they held nothing that would have been of use to her. She laughed softly.
"You are enough, my heart." She sighed, sounding happy and content. I leaned closer to her, my heart glowing from her love. Her magick shimmered around me, awakening my own magick. When had I last used my magick?

She began to tell me a story, taking me back to my room in Brimhaven. I wondered what it was like now? It had been so long ago that I occupied that place.

I sat and listened as she talked of the winter king who once ruled the north. It was a story I had not heard of in a few years and I revelled in the nostalgia. Like hands, our magick combined and held each other as my mother told the story, her words chiming with magick. I turned and nuzzled my mother and she paused.

"I missed you, Mother," I cried softly into her neck, embarrassed by the tears that fell. She shushed me and kissed my head.

"I missed you too, my love," she said softly.

"I don't want to sleep tonight." She clutched me tighter.

"Then don't. We can talk until morning," she said softly, her voice and magick comforting me. The feeling of Brimhaven returning to me again with a welcome embrace. My mother and I talked more. I shared with her my songs I had sang, and what it was like being at Carmilla's court. In turn, she shared the potions and vials she had prepared recently for the locals of Brimhaven. Casually sliding in ingredients that would aid me too in my service as a subsidium and advised lightly what the servants should get for me. I tried to tuck away the information to request when I returned. For now, I tried not to think on returning to Merlough's house.

Soon, we lulled into a soft song together, one we used to sing at home. Like a spell it carried me off and I soon fell asleep, the fire's flame dulled and the moon high above us. My mother gently led me to bed, my body tired but reluctant. She hushed me and I succumbed to her magick.

"Sleep, my precious boy, my brave faeling," she whispered, her hand stroking my face softly.

Azalea's eyes hardened as Élan lay asleep, helplessly at peace. Carefully, she placed two fingers to his neck as if to check his pulse. She clicked her tongue and clasped her hands together.

"Mighty Gods of the wind and sea, watch over him," she prayed. She remembered his weakness and his fading light, a harsh slam of reality as she greeted him earlier that day. Her clasped hands trembled, a silent tear fell.

"Protect him, I beg you," she whispered, her voice quivered, her hands trembling. Her magick swirled around them, pressed onto the sleeping faeling as if trying to get under his skin. Élan shifted with sleepy discomfort, causing her to ease on the pressure.

Mother woke me early, and together we had some broth using the package she brought. As I sipped the earthy flavours, I felt the nutrients charge my being. She smiled at me as if watching the effects it had on me. She sobered on her thoughts.

"Is he good to you?" she asked quietly, making me pause.

"I believe so. It is not so bad, he makes an effort to make me comfortable," I answered carefully. She seemed to buy it even though I felt it was not the complete truth. I wanted to avoid upsetting her as the promise of dawn was upon us, marking my time with her was over.

"When will I see you again?" I asked sadly, my voice muffled as I held her one last time.

"Soon, my precious. Be strong," she said softly. She pulled away, looking deep into my eyes. Her warm brown to my cool green gaze.

"Remember what I showed you; use your magick," she said firmly, referring to our days together in the sun, pointing to my heart. I nodded slowly, understanding that next time I felt the deep loneliness, I would call upon the warmth and connect our magick.

With this, I could create my own 'Brimhaven feeling' and comfort myself until I saw her again. It was a worrying thought, thinking how long it would be until I next saw her. But perhaps I would be in a better place. Surely, soon, I could sing again at court and be closer to my dream. Once I was recognised, I could be wherever I wanted to be.

The servant was waiting for me at the front of the inn, covered in a hood and cloak as before. As if returning from behind the veil of sleep, I returned to my master once more, the pleasant dream-like memories of my mother cooling in my heart.

As I returned to the town house I was familiar with, it now held some looming darkness I had not felt before. I felt my own light dimming as I entered and my mother's light now just a vain memory. I sensed it before I saw Merlough's impatience. Even though it was early for a full blooded vampire to rise, he had risen and was pacing manically. The servant barely had time to bring me in before he was upon me, gripping me like a viper.

"By gods, you took an eternity!" he hissed and my heart lurched as the servants all retreated.

Please do not leave me alone with him! I wanted to beg. Like sinister worms, his finger caressed my chest over my heart.

"Hush now. You are back with me, birdie. Such a good birdie to find its way back again," he muttered making my skin crawl. I resisted the urge to flinch, knowing it would only make him worse. My reality crashing back into me with sickening contrast to the Brimhaven feeling I had felt with my mother.

Too soon, I felt the slice of his fangs on me, heavy gulps pulling my body painfully. With the pain came the doubts once more.

How was this going to get me to sing to the world?

Sooner than I expected, he withdrew with a sigh. Weak, physically and mentally, I let him pull me to the couch where he held me quietly. I spied a piece of parchment on the mantle and recognised the crest lazily.

"We have been invited to the court for Yule, my sweet," he said softly, stroking my hair making it tingle unpleasantly. I still felt nauseous from the rough handling and dared not speak in case I vomited.

"It seems my cousin has appealed to Auntie's better nature and convinced her that we could be present for Yule," he explained, the brief image of Alain in my mind beckoned me like a moth to a flame. His nails tightened on my head briefly as he scoffed at the thoughts of his cousin.

"Bah! I do not know why my cousin did such a favour but I am glad. I am eager for them all to see your beauty. I want them to know what a precious bird I hold in its gilded cage," he purred, making my body ripple with repulsion.

"We will have a wonderful time, you will see." I heard his grin as my consciousness faded. I was at least soothed by the idea of going to court again. Perhaps the chance to sing at court would come not too long from now. With that in my mind, my body finally gave in to the restless sleep, now that the beast'd had his fill.

Yule with Vampires

If possible, I felt more nervous than the previous time I attended Carmilla's court. Fearing the unknown seemed much more appealing than fearing the grim possibility of what I was to face this Yule.

While my family was a world away, kept and warmed with love and songs of the fae, I was once again thrust into the dark, cold world of vampires. Merlough had hired a different tailor this time to adorn me in a suit fit for the Yule occasion. Unlike his usual attire, I was to wear something different, a colour more becoming perhaps to appeal to the Red Queen. I was made to wear a simple silk shirt and a suit of dark blue, which shimmered with small diamonds that reminded me of a clear night sky. It still felt tight and stiff to wear but felt more my own than being made to wear bright red like a vampire.

As I looked back at myself in the mirror, I took note of the thinning of my cheeks that were once full. My skin gaunt and slightly bruised, more translucent, showing the veins underneath. One might even have considered that I was a mere shell of the gleaming faeling that had entered the Vampire Nation last spring. This is just a small adjustment in order for me to sing in front of others, I thought.

As we arrived at court, I noticed the differences since I was last here. More lights adorned the spiked turrets, and brighter candlelight that beckoned you in. Warmth accompanied slow, steady, beating music. It woke something within me and despite the sinister claw of Merlough's hand upon my shoulder. It was its own kind of magick that I was eager to explore as I followed the music, finding comfort in it.

As we drew further into the halls, the candle sconces burned brightly alongside gleaming smiles to everyone who greeted us. Instead of red, there were a mixture of colours ranging from greens to purples, holding the shapes of the vampires around us. The music grew louder and I felt my own magick respond as if waking up from a long sleep. It tingled in my toes and fingertips, and I revelled in the sensation. It felt as if the magick here, mysterious as it was, was trying to connect with my own. It was more unfamiliar than my mother's or even Diafol's, but it was still more welcome than the absence I had felt. Unlike before though, the connection felt smoother.

On my last visit, it had tugged and pulled me in my confused state. Now I did not feel confused but warmed. It danced with mine as the vampires danced around us. Spiced smells of cinnamon and sandalwood swirled around us as the lights glowed. It allowed me to see more detail than before. Instead of being lost in a sea of red and gold, I was in a hall of artistry and tradition. The walls were lined with tapestries depicting mythical beasts and beauty. Roses bloomed and curled on sconces, perfuming the air with romance. The fine tune of the harpsichord set the eager pace of the dance around us. It wasn't home, but it was exciting to behold.

Like lovers, the vampires clasped together, embracing and dancing with passion. As I admired the moving beings, I was pleasantly surprised by the presence of faeries. There were still hundreds of vampires, with only an occasional faerie presence, but it was welcome to me nonetheless.

The music slowed and a range of voices rose in a beautiful harmony. I was led to a dais where a group of vampires stood in gold garments of the finest silk, their voices smooth as they shimmered in the light. The choir sung a slow, soothing melody of yuletide. It was beautiful and I felt my own heart flutter, my magick reaching out to join the melody. I felt a small slice of envy, why was I not up there with them? Surely this was why I was here?

A caress at the keys of a harpsichord, which blended with the voices beautifully, drew me back. I watched this new vampire with interest, his love for music apparent on his face. Where the voices lulled my magick, the strings on the harpsichord commanded my presence, pulling me closer to the dais. I felt as if this musician was pulling me with a solo string from my chest towards him. Yet he neither stirred nor acknowledged this connection as he enslaved all those present to his mastery.

Merlough had lost me again. As I briefly began to wonder where he was, Doric appeared, chuckling.
"How is it every time I find myself in your presence, it is in the most unlikely of places?" he asked, greeting me warmly. I smiled and explained softly of our invite from Alain still half listening to the choir's song.
"It is not everyday someone catches the attention of the Blood Prince, especially a faerie," he clarified, making me swell.

Before we could discuss further, a round of applause erupted as a flurry of red entered, the Red Queen herself. Adorned in a huge dress of scarlet, it glittered in the candlelight. No one could doubt her beauty as she smiled humbly at her adoring subjects. After moments of admiration, the noise quiets down to allow her to speak.

"Greetings to you all, my beloved people. In the darkest hour of the year, I am eternally grateful to share it with you all." My own heart thudded as it recognised a flurry of magick dancing around us. Should I be worried about this magick and its effect on me?

"And this year, not only do we have the grace and honour of sharing this fabulous time of year with my beloved Alain, your Prince…" She paused as the crowd applauded again. I struggled to see him as the crowd celebrated around me. "But my beloved child of the North, your sovereign, Enkil," she announced, causing an uproar of applause. I frowned in confusion for I had never heard of this being.

Amongst the celebrations, Doric tapped my shoulder and led me aside, outside the hall. I caught sight of Alain as I left the room. His beauty was stunning in his scarlet red coat, his fine clothing underneath shimmering with wealth. He was smiling and my heart fluttered. I blushed as I realised those near me had noted my reaction and had stopped to look at me. I moved quickly but not before I saw another blonde male join the stage. Unlike Alain, he was huge in build. Where Alain was tall and graceful, this being was wide and strong. He oozed strength and a menace that trumped even Merlough's. His fangs had their own glint and his hair and skin, a different sheen of pale, more threatening. His very aura caused my magick to retreat and I left quickly, flustered by my own reaction. Doric was waiting for me patiently outside the hall.

"Gosh it feels…" I began to gasp as I caught up to him. He smiled.
"It's a lot, isn't it?"
I nodded breathlessly in reply.
"Again, I'm impressed by how you're handling it, to be honest. Not many faeries can be in there without feeling overwhelmed."
I shrugged.

"So, who is Enkil?" I asked, making him laugh with my forwardness.

"Curious as always. Not that I blame you. He is a commodity, even in Carmilla's court. For this though, I need a drink and a seat," he said, though he did not notice my sudden discomfort at his reference to his drink. He takes a glass from a nearby waiter and sits on a chair near the wall. The sconces nearby highlighted him like a halo and I joined, sitting opposite, turning to face him. I tried not to think on who's blood swilled in his glass as he sipped so casually.

"So Enkil, hm, where do I begin?" he mused out loud, tapping his free hand in thought. "Did you notice his aura? How different he is?" I nodded eagerly. "And do you remember our last conversation about pixies?" he asked.

Again I nodded, feeling my impatience brewing. It was at this point I noticed his usual serious, tense exterior was lulled and calm. I was unsure if he was intoxicated or just in the celebratory spirit.

"Well, you see, Enkil is a pixie. And not just any pixie but a sub-species called a Blondie." He frowned as he tried to think on how to continue.

"It is a long story, actually, but basically he was brought up here at court. Pretty much as Carmilla's adopted son. He and Alain are very close. And for a pixie, it is very unusual to be this integrated with society but then…Enkil is quite unusual anyway," he mused more to himself as he struggled to explain.

"So he was raised here from childhood? With vampire habits and everything?" I asked, trying to draw Doric back.

"Why yes, I am pretty certain he has been here since he was a youngling. His mother had died giving birth to him and although the details remain vague on his father, he was brought here to be raised under Carmilla's discretion. You see, everyone knows she is unable to bear young herself…" He stopped himself as if remembering who he was talking to. He coughed uncomfortably. So that is why she reacted the way she did when we first met…

"Anyway, he was welcomed here and has been treated as one of our own. And to be fair to him, he has returned the favour by embracing our lifestyle to the fullest. Some say he is even more 'vampire' than most out there." He chuckled in admiration.
"How is he more of a vampire than most?" I asked, confused. It made no sense. A creature, not even a vampire, behaving like one! My question made Doric pause again and hesitate to answer.

"Well, you see…he um…has a rather decent appetite for such ways…as vampires," he explained lamely, looking away from me. I swallow as I realised what he was referring to.
"So he drinks blood, and lots of it," I commented, sounding more bitter than intended, making Doric cough again awkwardly.
"Well not only that, but I guess he embraces our laws, follows our ways. I guess you could say he is much beloved by the queen and therefore loved by us." Doric shrugged, setting down his empty, red stained glass before standing.

"Anyway, that's Enkil, and if I were you, I would avoid him. Merlough hates him more than Alain and I would hate for you to irritate him as such. For now, let's go and enjoy the festivities." He nudges me out of the seat and back into the hall.

What was it like for Alain and Enkil growing up here? The walls seemed so close and looming to me, compared to the open fields.

Vampires danced so gracefully, moving fluidly with each other. The music was refined and held a pace that encouraged the movement around me. Seeing vampires gathered in these numbers in such close proximity should have scared me or even worried me, but the magick wouldn't let me. The lull of desire and ease of the music made me feel I deserved to be there. That I belonged amongst them and was welcomed into the arms of the darkness.

I smiled to myself as I caught a glimpse of scarlet Alain dancing with Queen Carmilla. The relation was obvious and there was true admiration in their gazes as they were admired by those who surrounded them. Beautiful to watch such grace and elegance. It was easy to forget the dark and dismal times I had experienced with a creature related to them. I felt my magick swell and merge with the other magick around. If only I could sing here!

For a split second, I felt Alain's gaze snap to mine, but it was so quick, I felt it was a trick of my mind. I no longer felt Doric's presence near me as I followed the magick.

I soon found myself in a hallway that was unfamiliar to me. The magick pulsed here in lines as if they were veins within the walls.

It radiated warmth and comfort that I had not felt since I left home. Doors opened as I walked past them, though I did not enter. I felt no pressure and felt guided into the hall.

Soon I ended up in a room that swirled with purples and velvets. It was darker here and sensuous. The magick thudded, heavier, as if eager for me to continue and so I did. The room was lined with private booths and sheer fabric. Breathy gasps and sweet scents surrounded me. The atmosphere was different here, one that was more private and secretive.

Despite the lure of the magick, I decided I should not be here and tried to leave, unconcerned by how I had gotten here. A breathy moan caught me off guard and halted my course. Whispered words from a voice I will never forget, tugged me back.

Alain's blonde head was bowed as he drank from a brunette male vampire's neck. The male's face was frozen in ecstasy as Alain drank from him so carefully, cradling him with such care it made me ache.

Why was it not like that for me?

Even as I witnessed the forbidden scene, I felt a new emotion emerge in me.

Why was that not me?

In a flash, the brunette's face changed to mine and I felt my body respond in the vision. Feeling his lips upon my throat as he drank, the breathy moans became my own as he drank from me.

As if lost in my vision, I saw a small smile creep onto Alain's face as he drank, though our eyes did not meet. Why did he not smile like that against my throat? Hold me and cradle as he did him?

For one moment, I had a crazed urge to rip him from Alain's grasp and offer myself in his stead. It was then that I observed the magick again. It had begun to retreat from the other magicks' embrace.

As if to reflect my feelings on the scene, it snapped fully back into me and I turned to leave, my face burning with shame over what I had just witnessed, my heart heavy with jealousy and hurt.

Immediately I bumped into Doric again, who grasped me, looking flustered and worried. He sighed, relieved as he looked at my neck.

"Thank the gods! I am so sorry I lost you! You should not be here; it is not safe. It is best I take you to the other faeries now, things are ramping up," he said mysteriously, tugging me back down the corridor. I followed numbly, my mind lost in confusion and my heart dwelling on the blonde prince.

We reached a room that was guarded and Doric spoke to them quietly which was inaudible to me over the music from the hall nearby. They nodded and we entered, coming to a smaller hall that was decorated with a wooden layout and alight with small candles along the walls. The magick was dulled here and I tried not to panic as I felt my own senses numbing the further we entered.

"It's okay. You will be safe in here," he assured me as he sensed my fear, perhaps smelling it.

"Doric, can vampires feed from other vampires?" I asked, the image still burned in my mind. He frowned at me, surprised, as if he was expecting a different question.

"They can yes, and some do. It is a practice that is only a temporary fix and dangerous if it is in close relation to the other but if paired correctly, it can be a useful technique to stave off hunger. Why in the gods do you ask?" his eyes burned with curiosity—or was it concern? The scene from earlier replayed in my mind yet my mouth could not summon the words.

"What did you see?" he asked, grasping me desperately. Before I could reply, an echoing thud stopped me and made me jolt.

"There is no time. We will talk later," he said hurriedly as he led me to the room at the end of the hall. The door opened with a creak and he stepped aside, indicating to let me in.

"This is where I leave you. You have my word you will be safe here. Do not leave here unless I come to collect you. Do you understand, Élan?" he asked me carefully. I took in the room before me, quiet with a woodsy smell and a fire burning somewhere inside. It was welcoming but I was hesitant as the presence of magick dulled. I turned to Doric and the seriousness in his expression encouraged me to decide to trust him.

"Okay," is all I answer and he was gone before I could ask him more.

I entered the room cautiously and realised there were only faelings in here. I took in the small, sheltered room, where fifteen or so faelings were gathered, all adorned in similar clothing to my own. I shyly nodded to them as the door closed behind me. A small wave indicated a greeting and I moved to sit by the fire where a few were gathered. The woodsy smell was familiar and took me back to Brimhaven. I took in the walls around me, was is dully lit with small candles and simply decorated compared to the rest of the court. It smelled dusty and unused.

"That's Élan," I heard someone whisper. My face warmed as more mutters echoed around me.

"I can hear you, you know?" I said, suddenly feeling weary and sad. My first contact with the fae in weeks and I was bitterly disappointed. None of them felt my kin and I felt even more alone than before. A hush fell in response to my comment.

A few crept closer, joining me by the fire. A quiet settled over us that felt somber. It was easy to forget we were in the centre of a vampire court. I watched the flames dance before me quietly as others began to softly murmur together. I caught a few words relating to their blood experience and how it had been a rushed affair but their Yule festivities had commenced without them and they were sent here. My curiosity soon got the better of me and I turned to the faeling nearest to me.

"Have you been here before?" I asked them. At first they don't respond, surprised by my question. Slowly they nodded.

"Why yes, most of us have. That is why you are such an interest to us. We haven't seen a newcomer in a while," he explained softly and others nodded in agreement. I took in their pale faces around me. They were all not much younger than me, which surprised me.

"I see. And why is that? Are you all subsidiums to this court?" I asked softly, which was followed again by another chorus of nods.

"Yes, we all serve those above. It is not a glamorous life but we do what we can for our families." The faeling shrugged nonchalantly. I once again took in their young faces around me, feeling my sadness sinking into my gut. How long had they served if they were not new like me?

"And where do you stay? Are you housed with specific vampire lords like I am?" I asked, having not recalled seeing any of them near where I lived. The faeling shook his head.

"No, we live here at the court. Our families are from the villages surrounding the court in Roma. We were sent here to support our families, a lot are poor you see. It is an important job and the best for coin."

Gods they grew up here?! In the Vampire Nation? It was no wonder I felt little magick from them…

"Queen Carmilla is not particularly fond of the practice and has recalled all if not most subsidiums, to reside here. As much as she dislikes it, she has begun to request to oversee our treatment, meaning things have improved for us thankfully." The faeling smiled fondly. I felt my magick simmer, wanting to reach out to

them suddenly. Why was I not housed here then? The faeling read the question on my face and replied.
"Well, you are an exception, you see. Subsidiums of those vampires that are held in higher regard are more trusted. Vampires with the red eyes seem to have more control or at least, have more trust with Carmilla, for now. Is it true? How often are you used?" the faeling asked, suddenly feeling bold and curious. I swallow audibly, conscious that I was alone in my experience too. I explained my lifestyle with Merlough rather factually, breezing over the details of his rough handling and underestimated appetite. I watched as their expressions evolved into worry.

"Oh…well that sounds okay then. At least it is only with one vampire. Here at court, we are to serve more than one, whoever has permission really." I swallowed down my shock, imaging having to serve more than one Merlough made me feel sick and even more confused. How was this controlled? How was this better than before as Carmilla has planned?

"Although saying that, there are benefits. Those who get the luck of the gods, get to serve the Blood Prince at least once or twice in a blue moon." Another faeling grinned, getting my attention. The faeling closest to me chuckled knowingly.
"True. Any one of us would serve hundreds just to make it to the Blood Prince." He giggled, blushing. I smiled, edging closer, eager to hear more. The Prince's face bright and clear in my mind.

"Oh? Is he that good? What's so pleasant about it?" I asked, interested, making others giggle about me. An older faeling scoffed and moved closer into our little gathering.
"If you have to ask, I feel for you, friend. I know not what Merlough is like to feed but the Blood Prince…ahhh," he sighed, looking younger suddenly, his eyelids fluttering pleasantly.

"Heh, Laufrey here is a favourite of the prince's." The faeling closest to me nudged him playfully. I smiled, though it did not reach my eyes as I felt jealousy coil in me once more.
"Oh? It feels nice when he feeds?" I ask shortly, sounding sharper than I intended. Laufery scoffed again.
"Nice is an understatement. It is still in speculation on how he does it but the prince…he has this way of feeding like no other. It's so good even the vampires flock to feed him," he explained and the image I saw previously with the brunette vampire flashed in my memory. I blushed recalling it, something forbidden I had witnessed and how jealous I had felt in that moment, wanting to be in the vampire's place.
"Is that…unusual?" I asked even though I knew the answer. Laufrey seemed to be in a sharing mood and I was keen to learn more.
"Indeed. Oh, vampires feed on each other all the time. It can be pleasurable to them if done right. But it is not a secret what Alain does is…on a different level. Some even say it competes with Carmilla's own sensations, that he has his own magick that enables him so," he whispered the last part in a conspiratorial way, making the others gasp. I ignored the swell of jealousy in

me at the mention of Alain's name. Where others had referred to him as the Blood Prince, using his name felt more…personal.

"And how does it feel…exactly?" I asked, making the faelings around me giggle. Laufrey chuckled and shook his head.
"I couldn't explain it. No one can. It is a pleasure that you have to experience yourself. Something personal and secret. I hope for your sake, you do one day, my friend." He grinned cheekily. I huff, annoyed and feeling cheated. There must be some way to know!

"Well then, do you know why he favours you over others?" I asked, trying not to sound as jealous as I felt, which became more difficult as the faeling swelled with pride.
"I am not certain, but it must be the taste. From what we have learnt from other vampires, favourites start to develop depending on their taste. Some taste sweet, others taste more savoury. Mine is interesting enough to capture the prince's tastes more than once. He frequents me more than the rest here," he replied proudly.

Our reality hits me then. There is competition here. It is subtle and hidden from outside these walls, but here it is revered. If you are favoured by the likes of the prince, you are ensured more privileges and a better crowd. My mind swims with the new information, something I have been unable to experience thus far. Being tied to Merlough, I have been restricted and restrained. How different would it have been to have been given to the court instead of Merlough? What was my grandfather thinking, for surely residing here made more sense? How was I to sing at court if I was based away from it?

The faeling continued to chatter about their experiences without my intervention, leaving me to my confused and hurt thoughts until another blonde male flashed in my memory.

"And what of Enkil? I heard he is just as admired as the Blood Prince," I asked, my words slicing through the chatter in one fell swoop. Someone gasped and Laufrey looked ill suddenly. Finally the faeling nearest to me gave me a pat on my crossed leg, sighing in sympathy.

"He is to be avoided at all costs. Luckily, he does not feed from faelings any longer," he said softly and I observed a few faelings shudder.

"Is he that bad?" I asked, making Laufrey scoff angrily.

"Seriously? I don't know who you have spoken to but Enkil is not our friend. The vampires may adore him but to us he is more of a beast than a fellow courtier to serve. I say, anyone here who has fed Enkil, raise your hand." He gestured around as the fae fell still, staring dismally at me. Like a pebble in a river, I feel the dread sinking into my belly as Laufrey exposes my ignorance.

"Do you know why, dear Élan, that there are no faelings present who have fed him? I assure you it is not from his absence. Rather that every faeling that has left this room to serve him has never returned." Laufrey's words hung like a noose in the air. I swallowed heavily. Surely that could not be right? They would not be able to get away with such a thing. I began to mutter my disbelief when Laufrey cut me off.

“Of course they can! They OWN us, Élan! You really think anyone is looking for us? That anyone misses us back home? I do not know where you are from, but here in Roma, faelings are bred a plenty, and with poor families struggling to survive the harsh weathers, they are eager to sell us over.” His voice cracked with sadness and my heart swelled. Was that really true? Suddenly, the absence of my own family's letters opened like a hole in my chest. Surely, they missed me?

“But surely they are not…surely they are just moved somewhere else or…?” I muttered, trying to reason but Laufrey cut me off angrily.

“Do you really think that, Élan? Do you think there could be any possible explanation? And that is the worst of it, that these vampires are covering it up for him. All because he is their queen's beloved adopted son. It's disgusting,” Laufrey spat and the other faelings started to hush him, looking at the door nervously. We remained quiet a moment, the faelings half expecting someone to enter as if we were being listened to.

When moments passed and nothing happened, they began murmuring again. I was lost in my own dismal thoughts. If what they said was true, then Merlough owned me too. That meant that if anything happened to me, nothing could be done. Was I in danger? Surely my grandfather had arranged some sort of protection?

Or I was at his mercy. The sheer truth shocked and appalled me. How could my grandfather allow this to happen? To what end? What was he trying to achieve? Did he know about Enkil's crimes here?

Before I became lost in my despair, I recalled the last time I saw my mother and what she had taught me. I took in the pale young faces around me as they muttered and shared with each other in the dark, the weight of their fates looming over us like a dark cloud.

Unlike me, these faelings had never run the open faefields, never tasted the summer's pinnacle in our homeland. My heart hung with sorrow for them. I was lucky, despite the Laufrey's pride in being Alain's favourite; it seemed he has never felt the embrace of his parents' love. My jealousy for him then faded into sympathy.

There must be something I can do here, something I can do to help…

Without realising, my magick began to gather within me, drawing in the warmth from the fire before us and circling me. Despite whatever had dulled it before, it now gathered carefully, secretly within me. A few faelings noticed and fell quiet, observing me in silent admiration.

It was gentle at first, then began to swirl with a vigour of encouragement. Someone whispered about magick nearby and my lonely heart beat with the compassion of my kin. I felt no magick here aside from my own. So with that thought, I would share what I had with them. Here they were trapped, alone and isolated from the fresh fields of the faelands and the magick that the sunlight brought. As I envisioned this, I felt my magick click into place and a song sprung to my lips.

Lapsi dine rackai…

I began to share a tale in the ancient fae dialect my mother had taught me, unknowing if the other faelings knew what I said. I sang it quietly and gently, a comfort as my magick began to swell around us, drawing them closer, creating a barrier from the darkness.

Without looking, I felt their happiness that sprung from my voice, the lyrics ringing true. Some quietly joined in, while others hummed. Soon we were a small, sombre gathering compared to the bands that were sung in Brimhaven. Yet my body thrummed with energy as I felt a connection with each faeling in the room on some level. It was like a weight was lifting off us as we lost ourselves in the magick. It was no longer my magick but the magick of our blood.

This is what I wanted, this is what I am meant for…

It felt grotesquely ironic as the creatures above us revelled and drank blood; ours was hidden below, simmering fluidly together.

As we sang, I felt our strength grow, not in a physical sense but on a level that felt more personal and right. Soft smiles formed as we looked at each other. The bitterness melted away, even drawing Laufrey, who seemed the weariest, back to the land of the fae. Some began to laugh with happiness, though they seemed unsure as to why.

I felt the song slow and merge into a story of the North and the serpents that devoured the fire in the sky. A few quieted, listening to me intently while others swayed, lulled and happy.

Time passed unknown to us then, a small sense of Brimhaven having returned to me, and it seemed introduced to them. I was nearing the end of a story when a creak shattered our bubble like a pin.

The wooden door creaked open and some vampires entered. The faelings jolted, the light feeling fizzling away into the dim reality. Some faelings were collected quietly and I repressed a sigh, knowing they were withholding their reluctance to leave for the others' sake. Laufrey edged closer to me, showing the most reluctance suddenly. The vampires soon left with a handful and the door closed once more with a heavy sense of finality.

"I don't know how you did it, but we needed that. We needed you," Laufrey muttered, making me jolt in shock. I was surprised into silence, unable to respond. He patted my shoulder, a grateful smile on his lips.

Before I knew it, I felt the air grow cold again as the door creaked open. Gasps made me turn to see who had entered before my breath stuttered in shock. There stood the Blood Prince himself.

With great difficulty, I drew my gaze away, looking to all the faelings as their faces grew eager, soft smiles of encouragement directed at the tall figure who seemed to be the root of all our desires at that moment. The faelings had straightened and sat pleasantly, their eyes shining with encouragement. The prince himself seemed happy to see them, smiling warmly (well, warm for a vampire anyway) at each one in turn.

When his eyes fell on me, I felt my magick snap, making me shudder. It was a shocking sensation and before I could determine whether it was a good or bad sign, I had stood up, drawing everyone's surprised attention.

One of the prince's fine eyebrows arched as he stepped closer, his tall height towering over me, feeling more protective than menacing. It was as if we were having an internal conversation as our eyes remained connected, lost in each other. I tried everything to avoid the memory earlier but as I became lost in the red gaze, I saw myself in his grasp, my body lax with ecstasy as he drank from me. As if to read my mind, his smile tilted into a smirk.

"I was drawn down here after hearing quite a stir. The guards reported singing and were worried that you faeries were being… mischievous." He smiled fully at the last word, purring it and making it sound more sensual. I was dumbfounded into silence as were the rest around me. He shrugged, his smile bright and charming.

"But you are all good, well behaved faeries and surely no magick could happen in here?" He smirked as if keeping a good secret.

"I believe our last greeting was rudely interrupted by my cousin. Since then, I have not been able to let you escape my mind. I believe I owe you an official introduction." He offered me his hand, graceful and white in the low light. I almost took too long to respond, feeling the impatience of the faelings around me buzzing like insects. Laufrey huffed loudly near me.

I suddenly jumped into action and took his cold grasp. Unexpectedly, it did not make me shudder but my magick once again reacted. In a flash, I recalled the dream with him in daylight above me. Alain responded as if he didn't notice my heart beating erratically. He smiled, genuinely happy, and lowered so we were on eye level.

"Lovely Élan, welcome to Queen Carmilla's court. I do wish you good Yule," he said softly, his voice sounding intimate.

In that moment, all other faelings were forgotten in the room as I was lost in his touch, in our connection. I was blushing wildly as my magick tried to reach for him, my blood rising to greet him. As if in response, he slowly lowered and kissed my hand. I felt my flesh reach for his lips, which were firm and cold. His red gaze never left mine as he did this.

Then in a flash, as if waking from a dream, he stood and our connection was lost. He led Laufrey carefully out of the room, Laufrey looking back smugly. I was left with such a buzz that the jealousy was drowned out immediately. I swooned from his presence, as I watched Doric approach and carefully led me out.

Seeing Alain was the highlight of the evening and not even the thought of being reunited with Merlough dampened my spirits. Doric's guilt showed as he led me to a private room. "I am sorry I have to do this," he muttered, his face full of shame. I could only nod in understanding as I entered, knowing Merlough awaited, pacing like a lion. I was numb, still lost in my swoon as Merlough snatched me roughly from Doric, wasting no time in sinking his fangs into my throat.

As I felt my heart stutter and struggle against the assault, I imagined it was Alain above me. Warmth spread through me and I fought hard to imagine the pleasure, remembering his simple kiss and spreading it through my struggling body.

I faded further into darkness, the cackling of a nearby vampire, the smell of musty velvet in a used room. With what little energy I had left, I closed my eyes and tuned in to the music from my homeland. The sounds of the court and the feeding blurred into the warm hum of Yule in Brimhaven.

Sickness

"*Awake my youngest for it is your special day,*' my mother whispered, kissing my head. I smiled and stretched, the sun shining through my sleepy eyelids. I grinned, opening my eyes and disappointment crashed over me. I observed my small, dismal room in the vampire townhouse. I was not home. I was not in Brimhaven.

It was my first day of my fifteenth year and I was away from my beloved family still. I quietly rose and dressed, cradling the warmth that I had summoned from the illusion of my mother's presence. It was hours before any others woke in the household, so I decided to lose myself in the dusty books given to me by the Master.

I would find odd moments in the late afternoon, when a well of sadness would reveal itself to me, highlighting how different my life was to be now. I clung to my magick then, summoning the Brimhaven feeling like my mother had taught me. In some sense, I felt hers reach back to me and I began to see them at home, going about their simple yet fulfilling days in the sunny, wild of the Faelands. I would sit and breathe in deeply, feeling the rich earthy scent as if I was there. The heat from the sun's gaze shone through the window, reminding me of the rays that graced my homeland. My mother would be deep into the flowers that gathered there, whispering encouragements and secrets, my brother working hard in the field, working the land as he knew best while my father lay peacefully on his small boat on the lake, waiting for fish as he dreamed in bliss.

Yet as soon as I opened my eyes, I would be back to the dusty barren house of the vampire Merlough.

That evening, I entered his quarters with quiet determination. I allowed him to feed without a fuss, avoiding the slicing pain of his rough fangs, the sickening tug on my heart as he drank thirstily. Once he was done, I observed as he swooned, knowing the music in my blood soon followed. Keeping my voice low, I gave my request.

"Master, may my family visit for my birthday? It is spring after all? My fifteenth year and that makes it one year in your… service," I finished, watching him carefully as he swooned on the couch. He didn't respond after a moment and I waited tensely, knowing he heard me amongst the tune my blood sang to him. When he continued to remain silent, I tensed, worried about what to do. Surely I could not anger him?

Boldly, my magick began to swirl. It was a dangerous, deadly tactic but my desperation had captured me in that moment. I hesitated, seeing Merlough's jaw tense. He sighed after a long moment and my magick cooled.

"Agreed. But only your mother and grandfather. I have business with him anyway and he has ignored me long enough. You may summon them," he growled, waving me away in dismissal. I nodded and bowed respectfully before skipping away to write my letter immediately, my heart pounding with triumph.

They arrived a few days later, and as soon as they did, I sensed something was wrong. My mother's embrace felt distant and reluctant. I barely recognised my grandfather before me. He looked the same yet, the determined gold stare of his strange eyes was no longer on me. I began to wonder if the dark, cold isolation had made me paranoid as his eyes seemed to almost avoid my entire presence altogether.

Had I done something wrong? Was he angry with me?

Almost immediately, my grandfather agreed to meet with Merlough in his private study. I sat with my mother in the 'lounge', where the servants had kindly lit the fireplace, lighting the room for our daylight dwelling sight. My mother seemed almost nervous as she glanced around the townhouse.

"Mother, I am so glad you came," I burst, happily trying to squash down my sinking disappointment at her lack of enthusiasm.

"Of course, dear one," she whispered shakily, her eyes trying to find something within the flames. It was then I noticed her hands wringing impatiently.

"Is something the matter?" I asked shortly, confused by her distant behaviour. My words seemed to finally capture her attention and after what felt like a lifetime, her eyes finally met mine.

"Matter? Why no, of course not. I am here with you, am I not?" she asked, almost too hastily. And like that, her gaze moved from me once more, as if afraid I would see something in them she did not want me to see. That fact alone made my heart pound with panic.

"Mother, I am fifteen years now," I stated, the pride in my voice wavering. I was a year away from officially being seen as a full-fledged faerie. No longer a faeling.

"Indeed, such an age now, son. You have done well," she said, though the words felt false. Was she not proud of me? Was she disappointed that I had not managed to sing as much as I had hoped?

The air felt wrong. I could no longer sense her magick reach for mine. I slowly extended mine further than normal, eager to feel her touch even just for a second. A brief remembrance of reality.

My heart dropped as her magick retreated further and the clear rejection made my magick snap back. She looked pale and withdrawn, her normal warm, brown eyes glassed and hard.

As I quietly observed her before me, she felt more of a mirage of herself. Indeed, she may have been there physically but in spirit, she was somewhere else. Somewhere I desperately wanted to be too. I swallowed heavily, the bitter disappointment overwhelming me once more. I knew my mother. Whatever she was hiding, there was nothing I could do. She had been raised by my grandfather, the most secretive faerie known in existence, and I knew she had managed to keep things even from him.

Whatever she was hiding had to be bad, didn't it? But then shouldn't I know if that were so?!

Before I even realised, I had begun to hum. A gentle soothing sound, heavy with sorrow and woe. It was only when my mother hesitantly looked at me, that I hear my own voice. For a split second, I saw a break in her resolve and a single tear fell. I continued encouragingly feeling my own magick powering my own strength. Almost in rebellion, fuelled by my disappointment, I wanted to show her my own power. She would not hide from me.

My magick began to grow so much, I felt it envelope me in my own comforting embrace. If she would abandon me, I would embrace myself. Like with the faelings at court, I would embrace myself in my own magick. I felt my magick almost stutter in shock as a small smile broke over her pale face.

Was that pride I saw?

Before I could encourage anything further, the study door abruptly opened and loudly my grandfather strode out, closely followed by Merlough.
"It is time we take our leave, dear one," my grandfather grinned, ignoring my presence completely. His grin angered me then.

A smiling mouth in a rotten head.

Surely, he was the cause of this effect upon my mother. She was repressing something, something terrible, and he had trapped her once again. I felt my magick swirl angrily at this realisation but at the sound of his loud giggle, my magick retreated.
"Indeed we are no longer needed here." he said and my mother nodded solemnly, standing stiffly.
"But surely—" I began to argue and finally his gold gaze snapped to mine.

"Dear one, we have overstayed our welcome. Your master wishes for us to take our leave. It is rude to remain here any longer," he hissed almost threateningly to me. I looked at my mother pleadingly, but again, I felt her spirit completely shut to me. She shrank before my grandfather's presence. I couldn't help but believe this was a nightmare.

As I watched them leave, feeling frozen and trapped, I tried one last time to reach my mother through my magick. My heart lurched as she ignored my approach and I swallowed down tears as my grandfather cackled once more, that damned sound echoed in my dreams for days after.

What is happening?

As the grim realisation of my family's departure takes a hold of me, I half expected to feel the sharp fangs of my master. I almost welcomed it. I looked to him, confused when he returned to his study. His door closed with a loud slam that shook my entire being. I was left confused and hurt in the hallway.

The next day, I awoke with renewed determination to figure out what was going on. I felt the distance once more of my mother's spirit and decided to write a letter. I wrote exclaiming on a weird apparition who had visited me the day before. For I believed it was her, but that it felt so unlike her, I no longer believed what I recalled. I begged her to tell me if it was real or not. Was it some cruel trick played by my grandfather? For surely, he was there. I tried to sound kindly and open, weaving in my magick in order to convince her to share with me.

Something is hidden and it is rotting you, mother. I beg you, share this with me and together we can help each other like we have done so many times before…

I began to write some of my favourite memories. Stories she had shared with me, fearing it was a sickness of the soul. I hoped it was enough to convince her that I was still her son, her beloved faeling, and was able to assist her with whatever was ailing her.

My master's feedings began to increase in the coming weeks as did the fear gnawing on my soul. I had gotten no response from my mother and I noticed that despite being notified and invited to more court attendances, Merlough declined most of them.

To my dismay, whenever he did rarely go on a visit, he no longer took me with him. To worsen the isolation, he would return in the early hours, when most day creatures would sleep and would wake me in a frenzy, as if dying of thirst and drink greedily from me. Those were grim and frightening mornings in my fifteenth year.

Months later, I eventually received a reply from my mother. I couldn't contain my excitement as the servant handed it to me, my heart fluttering.

Élan,
I am well. You have your own battles ahead, my brave faeling. There is nothing for you to fear here. Keep your eyes in front of you. Your music is your gift. Use it.

My hands shook with the confusion coursing through me. Was she afraid for me? Then why didn't she do something? I moved to the window as if to find the answers to my troubled mind there. Even though it was daylight, a brief reprise from the Master allowed me to process this. I felt as though I was in the dark.

This then began to filter into my dreams; I would toss and turn, lost in a sea of fear and abandonment from my family, only to be awoken by a ravenous beast that was my master in reality, and he drank from me with no such regard.

Some nights I would welcome dreams of Alain and dared not speak of him in front of Merlough. This was from a day when I felt particularly bold, and as Merlough snapped at the servants, saying to reject another one of his cousin's requests to court, I asked him why.

Before my magick could anticipate it, I was flung across the room from his backhand, the sting of shock worse than the pain.

"Do not speak to me on my personal affairs, you ungrateful worm!" he roared, in such distress, his fangs elongated, and in that moment, he looked completely dangerous. I swallowed down my words of missing the blonde prince and locked them away in my heart, which pounded from the danger I was now in.

"I am sorry, Master." I trembled, making him growl, his red eyes taking on a bloody sheen. My heart sped up as I took him in, knowing the likelihood of my demise could be met at his strong claw-like hands.

After moments of tense silence, he seemed to calm and tilted his head, listening.

"Sweet melody," he murmured quietly, his snarled lips barely moving, his fangs retracting and I calmed.

From that day onward, I no longer asked to go to court.

A New Court

A miserable year passed that way. Then one evening, Merlough was absent, on a rare visit at court. I was reading a musty old vampire book out of boredom. Like many others in Merlough's collection, this contained stories of the courts and how they were formed, highly emphasising the 'justice' that vampires were delivering on their own terms. When faeries were mentioned, it was merely a note on the food source, or suppression of magick within the realm. The distrust of the fae was obvious and began to irritate me to no end.

I mused on what I had seen so far, and how little the fae knew their own species was being treated in other lands, when the flurry of servants distracted me. Whispered murmurs were heard before the front door slammed open, making me jump.

"Cursed ingrates!" Merlough growled. Servants rushed to attend, trying to assist him as he ripped off his coat and growled to himself. I stood quietly nearby, close enough that he could smell my presence, hear my heartbeat. Even that knowledge seemed to not be able to calm him that night. He muttered and snarled to himself and I strained my hearing to listen to his words.

"I will show them. I will teach them. No one looks down on Merlough! NO ONE!" he barked and the servants eventually left him. He stormed past me as if I was invisible and slumped into a chair near the fireplace, which was lit for my comfort.

In that moment, I wondered what it felt like to be a vampire, for it sounded dreadful to a creature like a faerie. Sure, the strength and wealth that came with it were nice, but to contend with the continuous hunger? The need to remain in the shadows and the night? I could not comprehend such an existence.

Quietly, I remained at the doorway, watching him silently, both of us aware of each other's presence. In that moment, I reflected on the time I have had with this creature, feeling a small pang of pity, as I knew the warmth of the fire would never reach his cold flesh, the hunger even now simmering just below the surface within him. I realised that in my time being here and feeling cursed, he was just as cursed as I.

Both of our families have abandoned us…

It was no secret that the courtiers had begun to disregard him. I had heard from the servants that the Queen herself had continued to ignore his presence, which influenced his social standing with the rest at court. These thoughts almost made me want to approach the tired, gaunt creature before me. For we were both so alone in this existence. All we had was each other now. My mother had clearly abandoned me. Whatever she held close to her heart, I would not find out. Letters had stopped coming from home altogether and that alone made me feel empty and hollow.

My master's back was to me as he faced the fire, his eyes glowing from the flames. Without looking away, he beckoned me closer. Like a puppet on a string, I felt his draw to me and was not frightened. Not anymore. This was my fate. I was his as he was mine, whatever that meant.

Even as I approached him cautiously, I felt my blood rush at the impending departure from my body. I heard him sigh, and I knew he could hear this. My body responding to his call. I swallowed the sick feeling of how true this was to me now, how closely connected we were, despite my reluctance. I knew the pain well, I knew the tugging sensation that would soon trigger my heart into another dance.

To resist was only to fuel the hunger more dangerously. I paused when I eventually reached him, close enough to touch.

"I see you have finally understood who you belong to. That is good. It will help you," he purred, and I recognised that edge now in his voice, the hunger was surfacing and soon the pain would commence. I felt calmer than I normally did, and it didn't seem to bother him as he drank. My heart gave in to him, providing and quenching him. I felt myself drift as he did this, my spirit searching, still sadly searching for my Brimhaven feeling, my family whom I missed still, despite their abandonment. And music, gods, I missed my music.

When did I sing last apart from in the calm of the day when everyone else slept? When had things gone wrong here? Why had I not reached my dream that was promised to me?

My throat grew cold as Merlough finally released and though I felt weak, I allowed myself to remain in his arms as he swooned.
"Damn them, damn them all." Merlough swooned drunkenly and no longer cared on who he was talking about.

Another week passed in a quiet fashion with feedings that were more often but smaller now. I could no longer remember a day that passed without a small piece of my soul being given to the beast I now belonged to. And soon this dreaded existence would only get worse.

One evening, as Merlough swooned after what I hoped would be the final feed of the night, he grinned, shark-like, as if an idea just came to him.
"Seems a shame to waste such a beverage," he chuckled and raked his hungry gaze over my weak form. "Such sweet melody does the blood sing to me. Perhaps, birdie, it is time your song be shared with others." he purred and my heart fluttered at his words for it had felt like an age since I had sung for him.

"Thank you, Master," I croaked, my voice dry and weak. He turned away, his grin still fixed on his face as if he had not heard me at all.

The next evening, Merlough had gotten up early to leave for court, his mood lighter, which seemed to encourage everyone in the household. As he turned to take his leave, he seemed to suddenly remember something and turned back to me, his eyes alight. It was summer, and with the lighter evenings, Merlough was usually sluggish. Yet now he seemed alert and sharp, which surely spelled my doom.

"Make ready for I shall return shortly." He smiled as kindly as a wolf and left. I had little idea what his plan was and had no will to ask, so I did as I was commanded, with the servants' help and dressed for company.

As I waited, heavy with dread, I thought of Brimhaven. Summer there was glorious in the golden light. Light that I dearly missed. Surely its absence affected my fae magick? Perhaps that is why I felt so weak despite it being the peak season for faeries. I thought of the summer fayre that was held yearly to praise the light for its power. How it rejuvenated us.
I missed the fresh smell of baked goods and brews. My heart sunk at how long it had been since I had sung with truth in my heart. With real joy and contentment. Was my family to attend this year? How were they without me? Had my mother returned to her beloved flowers once more?

I replayed my sun-soaked memories of her among them, a soft smile that flushed her youthful face. My father would be fishing in the large lake, which would be bursting with new catches, the balance from winter renewed. How were Rolo and Mary? I could barely recall them now, my thoughts soon faded, tarnished by my grim reality. Perhaps it was too painful to look that far into my past…

Upon his word, Merlough returned a few hours later, flocked by three more vampires in his company.
"Ah and here, as promised, I have brought you to share his song with you." Merlough gestured proudly and I stood as tall as I could, wanting to make a good impression. I had grown to reach Merlough's shoulders now. I felt a small beat of hope, getting the chance to finally sing again.

As red eyes set on me hungrily, I felt the blood rise into my face, making them chuckle. My throat was still warm from my earlier practice and I began to sing.

"Enough!" Merlough silenced me abruptly, barely into the song. I stared, shocked. How had I displeased him already?!

The other vampires, all non-distinct and unrecognisable, seemed impatient and annoyed. Merlough approached me fast and I flinched for an impending slap that never came.

Instead, he grabbed my wrist roughly which shook my entire being. He held it out to them and my heart leapt at the horror of my realisation. I began to tremble, which only sweetened my scent to them. Unable to pull from his gasp, I watched as they approached, their red eyes already glazed over as my pale flesh was reflected in their hungry gazes. It was the blood song they sought for an audience. The one I could not hear but seemed to entrance and make vampires swoon.

Like a siren, it drew them in. Never before had Merlough shared me and now I hated him for it, for the pain that I thought I was used to, escalated a thousand-fold. Like a sinister dance, my heart was pulled and tugged in multiple directions as all four vampires, including Merlough, took their drink of me. My heart kicked into overdrive and that only seemed to encourage their gorging on me. The tugging on my blood was so intense, I was painfully aware that I was passing out this time. The experience was so alarming all my senses were on high alert and I felt my magick swirl around me even as I physically began to weaken. Like a spark, I felt it just beneath my skin, beginning to threaten to surface when suddenly, all vampires broke away with a gasp.

I fought to stay conscious as I feared this would anger Merlough. I looked around, confused as they all seemed slumped, drunkenly grinning, my precious red lining their lips.

"Gods!" one of them gasped.

"Shhhhhh," another one slurred.

They were all drunk, drunk on my blood that betrayed me in giving them the song they wanted to hear so badly. It seemed that it was not only Merlough that my blood would sing for. A song that seemed to comfort and charm these damned creatures. I barely acknowledged the fact that their reaction indicated my increasing magick, for Merlough was not this intoxicated upon his first feed.

Before I could even get upset over what had happened, I felt the arms of a servant quietly pull me away. I passed out before I reached my bed.

The next day, I was painfully aware of the absence of my blood this time. I felt weak, I looked sickly, and my energy was barely present. Merlough let me be that night and I was glad. The servants seemed more concerned about me than normal and lit numerous candles to accompany the fire in my room. I stayed in bed, hoping for my energy to return.

I lost myself in fevered dreams of Brimhaven. I was amongst my family but none saw me. I was shouting and screaming, telling them I was there but none acknowledged me. None felt me there.

When it took a few days for me to recover, even Merlough showed concern. He was pleased when I eventually left my bedroom. He approached me and looked me over, almost as he did when he first set eyes on me years ago, in my grandfather's house. He grunted in approval and left for court once more.

Hours later, when the dreaded door opened again, I reluctantly noted there were four vampires accompanying my master this time. Surely not all of them would feed from me?

Sensing the approaching danger, my heart betrayed me once morc by pounding in my breast before them. Merlough cackled.

"Aw, your little birdie is afraid," the new vampire cooed. My instincts told me to run. Run away, fight, kick, and scream for these predators would drain me dry. I felt my magick simmering and I trembled at the pressure within me. My reaction seemed to somber Merlough.

"Everyone, meet us in the drawing room." He gestured politely, his tone serious and firm.

Obediently the vampires obliged, grinning at me greedily as they walked by. One even had the gall to run a nail along my shoulder before joining the others. This new one, he seemed bolder than the others and it frightened me. Merlough's sigh caught my attention.

"Master, I—" I began, but he gestured for me to be silent. He approached, a dangerous look in his eye, his fangs elongating dangerously. For once, I hoped it would be the only fangs that I would feel tonight. He looked me over carefully, his gaze penetrating; I was certain he could see into my veins. He watched me silently like that for brief moments of tense silence.

"You will behave yourself tonight," he gritted threateningly, and I swallowed down my confusion.

"I know not what tricks you spin on to my guests, but if I even sniff that faerie magick again, I will cut off your pretty hands and send them to your grandfather," he hissed and I swallowed a shudder.

"Master, I-I don't know…" I stuttered unable to summon the words, my voice betraying my fear. He gripped me on my arms quickly and with a vice-like grip, which shocked me into silence.

"Who do you belong to?" he asked with a terrifyingly calm voice. It took me moments to find my voice once more as it had abandoned me.

"You," I replied and I watched as his irises expanded, making his eyes almost completely black. Without another word, he pulled me into the room, where the vampires waited patiently for another feast.

"Ah, Merlough, the melody…it is divine!"

This time I stayed in bed for a week. I couldn't even move if I wanted to. I began to lose my sense of reality. My dreams swarmed with fanged beasts, biting and tugging my heart, making me squirm and sweat. I was trapped in vice-like grips as my body was used over and over again, drained beyond recognition.

When I awoke, my vision was blurry and my body aching even more than it had in my dreams. I no longer felt like a fae. I no longer felt like anything but a vessel. A vessel that succumbed to the beasts' nature over and over again.

Fevers claimed me endlessly, and I vaguely remembered the servants concerned faces as I barely registered their presence. The fever consumed me so much that I would be caught between the veil, between dream and reality, and the heat on my flesh would be from the summer sun in the faerie fields, the melody of birds and wildlife around me as I lazed about among my mother's flowers. To feel such a sense of calm and peace again, would be the only assurance that I had once again slipped into a dream.

"Is he awake? He is singing,"
"Ignore the poor boy, he is suffering and needs the help of his people now."
"I think we should call for Dr. Doric."

When I awoke next, I saw a figure beside me, his cool flesh contrasting drastically against my skin.
"Élan?"
"Mmmm…" I sighed. As I slowly returned to my body, I felt the discomfort and heat increasing within.
"Élan, can you hear me?" asked a familiar voice, more clearly now. It forced me to blink awake and take in the room around me, the evening fresh as the sun had only newly gone down. Doric sat next to my bed, looking vibrantly coloured and real.

"Is this real?" I croaked, my own voice barely recognisable.
"It is indeed, dear boy." Doric sighed sadly. He looked flustered and in uniform, that long white coat, casting a ghoulish sheen to his face. My bedroom door suddenly opened and Merlough swiftly entered, standing in front of me, blocking my view from Doric.

"As you can see, he is fine," Merlough growled, sounding hungry and tense. I fidgeted in bed to look around him to Doric. He sat

back and calmly took in Merlough's height as he dominantly stood in front of me.
"I wouldn't say 'fine' is quite accurate," Doric replied sharply, making Merlough scoff.
"The boy is changed, Merlough. Since I saw him last at court, he is losing his colour, his spark."

"Is he now? Hmm sounds to me like you have missed him, Doric. Perhaps you are jealous," Merlough replied snidely, making it Doric's turn to scoff.
"Don't be ridiculous, Merlough. Are you listening to yourself? Why not bring Élan back to court? It would do him good to leave this house," Doric calmly suggested and I watched as Merlough's shoulders tensed.
"Ah, you would like that wouldn't you? Well, I know for a fact that birdie doesn't like…court," Merlough snarled.
"Oh Merlough, please don't do this." Doric suddenly stood, looking at him beseechingly.
"Don't do what?!" he hissed, dangerously low. Doric moved closer to him.
"I see the marks on him. I know you bring others back here. What you are doing is—"
Merlough's snort cuts him off.
"Is what, dearest friend?"
"Is illegal," Doric finished quietly. Merlough remained quiet as Doric's words sank into both of us. I grew confused. Illegal? Something had changed then. Changed, which was why I was being hidden. I tried to meet Doric's eyes then, but he was

holding Merlough's gaze firmly. Both stood erect like two cobras poised to fight.

"Illegal? I see no issue here. I think it is time you left." Merlough said calmly, moving towards Doric, forcing him to retreat from the room.

As the distance grew between me and them, I became more desperate, the very weight of the situation frightening me. Something in Merlough's look broke Doric down and he eventually left, ignoring my desperate gaze.

With them both gone, the room felt cool and larger than before. I trembled and lay there, thinking on what had just happened, my mind moving too slowly to really piece anything together. The weight of my thoughts on my chest and my breath slows. Soon the veil would welcome me once more, and I was trapped in my own healing self.

In one last desperate effort, I called for my magick silently. At first, nothing happened, and my heart thrummed in panic. Then I sensed a small shift, a small wisp near my head. I was unable to move as the magick slowly woke around me. I suddenly heard my mother's voice in my head, her voice that I hadn't heard in so long.

'Mighty Gods' of the wind and sea, watch over him.'
'Protect him, I beg you.'

I felt the magick bellow stronger then, swirling around me, bringing with it the fresh scent of trees and the woodland. The earthy scent after a rainfall. I sighed and recalled the feeling once again, welcoming it. No longer was it my mother's presence, but my own that calmed me. The magick floated onto my skin, caressing, comforting.

Behind my closed eyelids, I felt the glittering sunshine, the warmth of the rays as if I was transported there. It lulled me into the veil even before I could stop it. My magick faded as I drifted further into sleep once more, as if calmed that it had done its job. And just before I slipped through the veil completely, I heard something.

A quiet voice. A soft, gentle cry. My mother was crying.

As I slowly recovered and began to leave my bed, I noticed there were fewer servants than before. My energy felt renewed. I decided to boldly ask Merlough why this was as he swooned from a solitary feed one evening. He shrugged, his eyes glazed drunkenly.

"I have no need for such. We are fine on our own," he cooed, petting my head heavily. I frowned at his words, but did not bother questioning him.

Nowadays he made less and less sense and I could not tell if it was my disorientation or his.

I took note that as the servants lessened, the days were getting brighter. The summer months were even lighter here in the Vampire Nation, though still darker than the Faelands.

With the light, I began to feel as all faeries do, their energy refreshed, with a newer spring in my step.

Though the house was impossibly quieter than before, Merlough was weaker now that the evenings were shorter. I welcomed the light in the new season, I also noticed how much hungrier he was when he awoke. Now he commanded me to be in his presence even before he arose. He explained it was like when I woke to the bird song, he awoke to his own within my blood. It was a grotesque idea to me, but I, of course, obeyed and stood quietly at the sweet spot of sunset. As I solemnly felt the loving comfort of the sun sink, I felt the rise of my master, ready and ravenous for my veins.

One particular evening, he asked me not to bathe, and when he rose, I trembled more than normal, feeling my own sweat gather on my flesh. I sensed him awaken even before I saw him move. I had never watched a vampire sleep and I could understand why. It was frighteningly disturbing. I never realised how alive we must seem to those dark creatures even in sleep. Vampires do not breath, do not move, nor make a sound. It's as if death consumes them completely and you can not distinguish between a corpse and a sleeping vampire. At least not until the sliver of sunset disappears and the first breath of consciousness is upon him, quickly, by a bite to my wrist.

On particularly hot days, when my heart was still pounding from worshipping the light and the musk of sweat was still fresh on my skin, my master swooned even before his bite.
"Gods, the songs are louder now," he groaned before biting me hard, making me jolt. His thick fangs sliced through my flesh like butter. I had yet to figure out what this meant.

Was this me ageing to a faerie? Was it my magick being increased by the season like other faeries? Had the sun finally reached me here in the south?

I worried over these thoughts over and over again, trying to avoid the increase despite Merlough's pleasure in the blood song. I feared how far this would go, how I could do nothing to stop the song my blood was singing to him.

Why was my body betraying me so?

Unfortunately, it was not long before the land cooled once more and Merlough began to bring back his guests, this time to take note of the heightened intensity of my blood song. As if to fight back, my blood song seemed to only entrance them further.

From the moment they would see me, the song would lure them to me. After they had their fill, which I seemed to sustain slightly better than before, I noticed the swooning afterwards was also longer. What took an hour before now took them almost until before sunrise, when they would rush to somber up and leave before the day was upon them.

One such evening, five of them lay there. I dared not leave as Merlough watched me like a hawk, even under his stupor.
"It'sssss ssssso unfairrrr," one vampire slurred. The others ignored him. "Why did she have to take them from us? They are meant for us!" he growled angrily but was immobile in his inebriation.
"The fae are meant to serve us. This boy proves it," another growled but none looked to me.

I sat quietly, observing the conversation, my heart having slowed to a calm rhythm from my concentration. I was tired and drained as expected, but I felt my curiosity begin to stir.

"Indeed he does," sneered Merlough, picking his teeth.
"Well, I say we hold our own courts then!" the vampire added, sitting up and falling back down again. Merlough chuckled.
"Our own you say? Is that not what I do here?" Merlough rumbled.
"Indeed, and we are eternally grateful for you, Merlough," another vampire mumbled.
"Mmm I want to bring mine next time. I want a snack after that high, plus it is better to keep them away from court now," another yawned and groaned. Merlough chuckled again.
"You are welcome to. Any subsidium is welcome at my court." He grinned and looked at me then. I repressed the shudder I felt. Bring more faelings here? I tried to calm my racing heart, but no one seemed to notice my distress, or care.

I suddenly realised in that moment, if Merlough stopped going to court, something had gone awry with my grandfather's deal. I recalled with sickening dread the whole point of me coming here, alluded to the fact that I had a presence at Queen Carmilla's court. I struggled to keep my heart calm as it thudded in protest at my horrid truth. I was in trouble.

Another week passed, thankfully with no visitors. Although Merlough continued his little but frequent sips from my wrists, I did not complain. I was glad to be alone, glad that the vampires stayed away. The bruises on my arms were fading and the sun in the autumn season seemed to renew my energy once again. I felt a new sense of calm as the routine set in.

Once again, servants were dismissed, leaving only one present during the day and one during the night. It was highly unusual for other households, but with Merlough's distance from court, I assumed that he could no longer afford them.

I stopped worrying about my family's silence. They had abandoned me and though I still cried at night for them sometimes, I knew they were safe, they were happy, somewhere far from here. As my mother had said, I had my own battles ahead of me now.

My magick would swirl and comfort me in those times. Supporting and strengthening me from the isolation. With my magick, I was not alone. With it, I felt the presence of all the faeries in Brimhaven and the songs of old. I was doing this for them and one day I would return to share my songs from this time.

In quiet moments, during the midday, when the sun was the highest and Merlough was far beyond the veil, I would summon the magick around me. Not for any particular purpose, but it felt like a muscle I was flexing each day, getting easier the more I did it. I was no fool to my situation. I was here alone.

On the worst nights, I was surrounded by six powerful vampires. If I had any chance, I knew my magick would save me. With the servants barely around, I knew no one would be aware of my daily practise and it felt a comfort to me that I grew this one my own.

Some days, the magick would swoop in so strong as if it had been waiting anxiously beneath the surface, and like a breath of fresh air, it would surround me, encouraging me to sing softly in an ancient fae language. It would float and drift, and I could almost feel like I was in Brimhaven once more. It was my last connection to my homeland. A strong and distant connection I held onto stubbornly. It was my hidden gift, that only I could see and I revelled in that. It gave me hope.

A dangerous and forbidden feeling in the dark townhouse, which I guarded more sacredly.

I failed to hide my dismay as four vampires again returned the one evening to Merlough's house. The bruises had just faded and I tried to ease the threat of my magick surfacing as a reflex. I was caught off guard as I recognised a shorter figure entering behind them. It was a faeling. I recognised him as one from court that I met at Yule two years ago.

Gods, I was unable to hide my horror at his gaunt pale face, his weakness as he was barely able to stand. He was ignored by everyone but me and I tried to steady my panicked heart as not to excite their hunger further. They had already begun to circle me like vultures as Merlough boasted and grinned at them. I could not tear my gaze away from the other faeling. I wanted to talk to him badly; after all, did he not live at the court? Why was he here? And gods, why did he look so ill?

I felt the first pair of fangs enter my right shoulder as I still struggled to comprehend the boy before me. He looked like a shell of his former self, and never once met my gaze. I felt the pulls and tugs as more fangs joined and I struggled to focus on him.

In my mind, I pleaded with him to leave, run away. Surely the servant would not stop him? No one took any notice of him now and it was his chance! My heart sped up, as if trying to fight the pulls though my focus was fading from him. I felt my knees buckle as the strength was drained from me and my vision began to cloud.

"Please…" I croaked, begging him silently to leave. Leave this cursed place, I wanted to send him my magick, somehow try and transport him away from here. But I felt Merlough's fangs tighten and knew the risk was too much to try now.

Painfully, they slowly broke away and I felt more drained than normal, having been more resistant to them, they had inadvertently taken more from me and I reprimanded myself for being so foolish. I could have done it by now while they were in their stupor! You fool, Élan!

Blindly, I tried to find the boy, but I felt drunk myself, though not the floating high that the five vampires around me were. I was trapped by my own weakened body, fighting the oncoming sleep which would make me bedridden for a further week.

A loud laugh suddenly jolted me awake, before I even realised I had lost consciousness. I looked around desperately. One of the vampires had the poor boy in his grip, drinking him greedily. The faeling looked like a broken doll, limp and small against the beast that fed upon him. I felt my magick swirl dangerously close to the surface.

"Any more you can spare, friend?" Merlough cut through my thoughts and I shut off my magick instantly. I trembled as I felt him stroke my head, almost approvingly. Another vampire laughed across the room.

"Opps," giggled the vampire holding the faeling. I turned and looked as he dumped the faeling on the ground, his body unmoving.

"Seems I had too much thirst for such as him… again," groaned the vampire and he slumped back down in the chair. Merlough chuckled.

"Ah you see. Once you have an appetite for my birdie, he spoils all else in comparison," he rumbled, his voice loud against my ear, my heart racing. I stiffened as the vampire stood and swayed a little.

"Merlough, my friend, I will need to come more often until…I find a replacement." He hiccupped. Merlough stood and replied as the horror swirled within me. Gods, they had killed him. They had killed the faeling and how many others? Why was I not dead?

In that moment, my hesitation and guilt overwhelmed me. I could have saved him. I know I could have, even with Merlough's wrath before me. It was then I realised the difference, why the vampires revered in me so much. Not only did my blood betray me by making a song so pleasant to them that they could not deny another taste, but that my magick was a curse. It cursed me in keeping me alive when others would have died. I was the ultimate subsidium.

Not long after, too weak to get up, I rolled over and threw up over Merlough's Persian rug. They were all so high, they just laughed in response.

From that night on, the other vampires' visits became a weekly occurrence. Coincidentally timed so that the day I recovered from the previous onslaught of blood taking, they were back for another round. They no longer brought other faelings, whether it was because they no longer needed them or there were no others they could salvage.

Further drunken talks were held about creating their own court, how the fae were rarely seen in the territory anymore. The Queen's distaste in the subsidium system had increased as such that the practise had been banned from court. I knew not what happened to the other faelings that I had met there.

Since witnessing the faeling's death weeks before, I felt myself detach from reality more and more, succumbing to my current reality, no longer practicing my magick daily, for I was too weak to leave my bed now. I was better off preserving my energy for the next time Merlough's 'court' was held. I knew I was losing weight as I ate little and moved less during the sunlight hours.

It was almost as if I had become one of them, perhaps in a vain hope I wondered if this would also weaken the blood song they were all so fond of hearing. Sadly this was not so. Whereas physically, my body seemed to weaken and grow paler every day, my blood song remained strong and consistent, encouraging the vampires to continue their despicable behaviour. I no longer dreamed of home or anything at all. I was so exhausted that even the veil failed to provide me with dreams to hold on to. I felt my actual voice was lost, rarely used anymore. I missed singing real songs so badly. I even thought back to songs I used to sing for Merlough, and felt rejected when he no longer was interested in them. My beating heart lost within the dark of my shallow, weak breast. I feared I would soon forget my home, forget the magick and all that I knew.
With each draining night of Merlough's weekly courts, another piece of my soul was broken away and cast into the abyss. When I tried to think of songs of comfort, no words were found for me. My mind, reluctant to spend energy other than on my own healing before another feast.

Weeks rolled into months, and time itself moved by in an ill begotten nightmare. Soon, my ill-state was recognised by the vampires themselves.

"Your birdie looks ill, Merlough," one snarled, wincing and hesitating from his normal bite. Merlough scoffed and bit into me as if to prove otherwise, making me sway unsteadily. My heart thumped off beat and I was dripping with sweat.

Merlough pulled away and frowned. Another coughed awkwardly as I turn and vomited onto the floor. My magick pounded awkwardly with my heart now, and I could no longer control it. I swayed drunkenly as I tried to regain my balance and could no longer sense anyone else around me.

"He tastes different…" someone muttered, sounding more somber than myself. The words struggled to leave my lips as I felt something wrong was happening. My magick was swirling dangerously close to the surface and I knew they could almost see it if they were watching me closely enough.

"Stand back," Merlough barked, his clear voice splitting into my head suddenly. The sound knocked me down and my magick fluttered around me, fighting myself to break free. I dared not in my state, out of control, and it took all my control to hold it close to me.

"Something is wrong," another vampire whined and Merlough growled.

"No shit. Call the servant. The court is closed for tonight," Merlough spat, his voice dripping in disappointment. I tried to steady my breath as the swirling magick made me dizzy. I would vomit again if only my stomach was not empty already.

I blinked around me, trying to focus on the scene before me, the bland colours of the floor and walls mixed into a blur. I smelled him before I saw him as Merlough approached me from behind. "Enough now," I heard him say, though I frowned. It sounded too soft to be his voice and I coughed, the effort alone was what finally made me pass out.

Bird cage

Coolness is the first thing I felt. Then I was rocked as if I were floating on the waves themselves. I was swaying but it was a comfort, no longer was I nauseous or sick. I had no sight or smell but it did not frighten me.

The presence I sensed calmed me. Soon, feeling returned in my body, I was surprised I was not sore from my bruises and aching bones. Instead I felt togetherness, warmth, and comfort. I embraced it, holding onto it tightly. I heard a sigh but could not tell if it I was my own or someone else's. Either way, the sigh eased my chest and my heart once more beat strong and steady. Wisps of cold air floated around my legs and move up to my stomach then my torso, leaving through my head. The path it left gives a cooling and healing sensation. I wanted to thank whomever was healing me, but I was blind.

Suddenly, there was coolness on both sides of my face as if to calm my thoughts.

"*Weary traveller, rest your one*," came a voice, disembodied and unrecognisable, yet at the same time, it felt familiar. I sighed again and this time I knew it was myself. The coolness left my face and repeated the movements over my body once more. Memories slowly returned and I became confused. Where was I? Where was Merlough? The other vampires? Who was this presence? My heart sped up with my thoughts and the movements sped up. Another breath, this time more of an annoyed huff, and the movements stopped.

"*All the relics of life long lived…*" said the voice, sounding regretful and sad. Before I could ask what they mean or other questions I was bursting with, the weight of consciousness pulled me back through the veil.

A thud and a growl made my eyes snap open. My heart slowed and dread sank in as the familiar bedroom was before me.

"The boy needs a real doctor. He is sick, Merlough," Doric sighed, gesturing desperately to him. Merlough's face twisted and snarled at him.

"Are you saying you aren't a real doctor then? What in the gods name am I paying you for?!" he hissed, his fangs sharp and threatening.

"Not for a faerie, no! I have always told you that, but you never listen! Besides, I may not be a faerie doctor, but I know abuse when I see it!" Doric barked back angrily. Merlough remained dangerously quiet. Tense heart beats later, Merlough chuckled darkly.

"I see what's happening here. You want him all for yourself, do you not? Jealous you haven't had a taste yet?" Merlough sneered.
"By the gods, Merlough, you are insane! The boy is dying. He needs food and rest, not another to bite him!" Doric clutched his head desperately. Merlough's growl sounded more animalistic than before and the noise alone made me tremble, my body already anticipating further pain to endure.

Bruises and aches had returned and they would make me moan if I had the energy. Doric suddenly seemed to remember my presence and turned to me. Merlough moved to intercede him and Doric huffed impatiently.

"Look, the boy needs food. If you are his master like you say you are then please, get some for him," Doric begged calmly. Merlough seemed to ease and to my relief, moved aside once more. Doric reached my bed and Merlough left the room swiftly. As Doric took me in, he sighed sadly.

"Do I really look that bad?" I muttered brokenly. Doric smiled and chuckled to himself.
"Sorry it's just…" have looked away, catching himself.
"It's not your fault." It only seemed to break Doric's resolve and he sighed, heavier than before.

"Is it not? I think it has gone beyond fault now, little one. What Merlough is doing is illegal and… Gods…" Doric trembled.
"You are strong though, the strongest I have ever witnessed…" he muttered.
"It is a curse," I spat bitterly before I could stop myself. Doric frowned at me in confusion and then slowly, the understanding sank in. He nodded slowly, his eyes distant. We were silent for a moment and I began to wonder where Merlough had gone. They must have had no food in the house.

"It may feel that way….for now. But…" Doric struggled to think of the words and I sighed hopelessly. Doric huffed impatiently.
"Look, as I have said, what Merlough is doing… it isn't right. It won't be long before he is stopped for what he is doing to you, damn the contract you have! Just… keep doing what you are doing… please?" Doric said with more determination and hope that I felt. I shrugged and pouted, knowing there was little else I could do.

I had little knowledge on what was going on beyond my prison of four walls and no idea how long it would take. Plus, I'd never seen my grandfather's contract. They were pretty unbreakable, despite law and political intervention.

For the first time in months, I considered my grandfather. Where was he? What was he doing right now? I had no idea if it was my sense of hopelessness or bewilderment in my circumstance, but the thoughts were entertaining to me. Doric's cool hand on my own wrist jolted me from my thoughts.

"I will find a way to free you," he hissed, his eyes alight with determination that shocked me.
"Why would you do that?" I asked weakly, fearing the hunger that he must be feeling, conscious of how vulnerable I was at that very moment. My magick was silent which was the only consolation I had that there was little danger with him.
"Because it is the right thing to do," he replied with such absolution I almost believed him.

Suddenly a roar shook me and Doric was thrown across the room.
"I knew it! Get out, GET OUT NOW!" Merlough roared. Doric was just as in shock as I was and it took a moment for him to stand once more.
"I will go. But be warned Merlough, this is not good." Doric took one last look at me, his eyes alight with anger and left. Merlough scoffed and to my dread made his way towards the bed. He sat where Doric sat, facing me on the chair before my bed. I tried to suppress the shakes in my body, my instincts sensing the menace beneath the flesh before me.

To my surprise, Merlough clutched his head, his long hair mangled and unkempt, his pale sharp hands scratching his scalp.
"Stupid bloodsuckers, all want my birdie, my birdie is mine! I should kill that fool," he snarled to himself. I remained deathly still, not wanting to distract him from his trance-like mutterings that have gradually become more frequent. I could do nothing but watch on in silent still horror as the madness spilled from his drooling, cracked lips.

The world had a smoky hue, making it hard to see things in detail. Before me was a huge, dark river. It was thick with cold water that moved slowly and pacing. I squinted as beyond the river, I saw three figures, dimmed by the smoke. I focused hard in order to see them, only to recognise my family.

I almost ran forward, forgetting the water before me. I ran down the river, straining to get to them. I saw my mother beckoning me, telling me to cross via the river. I struggled to will myself to cross, though my instinct made me hesitate. The water was so dark and black, I saw my own reflection hesitate.

"*Slow, love slow*," my mother's voice whispered around me. I slowed my breath and concentrated. Surely I could cross if my mother said so? I stepped onto the water, surprised to find it supported my weight. Was it magick?

I looked up and found that I saw them more clearly now, my mother smiling and my brother was beckoning me further. My father stood watching, pride alight in his eyes. Seeing them seemed to strengthen my resolve.

With a steady breath, I took another step onto the water, bringing me forward entirely over the river now. Again the water held me as though I was light and made of nothing. I smiled up to my family and they began gesturing excitedly.

In my earnest to get to them, I moved forward, confident in my steps now, enjoying the cooling wetness. I was about halfway before something stopped me. A giggle I had not heard in a while. It was distant but enough to make me pause. I looked down, seeing the doubt in my reflection. I could feel my family's panic and started gesturing wildly but my gaze was drawn to my reflection.

Who was I? Hadn't my family abandoned me?

With those thoughts I suddenly sank into the black waters below...

I was drowning.

Drowning far down in the river that pushed and pulled me into its darkness. No more was the calming gentle waves of healing. This was menacing and deathly. The blackness surrounded me as I was twisted and turned, completely out of my control. I knew what this was. I knew this river. This was the Ghost River, a tale from my youth.

A terrifying, frightful river that was somewhere in the mystical north. A place where lost souls go when they pass from this world. With no weight of memories or love to guide you into the afterlife, the river pulled you. Greedily it took you for its own. Further down and down you go, forever drowning in the black abyss.

Faeries young and old could be found, ghosts of the abandoned and lost. With connections to all bodies of water, it was a myth to be heeded by all young faelings. I searched desperately to see anything other than blackness before me. Grey shapes shifted past me as if I was falling at a great speed. I struggled to catch at them, hoping to slow my sinking, my lungs close to bursting.

Suddenly I halted, one of my arms caught onto something. I looked up and saw a grey figure, straight into sad eyes. It was the faeling that I had seen die in the arms of a vampire. I gasped silently but the figure did not respond.

Timelessly, I was locked into his sad gaze; he was searching, looking as lost as I was, feeling as hopeless as I did. I tried to speak but silently he shook his head sadly. His grip began to loosen and I panicked. As he let go, I felt myself begin to sink once more.

"*Never lose your heart, before you cross,*" my mother would warn when speaking of this tale. Even my brother would heed her warning.

"*When crossing a river, never forget who you are, question who you are, for the river will find you and pull you down, far deeper down until you drown,*" she would warn, and gods, I felt it then. Even as I was pulled, I could not scream, making no sound for help.

Gods, I missed my mother, my father, and brother. Why had they abandoned me? Why was I lost and forgotten?

The Ghost River had me in its grasp and forever I was drowning.

I gasped, my heart pounding, my body wet with sweat (or the river?) from its return to consciousness. Pain sliced from my left arm and with horror, I saw why. I was in Merlough's sharp grip, his fangs deep into the pale flesh of my upper arm, the area already purple from the strain and damage of the veins around it. Which was the nightmare now?

My mind swirled with nausea and once again, I was reminded of the Ghost River's grasp. Gods, which would I prefer at that moment? What had become of me? I choked a cry and Merlough released me, seeming to be just as surprised and waking from his own dream. He stood, frowning down at me, licking his lips, red with my blood.

"Hm," he grunted and scratched his hair, just as matted and messy as before. My heart pounded and I strained to calm it, resisting the urge to tempt the beast before me even more. Was he hearing the song now? I dared not ask and stared as he slowly backed away.

As he turned to leave, he began to hum to himself, confirming the song that must've been swirling in my blood. The resentfulness and betrayal rose in me once more and my magick startled me as it zinged to the surface before I could stop it. Merlough paused and my heart sped up once more.

"What was that?" he muttered. I didn't answer him and waited to see if the madness answered for him. My fright only seemed to fuel my magick and it swirled barely beneath my flesh now, spurring goose pimples over me. Merlough growled, which only spurred my magick further, fluttering my hair now.

"Mine! Mine!" he roared, speaking to no one.

"Yes!" I cried as he stormed out, his ravings fading with the distance.

As I slowly recovered, Merlough did not. More words would spring from him with conversations to no one but himself. It was alarming and disturbing to watch.

Sometimes, I tried to reason with him and respond but it did no good. I tried to avoid his presence but it would only draw him into my room where I felt more trapped. His raving would turn into arguments and again, as my fright grew, my magick seemed to respond. This only made him worse and I concentrated on calming myself, hoping to alleviate the danger I was in.

Blindly, Merlough would snarl and snap around him as if he was being pecked at and bothered by invisible birds. In my panic, when this grew to be too much for me to bear, I ran at him, trying to shake him out of it. This made him only fight me more and he repelled me back with the strength I knew and feared.

"You! This is your fault! Stop them! Stop them now!" he roared at me. I trembled, looking around confused, not even feeling my own magick now. I stayed still and calm, watching him as he panted and stared at me, his eyes red and glowing, his terrifying fangs erect and poised.

"Things are going to change around here," he warned and I was too terrified to move. I had no idea what he meant or how to reason with him anymore. I remained frozen as he stomped to the door, slamming it shut behind him. I stayed there as I listened to some rustling.

A metallic clicking sound raised the alarm in my head and jump-started my body into movement. Before I reached the door, it was already locked, bolted shut. The lock had always been there but never had he done this before. I sank to my knees, dizzy with terror and confusion.

"Birdie will stay in his cage from now until he behaves," Merlough's muttering voice beat through the door. I shook and cried, waves of emotion bubbling through me, being trapped with a madman too much to comprehend.

Sometime later, I found myself back in the safety of my covers, lying aimlessly, trying to remain present with myself. Ignoring the grey of the walls, the dimness of the window behind me, I carefully summoned my magick, waiting for the warmth to return. I was frozen in shock and sadness, the magick returning like the rays of sunlight.

No longer could I hate my magick, the songs within me, this is who I was and no one could be the same as me. The fresh scent of pine was over me like a metaphysical healing balm. I sighed and let the magick soothed me. It felt useless and unpredictable but it was mine. The last piece of my soul I had left. The images of my dally across the river haunted me, my magick swirled at my thoughts, bringing me back to myself. A song burst from my heart, I sang it softly to myself;

Small spring birds, so light and free to sing,
How can one be so happy for joy to bring?
My loving heart, is lost in the dark,
For hope I would give anything

Silent tears fell for me then. For my life and what it had become. I was a shell of the faeling from Brimhaven. My magick fluttered and flurried as if in protest. I left it to lull me and comfort me back into the dreaded veil of unconsciousness.

The next days were tense and anxious as I heard little movement beyond my locked door. Dry food was left for me while I slept and I no longer knew if it was the servants or Merlough himself who left it. I was soothed by the idea of being on my own. This meant I was safe from the madness and unpredictable behaviour. I used the time to reunite with my magick and use it to soothe my own isolation. I was alone and that was okay.

I had to survive this; I had to if not only to see my family again, but to prove to my grandfather he no longer could control me. I wanted to survive to share my story, to stop this once and for all. To finally sing and share with the world, to give myself what my young faeling-self had dreamed of. I would survive Merlough. I had to.

With my resolve strengthening, I felt my magick beckon in approval. They said the source of magick was from our kin, memories of souls and ancestors of the first all through generations. I felt that connection now, like roots in a giant tree with me being the highest point as a leaf. I reached down deep, willingly and encouragingly. I would not die here.

To my relief, our distance seemed to also clear Merlough. Though he still muttered and raved occasionally, he also began to see me for songs again. I was no longer allowed to leave my room without his permission (and such amenities were to make it so I didn't need to leave so often) but nor did I mind so much. At first, my songs were hesitant and raw in my throat. Merlough seemed patient with this and eventually my songs returned. I would sing for him and he would leave, wistfully avoiding the topic of blood and for that, I was grateful.

With each passing day, my songs returned in my voice, which only encouraged my hope and resolve. I was polite, quiet, and served Merlough as I had in my early days. I made more of an effort to dress, predicting his entrance now and preparing songs. Songs of hope and strength.

As I sang to him, he responded with little emotion or interest. The mutterings slowed with each day, and he seemed more himself.

When it felt as though a week had gone by, I knew his hunger must be at its peak. I tried to sing but was distracted by the idea and Merlough eventually gestured for me to stop.

"You are distracted, birdie," he growled and I nodded, blushing with shame. Even with his cruelty, I hated to disappoint him. My body's response seemed to remind him of his hunger and I saw the glazed look slowly return. I could do nothing but tense and try to remain still as I watched the beastly-look take over my master.

"It seems you are now distracted as well," I stated boldly, my voice shaking.

To my surprise, he only nodded and beckoned me forward. With great effort, I obeyed, suddenly wishing I hadn't said anything on the subject. I tried to withhold the tremble he found so tempting as I raised my bare wrist to him. I found it curious to watch him hesitate as much as I had.

Carefully, he took my wrist, which still looked small and pale in his sharp grip. But with ease, his fangs retracted when his red eyes fell onto the blue veins that lived there. I watched as they sliced through my pale flesh, my blood already racing to reach him. His eyes soon fell shut in bliss as my body betrayed me to him once more. The pulls and tugs were more gentle as if he was savouring me for the first time in a while. My heart fluttered and started at the slow teasing of his pulls and I almost sighed with relief.

As he broke away, I slowly moved, noticing my balance was better than it normally was after a feed. He stood swiftly as if he was barely affected by my blood this time and left quickly without a word or glance behind him. I frowned until I heard the mutters and ramblings, knowing the words were, once more, to no one. I shuddered and suddenly had a strange thought.

Was that lock to keep me in or to keep him out…?

Loss

I was standing on a shore. It was raining hard and there was a rumble of thunder in the distance. The clouds were grey and the water matched it, making the world a hazy, soft hue. The rain was unyielding, pasting my clothes to my skin.

On the water before me swayed a large, black, foreboding ship. The sails were torn and fluttering with an anger of the approaching thunder. The boat scared me for some reason and I tried to move away.

As I turned, I noticed a dark figure on the ship, which halted me. I recognised him not by looks but by the hat on his head. It was a captain's hat, which contrasted with the white of his hair. It was my father.

Even from the distance I was at, I could tell it was him, perhaps how I imagined him in his sailing days. The figure was busy working on the ship and I noticed the anchor being heaved from the water.

My father was to sail away? The thought worried me and my heart leapt as a flash of lightning slashed behind the ship, haloing it in light for mere moments. It was a menacing vision and though I longed to be with my father, I knew not to try and get on to the boat. I called for him but my voice was lost in the wind. Seagulls squawked and whined as the ship swayed heavily again, the waves crashing before me.

I tried again, feeling my own throat strain and constrict with effort, but to no avail. The thunder rumbled louder as if mocking me and I grew irritated. Why was my father leaving?

Suddenly, I was struck with an idea and recalled a sea shanty my father had taught me years ago. At first I hummed it and soon sang, my words stolen from me but it did not matter.

I saw my father hesitate and he turned to look in my direction. I continued to sing, encouraged by my efforts and soon I was in full swing of the shanty that reached him. My heart burst with joy as he raised a hand to me and I smiled widely, making my face ache. How long had it been since I'd smiled?

My emotions were as big as the waves before me, my eyes spilling with tears at the sight of him. He looked the same as I remembered and he was smiling sadly, his blue eyes watery. I continued singing despite the thunder and waves now trying to compete in volume. My love for him was renewed and the need to see him again was so great, I continued my song.

Slowly, my father placed his own hand onto his heart and my song lurched as I choked a cry. As if on cue, the boat began to sail away, though my father remained in place. I did not know who was driving it but he seemed regretful in leaving me there. His smile sunk into further sadness and I could not tell if there were tears or rain on his worn cheeks. I desperately wanted to reach him, assure him that I was okay. That I would see him again. I put that feeling into my song as I continued to sing even as he and the boat faded away, swallowed by the horizon.

I was startled awake by a knock at my door, which seemed pointless considering it was locked. This was followed by rattling metal noises before opening to reveal the pale face of a servant.

"Master Merlough wishes for your company in his study." He gasped, sounding as surprised as I felt. I bolted up and jumped into action, dressing quickly and followed him into the study. The house looked the same from my room and the sun had freshly set. I knew whatever I was called for would be important. As I flurried my way into the study, the servant quickly left us, and I saw Merlough himself looking roughly dressed, his shirt askew and his hair as messy as my own.

"You asked for me, Master?" I gasped out of breath and my heart pounded excitedly, hardly believing I was out of my room, sleep still slowing my mind. Merlough huffed.
"Indeed," he muttered and was writing speedily, even for a vampire, on parchment, his pen scratching so much, I feared it would catch aflame. I waited patiently, not wanting to anger him, unable to read his mood in that moment.

It didn't take long before he slowed and then stopped, put down his pen and looked up at me wearily from his desk.
"I have news from Brimhaven," he said firmly and I smiled, my heart fluttering. Finally my family had written to me?
"Oh gods, is it true? After so long? Oh my, I am so excited and so glad. I thought they had forgotten me. Oh thank you, Master, for telling me. I—"
"Your father is dead."
"…W—what?"

"Your father is dead," Merlough repeated, accentuating his words, his red eyes hard and cold.
"It can't be!" I gasped, the air abandoning my lungs, my dream haunting my mind.
"Indeed, it is true, boy. I asked you here to tell you in person. It is the least I could do," Merlough muttered and continued to write, which infuriated me.

"You're lying!" I screamed suddenly, making him pause to look up. I was shaking. Shaking and trembling, my blood rushing and my magick swirling dangerously.

"Calm yourself," he spat and began writing again, this time angrily. I knew better than to fuel it, yet in that moment, all reason was lost to me.

"I don't believe you," I argued. Merlough's mouth twisted into a snarl and he threw a letter at me.

"Call me a liar again and I shall rip off your legs so you can no longer walk, birdie. You don't need legs to sing." He chuckled darkly, eyes back on his writing. I read in silence, the dreaded truth before me, the only sound was my pounding heart and the scratching of his dreaded pen.

My arms trembled as I strained to read the cursive writing before me, the words feeling false on the page. I do not know who wrote it.

...perished from illness long endured in the winter months that lead through to the summer. Its deathly grip refused to leave him and he eventually succumbed...

I couldn't believe it. My father was gone. He was gone and had been sick for a long time. The sight of him leaving on that ship flashed in my head. I felt bile threaten to rise up through me. I tried to calm myself in order to strengthen my next words.

"I bid you permission to see them. To see my family and help with preparations of his passing." My voice sounded strong but empty, unknown to me. I couldn't believe I was even saying these words to him.

In agonising silence, Merlough seemed to ponder this as he continued writing. My heart thudded loudly in my ears as I waited, my body trembling with the tension and emotion.

"No."

"No?"

"Do I need to repeat myself?" Merlough growled.

"Indeed you do, sir, for I cannot comprehend your answer," I bit back boldly. Merlough snarled and stood, his pen dropping off somewhere with the speed of the movement.

"It matters not. You are *mine*. You do not have permission to leave," he said, then calmly as a predator, he approached me in his great disheveled height, making my stomach drop.

"B-but my family needs me—" My words are cut off as his arm snaps to my throat, cutting off the air.

"No, they don't. He is dead. There is no need for you there. You are remaining here," Merlough snarled and I struggled in his grip, my body fighting for air. Tears streamed from my eyes in disbelief over his cruelty.

"Stop fighting me. I own you," Merlough growled and dropped me moments before I passed out. I choked and coughed on the floor.

"I hate you," I wheezed, no longer caring for my life. Merlough chuckled darkly and knelt towards me on the floor.

"And I hate your grandfather. Aunty was right; she warned me not to trust him. He tricked me all right; he tricked me good with you birdie." He then dragged me back to my room. I struggled and wheezed, feeling weak against him.

Things were moving too fast for my magick to come, I was too emotional, my mind swirling all over the place. I scrambled and struggled in vain and once I was flung back into my room, I heard the lock turn and my desperation died, my body collapsing with exhaustion.

I pull myself up a few hours later and considered what has happened. I felt a void, knowing my father was gone, one not even the magick could fill.

Gently, I sat upon my small, squeaky bed and hugged myself. I let my eyes fall shut and fill my vision with my father—of the last time I saw him, of how he looked in his weathered clothing with his bright eyes and aged face. His proud smile, feeling the warmth of his pride like the sun. Emotion welled within me but I continued to recall the last letter he sent to me;

'I will see you soon, until then, stay strong, brave and bright like you always are. All my love, your father.'

That memory unleashed something inside me and I broke down, crying harder than I have ever cried. My magick flustered around me. With it, I reach out, trying to find my father's, which I'd felt all those years ago, when that letter was sent. I knew it was in vain and as my magick shook from the strain and tension of trying to find something that wasn't there, I beckoned it back, letting the loss wash over me like a wave of despair. As it returned, I let it sink back into me. My father was gone. And I would never see him again.

As I slowly faded into sleep, I saw one last glimpse of him waving on the descending ship on that stormy sea, knowing the gravity of that vision.

The next day, I was flung into another world of bewilderment. Merlough was pacing my room, having just requested to feed from my veins and then refusing it last minute in a panic. I stood, watching him, confused.

"I—I do not know if it is he. If it is he or birdie," he was muttering, his steps focused and certain.

"Is it Diafol? Would Diafol be here to do that? Tricking me again? Gods!" He growled, his pace speeding up gradually.

"Him and his blasted magick! I hate the stuff! So fucking tricksy," he spat, pacing still. He moved so fast I feared he would begin to mark the floor in his movements.

He thought I was my grandfather…?

"Hm but maybe that's it. Maybe that's why birdie is more rebellious, because birdie isn't birdie at all," he chuckled, wiping his forehead, his long hair knotted, tangled, and unkempt. I swallowed heavily, knowing better than to argue with him in this state. There was no argument to this insanity.

He stopped suddenly and rifled through his pockets, pulling out a crumpled letter which he thrust in my direction. I awkwardly scrambled to catch and read it.

"Tell me what this means. Surely, Diafol will know what Diafol wrote to me," he muttered as I read the words silently.

There, before me, was my grandfather's own majestic scrawl, commanding Merlough to reply. Asking him for a report on his grandson's wellbeing. If I did not worry too much on his motives, I felt almost touched by my grandfather's concern. I had no idea he was writing to Merlough all this time, and then perhaps, maybe my family had been too?

"I tried ignoring him and now look, he is punishing me with his tricky magick," Merlough hissed and began pacing once more. "It is *you,* Diafol, who is keeping me here in prison with this damned grandson of yours. This boy with song in his blood. My friends have died—DIED—trying to quench themselves from the songs." I bit my tongue, not wanting to turn loose this mad creature onto me. My grandfather's threats worsening his paranoia it seemed. His words confused me though.

His friends… were dead? Is that why they no longer visited here? It was a frightful thought for it was particularly difficult to kill a vampire. Merlough distracted me as he suddenly moved for the door.

"Well, he shall see. I will keep an eye on him. I will know if you are my birdie or not!" he barked and slammed the door, fumbling to lock it. I sighed as I tried to relax, feeling the imminent danger had passed. I was not fond of the madness returning in Merlough.

Though he seemed to drink less from me when he was like this. Somehow that seemed to make him worse, as if the lack of blood pulled Merlough further from reality, further into chaos and paranoia.

The next evening, Merlough did not come into my room. Yet part way through the night, I felt eyes on me. I moved carefully, internally trying to figure out the unfamiliar sensation of someone watching me. I was sitting at my window, my back to the door when I closed my eyes. I reached out with my magick, silently asking it to show me what I couldn't see.

Almost immediately, it shot to a space on the wall not far from the door. It poked and prodded, making me realise a fresh hole has been made there. I sent the magick through it and instantly sensed Merlough on the other side. He was crouched and deathly still as he watched me. I tried to not react to this knowledge and continued on as if I did not know he was there.

Seeing Merlough spy on me made me feel ill and the magick pointed down, highlighting his hands as he was scratching at his own wrists, which were bloody. Gods, what did this mean? Why was he watching me? What was he thinking?

He remained there for an achingly long time, and I started to wonder if I should say something to him. Suddenly his voice could be heard through the wall.

"What to do, Merlough? What to do… how do I know if it is birdie? Hm? Cannot drink, cannot drain him!" he muttered quietly, but enough for me to shudder.

"Gah! The songs, but the songs. The songs will stop then. Don't stop the songs," he whined, sounding in pain and I struggled to remain composed. I am still poised to listen for the door but relieved when moments later, he moved away, leaving me to my concerned thoughts.

A few worrisome evenings passed this way when one night, only a few hours into the fading winter daylight, the slam of a carriage door distracted me from my own thoughts. I looked out of the window to see a huge carriage, pointed and black with dim lights. It was lined with gold and I sensed him before I saw him step out of the carriage.

The Blood Prince! There he was in his red velvet glory as he stepped out. For the first time in an age, I felt my heart leap at the sign of hope. I felt Merlough watching me through his spy hole but I ignored it. I was more focused on the prince's stronger presence down below. Even the walls could not prevent the great magick and strength emanating from the great prince. Why in gods, was he here?

Now I was the spy, listening intently as I heard Merlough shuffle away, the insistent knocking at his door echoing loudly through the town house. Merlough hesitantly let his cousin in, the power shifting up to meet me as if seeking me out. It wasn't intrusive and I welcomed it. I felt it vibrate like a hiss as if discovering the door being locked to it. I pressed myself against the door, showing how badly I wanted to reach him, to show him I was here. I heard his silken voice question Merlough below.

"It seems your are ignoring your summons to court, cousin," he commented, his voice having a firm edge of warning to it. Gods, I had missed that voice!

Merlough scoffed. "Cousin! You come so suddenly and unannounced. It is only Doric who is stirring trouble, dear cousin. I have been busy with my estate," I heard Merlough's slimy reply.

"Hm. And why would your friend do that? Also, have you seen him recently? He has also has failed to appear at court lately…" he said, not falling for the lies spilling before him.

Doric was missing?

"Because, dear cousin, he is jealous and wishes to stir trouble for me. No doubt he has ran off," Merlough growled warningly. Unaffected, Alain moved aside his cousin and began to descend the stairs, making Merlough splutter and whine.

"I wish to see the faeling that is in your care," Alain replied, unconcerned as he continued upwards, making my heart pound and flutter within my ribcage as I felt our distance shortening.

"Alain! You are being rude! I cannot—" Merlough's gritty words were cut off.

"Do not *stop* me, cousin. This is by order of her Majesty herself." I could not see him but I felt the power behind his words, enough to make Merlough step back as Alain moved forward once more.

I flinched back from the door, waiting for him to ask for the key when he simply turned the knob. A spark of magick clicked and the door opened as if it was unlocked all along. I could not help but gasp as the door opened sooner than I'd anticipated and stumbled back.

For there he was in the flesh. His cold pale skin that warmed me like the light of the moon. His red eyes pinned me in place and a soft smile fell onto his lips.

"Dear faeling, do not be afraid," he murmured, holding out his graceful hand. My skin tingled at the idea of meeting his in anticipation and I took it. As he helped me up, I felt Merlough's grizzly presence behind.

"You see, he is fine," he growled, his red eyes alight with restrained jealousy that I feared would cost me later.

Ah but seeing the Blood Prince again, it was worth it! To feel his magick swirling around mine, not too unfamiliar to my kin. I clung to the feeling in those moments. I hoped with pleading desperation that he registered the danger I was in. Surely he could help me?

He was so tall and beautiful in his vampiric grace, words I never knew existed together before. For in this moment, I realised I did love him even though I was nothing to him.

The thought alone made my magick stutter and slump, which caused him to arch his graceful eyebrow. He turned to his cousin to say something but I no longer heard the words, feeling my energy ebb away as if I had used it all up in the simple interaction.

"Dear cousin, I take care of him well enough. As you can see, the boy is fine and perhaps in your delightful presence, I should offer a taste?" Merlough offered and his words pricked my eyes. Feed the prince? Would I be given such a luxury that the other faelings boasted about before? Do I have enough energy to not shame myself from such an honour?

"I am to politely decline, cousin, for I no longer uphold such tastes, under her Majesty's instruction," Alain replied, looking at me once more. Was that regret I saw in his eyes? Pity?
"Ah, stuck under her thumb, I see," snarled Merlough, taking offence at his cousin's rejection. Alain glared at him.

"This is our Queen you speak of, and I am following what others should follow, cousin. The fact you continue to ignore her instruction is what caused enough concern to draw me here in the first place. And now seeing the faeling in person before me, I have even more reason to be concerned," he commented, making me look up once more in alarm at his words. Our gazes met once more and I saw pity within the red depths.

"The faeling is sick, just as Doric reported to us, and his magick has somewhat dulled, which is a greater concern for this is a very hard task to do, even for you Merlough. The fact he is afraid of

you still does not put you in favour, cousin," he said, his voice sharp and icy cold.
"But I am feeding less now for such a reason, cousin. It is not my fault he is a gentler thing then what was first proposed to me. Plus, after your sudden entrance, no wonder the little thing is afraid, for you entered with such force it would make any faerie tremble," Merlough reasoned patronisingly. "Are you sure you do not want a taste, dear cousin? How long has it been since you sweetened your taste with faerie blood? Plus, you know how much this one was highly recommended at court." Merlough's sharp, shark-like grin was back as he saw his cousin consider me. I watched in silent awe as his red eyes began to glow then as if the idea was extremely tempting. His hunger widening his irises to blacken his eyes, I felt my own body respond, my heart pounding louder as if to tempt him, my flesh goose-pimpled in anticipation at succumbing to his sharp fangs. Our magicks gingerly touched once more and mine fluttered around his in a seductive dance.

Moments passed like this and Merlough patiently watched on until suddenly Alain closed it off, the magick dissipated as if it was never there. I flinched from the rejection as did Merlough.
"I am sure he is lovely, but I came here for business only," Alain responded, his voice distracted as he turned away.

I swallowed the rejection and shook myself. Was I that desperate that I was willing to give myself to another? I was suddenly terrified at my previous actions, even my magick betrayed my intentions to him. I blushed with shame as I sunk down in defeat. I tried to assure myself it was his duty, but could not help the hurt I took from being unable to tempt him. Which in turn shocked me further. What had I become? Is this what it was like to be a subsidium? To seek approval through offering oneself to the creature of the night?

Alain turned to leave when Merlough stopped him rather forcefully.

"Cousin, I do insist. It is terribly rude to deny one's offer at court, is it not?" Merlough hissed, eyes burning with anger now. I looked up despite my defeated state as I felt Alain's magick rise dangerously, causing my hair to prick on end, the air becoming static around us.

"Be warned, *cousin.* Do not lecture me on court manners when you have not yourself been there in an age. Let me pass before your bones regret it," Alain purred, his magick licking dangerously, invisible to Merlough. I watched, enthralled as Merlough struggled and trembled under the power and quickly relinquished his hold on his cousin.

I watched them leave, and the door shut once more and locked. The lock clinked loudly and I was hit with a wave of loss and regret. Why did I not say anything? Do something to convince the prince I needed saving? Had I done enough? What if I had blown it?

What could the prince do? For I knew nothing of the contract I was tied to.

Immediately, I felt dismayed at my own foolishness, distracted by my own spell on the Blood Prince.

I felt the prince linger down below as they continued to talk business and Alain firmly insisted that Merlough return to court as soon as possible. As the discussion continued, it began to heat up and soon turned into threats. Too soon for me to bear, Alain left quickly, in order to avoid further conflict and I ran to the window, eager to torture myself with the visual of him leaving.

I watched from the gloomy window, the darkness enveloping the carriage, the lights even dimmer than before. The coachman jolted as Alain appeared and let himself in before the coachman could move. Although as Alain opened the door, he hesitated. I watched him contemplate something and then he looked up, his red gaze clashing with mine powerfully in the darkness. I felt the hurt and regret sink away as I became lost in his gaze. We stared at one another silently.

Moments passed like this, my hand pressed to the glass, the grates outside the window obstructing my whole view.

Once again, I felt his magick drift up to meet mine. It was very careful, but with more power than before. As I gently allowed it to touch mine, his eyes hardened with a hidden sense of determination. I could not read his gaze, but I enjoyed the look as it felt more hopeful than anything else this night had entailed. I blushed as I became aware of how it must look to others to not be able to see the magick between us.

In that moment, I was glad no other magickal beings were around, as I allowed his magick further so that it almost caressed me. I knew not what this meant but I held onto it as my only glimmer of hope. I knew he will help me, he cared for me; I could feel it in the magick.

I have to survive this. I have to see him again.

Before I could savour more of this moment, he got into the carriage, shattering the connection. The horses were whipped and with supernatural speed, the carriage glided away, out of sight.

Truth?

With bitter prediction, Merlough's behaviour worsened after Alain's visit. Further ramblings to himself could be heard behind the foreboding locked door. More spying was done and like the hot air before the storm, I knew his entrance would mean further danger to me. The house was in the full depth of winter now, the windows frosted with sliced blades, clawing for entry.

I steeled myself as I heard the lock finally turn, the sound loud in the silent, gloomy house. He entered, growling and spluttering, pointing to me.
"Your grandfather is a cheat and a LIAR!" he started and soon I fell into argument with him, the glimmer of hope, fueling my boldness and bravery against the maddened, spluttering creature

before me. He paced like a beast and I stood firm, feeling hurt and attacked and tired of recoiling from his harsh words.

What was there to lose now? My father was gone and my family were far away. Alain would help me and until then, I had to survive.

I stood my ground and argued with him, defending myself. This only seemed to fuel Merlough further and soon he lurched towards me, trying to intimidate me with his height.

"Hmm I wonder, do you not know the story of your birth?" he hissed, his voice dangerously low and threatening. The question confused me and caught me off guard. What did he know that I did not?

"Do you not know of how your mother lost you? How she lost you before you were even born hmm?" He grinned evilly then and I was so confused I shook myself.

"That's impossible. You are lying," I whispered, my voice dry and hoarse.

"Hah! Lying am I? Are you sure you haven't mistaken me for that monster which you call *Grandfather*?" Merlough rumbled and I scoffed.

"Monster? *You're* the monster!" I cry, utterly upset and defeated, not caring for my own safety anymore.

"Bah! Me the monster? Ask that bastard of a grandfather, birdie, for you will see what it truly means to be a monster," Merlough grinned, enjoying this now. I trembled, at a loss for words, confused by why he was enjoying this.

"What he did, he did for us. He did this to help me achieve my dreams… If I am to be a subsidum in order to achieve it then so be it!" I barked, my entire being trembling with fear and pure hatred now. Merlough laughed so hard, his eyes began to run with small bloodied tears.

"I am not talking about that. You think you can become musically famous with *me*? No, no definitely not. I am talking about your dear mother and what happened all those years ago…" he trailed off, his voice quieting.

"I-I do not know what you…talking about," I stuttered, my teeth chattered, my mind swirling with confusion.

"No, no, you wouldn't, would you? She wouldn't admit such foolishness. Not to you, her dear little Élan. Her pride and bitter gift to the world," Merlough sneered and grinned, making me feel sick. For he must know the truth which I did not and this would mean the biggest betrayal I had yet endured.

"Enough!" I cried, suddenly afraid, not wanting to hear his words. I could not face the truth that threatened my entire existence.

"Did you know she was a slave hmm? I bet you didn't. Not many know this anymore." He sniggered and I flinched, clutching my throat without thought.

"Ah no but not a slave like you, no. A slave to her own father. Imagine this, having his own daughter be his slave. For years! He had her under that damned roof where you studied. For years, she had to serve him, trapped in that house, knowing nothing else in the world but what he taught her. Oh yes, many secrets he had and shared. Much sneaky magicks but nothing of the true world, the world of freedom. He used her talents to lure innocents to his door. It was well known and feared even as far as here in this land." he explained and I grimaced at it all.

Was this really true? Was this the life she knew before me?

"Innocents that he manipulated to obey of course. Ah yes, such sneakiness and cruelty," Merlough continued. He crouched low to meet my gaze and I knew something was to be revealed to me.

"And there was a day of course when she fell in love. Oh but not a sweet, fancy like in her youth type of love. But a real, true and defying love. She met your father and boom! She escaped!" Merlough gestured wildly at this for dramatic effect. I was bewildered at what this being shared before me, the story weaving a sinister twist to the one my father used to tell me all those years ago. How their great love was trapped under Diafol's cruel rule, and together they had conspired and defied him. I felt a foreboding then. How was this going to relate to me?

"She fled his house, slicing his magick with her own in such an unexpected move and most impressive for one so young. She took all she could carry, a few trinkets and of course, some of Diafol's precious gold." I recoiled then, the words lighting up my mind. I could not hide my shock and grimace.
"Ah yes, you see. You know the gold of which I speak! For all know this is not any ordinary gold, but the magick gold coins that spell trouble. Cursed some even say. It is said that they were

moulded using the remains of Diafol's own heart blood, distilled and frozen eternally. The last of his feelings transformed and withdrew from him, which is why he guards it so fiercely," he explained and I was too involved to stop him now, despite my reluctance and denial of this.

"No, it was most impressive that she stole this, perhaps naïve to the truth of it all." He smirked at me then, his expression wolfish and smug.

"Of course they were caught though, they made it as far as the forest behind his house. But like a ghoul of death, he swooped down, as an owl would hunt mice-lings. He had your father you see, in a deathly grip which aged him in seconds, draining his life force. Gods, what a sight that must have been!" Merlough panted excitedly, while I grimaced in horror. That was the truth behind my father's appearance? Oh gods' what a thought…

"No matter how loud your mother screamed and cried, her father, your grandfather, continued to drain him, leading him to his impending death." His words cut me, knowing how my father was now actually dead.

"Until the important words fell from her lips. That if he was spared she would give him *anything* he wanted," Merlough explained. "Anything?" he had sneered, those oily gears already working in his head. For what could she possibly give him that he had not already taken? Yes, she had breathed her magick and was already healing your father, though his hair never returned from white, the damage was too much even for her magick." I was still now unable to interrupt or deny the story unfolding before me. Things ringing too true to be a lie, no matter how ugly it felt.

"He thought and thought and oh! What a wonderful, hideous idea he had. Like a black venomous snake it slid through his mind. His mischievous mind spun a good one that day!" Merlough snorted and cackled at his own joke.

"His darkest contract he had drawn thus far. Can you guess what it was?" Merlough pouted as if mockingly in thought. He cackled nastily as he looked at me then.

"Their second faeling. That's all. Perhaps he knew the first would be a flop. Who knows? Once it was agreed, they were free to go immediately, on the condition that he would have their second child. That he would *own* them, soul and all. To own and to keep as was his right." Merlough explained it so matter-of-factly, which only exacerbated my nausea.

"Ah! But desperate and starved they were, the promise of freedom tingly on their dry lips. Your mother signed you over that very same day. Probably scoffing at herself that she would never conceive a second child and cheat him. There were work arounds and magick to avoid such a thing. Can you guess what day it was that they signed? Oh, it's a goodie!" He snorted excitedly. I swallowed but remained silent, knowing he wanted to tell me regardless of my will on the matter.

"The first day of spring! What a strange coincidence it happened to be the day of your very birth years later. Oh the fates are cruel! Perhaps you are a cursed family to harbour such a demon as your grandfather." He snickered and scratched his head. It was no wonder my mother struggled with me so much when I was born. It seemed like I knew somehow and was determined to stay within her forever. Merlough's voice broke through my thoughts.

"Now off they went on their merry way to their happily ever after. Their first son completed their family. Pah! Soon the fates would strike again and defy your mother's attempts at avoiding another child. When she heard that song, she knew, she knew what she feared had come to pass. And then so did Diafol."

"He must have watched her like a hawk, caring for the child as if it was his own. I dare say that is why you were born with such magick infused within your veins, magick to rival your mother herself," Merlough mused.

"Now, as you were born, the little screaming brat you were, must have charmed the old goat. As, for years, your parents were able to keep you under a false mirage of a normal life, away from the dark truth of your being, of who you really belonged to," Merlough explained, sitting back, observing my reaction. When I had none, he continued.

"So, to put it simply, your life is a lie, my little bag of blood." He grinned, trying to goad a reaction from me.

"Your very existence is a punishment for your mother's disgrace." He snickered, making my heart break further at the truth. This was why my mother never wanted me alone with my brother. Why she was so afraid for my safety growing up. The tension with my brother and my mother - how he blamed her specifically for what I thought to be my choice in leaving them. My magick tingled and simmered as I worried over this.

"And everyone around you knew it, your mother, father, Diafol and, I believe, even that brother whom he despises so much. So now here we are, both cursed from our parents' mistakes. We are not so different you and I." Merlough gestured, seeming to realise the horror he had shared with me.

"Apart from, I guess, you are much tastier than me." He chortled, leaning further into madness now his story was shared. It was the final cruelty that broke something within me, the reality washing over me in terrible grief and sadness.

"How do I know that what you say is true? How do *you* know?" I hissed. Merlough's red eyes slitted dangerously, sneering at my words.

"You're calling me a liar? Pah! I do not care if you believe me or not. For I tell the truth and what good would it do to make all of this up eh? I had heard your mother's part from stories at court, but it was the visit by your grandfather that affirmed the truth, why he could make this contract with me," he smirked.

My grandfather. Diafol. This was Diafol's fault. My poor parents were just trapped and tricked by him. Just like I was.

"Why?" I cried, unable to utter anything else.

"Why? Why didn't they tell you? Bah! Diafol implied it most often, I believe your father even threatened his marriage on it when our bond was sealed," Merlough explained and the thought of my father's efforts ripped another hole in my heart.

How he loved me! Even after everything I had meant to them, what I must have reminded them of from that fateful day.
I wanted to know the truth of my contract. What was it all for? What was my grandfather trying to gain? Intel on the vampire court? Gods only knew for even the contract may be false now. For what was I to believe in this mist of lies? Who could I trust now?

"I need to speak to her. My mother," I said, sounding stronger than I actually was. Merlough just scoffed and waved at me in dismissal.
"Whatever you have to say is long gone from her heart. She will have felt it a hundred times over looking at your little angelic face every day." He smirked in reply. Before I could argue, he continued. "Imagine what it was like for them, to have a little dark spot running around, taunting them, berating them of their mistake?" he asked and though I knew it was to taunt me, the truth was there.
My heart, though shattered already, began to break further at his words, seeing my childhood not as a farce but a desperate attempt to give me a happy life, to convince me and them that this was not to be. Had my mother held me longer than Rolo on those long, dark nights? Had my father told me more stories, despite his throat becoming raw and sore purely for my happiness and comfort? I now knew that my brother too had played with me long after he tired of my games, knowing that this was not to last.

All the efforts they had given to me, crashed into me at once. I couldn't breathe, I couldn't move, I couldn't feel.

I jolted from my thoughts as I felt a bruise begin to swell on my wrist from a fresh assault I was unaware of, my blood thudding angrily in me, brewing.

"You have the siren's spirit," they had said. I thought bitterly as I vaguely felt Merlough begin to swoon next to me from his fresh feed. The power in my song—what good has that done me? How can this be a gift?

Where was the fresh air of spring that I was meant to carry with me through these dark times, amid these dark creatures? This as all lies now; I saw them all before me. An empty hope, thrust desperately before me before I was snatched away from my childhood.

I could feel the darkness overwhelm me, dangerously swirling like a curious snake to my magick. I felt cheated and betrayed. I look down blankly at my own abused wrist. I had been condemned by my own family. And for what?

For a foolish mistake that happened years before my birth. Everyone who has ever loved me, has cast me away to this hellish land. This bitter slavery of the free and just. This was truly the Ghost River. The horror of the truth among my childish stories now sharing with me the bitter truth threaded within them. Did the faeries from my homeland know the truth of our terrible fate here? The brutal slavery their kin dealt with across the sea?

I needed to get out. I needed to survive this. Alain would come, and then I would face my family. I would repair this terrible truth. I would make it right and live my dream. I had to.

Merlough left me to my appalled thoughts not long after. I was numb and soon fell into bed, drifted into the veil of sleep and beyond...

I awoke within the first dream that I'd, had in awhile. I was in a dark, foreboding forest. The trees towered beyond sight, giant, bitter, and twisted. I was wandering aimlessly, not knowing my fate anymore. Even beyond the veil, my reality followed me into my loneliness and isolation. I was alone and only I treaded this path. A path unseen and unguided.

The space around me was full of mist and it was night time. Night time of the soul, I thought.

As I took in my surroundings, a low, slow song could be heard. It echoed, ghostly around me, but it was strangely comforting. For even if everyone had truly abandoned me, the music had not. Yes, I had felt betrayed as it lured and tamed the beasts of the night.

But could this not be harnessed for my own service? Was the siren's song truly a gift I had yet to fully embrace? Is that not what the beasts themselves feared? Is that why Merlough attempted to keep my energy low and lacking in hope?

Even as I thought these words, I felt my magick bloom like a rose in my chest and throat. The tiny thorns were curling and sharp but were secure and stable within me. The flower itself, bright as the moon above me, above the trees, only seeing the luminance that it presented past them.

Suddenly I thought of my father's face in my dream. His face full of sorrow and loss, the sea reflected in his eyes. A wide ocean of defeat and sacrifice. It emboldened me. We were all pawns in my grandfather's game. I no longer wanted a part of it.
The music thudded around me in either agreement or finality. I walked forward with the strength and determination I physically had not felt in a long time. Truly had I ever felt so determined in such a blind state?
The music followed me like a curious creature, watching through the trees. I listened but continued forward. I thought and thought, my mind winding and twisting at all I had learned before me. All the knowledge I held, all the truth I had to face.

"*Power is knowledge*," my grandfather had told me. How right he was in that respect.

I realised I had stopped and started forward again, but my heart slowed at the thought of those faelings I had met at court. How many were lost to us now? How many were no longer able to hear the music I had shared with them that Yule night?

At the corner of my eye, as if haunted, I saw what I thought were piles of bodies through the trees, the wind and fog making it difficult to see clearly and clarify if they were so. Everywhere was too dark and not enough light was present. I heard myself sigh.

How dare I whine of returning to my prior state, from most those never stir… I thought sadly of grieving heavily for the fae. My kin whom, like me, had been abandoned in a vain hope of protecting others. The selfish sacrifices of the fiendish and ignorant.

I felt my breath pant heavily at the weight of my kin. The brutal truth hard to deny.

*Fear is a choice you embrace, your only truth…*I thought next. I know not where this wisdom fed my soul but I was grateful, and the music continued to follow, as if fuelling and encouraging these thoughts. I no longer felt afraid. If my childhood had taught me naught of what I knew to be true, it was that I had my magick and my music.

Knowledge is power. Was my grandfather proud of my magickal ability? It was unlikely that was a lie.

I began to ponder his thoughts behind this—why throw his beloved prize to the wolves? Unless he knew…

I was ripped back from the veil as if the trail of thought itself was too dangerous for what it would reveal…

Defeat

Despite my dream being hopeful, I woke to a reality that I was truly challenged to face. I felt my body and its weight, almost too much to carry now. I knew I was closer to death than I ever had been. Merlough was insane, I knew this to be another truth I had to face. The bitter truth of my past being the last sane words to spill from his lips. As if the horrific truth itself was the last part to unravel his mind.

And close alongside this, I knew that if I were not to change, to continue walking that path in the dark forest of my mind, I would die here. I would perish in this darkness that I was cast away to. I did not want that.

Merlough's mutterings behind the door drew me out of my thoughts.

"Can't stop, can't…stop," he grunted, snarling to no one. I considered running from this place. Surely it would not be so hard to outsmart him by opening the door and making a run for it?

Ah, but like the beast he was, he would only give chase; the risk was too great. My knowledge I drew upon told me he would easily outrun me, even with magick.

My heart pounded, alerting me of the creak of the door as it opened slowly.

"Birdie, birdie, birdie," Merlough purred, grinning wolfishly at me. Carefully I stood to face him, my magick swirling, poised for my defence. My head ached, yet this just spurred my thoughts further into clarity as if straining to keep useless information back, allowing the important knowledge through. The knowledge that would surely save me.

With predatory grace that was truly a challenge for him, Merlough began to approach. If he sensed a change in me, he did not say. His smug expression was frozen on his pale, sweaty face. His hair a mangled mess as was the norm now. He had not changed his clothing in days either and it began to crease and hold a musty smell which must be the vampire equivalent of unhygienic bodily practices.

I steeled myself as he approached. Did I seem like frozen prey to his eyes? I hoped so as the magick was brewing inside me.

Could I kill him? Would I be able to? What if I failed?

Surely my life was at risk either way. I took in his red gaze, assessing me. Something was broken there. His mind and movements disconnected in a lurching manner. His fangs were out and sharp, my flesh crawling, resisting the feel of them again.

Enough was enough.

"Birdie, sweet birdie. Such songs sprung from you. They can't stop now, won't stop." He was mumbling, though I knew it was no longer to me.

Once again, my heart thudded as if wanting me to run, but I dared not look at the open door behind his approaching self. My magick crackled but he did not seem to notice. If I ran, he would catch me surely; if I stayed… I would perish. I could feel this truth now, for the hunger oozed from him like a sickness, springing my instincts to high alert. Never before had he felt this beast-like, yet so out of control with himself. I could see the hunger behind his eyes, cutting off his mind and any stable thought, leaving only space for primal needs now. He could not be reasoned with. He could not be spoken to, for there was no one left behind those eyes but a hungry beast.

"Stop, can't stop-ppp," he was now muttering, his voice low and threatening. My mind rushed, bidding my magick to do anything that it could now to protect me. I felt foolish and I flushed at the effort. I was like a child trying to command an ocean before me. Could I trust the power? I sought desperately in my head for I knew I was running out of time.

"*Help me, Gods. Help me,*" I prayed silently, feeling the magick respond to my hopes. I began to tremble, which only made Merlough growl appreciatively.

Abruptly, my magick seemed to react to that and I began to hear music. I frowned as I was not sure if it was in my head or not. I no longer cared as the beat, the slow swirling of it around my throat, tickled like it was trying to coax words from me. I hesitated only for a second. It was too late.

Merlough grabbed me, sinking his teeth at my throat, freezing the words there. I gasped at the shock and bitter disappointment in myself.

A tear fell as I felt my life being drained for the final time. I felt my heart fight furiously, my magick pound and rattle against my bones.

Without guidance, it watched, despairing as did I, as Merlough drank long, dangerous gulps. My vision began to blur and I began to see a golden glow behind Merlough. It was so bright in this darkness of my fate that I began to focus on it. Was it my entrance into Moria? The afterlife? Was I to see my father so soon?

The gold blurred into Diafol. *Diafol?* He was here? I shivered, my body feeling cold not only from the cold air around us but the heavy draining of my life's blood. I grimaced as I recalled winter being the weakest time for faerie magick.

I strained to focus on the blurred Diafol. I was too weak to truly tell what I saw. For surely, how could he be here so suddenly, after all this time? His face looked hauntingly blank as he seemed to watch the scene before him. His form seemed solid and more defined the further I focused on him, but my mind was panicked and confused. He was within a metre from my trapped self, as if to taunt me.

Was he truly here?
And if so, why was he not helping me?
Gods, help me!

I wanted to scream these words out to him, but my throat ached and was clutched deathly tight by the beast that held me. His drinking had slowed as if time itself had slowed. His movements blurred and sluggish. I blinked and I too seemed to be slowed in time.

Before I could ponder this too long, movement from Diafol caught my attention, and I focused hard on his form. He held up something and I blinked slowly again to refocus.

No, truly, it cannot be!

That damned gold coin glimmered between his fingers, his smile rotten, showing his sharp yellow teeth, the coin within reaching distance.

Gods, no! No! NO!

This could not be my only choice! To die and perish or to live trapped in servitude forever?! Was he truly the cruel master of fate? Was he truly so careless with the lives before him? Was that all I was to him? What of my magick? My music?
As I thought of my music, I heard it become louder in my ears as if in protest.
Diafol's eyebrow arched and the coin beckoned me closer, if I reached up behind the beast, I could take it.

Should I take it?
Would life over death really be so bad?

Truly, it seemed I needed it. For my magick still struggled. My mind rippled and wavered in confusion. The music louder and sounding more desperate, as if sensing the struggle. I felt Merlough's grip tighten on me, making my magick fluctuate for a moment. Diafol's expression suddenly changed with his own strain and frustration.

"Take it, dear one," he growled, his voice louder than anything else in my head.
"Take it and this shall all be gone. Save yourself, save your music!" he cooed and coaxed, the gold edging closer. I felt my own life force pulling then, the last parts of myself desperate to cling to this life.

I shall not die here!

I suddenly reached towards the gold and hesitated. Diafol's golden gaze bored into my own, willing me as much as I willed myself to live.

"This is your only choice, dear one," he said, yet my music convulsed in denial. I felt this wave so strongly, I hesitated further. I listened to the music once more and it begged me not to do it. I fumbled confusedly, not knowing what to do for I would surely die in moments. My vision clouded with darkness.

I reached forward further with renewed strength, the vision of my family and Brimhaven clear and delicately hopeful in my mind. I suddenly smelled the pine, the music almost encouraging this further. I saw past Diafol and saw myself; my younger self at my birthday party on my eighth year.

My family, and I, warm and safe. Innocent and protected from the dark fates of my parents' deal. I saw myself take the coin offered to me on that birthday and a further cycle of doom wheeled around in my head.

No, this was wrong.
I defeated this once before.

I embraced the image of Brimhaven around me, focusing hard on the coin, but not touching it. Diafol's face changed, sensing the shift within me, something wrong to him. His face turned into a sneer.

I ignored it and looked further, past him to my family once more. My family, frozen in time as they were when I was at the age of eight. My brother on the precipice of manhood, my father content and happy, my mother distant but wistfully so, seeing the darkness in the distance, but enjoying how far away it was in that time.

My heart stuttered, alerting me to my life draining further. I had wasted too much time! I growled, which came out as a broken, croaked groan from my throat.

Fight! my body begged.
Fight! my magick implored me.
Fight! my heart yearned, the weakest of all.

My hope began to spiral as my magick became a fuelling force within me, beckoning my weak soul away from death. I saw Diafol register this with piqued interest.

I looked to the gold coin and it beckoned me to it, taunted me with the promise of the life I once had. Of the life I wanted once again, the life that was taken from me. I only need to take it back!

But at what price?

My father was gone. I looked to the scene behind Diafol and saw it waver. My father was no more. There was no getting him back. Nothing would be the same.

Unexpectedly, a new feeling began brewing within me. One that accompanied my magick and the music, rising to the surface of my focus once more. Something new and dark altogether.

Something different from within, but familiar as the dark forest I walked in my dream.

A call came from my throat, a call that came not from the heart but from the very fibre of my soul. I felt it rattle and shift the vision before me, threatening to break through Merlough's skull, through the vision of Diafol and the vision of my family beyond.

The pressure and tension was great and threatening, but I encouraged it further. It rose with my hope and I lost the feeling of Merlough altogether. He was still there, but no longer took from me. He was frozen in time itself and I focused beyond. Diafol was a greater threat to me now. He watched me, a cruel smile on his cracked lips.

My magick burst through my fingers, reaching for the coin. But instead of taking it from Diafol, I watched as it started to misshape and fizz. Even Diafol seemed frozen now as I watched with fascination, feeling the magick tease and tangle the coin, pulling it, yet trapping it within Diafol's grasp.

Instantly, it glared bright green, almost blinding me further than when it was gold. I could not register this meaning, too distracted as I registered the shock on Diafol's face. I weakened at the burst of energy and was swallowed into darkness.

Was that pride I saw in his face?

Queen Carmilla prowled her hallways in the court, followed by the myriad of vampires, admiring her. The walls gleamed as Yule was upon them once more, everyone radiating the celebratory mood.

She barely took in the beauty around her anymore but she felt a crackle along the walls, making her perfect red eyebrows arch. She turned and Alain was already at her side, feeling it too. They looked at each other silently, avoiding raising the alarm, cautiously waiting to see what happened. When things quieted, they continued wearily, eyes searching.

The wind rushed by them and went out of her vampiric lungs, trying to steal breath that was not there. But her song, were she singing her song, would be gone and something was terribly wrong.

A *blast* of metaphoric pressure was felt through the kingdom then. It was enough for even the courtiers to feel it and they all turned to her.

"The faeling," was all she said and Alain was away. Guards flocked to him as he rode to the townhouses, armed with a warrant for Merlough. Guilt tore at him, ripped at him. He should have dealt with his cousin sooner! He should have followed his gut the moment Doric was reported missing.

If the faeling had perished, what would this mean? How could they have done nothing? How many others had fallen under his aunt's jurisdiction?

When they arrived at the bleak, dark house on the street, Alain shuddered. No light came from the house and he feared it too late. At supernatural speed, they burst into the house, finding a dead servant, the poor soul ravaged days ago. Vampires recoiled and lurched at the horror for killing their own kin was a horror within itself.

They soon found the culprit in the corner of the room.

Merlough feeding from his own wrists, making them blanch in disgust. For this was a true sign of madness for a vampire. Feeding from one's own wrists led to madness beyond repairs and they watched with horror. Merlough's eyes glazed and gone, his wrists worn and bloody, chunks of flesh hung loosely around his stained sleeves. His skin a dim, pale pallor of sickness, the slow agonising decay of his mind clear to those who witnessed him.

With bitter distaste, Alain bid those with him to arrest the maddened creature for insanity. His cousin was no more.

"My Prince, in here!" called a vampire from the broken bedchamber. Alain steeled himself and struggled to prepare for the scene before him.
The vampire pointed within the room, pale and with a haunted look on his face.
Alain was astonished by what he saw. For the faeling, Élan, lay in the small, shallow bed. Asleep and pale with weakness but alive.

Gods, how was he alive?

He was tucked in comfortingly as if someone had put him there. The sight was so unexpected and peculiar. Alain realised the other vampires were fearful of approaching the bed. Élan, though he looked pale and weak, his face was serene and gentle as if in recovery.

What in gods had happened here?

Unbidden to his vampire company, Alain sniffed as he felt a small remnant of magick. It tingled on his tongue, hairs raised on his neck.

Something magickal had taken place here…

But from whom?

From what he had felt coming from Élan, the great echos of magick that resided there…He knew the boy was talented but this felt as fresh as after a storm of magickal wonder.

Was this that blasted Diafol's doing?

Alain could not think of the consequences now. Nor could he blame Diafol if that were so, for he was relieved Élan was alive. He dare not consider what would it might entail if the results were reversed.

Did this mean that Diafol was after him and the Queen, for endangering his grandson?
Was his court in danger?
But then how did this tie in with the subsidium contract?

He pondered these questions worriedly as he watched the vampires remove his cousin and then Élan with fascinated concern.

Alain was certain he would not forget this night.

New Purpose

I woke up to an unfamiliar place. The scent reminded me of home, of Brimhaven, but I knew it was not so. A light blinded me. A light I recalled knowing so long ago—the sun. It was bright, making the air crisp and fresh.

The first promise of spring. Wasn't it winter? How long had I been asleep?

The sun was streaming through the unfamiliar windows and I could smell freshly baked bread. I continued to lie there, my memory blurred but I enjoyed the absence of dread or fear for what felt like an age. My body felt achey and worn.

What had happened? How did I get here?

Like a looming dark cloud in my memory, I struggled to remember something important. Something that led me to this place. A gasp distracted me and I saw my mother rush to my bedside.

"Gods, Élan!" she cried, hugging me tightly as I struggled to register her.

Was this a dream?

If that was so, why could I feel her magick, like a sudden stream of freshness rushing to reach me? The smell of lavender so strongly emanating from her? She sparkled almost too brightly before me, and I felt my eyes water. Despite my confusion, her presence washed calm relief over me. I felt safe for the first time in an age.

"It's alright, my darling, I am here now," I heard as I continued to struggle to remember what had happened.
"Mother?" my voice sounded broken and almost unrecognisable.
"Yes, yes, it is me, beloved. I am here now. Finally…" she sighed happily, oblivious to my confusion.
"You are here…now? Why?" I croaked. She sobered and straightened, taking my hand in hers, which felt so warm against my balmy skin.

"I was called to you; I felt your magick sweet. Diafol could not deny my need to comfort you. Gods, Élan! It was a blast I felt from miles away! Truly a wonder to those that are connected to you," she gushed.

Her words spurred my mind to rewind and suddenly I remembered the sight of me reaching for the coin once more.

It triggered everything that had led to that moment and I was overwhelmed with the sudden flood of information. I gasped, making my mother flurry to calm me once more, registering the realisation within me. Everything rushed and flowed through me once again as if I was reliving it at super speed. I was stunned and utterly confused when the memory cut off after seeing the green glow from my grandfather's coin.

"W-what…?" I struggled to make sense of what had happened in that moment. Azalea (whom I recalled had abandoned me) continued to hush me and I grew frustrated as my body grew tired from the rush.

"Enough now, you are safe, that is all that matters," Azalea murmured, stroking my hand calmly. But was that true?

"Truly?"

"Truly."

"What of Merlough?" I croaked, making my mother hiss in distaste.

"Do not speak that name, not ever again!" she growled, her eyes alight with warning. My mind swirled with confusion.

"Then..?"

"He is not your concern now. Things are being decided as we speak," she assured me firmly, patting my hand. I grew frustrated as my confusion continued to overwhelm me.

"But what happened to him, Mother?! What happened to me?!" I strained, my voice cracking with exertion. She sighed with great reluctance, her thin body bowing with sudden exhaustion.

"I know little of what happened. They would only tell me that you are lucky to be alive, my beloved son. When they found you, they expected you to be dead. Yet you were tucked away safe and sound as if the gods themselves bid you to sleep," she explained carefully.

"...and that…that beast! He was found and arrested, they are deciding his fate now for he is truly mad and kept you under illegal pretences with a contract no longer permitted by the court. The Queen herself is outraged and it is causing a great controversy. Dracula's court is even teasing to intervene if they do not reach a satisfactory conclusion soon."

"...so he is not dead?" I asked quietly.

"Not yet," my mother warned.

"You believe he will be put to death?!" I ask, startled. Mother scoffed in response.

"Of course he will be! Darling, he almost murdered you!" She gasped at me incredulously. I dared not tell her what else I saw at court. I realised then that was part of the issue that the Queen now had with my experience. I was a witness to such things. I had seen first hand the inner workings of the court and how faelings had been treated. How the lines had been blurred and stretched for the sake of societal status.

I looked around and noticed we were at an inn. Randomly, I wondered where Doric was. Would I ever see him again now? Had they found him?

"But it matters not now; you are no longer his," Azalea stated, matter of factly. I jolted in surprise at this new information, but then why would that be such a surprise? Merlough was gone. He was to be imprisoned or killed for his crimes.

Did this mean I was then… free?

I dared not venture that ideal. But what was I to do now? I asked my mother that very question. She laughed at my question, her voice tinkling with light and warmth.
"Why, my faeling, you will come home! Come home and be with us." She hugged me happily and I shuddered.

I was a faerie now, yet I did not correct her. I felt that after all she had missed, all that we had both missed—including my coming of age celebrations—I wanted to give her this small mercy. I felt she was not truly at fault here. We all played a part in Diafol's devilish game.

"Mother, I know I do not belong to you," I muttered and she lurched back as if bitten.
"I am his still, aren't I? I am Diafol's now." Azalea's mouth twisted and trembled shocked that I knew of this.
"You knew…?"

"Merlough told me," I stated and she sneered, looking away, blinking back tears. I felt her magick start to withdraw from me.
"Of course he did. And now you must hate me," she spits looking away, guarded and armed for my rejection. I searched within me then, trying to find the anger and hurt I should have felt.

But I found none. I looked at her with understanding and compassion. No more would I be a part of this entanglement with darkness and hatred. I had been through too much to harbour such pain and hate in my heart. She had made a choice, desperate to save her love, my father. I felt a glimmer of magick flare within me as if in assurance.

"I do not hate you, Mother," I said carefully but she snorted disbelievingly. I reached for her but she pulled away, pouting.
"Mother it was a mistake. What you did, what you and father agreed to...never make a deal with Diafol; isn't that what you taught me? I never have. I have never taken his gold coin."

For moments she didn't respond, but then the words sank in and she looked at me with surprised shock.
"Truly?" she breathed. I nodded and she hugged me then, her magick reaching for me with the same desperation, swirling around us, her body trembling.

"Gods, Élan. I was so afraid of what you would think…if you ever found out." She pulled back, tears clear and certain, falling on her face. She smiled, pride shining through as she stroked my dark bed ruffled hair lovingly, her view of me renewed. She laughed, relieved and overjoyed.

"You carry your father's wisdom. That is for certain," she said happily, though her voice shook with grief.

I smiled back at her, feeling a well of relief. I had her again, my beloved mother. No longer could she run from me in shame. It refreshed my strength and she arched a brow at my straightening and renewed strength in my posture.

"Mother, I will break this," I stated firmly.

"Break what?"

"His hold on us," I confirmed taking her hands into mine, showing her my seriousness. She trembled then, her flesh goose-pimpling as if the very thought of her father frightened her.

I leaned forward, my heart light and my magick dancing towards her, embracing her. She flushed as I felt her respond to it, her gaze widening in shock. For that moment, I knew she believed me.

We spoke together for a long time, my mother brokenly sharing with me about my father's death, how hard it hurt my brother and how he remained shut off from her now. He blamed her entirely and lost himself in the land, burying himself into his work. Only Mary it seemed, could bring him out of it, to eat and replenish.

My heart ached to see my brother. I now knew he had fought for me the hardest. Despite all our differences, I missed him the most. He was a true child of Brimhaven and I longed to be reunited with him once more. To reconnect to that part of myself again.

I knew now that I was no longer as whole as he. This new dark yet comforting feeling I first felt in that green light, I knew was my being, my magick coming into its own. I still did not know what it meant but I knew even in the darkest hour of my soul, I had managed to defeat Diafol. I had defeated him when my mother could not.

That truth alone, I protected closely to my heart.

I slept some hours later and my mother is there once again. This time I ask for my brother, but she shakes her head sadly.
"It is heavily guarded, sweet. I am the only one allowed to visit you. Queen Carmilla wants no further trickery or intervention until she has called her judgement on what is to be done, until your contract is fully reviewed and redacted," she explained uncomfortably. I nod understandably and rest back in the large bed.

"It is no matter Mother, I trust the queen."
"You do?" she asked surprised, making me blush as I suddenly realised it was Alain I thought of then. Had he heard of my state, of what had happened? Who had found me in Merlough's house? I sighed wearily.

"Indeed, she will see to this. She showed a clear distaste for my situation," I explained but mother chewed her lip worriedly, her mind elsewhere.
"Have you seen him?" I asked quietly and she knew of whom I spoke. She grimaced in distaste.
"I have not and do not wish to. I sense him always, yet he is far from us now and I wish for him to remain there."

She crossed her arms as another chill spread through her. It was in this moment I realised I did not feel the same chill, the same fear I once felt for him. Even though he remained a mystery, I no longer worried about facing him. I thought then that when I next saw him, things would be different.

I woke up and my mother was gone. The light was still bright outside from the promising sun but I felt a chilling edge to it. I turned and saw Diafol in the shadows, grinning, the source of my chilled edge.

"Hello, dear one."

I did not reply but sat up, more alert, startled that our time was to come so soon. My hair was surely ruffled as were my bedclothes. He read the surprise on my face.

"Ah! But you called for me, did you not? I heard it like a pretty little sing-song of a birdie," he said playfully, his use of the word made me shudder and he smirked at my reaction.

He strode forward into the light, it catching him, making it dance across his scaled skin. It glittered gold and sparkled like the magickal being he was. Sandalwood wafted to me and I noticed he was dressed in a fresher suit than ones I had seen him in before. His buttons shined and glistened like his eyes, the fabric newly cut.

Suddenly, the light brightened to the point of blindness and I squinted, struggling to see past my nose. The light burned my eyes and I blinked back tears.

In a flash, we were standing in a forest, though the air did not chill me. I did not feel fully present, my body no longer heavy and tired. I ignored the confusion swirling around me at the change in scenery, weary of his games now. I looked at him, still standing before me, grinning.

"You seemed well-dressed for such an occasion," I commented dryly and he cackled loudly.

"Indeed, dear one. Indeed! And why not, eh? For this is a joyous day!" he exclaimed, arms open and out. I remained still, quietly observing.

"Ah, but you are still recovering, yes? Still recovering. For this has been a long journey you have had, a long story…" he muttered. I decided to take his bait.

"Story?"
"Indeed! Story, yes!" He giggled, skipping happily. He sobered when I didn't react and shook his finger at me. "For this was a story of greed, my boy. Yes, greed! Ugly and stupid greed. The greed of beasts and fanged creatures. Ah for when they are presented with something they desire, they take it! Take and take again!" he explained, almost growling with anger. He seemed to shake himself and grin at me once more.

He moved closer and I stared, intrigued, my mind spinning with his words.
"For their gold coin my boy, ah *their* gold coin was your blood." He sighed, sounding almost sad, his buttons seeming to glisten at his words.
"Bah! And look what happened with greed eh? It isolates and destroys! Which is what your blood did eh? It isolated and it destroyed," he purred, grinning evilly. I frowned at him. Was he blaming me for what happened?

"Ah ah, but more to the point, it was your magick. Your magick was what wound the song into your blood, making the species go crazy for it. Turned even the most refined beast into a drooling dog." He giggled at that and I grimaced, as I had seen the truth in this firsthand.

"Ah! But what happens when they mess with it, hm? What happens when greed tries to take and take and the magick no longer wants to play, hm?" He tilted his head to me.

"Haha! Creatures like them are so silly, they do not look past what is before their own face, for they do not understand. They do NOT understand! Hehe, they never will," he said and I felt as though I would not either. I swallowed heavily, ignoring the similarity between my grandfather and Merlough in that moment.

Were we being driven by some being crazier than Merlough?

"Ahh and your blood...your sweet magick blood is the coin but your gift, my boy, your gift is the music." His smile softened and he stepped closer. I resisted the urge to take a step back.

"Like a siren's song, the magick in your blood either lures them into power or disaster. Only the carrier can decide. Only the magick can beget its true heart. Bah! And evil begets evil!" he shouted, shaking with anger, turning away in disgust.

Was that regret I read on his face? Again, he corrected himself and turned to me, approaching closer.

"Get it, dear one?" he asks and suddenly, I let the words sink in. He is telling me I can control my magick. To feed or destroy. That was the siren's song. To control and guide. My head was swimming in its own words and confusion, as he watched, grinning at me, taunting me.

"I think so; I think I am. Though I do not agree with the way in which you went about this," I said firmly, my hands trembling. He cackled again, stamping his foot this time.

"Ah! My dear boy but this was the hardest of your lessons, the most important... But look what is before you now! Even the princey is working to abolish slavery of the fae in all vampire territories."
I gasped at the mention of Alain.

Could it be true? Had I started this?

"You see, dear one, I know what is in you... Bah! But the power and such knowledge! And the music... Gods! I have not seen this in many, many years..." He shook his head and turned away, pinching his chin in thought.

"For you see... magick is a funny, wormy thing. Especially yours, suppressed under my own doing, I was unable to see potential... but add pressure... and let it build and build and build... Eeee, then POOF! It bursts through like a giant volcano, angry and vengeful!"

He fell silent and I watched him, grimacing at his reasoning for it all. This was no reasoning at all. This was all for my benefit? I could not believe it was so. I sneered at him then.
"Angry and vengeful, yes... even I felt it then..." I heard him mutter, having turned from me once more, I caught the regret felt in his words and the meaning behind them.

"You were there then," I confirmed, referring to my last memory of us together, me trapped in the arms of a beast.

He remained still for a long time, neither confirming nor denying what I had said. I sighed, feeling worn from his presence suddenly.

"Then if that were so, Grandfather, you are not to take credit for what happened. I chose to defy you once again," I stated firmly, watching as he turned back to me, pouting.

"I chose to defy you. I chose to save myself. I did not take your gold; I created my own," I explained, the memory still blurred but the green light clear and vibrant behind my eyes.

I felt it now within, thudding and powering my heart and soul. My music was my own, my magick like he said, I could use and I refused to let him take credit for that.

"Even in the face of death, I shall not deal with you," I gritted out, my eyes burning dangerously, my previous promise to my mother burning in my chest.

He faced me fully then, his eyes aglow. He stared at me, his face blank. "Mmm...indeed you did not. Even with a promise to return to where you once were… it did not pull you from your destiny… And now we are here, dear boy… I cannot help but be... fascinated by your fate."

Did he just admit he had no control of me now?

As this new hope grew, he giggled, cutting off my thoughts.

"Ah but you are still mine! Yes you are still mine dear one, until you are eighteen years, for that is what was agreed long ago. Those fanged beasts can try, oh they will try! But they cannot take you from me. No one can…" His words dropped like a stone in my stomach.

Why until I was eighteen? What did that signify?

"For now," I said boldly and he recoiled in shock. I resisted the urge to smirk back at the slippery fellow, feeling proud, knowing I had surprised him again.
"Why, who is this boy?! Who is this before me eh? Gah! Even now the magick flutters within in you… Gods… What chaos we can create together…" he purred, seeming pleased with my reaction.

I was weary of his words; I knew the truth. I was certain he would have made a contract so binding even after Merlough's, I would still be his. It would be unbreakable until I was in my eighteenth year; I had two years to go.

And so, until then, I would wait.

Carmilla's Verdict

A few days blurred passed in restful sleep and gentle stories from my mother, when guards arrived causing us to stir. They confirmed that I was recalled back to court. My mother was quiet as she helped me dress, my own feelings mixed and swirling. So much had happened and I no longer knew where I stood in the world.

She handed me a suit of dark green velvet that resembled the one I wore for my eighth birthday. No doubt this was also made by her. This one held a certain finesse to it with small sparkles that caught the light as I moved, yet it still retained that earthy freshness of my homeland, the vibrancy and fresh smell of those near me. I was relieved to find this felt less stiff than I expected, and I breathed easier as I made my way to court alone.

As I travelled in the sleek car, I took in the sight of the court before me once more. The spires pointing up into the grey sky, its looming presence I recalled with bitter familiarity. Were there any faelings in there now? I doubted it, yet I wondered what had become of Alain's quest to abolish slavery of the fae? Was I allowed to ask this or know?

At the simple mention of him in my mind, the image of Alain bloomed there, beckoning, making my heart flutter. Gods, I could not deny how I felt for him.

Despite his kin and what they had done to my kind, and furthermore, his relations to my old master, I knew there was something there. Something to discover and pursue. At least this is what my heart encouraged. I could not deny that his magick knew mine, that there was some connection completely unexpected and unknown in great detail.

As I was escorted past the large double doors of rich oak, heavy and towering above us into the dark ceiling, I took in how different the place looked. I had not been here in over a year and yet the place seemed emptier, quieter, more recluse and withdrawn. It no longer held hundreds of vibrant tall beings with their rich clothing and eccentric accessories.

Now the space felt more secretive, but I appreciated the sconces that brightly shone for me along the walls with intricate golden patterns. Our steps echoed as we walked the long halls, demonstrating how truly alone we were. Had I ever seen it this way before? Was this the norm?

My guides suddenly veered off into a side door and my heart thudded in surprise.
They stood waiting for me patiently to enter and when I hesitated one spoke; "You are to have a private audience with her Majesty," he explained in a soft patient manner which calmed me. I smiled gratefully and carefully entered.

The room before me resembled a grand library, a study of sorts. The floor was made of dark wood, lined with elaborate rugs and furs of great beasts from far north, way beyond the Faelands. The walls were lined with countless books, the walls a dark purple where bare. Portraits of vampires unknown to me hung dotted around the room; all seemed to be watching me as I approached.

In front of me, a grand carved marble mantelpiece with a fireplace that crackled and purred at me. I was almost halfway into the room and could already feel the warmth from the fire, I could not discern whether my heartbeats or footstep were louder in that moment.

The Queen herself sat on a velvet chair that did not look particularly comfortable but she remained perched on it as if it were a throne. As always, she stood out remarkably, her pale skin resembling marble, contrasting with the bright red of her gown.

As I got closer, I observed small rubies dotted on the fabric of her skirts like drops of blood. Her crown stood tall and sharp upon her head as if resembling the courts spired structure itself.

Despite my nerves, I could not deny her ageless beauty, her face frozen and blank as I took her in. Her lips as red as her dress and hair, her eyes glowing with a sinister power that was both bewitching and frightening to witness. A deep hum of magick radiated from her that made my own shudder and retreat. It was then that the doubts started to creep in. Did she blame me for what happened to Merlough?

I halt a metre away from her, feeling her magick reaching out to me tentatively as if trying to sense a threat. I remained calm as I allowed her to do this, enjoying the fire's warmth from behind her. I felt it flush my cheeks and suddenly, a smile cracked onto her face, which brightened her.

"I am curious, what do you believe should happen to Merlough?" she asked, her voice light, yet it cut through the silence around us. The mention of his name made me tremble. She watched me as I hesitated.

"'Truly?" I asked softly and she scoffed.
"Ah you see?! Too hesitant!" she growled, slapping the arm of her chair in frustration, the sound shaking me. She cooled as she saw the alarm on my face, hearing my heart pound in fear.
"That's your problem young one. With powers like yours, you should rely on those instincts! No doubt it is what has kept you alive thus far…" She trailed off, her voice softening. I remained silent, stunned by her words.

"My dear, do you know what you have done? You have reduced my nephew to a blubbering blood-hound. There is none of my family left in him now," she stated and I grimaced at her words.

Gods, she does blame me!

"Your Majesty, I-I'm sor—" I stuttered.
"Which is why he is to die," she cut in, gesturing flippantly. I gasped in shock and she seemed pleased with my reaction.

Does she jest? Will she simply kill her nephew like that? What will become of me? My blush deepened at my selfish thought. Her chair creaked as she leaned forward, her red gaze boring into mine.

"My boy, he has been driven mad. I have seen it far too often. He is lost to us and it is the merciful thing to do at this stage. He no longer resembles the vampire he once was," she commented, again, her voice firm and matter of fact. I fell to my knees, the truth overwhelming me.

Oh gods, I had done this! I tried to apologise again and she laughed in surprise. She took me in, as if speculating something.

"I'm surprised. You actually feel guilty, don't you? After what he did to you? I assure you, no details were spared when Alain recounted what he knew of your torture to me. Of the abuse you have endured." She laughed again. "Though, my darling Alain seems quite taken with you." She chuckled, looking younger for a moment. I bowed my head in shame.

"Your Majesty, I-I didn't mean to do it. The music… I had no control, you must believe me! I had no idea it would affect him as such!" I burst suddenly, desperate for my defence. She arched a slim red brow in interest.
"Oh?"
I nodded, ashamed, trembling some more. She sighed and leaned back into her chair.

"There is no doubt you are gifted. But young, yes, so young…" She trailed off, looking away distantly as if remembering something, seeing something that wasn't there. Her was voice soft and wistful, a rare smile on her lips. I remained silent, unwillingly to disturb her reverie.

"You see, this court is no place for a child. Especially a faeling. I have seen too often the issues brewing within my court and done nothing. It is a regret of mine. No, children, which are rare and precious to us vampires; that makes us less of beasts and more creatures. I myself can never have children, which pains me everyday." Her voice was soft and sad. She seemed to come to a decision within her thoughts and stand smoothly.
"Come Élan," she commanded and I obeyed swiftly, startled by her change in mood. She began to approach me and I remained still, bidding my heart to calm down.

As she moved closer, I smelt fresh lilies around me, her eyes even more luminous up close and I noticed the irises widen as if taking in my own scent with interest.

"When I saw you that day, hearing your song, I heard your mother's pain. The loss that I have felt myself. A pain that I no longer wished to be reminded of, a wound you reached within that I had buried long ago. It threw me, the power." She raised her hand slowly as if to cup my cheek, but halting mere centimetres from my flesh, feeling the coolness of her hand cooling mine.

"You, child, have a gift. You made me feel again, I felt something else rather than hunger or pleasure. Something real and important. And I am starting to see something in my beloved Alain." I swallowed in surprise at her words and she smiled at my response to her mentioning the Blood Prince.

"Ah yes, I see the connection between you two. It is young and innocent as you are...for now," she explained and before I could respond, she moved away from me.

"But he is to be warned. After all, he has seen firsthand the… dangers when dabbling with your kind." She turned, her face twisted in distaste. I grimaced then, my guilt returning.

Despite the horrors I had endured, I truly had not intended any harm to befall Merlough. I was just trying to survive! To escape and live my dream.

"Which is why you are free to go. I assume you are eager to return to the faerie fields of your land, and I shall not stop you. You have been gone too long." She called behind her as she returned to her chair, once again sitting upon it with majestic grace.

"Now, please leave, but before you do, know this," she added, raising a sharp, pointed finger. "You have a friend and ally here at court. Should you need it. You are gifted and I do not observe this lightly. You are a force to be reckoned with even compared to that blasted grandfather of yours. No, he may not show it, but he is indeed afraid. And he should be! He has control over you, but it is limited." I silently listened, shocked by her words.

To be allies with vampires?

"What you did back there was something very few have done. You defeated him and he shall not forget it. You were able to save yourself when he thought it was not possible. He wanted to trap you further but you managed to cross him in that regard. Which is why I believe us to be worthy allies, you are welcome here - upon invitation of course," she grimaced at the last words.

I dared not ask her how she knew about what had happened between me and Diafol that day.

"As far as the fae are concerned, I am determined to make up for the irreplaceable damage my species has done to yours, dear one. You have caused a movement and now you must follow it," she explained and I felt my breath catch.

I could not believe the turn of events, but the power of her words strengthened my resolve. She was right.

"And in terms of your music, I can help you there also. In fact, I insist upon it. As you know, I share a great love for music and have many talents under my wing. You are free to use them at your leisure, even outside of this court. I wish for you to join forces and use your music with ours to change the world." Again, I was stunned into silence.

I recalled seeing a few of those she was referring to and felt overwhelmed at the idea of creating music with them. This only reinforced her words earlier on wishing to join forces, knowing she was willing for me to use her musical talents at my will was… astounding. And interesting. Such music we could accomplish!

I stuttered a shy thank you, lost for words on what else to say apart from that I would do my best. She smiled at this and nodded, her fangs gleaming in the firelight.

"I know you will. Now please leave. I do not wish to see you for some time."

I retreated outside the room, feeling strangely elated. Such events have fallen that I never imagined from Carmilla's judgments. Was she really taking my allegiance seriously? It was unheard of. I grimaced at how pleased Diafol would be by this news, and how difficult it would be to ensure he did not manipulate this to his own games again.

I sighed but smiled as I remembered the vampire pianist I had seen at Yule during my first year in this land. I would certainly enlist him first.

Ah, such possibilities we could accomplish together! He was world renowned for being such a talent. Vampire and faerie music together? No one had heard of such a thing, yet already, I heard the songs in my heart begin to emerge.

This felt right, it felt meant to be. This was my calling now and we would share it with the world. Songs of dark faerie stories from the north mixed with the melodic, wistful beats of the vampire music. Finally, my dream would be a reality.

Recovery

I was entirely consumed by my thoughts as I was rejoined by my guards. I was surprised when I realised Alain was calling my name. My heart jump-kicked me into reality and I blushed up at him in surprise as he caught up with us. He looked flustered but graceful as ever, his velvet coat matching his aunt's, a vibrant red in the dull hallway.

"I am so glad I managed to catch you! I wanted to ask if I could possibly have an audience with you before you leave for the Faelands?" he asked imploringly.

"Oh? Yes, of course," I replied, still shocked and confused by what had just happened. First there was Carmilla's surprising speech and now seeing Alain again? Gods, it was too much! Alain gasped with relief and kissed my hand swiftly in thanks, making me blush as crimson as his coat.

"Excellent! It won't take long, I promise. I ought to speak with you before you are away with the fae once more." He almost sounded sad at that truth.

"Will you meet me at my townhouse within the hour? The guards will know where to take you." Alain was already turning distractedly as someone called to him. I agreed and he smiled as he turned to receive the vampire that called to him.

I anxiously followed the guards once more, noticing the change in direction as we led a quicker route to the exit. They remained quiet, leaving me to my swirling thoughts. I was excited to see his house, though I was once again mystified by his need to see me. What could he so desperately share with me?

It seemed urgent and yet it quickened my being having not seen him since my recovery. His beauty was radiant as ever and I was suddenly relieved I was able to share this time with him before I left this place. Who knew when I would return…

As we arrived, I noticed the house sat on a similar street to one I had been to before. It didn't look much different apart from the brickwork certainly looked fresher and cleaner, the outside having a more manicured appearance that was regularly tended to. The guards led me to the door and I was handed over to the house servants who already knew to receive me.

As I entered, I took in the house around me, noticing the familiarity in decoration, not too dissimilar from the court itself, more simplified and narrowed down. As with the outside, I could tell the interior was well looked after too; no passing of time or aged dust could be seen. Even though it felt more homely and decorated than the one I had resided in before, I could feel the emptiness was still the same.

How often did Alain come here?

I was silently led to a drawing room which held more soft furnishings lined with gold. The servants had already lit the fire, warming the room and offering further light for my benefit. I thanked them though they left me without a second look. I waited patiently, unsure of myself or how long Alain would take to arrive.

I took in my surroundings, sitting in a chair near the fire. I admired the artwork along the walls and smiled as I noticed the chair smelt of him. How familiar I was to this smell, yet how little else I knew of him. It was so quiet I could hear the clock ticking nearby on the mantelpiece and small movements of the house servants scurrying about elsewhere.

Soon, I decided to go to the window and watch the streets. I noticed it was early evening, yet the strange mixture of cars and horse-drawn carriages were already bustling on the cobbled ground.

A shiver ran through me as I noticed the frosted glass, how it was the same as Merlough's house. My body remembered the imprisonment I felt and backed away. Gods, it already felt so long ago, yet not far enough. When was he to die? Had they already done it? Was it quick and painless or did he struggle? I returned to the fireside in order to warm from my chilled thoughts.

Moments later, Alain rushed in, looked around, flustered, and was washed with relief when he saw me by the fire. His smile warmed me more than the fire ever could.

"Ah, I am relieved you have made yourself comfortable; my apologies for the delay," he said, joining me near the chair.

"It matters not." I smiled, feeling relaxed and melancholy.

"Would you care for a drink or…?" he asked awkwardly but I shook my head. He sat in a chair opposite to me and seemed to change his mind, then moved to join me on the two-seater sofa. He was closer now than I had anticipated and I felt myself become flustered, his scent overwhelming now, warm and welcoming like cinnamon and sandalwood.

"I hear you are to make music with my aunt's talents such as Mastuo," he started and I smiled at the idea of pure elation at this. Mastuo was the pianist I was familiar with, who I had first admired at Yule two years prior and who regularly played at court for the Queen's pleasure.

"Yes! And Gods, I am so lucky. I have never worked with such masters before so you can appreciate I am a little… apprehensive," I trailed off, worrying my bottom lip.

"Worry not, for he is most eager. He heard you too those years ago. He remembers. He is inspired by you… like many of us," Alain explained, making me blush.

"I inspire…?"

Alain chuckled at my disbelief and slid an arm around my shoulders, pulling me closer to him. I was immediately enveloped further into his scent and sensed tingles of his magick, which soothed me.

"Indeed you do. You have inspired many, more than you may realise. Parading you as he did, I know it was not his intention but seeing you, well, it's triggered something in all of us. I know for me, I am ashamed to say, I realised how wrongly we were treating you," he explained, his words tense at the mention of Merlough. I repressed a tremble from revisiting such memories and Alain pulled away.

"Though I am surprised my aunt has allowed you to use Mastuo outside of the court. Very few close to her have been allowed to leave for… such matters. She likes to keep what she holds dear close."

"Do you mean like yourself?" I asked, curious, surprised at his jealous tone. He huffed an annoyed sigh, making him seem suddenly younger for a moment before nodding reluctantly.

"If I am truly honest, I am jealous Mastuo gets to go with you into the outside world. It was something I desired myself," he confessed and I could not help but smile at this. He wanted to leave with me? But surely this was for his political movement, not for the reasons I had hoped?

"But if you want to… Why can't you?" I asked hesitantly, unfamiliar with these workings in court, not understanding that as a prince, he seemed more restricted than most. It felt backwards to me.

His sad sigh made my heart sink as he sat back in thought.
"I am the Blood Prince. My place is here," he replied bitterly as if having rehearsed it, making me frown.
"But surely, you can leave? Are there not blood banks all over the world to accommodate vampires? Surely they are needed to be attended to, not just your own?" I asked, confused.

From what I knew, blood banks were managed and directed from the Vampire Nation, so I was surprised that this meant Alain had little connection, despite being responsible for them. It didn't make sense.

"Believe me, dearest, I have tried. I do feel responsible as I should, being the Blood Prince. But… there are things you do not know. Things that have happened to my aunt that make her... protective of me." He shrugged, embarrassed by what little he could offer in her defence. I felt then that this debate had been going on longer than I thought. This was something he clearly wanted but, envisioning the queen, I understood her word was final in all matters. He chuckled darkly.
"Though I confess, I have pushed very little before now. I have never really had as much interest to leave until… recently." Was he blushing? Did vampires blush? The dancing light from the fire made it hard to tell.

"Oh," is all I could reply, feeling the rising tension between us. He sighed again, defeatedly.
"Enkil is the one who leaves. He ventures off and handles most affairs outside the court. Being a pixie, and not of our blood, I

assume my aunt feels little need to protect him. His need to explore the world grew much earlier. I assumed this came from not being born at court. But now I feel myself having the same…need," he explained, referring to the adopted son of Carmilla, someone I recalled having aggressive and threatening energy.

It was intriguing to think that though Carmilla considered him her 'son' that he was given special freedoms that clearly Alain had been denied. It distracted me that though I had shared a world with them for almost three years, I knew little of what happened there. It saddened me; I had been shut out and denied that education I had so eagerly sought in my early days here. But the pull to go home was stronger now, and I knew I would follow it.

After quiet moments of being lost in our own thoughts, Alain jolted as if coming to a decision of his own.

"Perhaps I will go and see your first concert in order to report back to my aunt. She knows I will detail it much more accurately than Enkil could comprehend." My heart fluttered with happiness. He wanted to see my first concert? I felt so excited then at the vision of it all.

"Of course! You must. I would truly love it if you…" I trailed off, my blush spreading as I heard my own words spilling out. I smiled shyly and he grinned back encouragingly. He took my hands into his suddenly, my rushing warmth contrasting with his cool touch, our magick having been stoked by the connection.

"I must confess something to you," he croaked, sounding strained. Before I could stop myself, I tensed resisting the words. Could he have such a terrible secret? What could he need to confess that made him strain so? The calm and sure Blood Prince?

My silence made him look into my eyes, a worry forming on his handsome face. I was sixteen now, considered a faerie and no longer a faeling. Yet what was I to a Blood Prince who was much older? That fact I didn't even know his age clanged in me.

In some respects, I still had much to learn. I swallowed heavily, trying to form the words.

"What would an influential Blood Prince need to confess to a mere faerie such as myself?" I asked, sounding sharper than intended. If it cut him, he did not show it except for a small arch to his brow.

"I must confess that despite my efforts in trying to do what is best for you, I find myself…" he trailed off, hesitating, his red eyes darting away from me. I withheld a tremble as my mind raced with the possibilities of what he intended to say, my heart hiding from the possibility of being broken. In the face of truth, I could not avoid these feelings for him any longer, and it tore at me. He seemed to sigh. frustrated, at a loss for words, which was rare for him, that I knew.

"Élan, I am guilty of not putting your desire before my own. My own in which I—" He suddenly held my face. My body was a slave to his will as always. His eyes dropped to my lips, which were now dry in anticipation.

"I wish to always have you near. Not for political needs or publicity, but for the sheer hope of having you as my own," he whispered, the words gushing out, shocking me. The possession in them should have stung, or at least warned me against my previous experience, yet I felt my own possession draw nearer to him. His breath reminded me of cinnamon.

"As your own…?" I was repeating his words, unable to make sense of what he meant. Hope bloomed in my chest.

"I know I shouldn't. Especially with the horrors you have been through. The fact you allow my presence at all in isolation is enough to… impress me," he explained, remaining turned away from me, avoiding my gaze. Gently, his hand found mine once more, making the hope inside swell again.

"But I can't avoid how I feel. I never have before and despite the… controversy this brings, I am willing to…pursue this." He sighed again and kissed my hand, making my heart lurch. I had never seen him struggle so much and it unnerved me as well as excited me. "Please tell me how you feel? There is no point unless I know how you feel." His gaze hesitantly met mine once more, dimmer than before, worry painted in every line of his face.

"How I…feel?" I asked stupidly, my mouth unable to keep up with my feelings. How did I feel? What was he actually saying? That he wanted my blood? Why did I want that?

A part of me raged at this, how I could easily give myself to him. Had I not learned anything?

A larger part of me was adamant that this was different. Convinced of his good nature, that I was drawn to him from the start for a reason. An illogical reason, but something I couldn't explain away.

"I have shocked you," he gasped bitterly, his own conclusions drawing together in his mind. As he began to draw away from me again, I seemed to unfreeze from my mental shut down. I leaned forward and took his hand back once more.

"Indeed I am, but for good reason," I explained, sounding calmer than I felt, smiling gently. His straight eyebrow arched at my words.

"I must admit, I find it hard to understand your true intentions, and understand my own. But from what I can determine, you mean well. Plus, ever since the moment we met, I could deny the magickal connection." I kissed his cool hand, feeling the blood rush to my hand as if urgent to reach his flesh.

"Gods… you did feel it too then? I thought it was…" he mused.

"It's true. I didn't even know vampires had magick," I said and his guarded expression paused me.

"Not many do… it is rare for us. I know little of my abilities, only that I know my lures are stronger and my venom gives the receiver a more pleasant feeding experience," he explained and I blushed as I recalled seeing that youth he drank from. My heart pounded with desire; he could surely hear it too.

"Bah I don't know what you do to me. Here I'm spilling you my secrets…" He scoffed and smirked devilishly.

"I won't tell anyone, I promise."

Alain sobered and nodded thankful, his curtain of blonde hair brushing my arm.

"You can trust me. I know you have always meant well for me. I guess that is why I trust you above other vampires, why I feel safe with you…" I hesitated to meet his gaze, unsure of what expression I would find there, his silence sowing doubt inside me.

"You feel safe with me?" he asked though his pleased expression made it seem like more of an acknowledgement.

"Yes, I had hoped now for weeks during my recovery that I was not a burden to you. I am relieved this has not been so," I confirmed, blushing as his eyes dropped to my lips.

He wants to kiss you.

My own thoughts shocked me.

"Élan, I care for you. But I also need you," he said, the last part sounding strained. As I pondered his words, I how close we had drawn to each other. His eyes still were to my lips, which felt more dry. My heart pounded as his cool presence could be felt in closer proximity, my earlier thought blooming.

"For blood?" I asked him, realising I hadn't replied. My words seemed to jolt him, my stomach dropped as he drew away, a strange look on his face.

Was he disappointed? Why?

He sighed and seemed to renew himself. Slowly, he turned back to me and took my face once more, cradling it gently as if I were made of glass.

"You would…do that for me?" he asked softly, his cool breath caressing my lips. I swallowed holding his gaze. I nodded and licked my dry lips, his eyes drawn to them once more. I swore he could hear my heart, waiting for the moment he complained at its incessant beating like…someone else.

"And what would I give you in return? It requires an upfront transaction now with the direct faerie, according to the new law passed. No longer the outdated form of 'family offerings' and such. Plus I can assure you we will be looking at these closely from now on. The Queen insists on every new contract to hold my magickal seal in approval as part of gatekeeping this," he said almost neutrally, his eyes alight as he continued to gaze at my lips.

I felt more blood rush to my face, greeting his cool flesh, his words fading in my distraction.

"Then a kiss?" my heart skipped as I realised it was my own voice that had said this.

Before I could even reply or recant from the slip of my tongue, I felt his cool lips meet my own. I gasped onto his mouth, my arms boldly slid around his neck. A rush of pleasure heated my whole body.

I felt him begin to pull back, and I felt myself pull him back towards me, manners forgotten. His strength seemed my own as he gave into me, our lips beginning a slow dance. My hands were brushed with his silken hair that had been tied at his nape. I had the urge to brush my hands through it as he pulled me closer.

A wanton groan that I had never heard myself make before, vibrated between us as I felt his strong tongue enter my mouth. He sighed as he explored my mouth and I felt our bodies respond to each other. Gods, what was this? This undeniable connection. I felt our magick twist and twine in a sensual dance around us. I was entirely new to this yet knew what we needed at the same time. It was maddening yet soothing all at once. Was it our magick or something more? It was hard to tell as my mind scrambled over what was happening.

"Gods," he gasped as I felt his fingers find the flesh at my hips, where my clothing had revealed me. Before I allowed another breath, I connected our lips once more, getting a delighted groan from him. I felt his weight on me and was not frightened but aroused.

As if my body commanded his needs, I felt his lips drift to my throat. I felt my pulse throb to his lips as my magick swirled around us, coaxing his magick forth.

"My prince," I purred, not recognising the possession in my voice that oozed in pleasure. Gods, I needed him. I needed him to— needed him to *bite* me.

I grew frustrated as I felt his hesitation at the key point at my throat. The place I have felt the pain so many times. Pain that seemed drowned out by the pleasure I now felt.

Gods, bite me already!

He pressed a kiss to the artery before sighing and drawing away. I mewled in disappointment.

"Why?" I pouted as he pulled away, my arms still around him, refusing to let him go. My magick soothed and ebbed slowly to a simmer. My awareness returned and I was fully on my back. His sharp, regal nose nuzzled my cheek softly.

"I can't. It's not right." He sighed, kissing my cheek softly. It felt lovely, despite the frustration.

"But it's okay. We agreed and—" I cut off as he shook his head at me.

"Despite this, I cannot…I shouldn't do this with you. Such a transaction… Élan, only weeks ago this act caused you to suffer so." He sighed, his fingers running gently through my wavy locks.

Despite his words, I felt calmed as I felt his magick reach for me tentatively and almost purred with the sensation.

"I care for you. I want to protect you and that should not come at a cost." His words soothed me even as I tried to pull him back to my lips. He resisted when he was a mere breath from me, a crooked smile playing on his lips.

"Not yet," I replied softly, making him arch his eyebrow at me.

"I want to. I care for you too. I trust you, Alain. No doubt it is a crazy admission as you say, merely weeks after…*him*." He grimaced at my words, which made me pull him close again. I felt a swell of smugness as I watched his eyes move to my lips once more.

"I rather enjoy my name on those lips," he purred, his red eyes alight with desire. A desire I did not shy away from.

"I would enjoy your lips more on mine," I whispered before pressing my lips back to his. Pleasure pulled in my gut as he groaned back into another kiss. One that began to grow faster, our breaths mixed, hot and cold tasting the same.

"Élan," he purred as I kissed his throat, my name sounding a prayer on his lips. His throat felt cool and soft. Softer than I expected and it oozed with his masculine musk.

In my passionate state, I softly bit him there. I felt his body alight with pleasure and our magicks met again, renewed. He gasped as I kissed him again, our bodies melded together feeling connected everywhere. I felt his hunger, his need.

"Alain," I sighed, tasting his name on my tongue, smiling as I felt his magick careen in response. How it sparked and fluttered against my own. I watched in silent awe as his eyes began to glow brighter and his fangs seemed to elongate.

A sign I knew for vampires as showing a deep desire, something they only did in intimate moments. It was a beautiful sight and I felt my own body respond with him as well as my magick. I observed that though fangs and glowing eyes had previously meant danger, it seemed with Alain it meant something else. His magick seemed to pull and ground against mine, making us both purr with pleasure.

"Gods, you are like no other," he growled, his voice a deeper timbre than before. I giggled as blood rushed to my face once more. No one had said this to me before. Let alone the Blood Prince himself! For a moment, I questioned if this was real.

"I must be dreaming." I sighed out loud, my tongue possessed and determined to share all my secrets with him in return. He chuckled and kissed my jaw.

"Oh? Do you have many dreams like this?" He grinned wolfishly, looking handsome.

"With you, yes, always you," I whispered and pulled him into another kiss. He sighed, content, into our kiss.

"I had no clue!" He chuckled, breaking our kiss. I sobered, blushing at my admission suddenly. He kissed my hot cheek softly.

"Don't be ashamed. It pleases me." He took my bottom lip in between his teeth carefully. He sucked and kissed until I felt swollen with need. I was gasping and squirming beneath him, and he enjoyed rocking our bodies together, despite the clothes that still restricted us.

"I dream very little. But I admit when I do, it is of you," he suddenly admitted in a hushed tone. I silently urged him to continue and it was his turn to blush.

"They are not always pleasant. I still bear the guilt of what befell you." He swallowed, his movements slowed. He smiled gently down at me. "And sadly the pleasant dreams are never enough. They are shamefully selfish in how you offer yourself to me. Just how you are now." His thumb brushed my lips. He dreamed of me too? Gods' that fact alone almost made my pleasure crest.

"Tell me about them—the pleasant ones," I requested, sounding almost desperate in my breathless manner. His warm chuckle threaded my body with further heat.
"I don't think so. I can barely hold myself back from you now as we are. For you to know my secret desires would be my undoing. No, you have enough secrets today, beloved," he replied gently, his hand going to my locks once more. His soft caresses made my eyelids flutter with pleasure. He laughed as I pouted, realising what he had just said.

"Maybe one day, for I cannot deny you for long," he purred, kissing my throat, making my heart lurch up as if jealous. Our magick lovingly entwined also.
"You make it sound as if I have spelled you." I chuckled nervously.
"Perhaps you have." He leaned back, eyes serious and searching. I bit my lip in worry, only half concerned that I had done this. It seemed impossible and even if there were an enchantment, I knew nothing of it. Could I have done this subconsciously? Could it happen to even a powerful vampire like him? His soft laugh broke my thoughts.

"I am playing with you. I know you haven't, sweetness."
"How?" I asked carefully, fully doubting myself now. His smile slipped to concern at my caution.
"You truly worry about this?" he asked carefully, making me shrug with a blush.
"It is just…your confession seemed too convenient for me. And the way Merlough turned mad from my blood…" His growl

made me pause and he withdrew further from me, his body tense and cold. His magick snapped away from mine.

"Don't even compare me to that vile creature. He was half mad even before he started using you," he hissed, his eyes glowing angrily. Very rarely had he shown me his temper though it was notorious in the court. I shrank back, which sobered him.
"Half mad or not, I certainly didn't help his condition, did I?" I hissed back, feeling hurt. Alain now sobered completely, the glow fading from his eyes. He hesitated and sighed before edging closer to me again.

"I am sorry. You are right to be cautious. I promise you, Élan, what happened to…my cousin, will not happen to me. He should have been stopped a long time ago. I will never forgive myself for letting him slip further than we would with any other member of the court. We were careless and before you, I am ashamed to admit we had little concern on the ramifications of his actions," he explained. I remained slightly unconvinced but was hopeful of his reassurance. I felt his magick tentatively swirl around mine once more. I was still unsure on how the blood works in vampires and how it affects them from one to another. For surely, he was a blood relative and made Alain just as vulnerable. The red eyes were a sure sign to me, and once again, I found myself annoyed that I had trusted another so quickly.

"As to my confession…" He started getting my attention once more.

"It is just a blessed coincidence that it is convenient for you. I truly mean what I say and it started long before you regained your full strength. I know my own mind and I know that it is my heart that governs this need, not an enchantment of the mind," he explained, convincing me further that he knew what he was talking about. I was aware of his vast education and in that moment, I realised it far outplayed my own.

The fae knew so little of the other species whereas vampires such as Alain himself, seemed to know full well about enchantments and other faerie specialties. I knew that it would worry and even frighten some faeries like my mother, but I found it a comfort.

Particularly in this moment, where so much was still uncertain to me, but to have his feelings be genuine and real, made me smile.

"I didn't know vampires had hearts." I pouted playfully, making him huff and kiss my cheek.

"You didn't know a lot of things. But like all curious faelings, you will soon find out." The comment seemed innocent enough, yet my mind twisted it to a cruder nature.

"There are some things I am particularly curious about, Prince," I purred, edging closer to him, knowing full well my green eyes appeared half mast and hungry in their gaze. "Also, I'm a faerie now, no longer a faeling…" I added smugly.

"Oh, are you? Well perhaps I shouldn't indulge you too soon for this is far to enticing," he teased, making me frown. It soon melted away as he leaned in and kissed me passionately, stealing my breath away. He broke away too soon and I couldn't stop the disappointment clouding my face.

"Beloved, it warms me to know how much you want me, but in this we should proceed with caution. It is early for us and we can take our time, yes?" he asked softly, kissing my jaw afterwards to sweeten his words. I huffed in frustration, making him chuckle.

A knock and awkward cough broke our reverie. A vampire server stood, headed down to greet the prince.

"My apologies for disturbing you, my Prince. Your presence is requested in the great hall," he said softly, head remaining bowed.

"Of course, my thanks. I will be there shortly." Alain sighed tiredly, turning back to me.

"I hope to continue this later. I shall write to you, sweet one," he whispered hotly against my face before kissing me softly as if to savour it.

The blush spread over my face as I caught the gaze of the vampire behind him. His eyes stared hard at us, his face expressionless, making me shiver. Alain drew away, smiling softly and turned to the vampire who looked away once more as he left the room swiftly, our exchange just a warm memory.

I was left with the vampire servant who remained still as the prince's steps faded away. The vampire murmured softly although it was too quiet for me to catch. I remained still, feeling the tense atmosphere.

"Is everything okay?" I asked softly, making him flinch and look up at me. He began to shake and muttered, staring at me once more.

"Can I help?" I asked worriedly, though I knew better than to approach. For a moment I considered calling out, though I knew this would only make things worse. He snarled at me and flitted from the room. Only when I knew he was gone did I shut the door and tremble against it, feeling the tears rise.

That hungered look, like so many others, terrified me, bringing me pain and misery. I hugged myself as I slid down the door, paralysed by what I had witnessed. It was like he had struggled for control, his gaze imprinted on me alongside the other ones I remembered.

A red gaze that haunted me, sickness coiling in my belly. Why did I do this to myself? Why did I have to fall for him?

I waited anxiously for the guards to return me to the inn once more and I wondered, did I love him? Or did I love my own *idea* of him?

I watched the world flow by in silent calm as the car took me to the verge of the Vampire Nation. I was going home. This time I would be awake for it, though it would take a few days with little sleep; I felt myself barely wanting to miss what was before me.

Finally, I was going back home after all this time. But as before, I was to make this journey on my own. My mother had left a few days earlier in order to collect supplies on the way.

Despite the pain, I could not help but revisit everything that had happened since the three years I was home. I had left a faeling and returned…a changed faerie somewhat.

As I thought this, I felt the new feelings summoned with my magick gather within me. The green glow in my peripheral vision. It sparkled and circled my skin as if to embrace me, and surround me with warmth. I had yet to explore further this feeling, this side to the magick I'd not had before. All I knew was that it was growing stronger, especially as I headed closer toward my birthplace. This magick that had grown with me in the land of dark creatures.

I knew that I was returning with the renewed feeling as well as the burden of what had happened to me.

What was the extent that Rolo understood? Would he even want to see me?

I avoided these worried thoughts as the worse option felt too painful to bear. What would Brimhaven be like now that I was changed and my father gone?

Would the food contain the vibrancy I had loved and cherished? Would it hold a closer value to me now to taste such bursts of flavour? Or would the tastes be too overwhelming for me to endure after all this time?

I noticed the light getting stronger the further we travelled. When we crossed over into the Faelands, I felt the difference in the air pressure. It was lighter, as if I had been holding part of a breath for three years.

I took in the fresh air and sighed as the wind caressed my wild curls. I was almost home, the rolling hills started to appear and rush by as we approached, closer to the forest region. I felt my throat tighten at how beautiful I found these hills now. I could almost see my brother in my mind's eye, his clothing torn and dirty as he worked the land.

Gods, I had missed him! It was not long now until I could see the hills that held in my memory so strong. The ones I knew and had climbed daily in my childhood, the scent of pine already increasing, the flowers beckoning and promising bolder colours as I proceeded further into the land.

Mercy

Alain

The Blood Prince approached the cell with grim determination. He could smell the bitter and sour scent of insanity oozing from within.

"Welcome cousin," hissed the voice from within the darkness. Alain sneered, barely recognising his cousin's voice any longer, reminding himself the creature within was sane no more. Again, visions of Élan's torture rushed through his mind, driving his next words with assurance.

"Merlough Marquis, you are condemned to death as deemed merciful and just, for the crimes you have committed against the fae. As passed by the new laws, you have chosen to defy and disregard our vision as a species to do what is right with those we share our lives with. The Queen herself has decreed that putting you to death is the merciful act upon your damned existence," Alain paused for effect before continuing. He knew little of whether the creature within acknowledged what he said but as was right, he felt the need to deliver the verdict regardless.

"You are to be put to death by injection of silver into your veins, followed by sunlight overexposure until you are engulfed and deemed dead to this world." Alain shook from his own words. Very few were killed this way. It would be a slow and painful death. He was surprised his aunt had chosen this, despite Merlough's clear insanity, wanting him to suffer despite him barely knowing what he had done anymore.

The very idea made him sick and knowing he had to witness this, shook Alain to his core. It was to be a harsh reminder of what was to come of those who crossed the Queen. Especially when concerning a blood relative.

When no response came from the cell, Alain coughed awkwardly.

"What say you?" Crazed giggles came as a reply, which angered him and confirmed his vain attempt at reaching the creature.

"What say you?!" Alain barked, his magick pushing toward the creature for obedience. Rarely did he use his magickal abilities to enforce others to obey him, but now he grew weary of his cousin's fate.

"I say FUCK YOU arse kisser!" snarled the response. Alain's magick retreated as he recognised a semblance to the voice that snapped at him so.

Guilt and hurt wormed into his heart, knowing his cousin's soon impending pain and torture. No doubt, he deserved it, but still, as a creature that barely knew his own thoughts now, he felt the verdict was… extreme for his tastes. Queen Carmilla had chosen to use his cousin more as an example now rather than a merciful death. A bitter reminder of how cold and deadly the Queen truly was when she was betrayed.

"Well then I say to you, if you are still sort of there in some form, Merlough, I mourn you cousin. I grieve for you. We have shared a few times together, but I had nothing but love for you. You have lost your way and in turn got burned with magick far superior to you. This is your consequence and now you must die." The bitter irony of how almost an age ago, his uncle, Merlough's father, had shared the same fate. Were we all to suffer the sins of our parents? Fall for the same fatal endings as those that made us begin?

"I shall mourn you. If no one else will, dear cousin, I shall."

Alain walked away quickly, his footsteps echoed as he went, reflecting the fast pace that he took. He no longer wanted to be in this dark place.

He decided to ignore the quiet sobs that his sharp hearing picked up.

Brimhaven

My heart leapt and my magick fluttered with the feeling of release as we changed from car to carriage, the land now too rural for the travel in machines. My spirit sucked in the air around me as if lost for breath and suffocated as I took in the freshness.

As I breathed it in, I felt it flush through my system, like a deep cleansing of the soul. It was springtime now in the Faelands, the promise of magick and growth invigorating for any faerie that came into contact with it.

As I sat in the carriage, the movement made me lurch forward and I surrendered to the welcoming flow of warmth and crackling energy that fed my soul.

I looked out the window, enjoying the sunlight as it kissed everything in sight, bathing the scene in a warm glow. The breeze was peppered and spiced with the flowers and plant life that thrived and ruled the lands around us. The roads were rocky and bumpy as the carriage struggled forward, not used to such wild lands.

I couldn't help but smile as I began to recognise a nearby tree, a specific blue flower that greeted me as we went by. I was home, and with each step, that old Brimhaven feeling that I had clutched to with desperate memory revived.

Eventually, the excitement grew to be too much, my heart rattling the cage of bone as I bid the carriage to a halt. I thanked the driver, having paid him and assured him that I knew my way from here. All I needed to do now was follow my feet.

I waited for the carriage to turn and leave, then I felt the magick burst from me in my laughter. With a moment of delirium, I removed my shoes, letting my bare feet be welcomed by the crumbled ground underneath. I felt the breeze swirling around me, noticing the change in my magick, but greeting me all the same. It assured me I was home, I was invited to proceed. I did with great enthusiasm, barely able to contain my stride from running.

The sunlight felt large and imposing now, as I was not used to such light. Yet I surrendered to it, enjoying the feeling of it empowering my cells and gracing my pale flesh. I soon became accustomed to it once more. I knew these lands, I was born on them. I knew where to go.

Birds greeted me above and rabbits rushed by me, their pace encouraging me to break into a run. I relived my faeling-self as I ran, almost feeling the spirit of my old self running alongside me, reflecting my magick within me, guiding me home.

I felt him before I could see him. Rolo, my brother. I swelled with the need to reunite with him once more. Could he sense me near? Did he know I was reaching for him?

My magick, faster than myself, rushed to beat me to him. Through my magick, I felt him closer and emotion started to swell. Gods! This was real. I was home. I was alive.

These feelings were pushed towards my brother, not far from sight now. I sensed him in the tall fields, the perfume of the earth and wheat engulfing me fully. I rushed forward harder, enjoying the feel of exertion on my body, every breath filling me anew with a sense of hope and light.

As I came to the field, seeing the first sight of him, the surprise made me slow in pace. His frame was taller and wider, his back to me. He was a faerie in his prime now, a male of twenty three years. Here he was, working in his element of the faefields. Gods, in that moment I could see my father in him entirely. The vision, so overwhelming, I took a deep breath to steady my thundering emotions.

I watched him working, so content as my doubts began to seep in. What would he think of me now? Did he even want to see me?

I allowed my magick to reach him tentatively, having slowed as I had, trying to sense for him, uncertain suddenly. Did I even know this faerie anymore? I swallowed heavily. He was married now and had a wife, Mary, with the flame red hair. Perhaps he no longer wanted to be reminded of the shadow of our past…

I stuttered to a halt as I felt my magick reach him and panicked in anticipation, knowing he would feel it on some level. I saw him physically jolt and turn my way, shocked.

We stood there, staring at each other, paused in time and hesitation. My distance still over a hill before his field, knowing I was barely visible to him. I could not see his face but I knew he stared, wincing in the bright sunlight above us. He allowed my magick to cover him further, which assured me.

"Élan?" I heard his whispered word carried over the air to me. His voice was deep with more maturity than I remembered.
I uttered a cry with emotion overwhelming me; this was Rolo! I started to run, no longer afraid. This was now or never! I felt the breeze alongside me, running with me, butterflies flurrying, having been disturbed from my trail. I reached with my magick, portraying my need, my hope to him. I ran faster, my lungs straining as I watched him start to walk towards me. I saw confusion and bewilderment on his face.

"Gods, this can't be," I heard him say as I closed the distance, noticing further changes and details on him. His hair filled and longer, his height was tall and strong, his clothing looking simple to me now, but so familiar.

I ran into him, barely slowing, and embraced him hard. My height barely reached his strong shoulders, his body hard like a tree trunk. His scent mingled with the fields and I cried at the familiarity of it. I trembled when I felt his arms slowly go around me, like branches of safety that I had not felt before.

"Truly, it is you?" he asked, his voice wavering. I pulled back, looking up at him, my face already wet with tears. My green gaze found his brown one that radiated home.

"Truly, has my lost little brother returned to me? Élan, is that you?" he asked, still in disbelief, making me chuckle. He laughed back and embraced me tightly once more, the strength in him making it hard to breathe, yet I welcomed it.
"Gods' piss!" he cursed, his chest rumbling deeply against my cheek. I giggled, knowing for certain this faerie was Rolo, for only he would use such a childish curse in this moment.

"It is I, truly!" I laughed into his chest, unable to pull away from his strength, not that I wanted to. I took in his woodsy scent, the rough fabric of his shirt, the warmth from the sun's blessing above. It felt so perfect, I worried it was a dream. My heart pounded at the horror this was some dream and I was back imprisoned in that dark place of my past. Rolo drew back, pulling me away from my stressful thoughts.

"For so long, I had…" he trailed off softly, staring openly at me, taking me all in as I did him. He shook himself in disbelief again and laughed.

"But you are here!" He huffed, delighted, his warm eyes sparkling with joy. I hugged him once more, feeling more belonging that I had felt in such a time.

I was home.

We held each other for a long time, feeling our hearts thudding together. Slowly Rolo pulled back and smiled down at me.

"I am to work the land some more, then you must come home with me, yes?" he asked shyly, as if I would decline!

"Of course! Can I watch, if you don't mind? It has been so long…" I trailed off at my own shyness. Rolo scoffed and laughed.

"I thought it'd be boring for you, new worldly brother, to watch such simplicity." He flicked me playfully, making me swell with warmth.

"Of course not! In fact I would find it...rather comforting," I said, withholding the dark truth of being at such a comfort with the simplicity before me. Rolo nodded and slowly returned back to his spot and resumed his work, his movements more confident now, invigorated as he knew I watched him with a similar fascination to when I was a young faeling.

With new eyes, I watched him work the land with confidence and wisdom only my brother would know. He had done this all his life, managing the land, nurturing it and guiding it to his will.

His hands and movements like a dance, poised and assertive as he manoeuvred the land around him, coaxing the crops and planting new seeds. The flow was mesmerising to watch. Pride rose in me as I watched my kin do what he was born to do. This was his land, this was our place. Our place of safety and comfort.

It was already past midday, so I knew the afternoon would roll on by, watching him this way, sitting on a hill over his work. It was so serene and tranquil as the clouds crawled by, making shapes in the sunlight over the land. The flowers danced and flashed me, the insects zoomed and buzzed, working with my brother.

"*Such a simple life*," I thought. Such a simple place… yet I could not deny I now bloomed with jealousy of it all before me. I was tarnished, tainted from the outside world.

Part of me would always remain an outsider to this land, created by the pain and trauma far from here. A dark part of me was not born here. Yet I was relieved that little had changed. My brother was where I had left him, where I had dreamed of him being while trapped in my own reality of horrors and darkness. He was safe and free from the dark creatures across the sea. I sighed heavily, feeling that what I had endured was almost worth it, knowing that. Almost.

I felt my father's absence, a small stain on the vision before me, yet I still felt part of him here with us. I could feel him in the land around me, carried through my brother. As my father had done, my brother now continued his work, and so with assurance, I knew my brother's work would continue even after he was gone.

I could not help but wonder, what part of me would remain here after I was gone? For surely, I could not work the land or do anything that my brother now did.

Calmly, I moved my thoughts onward, away from the shadows and back into the present before me. I felt another part of myself healing as I watched my brother move onto something else, sweat now visible on his shirt as he huffed.

Now and then, he looked up and smiled at me, as he had done when I was a faeling, watching him shyly. As if to assure me, a breeze blew up the hill and caressed me, moving my dark curls. I sighed into the freshness and smiled, welcoming the land's embrace to me.

Soon, the sunlight soothingly dimmed and it moved into its descent on the horizon. My brother stretched and sighed as he joined me on the hill.

"You okay?"

"Yes," I reply simply knowing there was too much to share now.

"Come home then." He grinned, holding out his muddied palm to me. I took it, giggling with excitement, my heart swelling with the use of the word home. His faerie-land twang I had sorely missed, emphasised that I was indeed home.

We walked casually to the house, the path as clear to me as before, my heart soaring along with the birds in the sky. The sunlight faded further into orange and red hues, yet I was secure in where I was heading. How much had it changed?

As we approached, I swooned at the familiarity of the house. It still stood with its humble height and familiar structure. A small fence had been built surrounding it, holding the wild flowers within its reach like a hug.

My brother opened a small green gate and mockingly bowed for me to enter. I laughed and walked in, feeling light and relieved. Rolo was still the same, though I had changed.

Beeswax candles in the windows flicked and beckoned at us as we approached the same front door. Rolo opened it and walked in first, calling to Mary.

Mary! Gods, I had forgotten how much my brother had truly moved on since I had left. I looked around, a small lurch in my gut as I noticed small details of things had moved or changed. Tables moved, furniture tweaked or replaced. Yet as I walked in further with my brother's encouragement, I still felt the same small, cozy comfort that it once held.

Mary came through and greeted me, her face I recalled warmly yet it had matured beautifully as my brother had. I gasped as I took in her large, pregnant belly and she tittered and kissed me. Her hair as I remembered, seemed a humble red of fire earth compared to Queen Carmilla's. Her dress handmade and practical, hugged her frame. Her scent, fresh and powered with ingredients from her cooking. She greeted me as if she had known me all this time and laughed as I took in her.

"Why yes, this one I believe to be a girl," she explained, stroking her belly. My brother moved around me to kiss her. Gods, he was a husband and a father! I swooned at the revelation of it all. I watched as he greeted her with the warmth and adoration my father had held for my mother, soothed by the familiarity of the scene before me.

Rolo leaned down, scooping up a small faeling who had been hiding behind a door, kissing his chubby cheeks, making him giggle. The boy's tension was eased by his father's embrace. The faeling looked to be around two years of age.

"Arlow, this your uncle Élan," he said softly and the boy's eyes widened with curiosity. I blushed and gasped. Gods, I was an uncle!

Another realisation that knocked me with shock. Rolo laughed at my reaction and Arlow giggled, blushing along with me. The boy had his father's brown gaze, wide and innocent, but his mother's red hair. Mary reached around the other side of the boy and kissed his cheek lovingly.

"Apologies, Élan, he is a shy one," she explained.

"Oh no need! As I recall I was too once." I chuckled and my brother ruffled my hair playfully.

"Dinner is ready, so please sit," Mary called as she waddled back to the kitchen.

We sat at the same oak table my father had made. I admired it once more, truly appreciating the craftsmanship and unique style. I had missed this place. We passed around bowls, ready to eat when I frowned.

"Will mother not be joining us?" I asked and Rolo flinched as it hit a nerve. Mary bit her lip and patted Rolo knowingly.
"No," he gritted and started to eat hungrily. Mary sighed, exacerbated, and looked at me sadly.
"She rarely visits us. She will probably come to see you tomorrow," she explained sensitively. I thought as the change set in. She no longer lived here then.

"Do you know where she lives now?" I asked quietly.
"I don't care," Rolo snapped, making me and Mary flinch. Moments then passed in awkward silence.
"Some say she lives in a cottage in the forest now. But we aren't certain," Mary explained kindly, her calm voice easing the tension in my brother. I swallowed heavily at this. Gods, this truly is what had changed.
"Sorry brother...I am still new to this," I muttered, blushing and embarrassed. Rolo eyed me sideways and sighed, guilt etched on his face. Mary patted his arm encouragingly.

"Things have changed here as have you," he commented blankly. I nodded sadly and continued to eat carefully, fully conscious now that this was no longer the home I remembered.
"But you are still welcome here, always," he explained, and Mary smiled, pleased. I smiled too and nodded appreciatively.
"And for that I am grateful, truly. I wish to make up for time that was lost to us," I responded, smiling. My brother snorted as if I had said a joke and continued eating.

Mary asked me a questions about the Vampire Nation to smoothly move on the conversation. I enjoyed the food as we talked, admiring the rich flavours but humble presentation. It took me back to my childhood and I embraced those memories fully now. I felt Arlow watching me quietly, shyly looking away when I turned to look at him, as I shared my stories of the vampire world - avoiding the grim underlying truth as to how I knew so much or how I had come to be there. My brother seemed to agree and avoided questions heading in that direction.

As we finished, my brother stood and helped Mary wash up, sneaking a kiss from her when they were alone in the other room. I was lost in my thoughts when I felt a small tug at my sleeve. I looked down to meet huge brown eyes, peering up at me.

"Are vampire's teeth really so big?" he asked shyly, making me smile. Gods how much he seemed like me! It assured me that I was truly related to Rolo as I had hoped. So much of this faeling reminded me of the Élan before leaving Brimhaven and it warmed me. I explained and we began having our own conversation, lost in our own stories when Mary called for bedtime.

Arlow rushed at me and hugged me tightly. The pure, innocent love overwhelmed me as did my need to protect him. Protect him from what I knew.

"I'm glad you came here, unkie," he said, muffled by my green suit. I swallowed thickly with emotion for a faeling I did not know existed a few days before. His pure and sudden trust in me soothed me that I was not so alien or tainted from this land as I had feared.

"I'm am glad too. I have missed a lot while I have been away."

Mary and Rolo led me on a familiar path to my room, and I gasped at how untouched it remained compared to the other rooms in the house.

"Rolo insisted we keep this here for when you returned," Mary explained and Rolo scoffed, blushed, and scratched his head. I hugged Rolo then, feeling like the young brother I was to him.

"So yeah, you can sleep 'ere, if you want." Rolo sniffed awkwardly, nudging me into the room. I took my room, the bed looking so small but comforting, the musk of forgotten childhood, welcoming me like an old friend.

"Rolo, you should talk," Mary muttered quickly as Rolo turned to leave. I watched him as his shoulders dropped with a sigh and turned back to me. Mary smiled at me assuredly over his shoulder and closed the door. We stood together awkwardly now, waiting for the other to speak. Rolo coughed uncomfortably.

"You must be tired. We can talk tomorrow if you like?" I asked softly, seeing his discomfort. He shrugged and gestured to the bed. We sat down awkwardly.

"There is just so much to say. I have no idea where to begin." He groaned and I chuckled darkly.

"Indeed. Though I have enjoyed this evening, Rolo, truly. Your family is beautiful and I am so grateful to see them." I smiled and he snorted waving it off.

"Despite what happened…You're still my brother," he replied, his voice wavering. I leaned into his arm appreciatively, taking in his scent once more, hoping it would be a long time before it is gone again.

"And so you know, I know what happened with mother… and father. Before I was born," I added and his sigh was mingled with a groan.

"You have no idea how many times I insisted on me being taken instead of you," he growled, his body tense with anger and frustration. His eyes blazed with a vengeful light. I sighed sadly, patting him assuredly.

"Though I am glad it was me, brother," I replied and he frowned.

"Why?"

Again I sighed, feeling the weight of my burden like a necklace of pain about my throat. Flashes of teeth and red haunting me behind my eyes. "Because it was meant to be. I mean no disrespect but if it were you in my place… I am not certain you would have survived," I explained though the struggle on his face. Slowly his thoughts turned dark and his eyes narrowed.

"What in the gods—"

"It doesn't matter," I cut him off, not ready to go there.

"It does! That—"

"It is done."

He growled in frustration. "What is this bullshit?! It was not 'meant' Élan. He is just insane, plain and simple," he barked, making me chuckle darkly. Very few I still knew would dare refer to our grandfather like Rolo does. I raked my hand through my curls tiredly.

"I am here now, am I not?" I replied wearily. Rolo huffed, annoyed.

"Yes, I guess." He pouted and his head fell into his hands. After a moment he looked at me, sadness in his brown eyes.

"But, you are different somehow. I can feel it in you. You are changed…" He trailed off, struggling to explain. I bit my lip worriedly. He had noticed?

"Is it…bad?" I asked nervously. Rolo looked at me then, squinting as if trying to find something.

"No. I don't think so," he said and looks away in thought. We remained quiet for a few further minutes, then I playfully nudged him.

"So, you married Mary." I grinned and laughed as he blushed.

"I sure did," he scoffed, huffing with pride.

"She is beautiful," I smiled at him warmly, laughing as his blush darkened.

"Yeah, she is. I'm a lucky guy." He grinned, crossing his arms.

"You are; you always will be," I replied wistfully, looking away in thought.

"And what about you?" He nudged me back to the present.

"Me?" I asked, my voice high with surprise. He chuckled.

"Yeah, any… interests?" he asked, gesturing vaguely. Now it was my turn to blush. Alain's face lit up in my mind.
"Oh ho! There is?!" He gasped in surprise and I turned away, embarrassed.
"Aw come on, you're old enough now ha!" He chuckled playfully and I grimaced.

"What?" he asked soberly.
"Nothing."
"You can tell me," he said, seriousness in his tone, his arm around my shoulders protectively. I sighed reluctantly.

"He's a vampire," I replied quickly, already armed for his response, hiding my face in shame. I knew it was not the fact it was a 'he' I had to worry about, but more the species.
"Oh." Rolo pulled away, disappointment heavy in his voice. We became stuck in awkward silence. Rolo huffed after a few moments and rubbed his eyes tiredly.
"Well… I guess it makes sense," he said and I looked up with surprise. Our eyes meet and Rolo groaned.
"Nope, no it doesn't," he whined. Despite not being surprised by his reaction, I was hurt by his rejection. He had not even met Alain!
"Just forget it," I snapped, hugging myself defensively. Doubts worming around in my mind. Why did I like a vampire after what I had been through? Rolo scratched his head, pouting. He slumped in defeat and pulled me roughly into his chest.
"Hey look, I'm sorry. I forget that I… don't really know that much about you anymore," he confessed and I scoffed at him.

"But I want to! Truly I do! It is why Mary pushed me to do this. I want this as much as you do. No way was I gunna let that toad ruin what we had." He hugged me tightly, his voice desperately determined.

"He kinda does look like a toad, doesn't he?" I smirked, referring to Diafol. No longer was I afraid of him as I once was. That was something that had certainly changed. I had proven my power. Rolo laughed happily.
"See!" He poked me playfully, making me giggle, the scene feeling nostalgic as if we were younger once more. I sobered as I recall something I want to address fully with him.

"So… Mother?" I asked and he huffed loudly, gripping his head in annoyance as he had done when he was younger and being made to be serious. He sighed after a moment's thought, considering his words.
"Yeah well, things got worse after father died. I can't stand her now. And she can't stand me, so it is just better… for both of us," he explained, gesturing hopelessly. I thought back, imaging how they were after I left, how tense they were and imaging my father no longer there to mediate them.
"I understand," I said sadly, patting him comfortingly. Rolo smiled sadly and hugged me once more. I was soothed by our closeness before he pulled away and coughed awkwardly.

"So listen… tomorrow, before my work, I was thinking that if it's not too weird… I could take you to father's grave…?" He shrugged dismissively. Like a heavy stone in my belly, I felt the thud of a huge aspect I had missed. Rolo took my silence as reluctance.

"We don't have to—"

"No, it's okay. I will," I assured him, my voice trembling. Rolo's large branch of an arm embraced my shoulders once more, his gaze warm with concern.

"Are you sure?" he asked softly.

"Yes," I replied with grim certainty. He smiled proudly at me and stood. He stretched, moaning tiredly.

"Thank you, Rolo."

"No problem," he replied gently, ruffling my wild curls like he used to.

"Good night, sprite." He grinned back at me.

I had forgotten how warm and pleasant the mornings were here. In springtime, the land greeted the light with fresh, cool air that balanced the heat and gently lulled one back from the veil of sleep.

I lay quietly, enjoying the sounds of the rising creatures, the shuffles of the lands and those that inhabited it.

A gentle knock and Mary entered. She held a simple shirt made to my size and placed it on top of my suit, blushing. I thanked her quietly, rushing to try it on as soon as she left. It was loose and baggy, like I remembered but I embraced the comfort of the wool around me. Simple trousers were placed with them and I wore them too. Already I looked more like the faerie borne of this land.

I joined my brother for a quiet breakfast, Arlow still asleep in the other room. He smiled when he saw what I wore and my heart swelled at his pride. The breakfast at the table was a familiar but distant scene. A simple porridge spiced with cinnamon and mint to greet the day.

I felt its weight in my stomach as I watched my brother prepare a horse and cart. I gingerly tried to help but ended up watching in contented peace as he smiled at me.

We said little as we rolled on our way through the fields in the early light. The land around us was contently lazy and sleepy to awake to the day. My brother hummed softly and once more, I was taken back to the morning trips I took with father. My heart sank like a stone in the river as I remembered his absence. I still felt him in the morning breeze and the rumbling stones beneath the wheels. I felt him in my brother's song as I recognised the shanty our father used to sing to us. I found myself humming alongside him, the familiarity overwhelming and healing to me.

When we arrived, I noticed the lake that once stretched as far as my small mind could reach. Now it didn't look as big, but was still impressive as it stretched across the land, small pines on the other side. I could sense the wildlife just below the surface, thriving and shimmering as it always had. The small dock where father's boat still rocked alone made me jolt sadly. My brothers strong, supportive grip helped me step from the cart.

Along the dock, I saw a shape that stood at the end. We walked along the dock, its creaking loud and groaning. The sky that reflected in the water, a soft pink and yellow as the sun eased its way out of the horizon.

As we approached, I saw the shape was an anchor, cleaned and shining a menacing dark silver. A hand-carved wooden plaque nailed to it, saying my father's name in dedication.

A deep hum suddenly found its way into my heart, a song I heard through my magick. It was a comforting, soothing presence that I felt was my father's spirit in that moment. Rolo sighed heavily next to me.

"His old fisherman friends came and gave me this, said it was from his old reliable boat. Seemed fitting considering his talents on the water," he murmured. I was silently impressed at the grave before me. Soft blue flowers threaded around the anchor, humbly brightening the place, my mother's influence, I presumed.

I knelt, the energy seeping from me at the reality of it all. I was before my father's grave. A death my brother and I endured separately, yet here we were, reunited in the spot my father loved the most in his life. I admired the life swimming beneath us as if in celebration of his spirit. Treasured in memory he was, in the waters and the air around it.

I smiled softly as I admired the carved name plaque, knowing it was my brother's handy work, sitting to fully take in the large anchor before me.

"He would have loved this, Rolo," I assured him and my brother sniffed. Slowly, he joins me by the anchor, the top reaching over his tall frame. We gazed upon it as if it was father himself, lost in our own memories, feeling his spirit with us.

"He fell sick just after the winter last year; it felt so sudden, one day he was strong and spirited, the next, bedridden and weak," my brother's sad voice cut through my thoughts.

"What sickness?" I asked shakily, not really wanting to know. My brother shrugged. My magick thudded at something hidden in secret.

"It started with him weakening, then a fever which reached his mind. I had not seen something overcome someone so fast as it did him. It didn't make sense as the weather was warming, usually strengthens faeries…" my brother said. He sniffed and flicked a piece of wood.

"I tried to work the land, like he wanted, like he did. But it was hard at first. The land wanted him, not me. I was still inexperienced and it was just as frustrated as I. That winter was the hardest I had dealt," he explained, his eyes far across the lake in thought. My chest tightened at the thought. My poor brother struggling, my father's impending death a great looming storm on the already harsh reality of winter before his young self. My brother suddenly snorted bitterly.

"Mother worked hard to revive him. She used everything she could, barely sleeping or eating. As I struggled with the land, she struggled with her magick. It seemed nothing would coax his spirit." He swallowed, grimacing at the memory. It felt so unusual for my mother to not heal with ease. Truly this was something that was meant, as hard as that was to imagine.

"Bah! Stupid magick couldn't heal him. Not even the land could bring him round, so I knew it before she did. She denied it right until the moment he passed." My heart lurched at his words, at my mother's denial in losing her true love. I could barely imagine what it must have been like, to watch him slowly perish before her, her magick failing her at a most critical time. My brother sighed again, this time more wistfully, looking back to the anchor.

"He didn't suffer though. He slept a lot and muttered about his fisherman stories. Sometimes I would go in at night, just to listen as though I was a kid again." He smiled brokenly at the anchor and I sniffed, feeling tears surrender and fall. His beloved fisherman's stories, what my father was famous for and I deeply missed them such that they tore at my soul. I wiped my eyes, the anchor's representation taking its full effect to me. My brother's strong arm fell onto my shoulders then, getting a choked cough from me.

"Father saw you, you know," he suddenly said, making me snap a look at him.
"He did?" I croaked in disbelief, trying to determine desperately whether he was just trying to assure me.
"Yeah." He sniffed, dragging his gaze away from the anchor to me.

"It was perhaps a day or so before he… was talking and then turned to me. I had stopped working the land that day, feeling him fading. His eyes were so clear when he said he had seen you," he explained, his own tears falling now.

"I knew it must have been a dream or something but he seemed so lively after that. It was to the point I thought he was recovering. Mother knew better though." He shuddered at the memory.

"He said he was on a ship and he saw you waiting for him on the shore." Rolo laughed bitterly as I flinched at his words.

The memory of the dream I'd had of him before I knew of his passing. The anchor, the ship sailing away… it all felt too eerily similar. Before I could think too hard about it, Rolo's words broke through to me.

"He never stopped believing you would come home again," he bit, looking back at the anchor almost angrily. He sniffed and wiped at his face. Guilt overwhelmed me from his words and my head sank to meet my knees in shame. The bitter weight of my absence that stained my father's death. Could I have saved him? Could my return have revived him?

"I was too late," I blurted brokenly to myself. The truth choked me with emotion. I felt my brother grab me then, pulling me into his embrace.

"Don't be a fool. You have no fault in this," he said, though his naïve sense of my understanding made me tremble bitterly. I had no energy to correct him, his kind, brotherly sense of me too warming at that moment.

"I'm not gunna lie, I thought you were dead too when he said that," he said and shrugged.

"Mother denied it of course, but then she was denying father's own fading that was happening right before us," he explained and sniffed loudly, turning back to the anchor. He patted the top bar of the anchor, known as the stock, and grimaced guiltily.

"After father had gone and you were not there...it was easier to believe you were both together somewhere else far away…" he trailed off wistfully.

"I'm sorry, Rolo," I mumbled, unable to contain my shame, for where I suffered, my brother had suffered his own reality. He grabbed my shoulders once more.

"Oh shush! You are back now and we are together again." He smiled down at me, coaxing a small smile from me.

We both turned back then, taking in the anchor before us, feeling father's spirit, embracing it. My magick swayed around us in time with the swishing lake water beneath us, a light touch of proud hands upon our shoulders.

As we slowly made our return to the small cottage further inland, we were lost in our thoughts and memories, the silence was a calm, healing presence in our reverie.

"I get it, you know," I began, mind still half lost in thought.

"Hm?"

"Thinking me dead, then separating from mother," I said vaguely. Understanding washed over him, relief sagging his shoulders. He chuckled softly; it carried away in the afternoon breeze.

"You always were understanding. You got that from father." He smirked. I blushed and hugged him tightly, making him laugh deeply.

"I can still feel him here," I whispered into his chest, my magick dancing around us.

"He always will be here. He is not lost to us," he muttered, feeling his heart pound against my cheek.

Word had soon spread of my return to the land. Tales were shared of my triumphs and endurance in the dark lands of the fanged creatures across the sea. Our distant neighbours and curious faelings began to approach me, asking me of what they had heard. It was mainly not true, making me blush and shy from the unwanted attention but my brother needed little of me, so I had nothing to do but inform them more on the truth.

Yet as some of the truth would spill from my lips, I found myself hiding the grisly details of my capture from my trapped and desperate time. I shared only the wonders of the vampire court and the glittering candlelight in the darkness.

It became clear that the villagers called for a party in celebration, as well as to celebrate my belated faerie transition. I was not surprised as the fae in this land needed little excuse to crack open the ale and ribbons, to stop work on the land for one day and celebrate the peace and contentment they shared. I was not allowed to be a part of the preparations, as they insisted I was to be the guest of honour. The term itself made me pout curiously. To be seen as a guest to my homeland? It truly showed the change in me then. I was greeted like a hero, the villagers bewildered and enthralled as they soon learnt of the abolishment of the fae slavery in the Vampire Nation. I still did not know who told them that this was my doing.

Mary giggled as she held her hands over my eyes from behind, excitedly ready to show me the party that anxiously waited to commence before me. I felt Arlow tug my shirt forward and we walked in slow eagerness to the open fields.

It was dusk; the light was already fading and I could smell the oiled lanterns being lit. With a whoosh of air, the sight was returned to me, as Mary removed her hands and I took in what was before me.

The fields glittered with lights, cheers of the villagers already on their second drink, swaying on wooden tables. Arlow ran with the other children, screaming with happiness. Some faeries had taken up their instruments and began to play softly.

"Welcome home," she whispered and kissed my cheek, making me blush. It had been the longest time since I had been to a celebration, my mind returning to my eighth birthday. Her hands gripped my shoulders warmly, easing my trembles.

"Thank you," I gasped, feeling a well of emotion. She laughed and was handed an ale herself by my grinning brother.

"This is for you, sprite," he cheered, gesturing with his own drink. I laughed then and took in all those around me. The humble party held in my honour, hastily pulled together but full of consideration and togetherness. I briefly wondered where my mother was, but decided not to concern Rolo with it.

As I entered fully, many called out to me, cheering me, congratulating or simply singing songs that I had written as a child. It was all wonderfully overwhelming. I was pulled here and there, villagers dying to ask me questions.

"Do you have any bite marks?"

"Are their fangs really as big as they say?"

"Do their eyes really glow red?"

All innocently curious questions that I struggled to answer without my own mind being pulled back into that dark past. The truth of how I knew these things was avoided with great effort, even from the most aged faeries.

I spent most of the night sharing what I knew, barely having time to sip my own ale that was hastily handed to me at some point. The faelings had slowed their games and the cheers and shouting had lulled into soft murmuring or drunken exclamations. As the questions began to wane, I started to search the gathering for my brother, finding him on a table, slightly apart from the others. He was sat with Mary as they talked quietly, Arlow falling asleep in her arms. I was about to ask if they had seen mother, when I was pulled away from the scene as a faeling tugged my shirt.

"Can we have a story?" he whined softly, the other faelings shyly looking up to me from behind the bravest. I smiled and drew them to the corner, placing myself on an empty barrel and began to share a story, not one of vampires but of mer and sea shanties that my father had shared. They listened intently, some sucking their thumbs, gazing at me with wide eyes as I spoke in my hushed tone. I smiled secretly as Arlow groggily joined and pushed his way to the front.

Soon my story seemed to revive them and they stood up, bursting with excitement and ran off chasing each other, squealing.

I was called over to a table of elders who drunkenly muttered to me on the changes I had made in the world.

"We always knew you would make a difference."

"Yes, yes, we sure did. Diafol never lies."

"Diafol knew of your greatness; it is why you were always treasured here as such."

"This land was blessed the moment that faerie walked into here," they muttered, the mention of my grandfather's name making me wince, though they were too wrapped up in their own conversation to notice.

"You changed the world, lad, saved hundreds of faelings from destruction."

"Indeed, for we are no fools to what happened across the sea," they murmured. I found myself too weary to defend myself, to argue at the cost of my own self, or why it was even allowed to occur if they knew so much.

I sat there, taking in their words, I now held the same respect to the villagers that Diafol had. It was a strange and jarring realisation.

"You haven't seen him by any chance have you, lad? We miss him greatly." One nudged me roughly.
"No I haven't, unfortunately." I apologised quietly, turning to leave the table when I bumped into Arlow, who stood close behind me.
"Is he scary?" he whispered, his fingers fiddling nervously as he looked at me with big brown eyes. I chuckled and knelt to his height, enjoying the fact I could at least do that to someone smaller than me now.
"You have nothing to fear," I replied, patting him reassuringly. He nodded, and ran back to the other faelings. I felt deflated, the talk of my grandfather had drained me.

It was then I heard a gentle song. I realised it was one that only I can hear. I followed the song, dazed, conscious that it lead into the forest behind my old home. I had a vague recollection of this happening once before, when I was younger.

A twig snapped, just a few metres within and I looked to the sound, my eyesight better in the darkness since I returned.
"It's only me." My mother sighed wearily, stepping out into the moonlight. I gasped and hugged her in surprise.
"Why are you hiding?" I pouted. Her shoulders drooped as I stepped back to look at her. Her form felt weaker than before.
"Rolo wouldn't be pleased. It's supposed to be a happy occasion for you both, dearest." She tapped my chin sadly. Her hand was cold. I realised she was avoiding a conflict.
"Have your fun with your brother. We can talk another time," she said sadly, already withdrawing from me.

"Mother? Are you okay?" I asked softly. She smiled sadly, the expression dim in the darkness.

"This land isn't the same for me since your father left us. I am glad it is still pleasant for you, dear one. You deserve this happiness," she said softly. A rise of laughter and childish squeals distract me.

"Are you—"

I looked back and she was gone.

I decided that since she wanted to be hidden, I searched again for my brother. I found him sitting on a hill, further away from the crowd which now had started to separate due to the late evening chill. I smiled and sat with him, feeling the relief of being away from the crowd.

"Is that father's pipe?" I chuckled as he blew smoke down below. He laughed, embarrassed, and shrugged.

"It suits you." Even in the low light, I see a blush spread to his cheeks, possibly from the ale and he nudged me playfully.

"You're not like him you know," he slurred. I frowned.

"Who?"

My brother snorted loudly.

"Toad man."

"Why do you say that?" I asked quietly, hugging my knees.

"I know you worry about it. His influence on you, his control," he explained, sounding more sober suddenly. I released a breath I had not realised I held.

"I was worried too. But honestly, seeing you come back here, despite how they see you below, no magick could hide you brother. You are you, despite that toad's efforts. You stayed true," he said, his faeland-ish twang carrying the soothing words to me, warming my heart. I smiled to myself as I watched the fading lights below.

"Truly?" I whispered. My brother sighed, turning to me then.

"You don't feel it?" he asked, puffing smoke over me.

I think on his words, feeling my magick simmering within me. The green feeling alight behind my eyes assuring me.

"I am not certain who I am anymore." I sighed, watching the green feeling wearily in my mind's eyes. Watching it as you watch a flame as it flickers and turns in reserved fascination.

My brother shoved me roughly, jolting me from my thoughts, scoffing loudly.

"You are the son of Maurice Avery! And speaking of that, it's time for music." He groaned, standing and swaying slightly. He held his hand out to me and I took it with a smile, aglow with pride and joy.

We rejoined the remaining folk down below, my brother taking up a lute and tuning it briefly, leaning against an abandoned table. A few drunken cheers from the surrounding faeries as they slowly gathered to my brother.

The remaining sleepy faelings huddled together nearby, also eager to listen to my brother play. I joined the crowd, eager and curious to listen to him play.

He started playing a soft tune and I lost myself in the music, my magick stirring, taking in his voice which had matured handsomely, the lute a servant to his story. It is only when I tuned in to the lyrics, that I began to pay closer attention:

Oh little lost brother,
Your heart is heavy in the valley of the soul
As you walk away,
From all the holds and dark you left behind,

But I will hold on hope for you
And I won't let you choke on the jaws around your neck

The land is lonesome without your song, dear brother
So come back walking
Find strength in your pain
So come back walking
And see the world for what it is
The truth being the rotten head of the toad

He straightened and eyed me openly, his voice louder with determination;

So make your sirens call!
Sing from your heart and soul!

For that is truer than what you say
You are freer than you ever were
Ever you believe to be

But I will hold on hope for you
And I won't let you choke on the jaws around your neck

A few cheers and claps break out, drowning out my shocked laugh at his words. I had no idea when he had written this but feeling the words, my music returning to me then, strengthened my resolve like a light in a dark tunnel.

I clapped and cheered loudly, feeling my own music well up inside me as a response, my magick reaching out to him in need once more. He gave a simple wave, beckoning me up and like the wings of a bird, my magick flew to him.

We were soon singing together—a merry tune; it was in such a blissful feeling I could no longer determine if it was the ale or my magick that made me swoon.

He led me onto the table as we sang a song our father used to sing, the remains of the ale passed to us in between choruses. Others began to bang and stamp to the beat, encouraging us further. We became lost in our memories as we danced and sang the rest of the night away.

I remember the end of the night was of me having laughed and cried so much they had blurred together within me. I remembered lying on the hill once more, the world quieting around me, dizzy from everything as I admired the vast expanse of the sky above me, swirling around me, and blanketing me as I fell behind the veil.

Further days passed as I relived my childhood from within my memories. Watching the grass green in the morning light, walking the forests I no longer feared that surrounded the land. I admired the gentle folk doing what they had always done, whether it be tending to the land, baking bread, or taking a drunken snooze on their porch in the warm glow of the afternoon sun.

I took in the peace around, feeling it comforting me, soothing my burdened soul. Beneath the surface, I felt my magick, new and hopeful, replenished from my surroundings. I felt it shifting and knew that the peace I felt was not the same as it was before I left here. I felt my music within me, fanning the flames of my magick. The peace here felt too still for it, too settled and rigid, set in its own way.

I began thinking about the music I had heard in the courts of the vampires, already piecing together my own with such low and thudding melodies. The need growing within me as the days passed by. The Brimhaven feeling combined with this new green magick, borne from my pain and despair in the vampire district, I needed to express it as it simmered and bubbled within me, feeling more right and assured than before, strengthening my restlessness.

As I was mulling over this one evening, my brother had noticed my growing distance, and he shared with me his concern over dinner.

We took an evening walk on the hill near the cottage, the same place where I had spoken to Diafol of my future almost eight years ago. I admired the dusky view below us, the glittering fireflies as they floated around to greet us. It felt calm and magickal.

"What is it?" my brother started, sounding worried as he sat next to me, the fireflies flurrying, distressed by his heavy movement. I sighed and he nudged me in encouragement.

"You said I had changed," I explained and he seemed to sober at that, turning to follow my gaze to the calm scene below us.

"You were right, I have. I won't tell you the details but my life was in danger once," I said, noticing him tensing at my words. He started ruffling his hair distractedly.

"It was real danger. I would have died, but my magick saved me," I explained and he grimaced.

"My magick and music are my purpose, that is still certain. I am but a catalyst to this force within me. It is my desire to share it with the world." My brother's heavy sigh made me turn to him, determined.

"It's not his Rolo, it is mine. My own magick. Do you understand?"

"I do," he answered wearily. Silence fell over us then. My brother sniffed and looked at me for the first time since we came here.
"So, you're leaving." It was a statement.
I nodded distantly, already lost to the music in the distance.

"Urgh, but you just got here!" my brother scoffed. Again I nodded sadly, the light fading further around us.
"I have to do this. I will come back; I always will." I turned back and looked to the horizon where the sun now hid itself from us.
"But it calls to me. I can feel it in my bones." I hugged myself as I whispered this, my heart already thudding to the music and the magick held within me. My brother sighed again, looking to where my gaze was.
"I know it's hard for you to understand."
"It is not actually. I have always seen it in you. Your eyes were always to the sky, whereas mine were on the ground. It's how I knew it would not be so hard for Diafol to take you from us." His words were sad yet he smiled in fondness to me. I returned it and he ruffled my hair playfully as he always had done.

Despite our differences, everything that our paths had divided for us, I still felt our connection as I had the moment I could remember. It was the most reassuring feeling I held alongside my connection, now smaller to the land around me.
"It is truly what you are meant for, isn't it?" he asked and I realised my eyes had already returned to the horizon.

"I believe so."

We sat and pondered quietly in our thoughts for a few moments. I hesitated to discuss further on what I must but soon it burst out of me.
"I am to make music with others too. Talents I have met in the south," I explained quickly.
"Vampires," Rolo spat, flicking grass angrily in front of us. I swallowed down my anger as his judgmental tone.
"Yes," I replied. My tone made him consider me seriously, then he sighed in defeat and rubbed his eyes tiredly.
"That's the part I don't understand, Élan, after what they all did to you?"

"It was one actually, and yes."
"Why?" his question made me turn to him fully.
"Because it is with them that I show the world," I explained though I could not define my meaning further.
"Now you *do* sound like him," my brother snarled, making me shrug defensively.
"They are not all the same, you know? I do not fear them. I can't explain it very well but I know I am meant for this," I replied, urging understanding to reach him. My brother shrugged me off indifferently.
"If that is what helps." He sniffed, making my heart sink. I shuffled forward, gripping his strong arms desperately.

"Listen, they can get me out there. To places I won't be able to go on my own, reach audiences that would not consider a solo faerie. The Queen herself believes she owes me that protection," I explained and my brother scoffed, pulling away from me.

His rejection cut me deep and my chest swelled with emotion. I looked down below, searching for the answer in the fields before us. I sank, my head falling to his shoulder in defeat. I sighed heavily, the glow of the fireflies softening me once more.

"What we shared that night at the party, I want to bring to the fae all around the world. Faeries and faelings that were never borne here, that don't even have Brimhaven bred in their hearts. I want us to share our father's songs and stories with faelings that were never graced with this land," I explained passionately. My brother jolted and looked at me.

"*Us*? You want me to go with you?" he asked incredulously. I winced and hugged myself, having been caught at my wish, which I now knew was hopeless.

"I am not sure. I know how much the land needs you here…just for my first concert, you know…?" I trailed off shyly.

"Yeah, but I have a family now, Élan," Rolo replied gently. I nodded sadly, turning back to look out into the distance, feeling the loneliness overwhelm me. I felt my brother watch me closely in silence.

After a few moments, he scratched his head noisily.

"But… if your first concert is after the summer, when the faeling is born…maybe I could… I do want to see you more." I turned surprised and hopeful.

"I want to help where I can. I can't stay with you longer than needed. My family and land need to be considered too. I won't be able to leave Mary with the faeling too long," he warned though my smile was growing with each word.

"I understand," I replied, fighting to restrain the excitement within me. I hugged him, making him chuckle. As I held him, his body almost too wide for me to fully grip, I considered all that he was leaving behind for me, even for a temporary time. The difference in our lives that once split in our paths like a river, now rejoined for such a time.

"I appreciate any support at this point, Rolo," I assured him softly. We both sigh contently, taking in the night air, our choice before us settling in.

I meet my band in the Middlelands, a decent five bed cottage big enough to house us. It was something Mastuo had suggested as a way for us to come together and rehearse. In the Middlelands, mainly humans resided here and with accessible bloodbanks for my bandmates, it was an ideal neutral location for us.

The land itself seemed rural like the Faelands but held little magick in comparison. There was little spirit to be felt in the breeze that greeted me as I arrived. This wasn't a problem as it helped me actually tune in to my own a lot easier.

Our first concert was scheduled for the beginning of fall, leaving the entire summer for us to work on the band. This made sense as it would be slow progress with adjusting sleeping patterns and living arrangements for the first few weeks upon our arrival.

Alongside Mastuo, there was Ville (on bass), Hector (on drums) and Marko (our lead guitarist). Being the only faerie, I should have been intimidated, yet I felt at ease with them as soon as we began to play. We were merely extensions of something greater coming through us. As they played, the words fell from me, tugged from my soul.

A month into summer, I patiently sat outside, waiting for my bandmates to rise, watching the blood orange succumb to the evening sky. It was then when our band name became apparent to me.

We would be called Nightfall, the transition between light to dark, where our music sat. I excitedly shared my idea with Mastuo and we happily agreed, his smile sharp but friendly.

Rolo joined us late in the summer, after Mary had birthed a faeling girl called Bellflower, or Bell for short. I felt a small smidge of guilt having not seen her, being her uncle, being too focused on my own dreams. It was soon driven from my mind as Mastuo played a new tune for me to write against.

As expected, Rolo was weary and guarded around my bandmates, only talking to me directly. I was thankful that they did not let his rudeness bother them, and that they were understanding of his reaction towards them.

We took our time, not feeling pressure but allowing the music to come to us. It seemed most natural despite this being something that had never been done before. It was a relief it went so well.

It was only a matter of time until we would find out if the world agreed.

Months later, I let my magick thread in my voice, vibrating with memories of Brimhaven and the feeling of home. Mastuo masterfully lured us with his pianistic talent as my song followed intimately behind with a soothing presence. My words I sang in perfect melody, spinning tales with the frequencies. Everyone was singing, dancing, or joining in, in their own way.

I looked around and my musicians were enjoying it as much as me, a relief and shared amazement at the phenomena that was being created around us. We felt ourselves feed off this power, this connection, and together, we take them on a journey. A world between the fantasy of faerie-tales and the passionate romance of vampirism.

As I reached our final song, the audience was already screaming for an encore, and I was reluctant to leave them. Already I wanted to do another, and by the feelings of my companions, they did too. When we walked off stage together, we were buzzing with magick and emotion.

With the audience still calling for us, we smiled at each other with relief and congratulated ourselves. The strong embrace from my brother eased me into the ground. As we walk together off the stage, the sounds fading behind us, I took in the fact that we had done it. This was the first step and now there was no stopping us.

This was my true power.
This was my recovery.
This was my music.
My magick.
My purpose.

I giggled, drunk on my new sense of freedom and relief as my brother avoided the pats of my vampire friends. Mastuo was already speaking to someone to book another gig.

Dizzily, I was led to my temporary studio by my brother. He halted me suddenly and growled, my eyes faced with red.
"Gods," I gasped as I realised before me was Alain. He smiled down at me, making me blush. My brother's grip on me hardened painfully.
"Ah this must be your brother. Rolo, is it?" Alain smiled dangerously, taking in my brother behind me, both standing a similar height above me.
"You came," was all I can gasp.
"Did I not say I would come to your first concert? It was truly remarkable," he gushed and all I could do was swoon at his

words. My brother flinched as Alain swept up my hand and kissed it.

"You sang with true magick and passion. It was amazing to witness," Alain said, his lips lingering on my hand.

"You're in the way, fang-man," my brother gritted out, making me jolt with shock. Gods! To say such a thing to a vampire prince? Was my brother mad? Alain just chuckled.

"I see I am un-acquainted with your brother. Rolo, I am Alain, Blood Prince of Queen Carmilla's court," Alain replied patiently, holding out his pale hand. My brother snorted.

"Fancy words and smart smiles don't impress me," Rolo hissed and I groaned, turning to him.

"Rolo you mustn't be rude! He is vampire royalty, you idiot," I barked, hitting him on the arm in frustration. Rolo frowned at my reaction.

"Are you blushing?" he asked, making me scoff and I attempted to shove him away.

"Of course I am! It is such an embarrassment to have you be so rude to the Prince after what he has done for me. I-I mean us!" I gasped, my face flushing entirely red now. Rolo's eyes narrowed.

"Ah so, he is the one you…"

"Enough!" I shoved him hard, which moved him barely a step back. He raised his arms defensively.

"Pardon my ignorance. Guess you have no need of me now?" he asked, making me growl in frustration. Alain chuckled as Rolo turned to leave.

"I am so sorry—" Alain cut me off by assuring me it was fine.

"Please do not worry. In fact, I am relieved you have such a diligent bodyguard. Otherwise I would insist you have one of mine," Alain explained and I smiled, relieved. He took my hand again, looking at me beseechingly.

"I kindly ask I take you for a late dinner, as a congratulations for such a successful first gig. Surely your band and um…brother-guard won't mind?" he asked gently.

"Oh of course, I will just change and we can head straight out!" I stuttered, my energy riding another high from this course of events. Alain nodded, moving aside for me to enter my studio. I shut the door with a slam as my adrenalin excelled my strength further than I thought. I sighed and bolted to change quickly.

I straightened my suit as I turned to open the door when a tinkling noise stops me. It had sounded as though something had landed on my table. I frowned and turned to inspect, having no clue what it could possibly be.

Straight away, like a beacon of light, the gold coin drew my eye and my skin went cold. A giggle behind me made me whip around.

"Over here, dear one." Diafol chuckled, making me turn back to the table. The mirror showed as if he stood behind me, tall and proud in his glittering terribleness. He wore a suit that looked newly tailored and not a material that I had seen before. We eyed each other in tense silence, frozen in time.

"That was a stunning performance, birdie," he murmured making me tremble. I felt a small swell of pride at his backhanded compliment.

"Do not call me that," I bit, eyeing him angrily in the mirror, his gold eyes menacing flames. He snarled at my reaction.

"Fiery now, aren't you?" he sneered, his eyes narrowing dangerously. I turned away, no longer wanting to see him, to acknowledge his presence.
"You are still mine, no matter how many vamps you wrap around yourself," he hissed, making me pause.
"Or even if the pretty prince does like you back," he growled.
"I know," I whispered, my body tense.
"Good," Diafol purred and I found myself drawn back to his image in the mirror, now pressed more closely to the surface, unable for me to see my own reflection now.

"What do you want?" I asked firmly, sounding braver than I felt. Diafol tapped his chin thoughtfully, grinning his pointed teeth mockingly.
"Want? Hmm…" He looked to me and the smile dropped.
"Nothing." I frown at him.
"Nothing?" At my question he spread his arms open, gesturing around us.
"Keep doing your music; that is all."

I stepped towards him in surprise and curiosity. He moved a clawed hand in front of him and gripped it slowly.
"Keep those beasts in your power," he purred, grinning openly now. I swallowed heavily, fearing the truth in his words. How much did I control them without my knowing? Were my songs simple spells to them? Diafol tapped the mirrored surface.

"Will you not take my gift?" he smirked, pointing to the coin on the table.

As soon as I looked to the gold, I felt its trapping gaze in return. The gold filled my vision, pulling and tugging my magick. Memories of the pain and suffering I had endured swirled and flashed before me in a terrible recall. I lurched, realising my hand was outstretched towards it and snatched it back, turning away completely towards the door.

"I'm sorry. I need to go," I muttered, realising Alain must still be waiting outside. The thought of him trying to come in here with Diafol present terrified me. I heard that horrible giggle.

"Then go," he hissed. I grabbed the door handle and turned it, determined to leave hastily.

"I will be watching."

Epilogue

Prince

Nova

The air was tense. I stood amongst the crowd as they eagerly waited for the music to start. The music that had spread through the land like wildfire, reaching even the farthest edges of Lut-Par, including the mountains in the north. This was why I was here; I must witness this.

Like a coiled snake, species from dark and light stood together to await for the gig to begin. Already small tinkles of the keys, steady beating of drums teased us. Soon it would begin.

I was nudged by an unknown person and tried not to recoil. I was not used to crowds. I had avoided them at all costs since my childhood.

I also hoped no one would recognise me; in a crowd this large and mixed, it was unlikely. Despite my unique appearance of dark blue cropped hair, my lavender eyes, my skin is a luminescent pale complexion from my northern breed. My clothing, which was humble for once, in order to blend in. Though I knew despite this, my timing would be limited. It would not be long before the presence of my faerie magick would stir those around me.

My small group of guards, also disguised, cast a wary eye around us. We were all on edge, we had not expected such a large crowd. They would have stood out like me if not for the vast expanse of those around us, which was currently working to our advantage. Such a gathering of fae and vampires, even a few pixies and humans could be spotted, the bizarre rarity drawing in more and more with each event. What was it that drew them in? I had my suspicions.

I huffed as the air felt tight and my hands began to sweat in my gloves. They were heavy velvet made for the harsh winds in the North, though I dared not remove them. They were the best material barrier I had against my magick that grew with each day. My fear of losing control of my magick in such a precarious place was too great. Still, it was damned stuffy and I strained to cool myself with my icy veins. I was not used to feeling warm and I did not like it. My magick whipped and snapped, reflecting my frustration. Soon.

I took in those around me, many talking and chatting amongst themselves, though I already had begun to notice a few faeries sensing a change in the air, a small shift influenced by my presence.

I jolted as the crowd roared in adoration as the gig finally kicked into its introduction. I was not easily scared and I shook myself from the foolishness. I was too on edge.

I looked below, onto the stage as he appeared, getting waves of approval and cheers of joy. A small spritely boy compared to his fanged bandmates. Huh.

So this is the Son of Song?

My discernment was quelled when his voice began to slowly roll over the crowd and in the air around us, melodious and beautiful. Like a purr it was across the organised talented keys of the piano. It was then that I felt the pull in his song, the pull in his voice.

That out in the midst of all this pain and despair,
I had been innocent and secure.

Now I am wiser but unsure.
I can feel this change within me,
I am stronger now, but still not free…

I took a steady breath to refocus, surprised by my own draw to the magick in his voice. I looked around and felt the energy, the magick that was intertwined with it. How unharnessed it ran free amongst us. I took in the large crowd, the dotted difference in species was truly a spectacle to behold.

As I watched the magick take its hold, I realised only a few like myself could truly appreciate what was happening here.

In faeries, I saw it revive and renew their souls, in some reawaken a magick, small and slumbering. In vampires and pixies, creatures of dark, I saw it lure and subdue them. I spied the Blood Prince opposite in the VIP boxed area, his smile proud and just as bewitched as the rest. It was in that smile I saw intimacy there, as his red gaze pinned the boy on stage, and I trembled.

My magick woke then, responding to my observations, simmering and dangerous. I fought to calm it, weary of how little I could manage it in this situation. Now was not the time.

Despite my restraint, my magick welled and oozed like a force, crawling towards the stage, its own draw to the magick that had its own release and freedom. At that moment, I was jealous.

I struggled to retain and keep mine hidden while watching a similar calibre dance free and relish in that. It made my fight less negotiable to my magick. As my magick reached the stage, I noticed Élan jolt, almost stuttering his song, though no one seemed to notice. He played it off as a roll on the stage and rapidly moved on with a cheeky smile. It was impressive, but I knew he felt it. It wasn't aggressive but I was certain it must have been a shocking presence to him, a difference in the air that would raise the hairs on your neck.

As he continued, I see him casually looking around, his tune lulling over the music like a lover, undeterred. I knew he could feel me watching. Like a hidden powerful interest. Do you fear it is Diafol? But surely he knows the difference. My presence is much more untamed than the master of mystery. Was Diafol in the audience? I could not sense him. Yet he could remain undetected if he wished. Another burst of jealousy as my magick had never been allowed that privilege. At least not in the presence of other magickal beings. My magick insisted that there was never a time to be hidden. Like a lured lover, it fought to be hidden now.

I resisted the urge to attempt to cloak myself, knowing it was a fruitless effort. A reflex that I had managed before, being undetected against lesser beings but this boy was different. We were the same. The magick returned to me with the same unbidden lease of strength. Like he, I too was a child born of legend. Many knew now of his grandfather, the alluded Diafol, rumoured to be the descendant of Pan of Peter himself.

Yet mine was a more prominent issue now. There were already songs of my mother, The Ice Queen in the mountains, and my being, fathered by Jack the Frost himself. Northern borne I was, hidden in the mountains, where the tales were spun, however my enemies saw fit.

I felt my magick's resistance and realised its course. I wanted to be known to him, I wanted him to know I was watching.

A few faeries nearby started to sense my magick further, though they themselves did not know what it was that tingled their senses. They looked around, sniffing the air, looking around curiously. You could always guarantee the fae to be the first to sense you, their curiosity too strong to ignore. I saw a few flicker their gazes towards me distractedly and I resisted the urge to grimace. My magick sizzled and spat in rebellion. Time was running out.

My guards smoothly began to move closer to me, closing in as they interpreted the notice I was giving. *Just a little more,* my magick whined silently and I relented. I wanted him to see me. Was it the pull of his music or my sense of pure loneliness in the world? Was this my brother in magick?

"Prince Nova," the nearest guard called softly, his voice travelling by magick only to my ears, underneath the strong current of the music. I nodded to him reluctantly; it was time to go.

A few faeries had stopped to watch me then, realising who I was. I turned and fought the crowd, leaving in the opposite direction of the stage, the song pulling and tugging me back, the magickal connection reluctant to break.

"Your Majesty," a faerie breathed, halting my path, their eyes staring at the translucent crown of stars that must be barely visible upon my head. I nodded and moved aside hastily, snapping my magick back to me just as the song ended.

19th October 2018 - 18th October 2020

Before you go…

Thank you for reading my story and I hope you enjoyed it. This has been a journey and I feel relieved to have it out into the world.

If you did enjoy this book, please review on Amazon or Goodreads and recommend to a friend.

Turn over for Exclusives!

These exclusives include:

- An extra chapter following on from the story
- Alex's inspiration behind the book
- A map of Brimhaven - Élan's home village
- A lineart illustration of Élan'
- A preview chapter of Vatican

Newsletter Sign up

For more updates and details following Alex's writing please sign up to her bi-monthly newsletter on her website at www.alexwolfonline.com.

Extra Chapter

Brothers in Magick

Élan

The news of my band, Nightfall, soon swept through the land. A fresh wave that followed the new year beckoned the species to embrace the change. It wasn't long before our schedule was fully booked, months in advance. I couldn't help but feel overwhelmed and humbled by the wonderful response. It was better than any of us had imagined.

Reviews spilled through the land of how it affected all those who attended. How the fae felt revived and renewed, a fresh expression of culture reminding them of what they were capable of.

For the dark creatures like vampires and pixies, it lured and subdued them in awe of the beauty and delight that was shared, while soothing them with the familiarity of their music.

Rolo had continued to remain by my side for a few more months through the winter, which was longer than I had truly hoped. As the new year approached, I could sense my brother's need to return home, surely as he had sensed my distance when I felt the need to leave Brimhaven. With a new faeling in his family, it felt wrong to make him miss them.

With that in mind, I had bittersweet feelings for his upcoming departure, as I knew he was slowly becoming accustomed to the presence of our vampire companions. It would have been nice for them to get along better, perhaps that was a hope too far even for Rolo.

"It is time, isn't it?" I asked softly one day as we shared a quick meal following another amazing gig that still left me buzzing with excitement. Rolo's sigh confirmed it.

"I'm sorry-"

"No. Don't be, Rolo. Truly, you have given me so much these past months. Being away from the land, your family—for me. I couldn't have asked for more," I responded, gripping his arm opposite me in assurance. His response was one of relief and anticipation.

Later, Rolo's farewell hug was crushingly comforting. I savoured the embrace, promising myself that it wouldn't be years before I felt it again.

"I am going to miss you," I said, choked with emotion.

"Me too, but this is where you are meant to be, sprite." His firm reply rumbled in his chest with emotion. His words were the final stamp of reality that assured me of what I had been beginning to feel for a few weeks now. That I was established in my place, in the band, in my purpose. He could leave me now.

I smiled fondly as he gingerly entered the sleek car that would take him back. Truly, it showed such differences between us, as technologies and beings outside of Brimhaven, I seemed to get accustomed to a lot easier than him. My magick swirled around me, a soft tune already driving my thoughts to a new song I wanted to write. A song that would well wish my brother as I explored the world further.

It became apparent that Rolo's absence was exactly what I needed. It was easier to breathe around the vampires, not worrying about my brother's judging eyes.

Also, the direct connection to home always loomed as I embraced the new world around, which seemed to remind me of what I had lost. Without my familial crutch, I spent more time getting to know the interesting creatures I worked with. Learning more about their stories and pasts, what brought them to music, what inspired them.

Then Enkil arrived.

After we toured the first few venues, Alain was recalled to court once more. I had not seen him since, though he wrote to me often. Within a day or two of my brother leaving, Enkil appeared, carrying a letter with Alain's seal saying he was to oversee the band and help with arrangements. It wasn't long before Enkil also decided to make himself our head of security. He explained that his cousin had voiced his concern with such a mixture of dark and day creatures present, something that hadn't happened before. Alain's hope was that my safety was a priority.

At first, I didn't quite know how to take it. This huge pixie, whom I barely knew (but was obviously very close to Alain) would be my new guard? He seemed intimidating and was regarded highly by my bandmates from being Queen Carmilla's adopted son.

"Alain would feel better having someone look out for you, sprite," he explained offhandedly. His use of the word 'sprite reminded me of Rolo instantly and I soon liked him. Whether it was his close connection to Alain or the fact I found his aura to be more protective than threatening, I could not tell.

All I knew was that I soon became fascinated with him. I had so many questions to ask him regarding his unusual upbringing and the obvious fact that he was a pixie. It was apparent that he did not hold the same grace or regality that his vampire peers did. Yet, I couldn't deny his confident swagger and uniqueness appealed to me.

In some ways, I found a kindred spirit in this being. He too, was considered an outsider from his own kin. He understood what it felt like, to be expected to be one way when he was another through his circumstances.

A couple of months into the new year with spring and my eighteenth birthday looming, we were playing a gig in the Faelands, further South than Astoria. This gig felt different though as I warmed up; perhaps it was the higher presence of fae than usual?

As the concert began in the usual way. I sang my start, reaching outward with my magick to gauge the audience. What returned, jolted me from my song.

A strong force had responded and I quickly continued, though now on edge as I took in the audience. It hadn't felt aggressive but more shocking that there was something here, something that radiated with the same strength in magick, if not more than what I had observed before. This certainly felt different and I was curious as to what brought it here.

Was it my music? Or something more?

As our music continued, I felt it watching, observing with powerful interest. I knew it wasn't Diafol; it felt stronger, not afraid to hide, and I wasn't sure if that was a good thing.

At the corner of my vision I saw Mastuo eye me, nodding as he too felt the presence. It assured me that whatever it was, we would be safe enough to continue.

After the gig, I lingered in my temporary changing room, feeling the need to, my curiosity still on a high from what I had felt. Enkil insisted on being present with me afterwards. As I changed out of my concert clothing, a dramatic sparkling outfit, the room around me felt static with silence.

What was I waiting for?

I decided to pass the time and read my recent personal letter from Alain. A comfort that I normally enjoyed after a performance, to help ground me. This time, I hoped it would calm me from this niggly feeling I felt.

Dearest Élan,

Many glorious stories of your concerts have reached the court again. I revel daily in hearing them. It seems your success has reached far and wide. My Queen is wonderfully impressed. I hope this means I can see you again soon.

I hope my brother Enkil is being good to you? He can be a brute but like me, you seem to have charmed him also. How am I not surprised?

...

A grunt at the door drew me from my thoughts. My door was opened and Enkil was standing, facing whomever had knocked.

"Step aside beast," spat an unfamiliar voice. Enkil snarled in response.

"That's enough," cut an authoritative, different voice, which made me stand. That voice, it was unfamiliar to me yet the power underneath it…

Enkil moved aside stiffly as if reluctant but also unable to deny them entrance.

A faerie entered, barely taller than me, yet held the air of someone much taller. I took in his midnight blue hair, which contrasted sharply with his pale face, his startling lavender eyes fixed on me. He wore a heavy coat, as if coming from lands much colder than here. The power clearly bled from this faerie, though his age looked barely a year older than mine. His maturity and presence seemed to even subdue Enkil into surprise.

He entered calmly, his power drawing me closer like a magnet, leaving a sharp lemon taste on my tongue. As he took me in, his look seemed to stir and crackle my own magick.

"I am Nova, faerie Prince of the North." His words accentuated and vibrated with power.

As I took him in, he dismissed his guard, the one who knocked and a few that had trailed in behind him. His eyes then shifted pointedly to Enkil.

Enkil smirked and crossed his strong, pale arms in defiance.

Tense moments passed in challenge and I coughed awkwardly. In the small time that I knew him, Enkil did not take authority well.

"Enkil, it's okay," I said, which sounded weaker than I had hoped, my voice drained from the concert. Enkil turned to me, his pale gaze narrowed in consideration, assessing. Prince Nova remained undeterred, and stood still patiently. I swallowed and nodded to Enkil, who sighed. He turned and made a silent promise in his warning gaze as he left the room.

Prince Nova moved carefully aside as if to avoid Enkil's touch and nodded in thanks. The movement caused a flicker over his head, but it was gone again, too quick for my eyes to settle on what it was.

Despite the mysterious encounter and the obvious power he exuded, I was too curious to be afraid. After what I had survived, I felt accustomed to being in unusual situations now.

"What a charming specimen," Nova mused, his eyes glinting with attraction as his gaze followed where Enkil closed the door.

"He is a good guard, takes his role seriously," I replied carefully.

"Ah yes, I can tell." Nova approached me then, holding out his gloved hand. I took it slowly and shook it.

Quietly, I was in awe at the dulled power I felt beneath the glove. *Interesting.*

"Élan, I have much anticipated our meeting. It is a pleasure to meet such a great match to my own." His voice sounded firm in confidence, which calmed me. There was no threat to be found here.
"Match?" Nova smiled at me secretly, making him look years younger. It charmed my magick and I was stunned at its response to him in such a way. As if it recognised him in a way I did not.

"Few faeries with magick like yours remove themselves from the shadows. I cannot help but be proud of you achieving such a feat," he explained.
"Magick like mine?" I echoed dumbly. He seemed to be able to make me feel naively younger than him despite us being close in age. It made me wonder where he grew up. What did he know?
"Indeed." He sniffed and straightened, tugging the large coat around him. The movement distracted my eye again. This time I was ready for it and honed on at the top of his head. I knew it was rude to stare but I was in awe as I realised what I saw.

Tiny, glittering stars floated into a translucent crown, barely visible on his head, contrasting with his dark hair. It seemed to trigger a memory within me then, like a spell in itself, freeing from the depths of my mind.

"I have heard of you, my mother said you were borne of the legendary Ice Queen and Jack the Frost himself. You came from within the hidden mountains in the North. No one knew you existed until a few years ago," I stated, and he laughed self consciously, shrugging. It was then that I noticed his heavy gloved hands. How handmade and intricate the detailing was, how even they seemed threaded with magick in the fibres.

"Such stories spread like wildfire, especially for fae like us."
"Why are you here?" I asked quietly, making him pout thoughtfully.
"Ah that is a good question." He folded his hands behind him as if to hide them from my distraction, the star crown glowing a little brighter.
"You see, I believe we have the same goal, you and I," he stated, beginning to pace in front of me in a serious manner.
"We do?"
He stopped.
"Indeed. We desire the equality of faeries among the dark creatures and humans—do you not? That is what your experience has shown you thus far?" His eyes were aglow with passion, as if staring into my soul, seeing my very past there.

It should have felt intrusive, alerting me of whom I was up against here, yet my magick seemed to beckon no danger. Unlike in the past, when vampires or even Diafol threatened me, my magick would respond. Yet in Nova's presence, it seemed lulled and charmed.

Was this a sign of a powerful spell at play here?

Should I be afraid?

He took my silence as confirmation and nodded briefly in understanding.

"You see, it is beings like us who demonstrate that we are a species to be reckoned with. Many, I believe, had hoped they had wiped out powerful fae an age ago. Now, we are starting to be feared as our rumoured ancestors were, like mine, Jack the Frost, and your Pan of Peter from your grandfather's blood." His mention of Diafol made my heart sink with worry. That damned contract felt like a brand on my soul. As I began to wonder, Nova's voice cut through my thoughts.

"Ah yes, I know of your… ownership issue. A terrible curse really," he commented, tutting in pity. He looked off to the side, as if caught in a memory, his crown glinting in the low light. He seemed to shake himself from it and awkwardly patted my shoulder.

"I have had a…similar issue," he added, making me jolt in surprise and he removed his hand quickly.

"You did?"

He nodded sighing defeatedly, sounding as tired as I felt.

"But no matter. You have barely a few months left." He waved it off and moved to my table, pretending to be interested in my trinkets.

"How do you know this?" I spun and asked him, feeling annoyed by his vagueness. So much I had already endured in the elusiveness of my situation, and I felt less patient to it now.

"As I have said, I have anticipated our meeting," he murmured, picking up a small hand mirror.
"I am afraid of what Diafol wants from me; his plans are his own." I wringed my hands nervously.

Could this prince truly help me?

I looked up and met his violet gaze in the mirror he held up.
"You cannot run from him," he said firmly.
"Then what do I do?" He replaced the hand mirror and turned to me, his eyes thoughtful.

After a tense moment, with me silently begging for an answer, he straightened with a decision.
"Do what you have done before," he replied, making my shoulders slump. He tutted and moved towards me then, a small, understanding smile on his face. I felt this was rare for him, as smiling looked awkward to him. His hand went to my shoulder once more, our gazes met.

Brothers in magick.

"Keep your eyes and ears open. Trust your magick, follow your music." I stared at him, taking in the details up close, letting the words sink in.
"Once the year is out, that is when we shall meet again. I have high hopes for you. We can join forces and accomplish what we desire. In a peaceful manner of course," he added, and moved away as if to leave. I frowned and turned to him, disappointment sinking in my stomach.

"You will not help me?" I gritted, moving fast and touching his sleeve. It was so ice cold that it burned, and I flinched away. He looked back at me sadly, his crown glinting in mockery.

"You must face this on your own," he said calmly. I tried to summon my magick in frustration, but it refused to obey, as if stilted.

Brothers in magick.

"Why?" I whined.

Must I always be on my own?

Nova fully turned back to me then, his face serious in sympathy.

"Have you not come this far on *your* own?" he asked firmly. Before I can reply, he gingerly removed his left glove. Black inked tattoos lined his hand in delicate swirls like small veins, his nails black. The temperature around the room suddenly dropped, making a shiver skitter up my spine. I was too enchanted to run away, though part of me screamed in warning.

Nova's eyes glowed a soft hue and he gestured with the hand to me. I felt a tug to my magick. It took me a moment to understand what he wanted me to do, and I took his hand carefully.

I tried not to flinch at the coldness of his flesh, a sharper feeling than a vampire's touch. The air around us moved our hair with some unknown gust. My magick simmered underneath my skin, tentatively reaching for his, which loomed, a large presence before us. A soft, flute-like tune began to play as we connected, making me gasp.

Whatever was happening, it felt right.

My magick glowed its neon green from our clasped hands, swirling around us. Tenderly, I saw his magick, a neon violet, stutter and writhe around mine, like it was being held back on a leash.

"I thought so." Nova chuckled, looking up to me, his eyes glinting with humour at something he knew that I didn't. Before I could ask, it was over.

He pulled his hand away, the glove already back on, dulling his magick once more. The absence shocked me, leaving me dazed.

"I look forward to seeing you again soon, Élan Avery. Our alliance will be the new wonder of this world," he called over his shoulder, already back to the door, leaving too quickly for my mind to react.

"I would very much like that," I murmured breathlessly

As the door softly snickered shut, it was like I was awake again. My mind flooded with questions and frustration. First Queen Carmilla's allegiance and now a faerie prince. How was this going to work? It was all still so new and strange to me. I was still in awe over the power I had just witnessed.

Was my own magick enough to prevent my grandfather's control?

Whom could I trust, but myself?

Inspiration behind Élan

I first dreamt of the character Élan when I was around fourteen years old. I was intrigued by a forest spirit being a young boy with dark hair and light eyes. It wasn't until years later when I first heard the band Nightwish's new song 'Élan' came out, when the idea expanded. The lines 'come taste the wine,' intrigued me. What is this was a fae singing about his blood? Then it was all go from there.

It further drove me as I decided to look up the meaning of the word Élan:

'vigorous spirit or enthusiasm.'

This along with my own personal experiences made me decide that no matter what happened to Élan in this book, that he must save himself. He must find his own personal strength.

Furthermore, I wanted to see vampires through a faerie's eyes, who in some cases were just as naive as we would be.

I have already written two books in this world of Lut-Par. They were very vague in comparison. Élan opened the door to the Lut-Par Saga and I cannot wait to explore further with you.

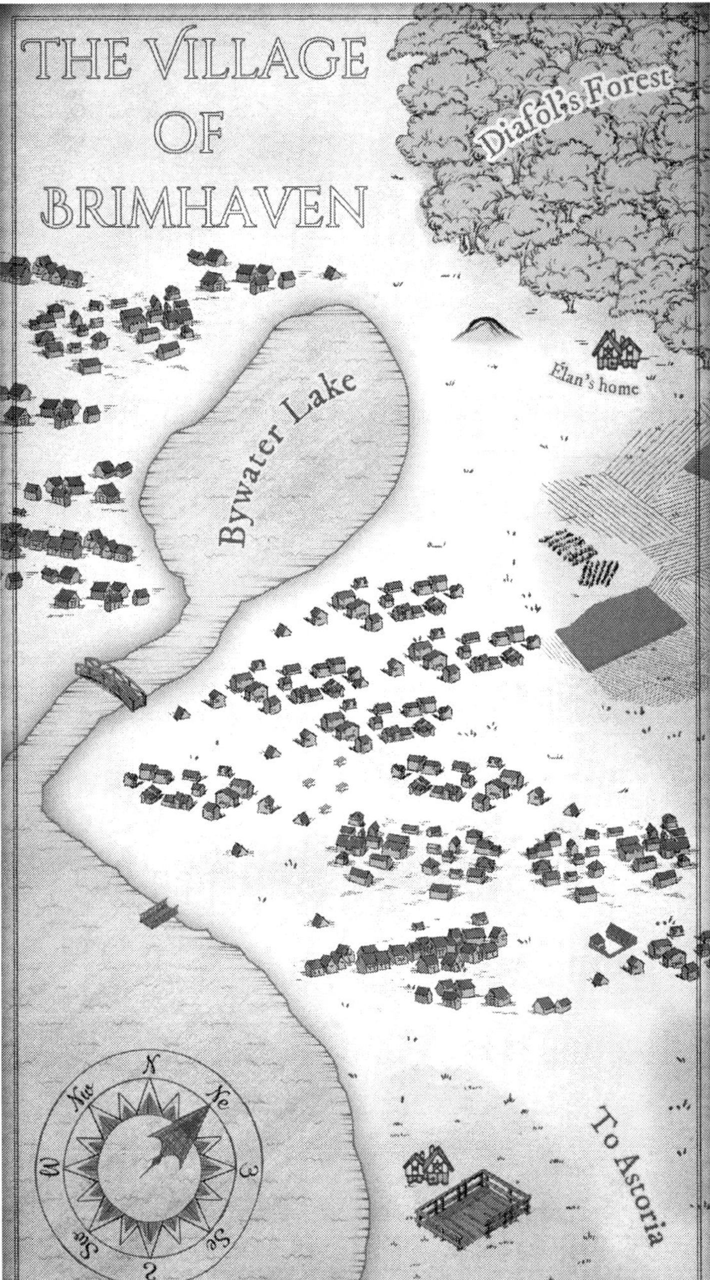

THE VILLAGE OF BRIMHAVEN
Diafol's Forest
Elan's home
Bywater Lake
To Astoria
N
Ne
E
Se
S
Sw
W
Nw

Sneak Peek at the first chapter!
VATICAN
By Alex Wolf
Available at amazon

Vatican

Luka Vatican is at the prime of his life having political influences in one of the largest capitals in the world. With power comes riches, he soon falls into an obsession with blonde Fae males, risking his immaculate image.

Mari has been a Fae-slave all his life. Numbed by the emotional and physical toll that life has thrown at him. A new customer gets his master all shaken and he is thrust into the dynamic world of the Pixie Capital.

Luka

"Lord Vatican, you need to marry," Gerald whines. My head hurts from last night and his voice grates on me. "After what happened with Mr. Kieler…"

"Cut the bullshit Gerald… you know that's not an option," I say through gritted teeth, feeling queasy. I gulp down my bourbon.

"But my lord, it would be good for publicity. Plus, you need to have children. Who else will take your place?" he stutters like a bloated toad. He looks like one too, reminding me of the rumour about me employing people uglier than me to feel more attractive. I chuckle at my own thoughts and he falls silent.
"Children? Seriously? You think *I* could father children?" I look at him incredulously.

"W-well of course, sir. Every Vatican…" he trails off at the dark look on my face.

"Gerald, you know I have people to replace me. What is this really about?" I spit, irritated with him jumping around the point. I breathe through another wave of nausea. He swallows audibly, appearing to choose his words carefully. I don't blame him. I am not in the mood for this.

"My Lord Vatican…you were seen again last night by the media. You need to hold off from-" he trails off again.

"From what? Fucking faeries? Are you kidding me?!" I am getting angry now. I stand, making him shiver with fear.

"It-it's not good for your image," he stutters, sweat dripping from his brow. He wouldn't feel half as threatened if he knew how shitty I felt. I am getting too old for this.

"Bad for my image? Are you serious? Isn't that why I fucking hired a publicist?" I grit. He nods, wide-eyed. I feel too dizzy and sit down again. He does have a point. I have been too careless lately. Perhaps going to the clubs on my own isn't a good idea.

"Are you feeling ok, my lord?" he asks, probably surprised that I wasn't fighting it more.

"Yeah yeah, I'm fine. Forward it to Gustav. Now tell me about today's reports," I wave off-handedly, picking up my pen. I take notes, letting sobriety overtake me. I need to stop this shit. I can't remember parts of last night and that's becoming a norm. How many was it? I can remember three.

Katze swaggers in, eyeing me. As my bodyguard, assistant *and* driver, Katze generally makes sure I eat and sleep regularly, since my lifestyle of endless work and partying tends to get in the way of my health. I sneer at him and turn back to Gerald.

"What do you want?" I hiss when he comes to stand next to me.

"Late night, was it?" he says casually, unfazed by my dark mood. He has experienced this many times. He is younger than me but stands taller. His spiked hair is bright red, and he reminds me of Kieler, my old business partner.

I had hired Katze during my first year as Vatican. His skills had been renowned. He'd had the ability to command an elite group of assassins back in the day. His background was vague, making me suspect that his family didn't hold a high status like mine. He had guts and wasn't afraid to challenge me. I liked that about him. I was attracted to him at one stage as well (yes, I do prefer blondes but fancy a change every now and then). Maybe that's why I had hired him. In any case, that desire had burned out long ago.

On a day like today, however, his gutsy attitude is not what I want to be faced with. He takes my silence as an answer to his question. I had forgotten how reliable Katze was, the bastard.

"Anyway, I came here because we are having problems in The Pits again. They have found another rat hole," he mutters over Gerald's voice. I groan, causing Gerald to pause and look at me.

The Pits was a district just outside of the capital. It was infested with criminals, as well as the poor and victims of slavery. It was a thorn in the Provinces' side and a politician's joke to assign me to look after it.

"I am not in the mood for this shit, Katze," I growl, losing my cool. He huffs, irritated. Now that I think about it, I am pretty sure The Pits is where he comes from. No wonder he is so concerned with it. The bastard probably convinced the other parties to assign it to my jurisdiction, just because he likes fucking with me.

He slaps down a document. "Just sign it and I will handle it," he bites back. I sign and watch him storm off. That boy is too smart for his own good.

"Continue, Gerald," I sigh, realising I have only been here for an hour. This is going to be a long day.

***

Mari

"Get up, shit bag," he grunts and follows it with a kick to my stomach. I roll over, feeling sick again. Is it worse today? What did I do yesterday? I can't remember much anymore.

I groan weakly as he pulls my face towards his. I can barely see him, my eyes are too heavy. I feel a waft of smoke hit my face from his cigarette, making me cough.

"I need you to be awake today, we got a new opportunity for you," he says. I feel the white powder drug assault my nose. As I inhale, my senses go into overdrive. My heart starts pounding and I begin to sweat.

He drops me back, chuckling. "That's better. Get cleaned up. We haven't got much time," What time is it? I don't even know what day it is. I scramble towards the showers, aware of him following me. It puts me on edge.

I was already naked, so I let the spray hit me as I walk under. All I can hear is the sound of the water. The cold slices my skin. I hear him growl. He starts washing me roughly, focusing on my lower parts.

"This isn't a holiday," he hisses in my ear, his hands lingering on my body. I shiver from the cold, feeling more awake. It must be someone important if he has got this involved.

"Mmm, I had forgotten how smooth you were," he sighs, his breath warm on my cold skin. His hands run over my body, no longer washing me. I lean against him, feeling weak again. "Ah I missed you pet, you're always such a good boy for me," he sighs, contented. My heart slows down at his voice. He is nice to me when he is happy.

It takes me back to when I first met him. How long ago was that now? I had fallen in love with him immediately. He had made me feel like a faerie prince or something, raving about how attractive I was.

I feel his hand slide over my body, kissing my shoulder softly.

When did everything get so twisted? So out of control?

"Master…," I sigh, knowing it would please him. I no longer called him by his name, I have forgotten it. When I used to, I was beaten. When I cried, I was beaten. I feel him smile against my neck at the sound of my voice. I barely speak anymore, so when I do, he knows it is a good sign. I lose myself in the past as he takes me roughly in the shower. He pleases himself and washes me again afterwards, whistling happily.

I am dressed in tight underwear that exposes my body erotically. He takes extra care to comb through my short, white hair. There is a knock on the door.

"Roland, your sister's 'ere," says the voice. I hear him growl. I feel sad; it is rare for him to dote on me like this. He drags me with him, buzzing with anger. I am thrown onto a couch next to him as he sits opposite the sister lady. She is too glamorous for these parts, with long nails and perfumed hair.

"You took too long," she whines, eyeing me, her mouth twisted in disgust.

"I can do whatever the fuck I want. He's clean now. So, who is this customer?" He cracks his knuckles.

"Not sure, but he's fucking important enough for them to withhold his name. The customer wants to remain anonymous and has paid well for that. Is he awake?" she snaps at the last part. A slap on my face brings me back to the room. She tsks at me as our eyes meet.

"It's just the Pixie Dust, it will wear off soon," I hear him grumble.

"Well, better sooner than later. Apparently, our customer doesn't like them all drugged up. It's bad for his image or something," she mutters, looking at her nails.

"No kidding?" Master chuckles. He rubs his hands together, jittery from his own withdrawals. "This guy sounds like big bucks, how the hell did you hook him up with us?"

The sister smiles. "Yes, indeed he is. I know his publicist, so he is the one to thank. Are you sure it's him that should do this?" she asks, turning her nose up at me.
He pats my head roughly, startling me "No doubt sis. He is the most obedient. Even you can't deny that he is pretty to look at," he says, his hand still resting on my head. My hair is white and fluffy. My eyes, when focused, are large and hazel. She snorts, looking bored.

"Whatever. As long as he is light-haired and has a good face - that's all the customer wants," she stands up with a sigh. "They will be here soon. Is that the best you could dress him in?" she points to me. I look down, confused.

"What's wrong with it? It shows everything he has got, the males love it," he responds irritably. She shrugs, uninterested.

Three suited pixies enter and she panics. "Greetings, gentlemen. We're surprised to receive you so early!" she chirps. Her voice hurts my ears.
"Is that him?" one of them asks with an accent. I feel eyes on me and squirm. My clothes feel tight and my head is pounding. I feel Master pull my arm roughly to get me to stand next to him. He fusses with me, showing my face to the men who stand opposite us.

"That's enough, Roland, just hand him over!" she hisses, pulling me away from him.

"Wait! Where's the payment?!" Master shouts, pulling my other arm. I feel nauseated and close to fainting.
"Roland! Don't be an idiot. I will sort it," she barks, pulling me roughly towards her. I fall into the men as the pounding in my head gets stronger. I feel strong arms pick me up and steady me. I watch Master and the sister lady squabble, while the two male pixies behind me mutter to each other in Hasser, the language of the Pixie Capital, Burlyn.

We are going to Burlyn?

"We are leaving," one of the pixies states, pulling me by the shoulder. Master and the sister lady are still bickering when the door closes behind me. The pounding in my head fades with their voices.

We walk to a shiny black car, with flags at the front. My heart lurches as I realise how important it looks. It feels sorely out of place and I freak out as they push me in. I yelp and bang the window in confusion.

This is just another job Mari, keep it together, I assure myself as the car pulls away.

The back is closed off from the front and the leather seats are cold on my skin. "You should sleep, it's going to be a long journey," a voice calls through a speaker. I oblige, and the last of the pounding ceases as I lose consciousness.

Read the rest for free at alexwolfonline.com

ACKNOWLEDGMENTS

As an author, self publishing a book isn't easy. Early on in this books development I learnt that this was a group effort. I am so lucky to have the following people help me make this dream come true.

Thank you to my friends and family who saw me through the writing and editing of this book while going through being jilted and my life changing forever.

Thank you to my beloved beta readers including; Christine, Andi, Mia, Kate and Josephine. You were my first ever beta readers and gave me the amazing support and encouragement that this was actually worth publishing.

Gabrielle for creating my vision for the cover art. Again, this was my first time working with someone else on the cover art but you completely delivered it, so thank you.

Finally, thank you to Kate Studer for editing this story. You managed to polish and refine something that I felt did not make sense at times - really appreciate your expertise!

ABOUT THE AUTHOR

Alex is a creator based in the centre of England who enjoys writing fantasy novels. She also illustrates fantasy-style portraits and draws commissioned pet portraits. Writing and drawing have always been her passion since she was five years old.

When she is not creating, she is either working her day job or reading various genres such as romance, true crime and dark fantasy.

Website: alexwolfonline.com

Connect with her on the following socials:

Instagram - Alexwolfauthor
Goodreads - Alex Wolf